KATIE'S JOURNEY TO LOVE

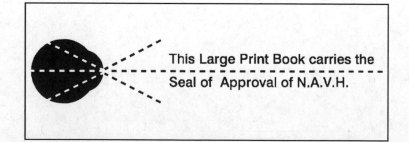

This Large Print Book carries the
Seal of Approval of N.A.V.H.

KATIE'S JOURNEY TO LOVE

JERRY S. EICHER

THORNDIKE PRESS

A part of Gale, Cengage Learning

GALE
CENGAGE Learning·

Detroit • New York • San Francisco • New Haven, Conn • Waterville, Maine • London

GALE
CENGAGE Learning®

LIBRARY OF CONGRESS CATALOGING-IN-PUBLICATION DATA

Eicher, Jerry S.
   Katie's journey to love / by Jerry S. Eicher. — Large print edition.
     pages ; cm. — (Emma Raber's daughter series ; #2) (Thorndike Press
   large print Christian romance)
   ISBN-13: 978-1-4104-6074-5 (hardcover)
   ISBN-10: 1-4104-6074-6 (hardcover)
   1. Young women—Fiction. 2. Mennonites—Fiction. 3. Domestic fiction.
   4. Large type books. I. Title.
   PS3605.I34K38 2013b
   813'.6—dc23   2013017288

Published in 2013 by arrangement with Harvest House Publishers

Printed in the United States of America
1 2 3 4 5 6 7 17 16 15 14 13

KATIE'S JOURNEY
TO LOVE

CHAPTER ONE

Katie Raber awoke well before dawn in the stillness of the old Amish farmhouse. Something seemed wrong . . . unfamiliar. Where was she? The question raced through her mind. The familiar shape of her upstairs bedroom was gone. Where the dresser should have been there was a window, and where the dark outline of the dresser was there used to be a closet door. She sat up in bed, listening as a door banged downstairs. The sound was soon followed by the muffled voices of people stirring below. There was also a soft clatter of dishes being moved and *Mamm*'s voice being overlaid with the deeper tones of a man.

Katie lay back in bed and smiled. Of course! *Mamm* had married Jesse Mast last week. The wedding had been held at Bishop Jonas Miller's place, with all the relatives and friends gathered for the great day. In the evening, the community youth had sung old hymns until after nine o'clock.

Today was the Friday after Thanksgiving, and the whole family was together for the first time since the wedding. They had given *Mamm* and Jesse some time alone, including Thanksgiving Day. The newlyweds hadn't gone off on some honeymoon like an *Englisha* couple would, so they were entitled to extra consideration — what with children from both sides of the families joining the new union and with a farm to take care of. Katie had also taken the week off from work at Byler's Store and had spent Thanksgiving Day with her Mennonite friend Margaret.

Mabel, Jesse's oldest daughter, had thrown a royal fit about being bossed around by *Mamm* last night when they'd all arrived after supper. And all *Mamm* had said was "It's time for bed, children." But thankfully Mabel had eventually calmed down. She'd been a wild card ever since *Mamm* had accepted Jesse's offer of marriage. At first Mabel had refused to even consider *Mamm* as her new *mamm*. It wasn't until *Mamm* was well into her engagement with Jesse before the feelings between *Mamm* and Mabel thawed out even a little. And even then Mabel gave in only after her *daett* brought great pressure to bear on her.

Katie took several deep breaths. The feelings of hope and joy that had been rushing over her at the memory of *Mamm* and Jesse saying their vows were fast disappearing. She really had to stop letting thoughts of Mabel's bad attitude affect her this way. After all, this should be a *wunderbah* new beginning for all of them. For one thing, she would no longer be known as odd widow Emma Raber's daughter, the strange girl with a yet stranger *mamm.* The wedding would surely change all of that.

Certainly Jesse and *Mamm* were persuaded things would turn out well for all of them. The past was behind them. Even *Mamm*'s past that had caused her to be thought strange by the Amish community — all because of that crush she'd once had on Daniel Kauffman, the most popular boy around when she'd been a teenager. *Mamm* had held on to her foolish hope that Daniel would return her affections right up to the moment he said his vows with Miriam Esh. *Mamm* had dashed out of the services and drove her buggy right past the couple and the astonished eyes of the bishop himself. She'd never lived down that action or gotten over the bitterness of the memory of Daniel.

Mamm had frozen her heart. In fact, she'd

9

married Ezra without expecting she would ever again feel love for a man. When her heart had opened to Ezra after their daughter's birth, it was made all the worse when he'd died suddenly. His early death had driven *Mamm* back into her shell. That Jesse Mast had been able to break through was a miracle indeed.

Now the joy was coming back. Katie belonged in this family — Jesse's five children and her. *Yah,* it was still a little unfamiliar, just like the room she hadn't recognized this morning. But she was here, and she was part of this family now. True, it didn't seem quite right that she should have this room that had been Mabel's. But Jesse had insisted. Katie was the eldest, so she deserved her own room. Katie dared not look at Mabel when he'd made that announcement.

At the wedding, everything had seemed to fall into place. There had been great love flowing from everybody. *Mamm*'s brothers from Lancaster had all taken time to speak with their niece, and they wished her well in her new life. "You're a Mast now," they'd teased, even though she really wasn't. She was still a Raber. *Mamm* marrying Jesse wouldn't change that. Only her own marriage would change her name.

That thought turned her mind to the dashing Ben Stoll, the boy she had her heart set on. He hadn't paid her any attention at the wedding. He'd taken Tina Hochstetler to the table at the evening hymn singing. Katie had been left with no choice but to sit with her young cousin James, who lived in Lancaster. At sixteen, he was too scared to take a strange girl to the table. She mustn't think about Ben now, Katie told herself. There were other boys in the world besides him, even though her heart would never be quite convinced of that. Maybe she could get over her crush on him if she tried hard enough. *Mamm* had found love beyond Daniel Kauffman, had she not?

Right now what she could be thankful for was that all of Jesse's children — except Mabel — had accepted *Mamm* and her with open arms. The change had been slow at times. Mabel hadn't been the only one of Jesse's children unwilling at first to accept the idea of a new *mamm* keeping house for them. But they had eventually come around. And Mabel had also — sort of — after she'd been told by her *daett* to straighten out her attitude and accept Emma as her *mamm*.

Well, even if Mabel made trouble for her, Katie was still much better off than she had been before. She now knew what it felt like

11

to be included in the Amish community and spoken to as if she were a normal human being. Of course, it hadn't been just the wedding that had accomplished that. It had really started when she accepted an invitation to a Mennonite youth gathering. There she'd become friends with girls like Margaret Kargel and Sharon Watson. Both girls had come to *Mamm*'s wedding at her special invitation. They were the only Mennonites there besides Esther Kuntz, who worked at Byler's Store with Katie.

Neither Jesse nor *Mamm* had any Mennonites in their immediate family. All the brothers and sisters on both sides of their families were Amish. That had made Katie's relationship with the Mennonite girls a troublesome matter for *Mamm*. Jesse too seemed a bit concerned about it, though not as great as *Mamm*.

She would continue to leave that matter in *Da Hah*'s hands, Katie decided. Much *gut* had come out of her friendships with Margaret and Sharon. And *Da Hah* had blessed them in spite of *Mamm*'s fears. How that all made sense, Katie still didn't know. And she might never know. It was enough that both *Mamm* and she were finding their way out of a life lived alone with closed-off hearts.

Back in the "old" days, *Mamm* had forbidden Katie from participating in the usual *rumspringa* the rest of the Amish young people in the community took part in. But to *Mamm, rumspringa* was a mild offense compared to attending Mennonite youth gatherings. But Katie had continued to go to them. She sighed and threw off the bedcovers. She knew Jesse and *Mamm* wanted her to stop attending, but she would have to see. *Da Hah* had been with her so far, and she would keep believing He would be in the future. It was true that living with Jesse and his family was going to be a great joy in its own right. Jesse had told her before *Mamm*'s wedding, "I love you, Katie. Just as much as I love Mabel and Carolyn or any of my boys. You'll be living at my house as my own daughter."

She was so thankful for that, and she appreciated the man from the bottom of her heart. That wasn't something a person just walked away from. She now had the chance to grow up for a few years with a *daett* who cared about her. There might now be less reason for her to attend the Mennonite youth gatherings, though she would always keep up her friendships with Margaret and Sharon.

Katie walked over to the unfamiliar

dresser. She opened the top drawer and ran her hands around the front edge. She found the matches and lit the kerosene lamp. The flickering flame had just caught when Jesse hollered up the stairs, "Time to get up, boys!"

Katie smiled at the sound. *Mamm* sometimes yelled up the stairs at home, but she'd never heard a man yell the morning wake-up call. It sounded *gut.* She pulled on her work dress as footsteps rushed past her bedroom door. She finished putting in the last pin and took the lamp with her as she stepped into the hallway. The light played on the walls as she found her way downstairs. No one was in the living room, so Katie peeked into the kitchen. *Mamm* had her back turned toward her as she worked over the stove.

"You should have called for me," Katie told her.

Mamm turned around with a smile on her face. "*Gut* morning, Katie."

"*Gut* morning to you." Katie set the lamp on the kitchen table. "May I help with breakfast?"

A look of uncertainty replaced *Mamm*'s smile. "Perhaps we'd better wait until Mabel comes down before we get too far along. I don't want to take over her kitchen on the first morning she's here. Not without talk-

14

ing with her about it first."

Katie sat on a kitchen chair. This was an unexpected turn of events, although she really shouldn't be surprised now that she thought about it. *Mamm* had always been in charge at home, but now she was in another person's kitchen — Mabel's kitchen. "But you're Jesse's wife," Katie protested. Everything has changed, she wanted to add, but she didn't. *Mamm* looked troubled enough without adding undue pressure, and obviously everything hadn't changed yet. There still would be bumps in the road. She could handle it.

Mamm was trying to smile. "*Yah,* I know. It takes some getting used to."

"You should call Mabel," Katie said. "She shouldn't sleep in on the first morning we're all together."

Mamm lifted her head from the stove, seeming to ponder the suggestion for a moment. Then she went to the bottom of the stairs.

Yell loudly! Katie wanted to say. Wake the girl up!

"Mabel!" *Mamm* called up the stairs, her voice gentle.

Long moments passed, and *Mamm* looked ready to call again when the sound of a door opening came from upstairs.

"What do you want?" Mabel's voice sounded irritated.

"I need your help in the kitchen," *Mamm* said.

The door closed upstairs without an answer.

Katie watched *Mamm*'s face as she turned back and went to the stove.

Mamm glanced at Katie. "Perhaps you shouldn't be in here when Mabel comes down."

Katie looked away. Had she heard correctly? *Mamm* didn't want her in the kitchen? *Mamm* must have seen the look on Katie's face because she came over and gave Katie a quick hug. "It's not what you think, Katie. I'm not rejecting you. It's just that we must think about the larger picture right now. Mabel is used to running the household, and we need to give her an opportunity to adjust. It might be difficult enough for her with just me in here. And she might think ill of us if she finds you here too, both of us working in her kitchen. Especially because we didn't take the time to call her before we started breakfast."

Katie kept her eyes on the floor. What in the world was she supposed to do now? The pain was throbbing something awful in her heart. She'd never been told to leave the kitchen at home.

"Come on, Katie," *Mamm* whispered. "We need to think about how Mabel will see things. If we're both here, it will look like we've taken over."

"Where am I supposed to go? What am I supposed to do?" Katie got to her feet.

Mamm looked around but didn't offer a suggestion.

"I'll slip outside for a bit," Katie finally said, opening the washroom door. Already she could hear Mabel's quick footsteps coming down the stairs. Katie walked past the faint outline of the wash-basin and towel in the darkness, and then she stepped outside. She stood on the porch with her arms folded and looked up at the splash of stars still visible in the heavens. Toward the east, dawn was breaking, the light still hidden in part by the corner of the house. In the other direction, the barn windows were lit with the glow of gas lanterns as Jesse and his boys worked on their chores. Katie looked at the soft light spreading across the dark lawn for a long time as tears stung her eyes.

Not that long ago she would have been out in the barn with *Mamm* doing the few chores they had at their place. Their two cows, Molly and Bossy, had been brought over and would be milked along with Jesse's herd. She wouldn't be going to the barn again for chores anytime soon. Jesse and his boys would take care of the farm jobs. So much had changed, Katie thought. And so quickly. She hugged herself tightly as she heard faint sounds of laughter coming from inside the house. That was *Mamm*'s voice laughing with Mabel. They were hitting it off big, apparently. Katie felt shut out. How could this be happening with all the hope that had filled her heart only moments ago? Surely *Mamm* hadn't planned on sending her out of the kitchen on the first day they were all here after the wedding. Katie told herself she needed to think the best possible thoughts right now or she was going to burst into tears and totally embarrass herself when she did go back inside.

Was all this part of *Da Hah*'s way? No doubt He was continuing to lead her on paths she was unfamiliar with. Instead of being bitter, she should be thankful that *Mamm* was adjusting so well in her new role as Jesse's wife and as *mamm* to his five children — especially Mabel. Wasn't Mabel the hard case? Any progress in that area was all the more reason to give thanks. In the end, Katie decided, she would fit in some-where. *Mamm* wouldn't forget her own daughter.

One thing was for sure. *Mamm* and she would never slip back into what they used to be. That was in the past — and would remain so. No more feelings of being passed over by everyone or going unnoticed in Amish youth gatherings. Some of that would still happen, but she now had her wonderful memories of the evenings spent with the Mennonite youth to counter the aloneness. Margaret and Sharon had accepted her so quickly, and she'd met many others who were friendly too. Even the Mennonite boys who played beside her at the volleyball games — young men she'd never met before — had taken the time to say a few words of greeting and inquire how she was doing. They were all nice people who had welcomed her into their homes and hearts.

She had them to go back to in addition to whatever new blessings *Da Hah* had waiting for her with her new, expanded family. Mabel was the thorn with the rose, but Katie didn't wish to destroy the flower because of the pain that stung her hand. *Nee,* she would not. She took deep breaths of the cool morning air and gathered her courage to return inside.

CHAPTER TWO

Thirty minutes later, Katie was on the way down from upstairs, taking firm steps, making sure each one creaked if possible. She'd sneaked up through the living room once she came in from outside through the front door. *Mamm* and Mabel had been talking in the kitchen, laughing as she'd tiptoed past the doorway. Sneaking up had seemed like the decent thing to do. She couldn't possibly have gone out to the barn with Jesse and his boys out there. That would have raised eyebrows. And barging back into the kitchen would have raised questions with Mabel she didn't wish to answer. *Yah,* I'm feeling hurt, Katie admitted. But I'm trying hard to do my part in this family, which included not provoking Mabel.

Only moments ago she'd heard Jesse and his boys come in from their chores and bang around in the washroom as they cleaned up. No one had called her, but how could they since even *Mamm* didn't know where she'd gone. Katie was content to let it appear to Mabel and the others that she'd overslept.

Mamm's face showed relief when Katie walked into the kitchen.

"*Gut* morning," Mabel said, all smiles.

"*Gut* morning," Katie replied.

Mabel was carrying a plate of eggs to the table, and she'd obviously been frying bacon. Mabel looked quite pleased, so *Mamm*'s decision about the morning routine must have had the desired effect. "Is there anything I can do to help?" Katie asked.

"I think we're almost done," Mabel said, managing a smile. "Maybe you can set the last of the table. *Daett* and the boys are almost inside."

I know that, Katie wanted to say. Their loud chatter in the washroom was obvious. Mabel was treating her like a small child, offering her the lowest of tasks, one worthy of her youngest sister, Carolyn — not a soon-to-be-twenty young woman. But Katie kept smiling as she took the dishes to the table, thinking how much worse things could be this morning. Mabel's red-faced outbursts before the wedding had been common occurrences. Even for a sixteen-year-old she hadn't been afraid to make a

21

spectacle of herself once her *daett* had chosen *Mamm* over the children's choice of teacher Ruth Troyer.

The washroom door burst open, and Mabel's two oldest brothers, Leroy and Willis, spilled in. They were soon followed by Jesse. Leroy and Willis stopped short at the sight of Katie and *Mamm,* as if they hadn't been expecting them. *Yah,* this would definitely take some getting used to by everybody.

"*Gut* morning to everyone!" Jesse exclaimed over the silence of his sons. "What a sight for sore eyes you women are. Isn't this wonderful? I can't say how blessed we are that Emma and Katie have come to live with us. Have a seat boys, and stop staring like you've never seen women before."

Leroy and Willis grunted and took their seats on the back bench. The two boys hadn't been staring at *Mamm,* Katie thought. They'd been staring at her. It was the shock, no doubt, of seeing strange Emma Raber's daughter in their house.

Katie smiled as she stood by the table, her hands clasped in front of her. She wasn't quite sure where she was supposed to sit. When no one said anything, she took a chair beside the one she assumed her *mamm* would sit in.

"Where are Carolyn and Joel?" Jesse asked, taking his seat at the front of the table.

"I'll call them!" Mabel jumped up to rush to the bottom of the stairs. She hollered up, "Carolyn, Joel!"

When there was only silence, Mabel took off up the stairs.

"How's Mabel doing?" Jesse asked *Mamm* when his daughter's footsteps had faded.

"Okay," *Mamm* said, taking the seat beside Jesse. She reached over and touched his arm.

Across the table, Leroy quickly stared up at the ceiling. A smile crept across Willis's face.

Mamm noticed and turned bright red as she pulled her hand away from Jesse's arm.

Jesse, taking it all in, laughed and took Emma's hand in his.

"Now, boys, this is your new *mamm,*" Jesse said, his eyes twinkling. "Get used to it."

There was no doubt that Jesse was working to make *Mamm* feel comfortable. Katie allowed a smile to creep over her face.

Soon *Mamm* joined in the shared laughter. She leaned toward Jesse as footsteps came down the stairs. Mabel appeared, leading six-year-old Joel by the hand with Carolyn following close behind.

Katie held her breath. Would Mabel object to this open display of affection between *Mamm* and Jesse? Would all of *Mamm*'s careful work this morning be lost in seconds? Perhaps Mabel would see something in her *daett*'s actions to remind her of her lost *mamm.* Might this open wounds that hadn't yet healed?

Mabel paused for a moment as she took in *Mamm* and Jesse's postures. She grimaced but then glanced away. Without further ado, she helped Joel into his chair, where he sat and rubbed his eyes. Carolyn took her place, smiling at *Mamm* and Jesse.

Jesse beamed back at Carolyn but he addressed all of them. "Do you think we should pray before the food gets cold?"

"*Yah,* let's do," Mabel spoke up. She had folded her hands in her lap like she didn't quite know what to do with them. Jesse gave Mabel only the briefest of glances before they all bowed their heads.

"Dear *Gott im himmel,*" Jesse prayed, "You who made the heavens and the earth and all that is within them, look down again upon us this morning in mercy. We give You thanks for Your many and great blessings You have given to us all. You have brought joy and laughter back into our home. You

24

have again allowed love to grow in my heart for Emma. You have not allowed either of us to stay in our former state of sorrow. Rather, You have given us new life again. For this we cannot give You sufficient thanks. Have mercy again today on our trespasses, and forgive us as we forgive those who sin against us."

Katie stole a look at *Mamm*'s face. It carried a touch of red, which made sense. She too would be sending off flames of red if such words of thanksgiving and praise were being offered on her behalf. The years of living alone hadn't been kind to *Mamm*. They had been long and lonely, full of suffering. Now the tide had turned and this was her time of miracles. *Mamm* hadn't been sure that she was in love with Jesse before the wedding, but that had also been the case with Ezra, Katie's *daett,* too. And just like with Ezra, Katie had no doubt that her *mamm*'s feelings for Jesse would match the love she had for *Daett.* With a man like Jesse, *Mamm* wouldn't be able to help herself. Katie bowed her head again.

". . . now be with us today, O great and holy Father," Jesse said. "Continue to bless us and to bestow Your grace upon our lives. In the name of Your dear Son, Jesus. Amen."

They all raised their heads, and Leroy

made a dive for the plate of eggs. Mabel slapped his hand, and he dropped the plate with a clatter, causing several eggs to slide off the platter onto the table.

"Enough of this," Jesse corrected sternly. "You're behaving like savages after such a *gut* start this morning."

"He's only being his usual self," Mabel stated.

"Pick up the eggs from the table," Jesse ordered Leroy. "And those will be yours. Next time be more careful. I've had enough of this."

Leroy groaned but gathered up the eggs one by one and slipped them onto his plate.

Jesse turned to Emma with an apologetic grin. "I'm sorry about my children's behavior. I guess you see why they need a *mamm* around."

"I understand," *Mamm* said quickly. "It's okay."

Jesse patted her on the arm. "Now, don't be too easy on them. They're also in your charge now, and they are to listen to you." Jesse turned toward his children. "Did you hear that?" he asked.

They all nodded, including Mabel. She appeared subdued for a moment, and then she passed the bacon around. Breakfast settled down into a family routine. *Mamm* joined in where she could, but Mabel clearly was running things.

Katie watched to see what *Mamm* would do. Out of the corner of her eye she noticed Jesse was doing the same. When the plate of eggs came around to little Joel, Mabel reached out to help him.

Mamm said, "I'll help him."

Mabel blinked a few times and glanced at her *daett*. When Jesse nodded, Mabel backed down. She attempted a smile and said, "Of course. I'm so used to doing everything."

"*Yah,* I understand." *Mamm* smiled at Mabel. "How many eggs does Joel usually eat?"

"Two!" Joel announced.

After Mabel nodded, *Mamm* pulled two eggs off the serving plate and put them onto Joel's.

Mabel looked so pleased *Mamm* had consulted her that Katie thought she would burst. But this is a *gut* thing, she reminded herself. She must not become bitter over *Mamm* and Mabel developing a good relationship.

When they were finished eating, Jesse bowed his head in silent prayer before standing to lead the way into the living room for morning devotions.

Mamm seemed to notice Katie for the first time since breakfast had begun. A troubled look crossed her face. As they both stood, *Mamm* reached over to squeeze Katie's elbow as they walked together into the living room.

Katie whispered, "It's okay, *Mamm.* I understand."

Mamm's face relaxed, and by the time she sat down on the hickory rocker beside Jesse, she was smiling again. Katie listened to Jesse read the morning scripture, a section out of Psalm 147: "Praise ye the LORD: for it is good to sing praises unto our God . . ."

That was so true, Katie thought. She was glad *Da Hah* had brought them so much joy.

". . . he gathereth together the outcasts of Israel. He healeth the broken in heart."

Kate thought again how glad she was to finally have a *daett.* She was happy *Da Hah* was healing their hearts, and she was pleased He had given her a small part in it. Hopefully they would become a strong, loving family. No matter what, she would trust in *Da Hah* to lead the way.

CHAPTER THREE

An hour later Jesse and the two oldest boys had left the house to begin their work in the fields. Katie walked into the kitchen to find *Mamm* up to her elbows in flour as she stirred a huge bowl of bread dough. At home *Mamm* had baked only a small batch of bread each week, but here it looked like she would have to make three times as much with so many mouths to feed.

"I'm leaving early for Byler's," Katie announced, pausing to give *Mamm* a quick wave. "They're expecting an extra busy time since it's right after Thanksgiving." She saw no sign of Mabel, but Katie could hear the washing machine running downstairs.

"Bye!" *Mamm* said, looking up but not lifting her floury hands from the bowl.

Katie closed the washroom door behind her and crossed the yard. Before she reached the barn, *Mamm* came running from the house, wiping her arms on the apron.

"Katie!" she called out. "Katie, I need to talk to you."

Katie didn't pause. "I have to harness Sparky, *Mamm,*" she hollered over her shoulder. "Can you come to the barn?"

Mamm followed her into the barn and watched as Katie brought Sparky out of his stall. She threw the harness on his back. "What is it, *Mamm*?" she asked.

"Katie . . ." *Mamm* stepped closer. "Katie, I'm sorry for how things went this morning. I'm so caught up in everything that I feel I've neglected you."

"I'm okay." Katie looked away. "I really am."

Mamm touched Katie's arm. "*Nee,* you're not. A *mamm* can tell. I'm sorry I asked you to step outside this morning. That was awful of me, regardless of what I was trying to accomplish."

"*Mamm,* it's okay," Katie insisted. "*Yah,* you are right. It did hurt a little, but it was for the best. And at least Mabel didn't blow up. Maybe she would have if we hadn't been careful."

"We'll have a good, long talk tonight when you get back," *Mamm* said with tears in her eyes. "I love you, Katie. Nothing is going to change that."

Katie met *Mamm*'s gaze. "Thanks. I love

you too. You've always been *gut* to me, and I know we have adjustments to make."

"Oh, Katie . . ." *Mamm* touched her hand. "Thank you for seeing so much more than I do sometimes. I know you will love Jesse and his family. *Da Hah* has given us a miracle, and you are part of it."

Katie slipped Sparky's bridle over his head. Words of warning on what conflicts might lie ahead sprang up in her mind. There were the Mennonite youth gatherings and also Mabel's true feelings. But Katie held the words back. None of that would benefit either of them right now. *Mamm* loved her, and she loved *Mamm*. That had been enough in the past, and it would prove enough now and in the future. She couldn't ask for more.

"Keep your courage up," *Mamm* said. "I know living with Mabel is difficult, but you're my shining example that all will work out. Soon things will go much smoother — once we've settled down a bit."

"I hope for the same thing," Katie responded.

"I'm so glad to hear that." *Mamm* touched Katie's arm again. "Come, let me help you get on the road."

Katie led Sparky outside, and *Mamm* closed the barn door behind them. They walked to the buggy, and *Mamm* lifted the shafts. Katie backed Sparky in, and when they finished tying the tugs, Katie climbed into the buggy while *Mamm* held Sparky's bridle.

Mamm was smiling and waving as Katie took off. She waved back, taking one last glance toward the house. Mabel had come out of the basement doorway to watch her leave. Katie was sure there was a frown on the girl's face.

Looking back at *Mamm,* Katie waved again before turning her gaze to the driveway. She looked both ways and then pulled onto the main road. The look on Mabel's face stirred feelings of bitterness in her . . . feelings that shouldn't be there, but she couldn't stop it right now. Who did Mabel think she was, anyway? Some special child who had a right to make demands? *Yah,* so Mabel hadn't gotten what she wanted when Jesse married *Mamm.* So what?

Mamm was almost crawling along on her hands and knees right now to try to keep Mabel happy. The girl was spoiled, that's what she was. She'd gotten used to running the household on her own since her *mamm* had died, and it had gone to Mabel's head — all that bossing of her siblings. And Jesse, with his kind heart, probably wouldn't see this fault in his daughter. Of course things had gotten out of hand. Katie sighed and gently slapped the reins against Sparky's back. She had to stop thinking these nasty thoughts about Mabel or she would be all out of sorts when she arrived at Byler's.

Katie was determined to get along with Mabel, but clearly Mabel wouldn't be easy to live with. Katie had already known it would be difficult, but there was nothing like seeing it firsthand. And Mabel probably wasn't above spreading rumors around the community about either *Mamm* or her, Katie thought. Now that Mabel had intimate access to their lives, she might see something she'd deem questionable. They might well be in deeper trouble than *Mamm* and she had imagined. Katie shivered at the thought. Part of getting along with Mabel meant that Katie needed a life of her own that Mabel couldn't touch. And that was exactly what she had in her relationships with Margaret and Sharon. How *wunderbah* of *Da Hah* to have looked out for her in this way. She would at least be safe from Mabel's touch with them. Even Mabel's strong ally, Ruth Troyer — the schoolteacher Jesse had rejected in choosing *Mamm* — couldn't reach the Mennonite youth group with her wagging tongue.

Now that Katie had more time to think about it, this morning's decision by *Mamm* had indeed been the wise choice. There were reasons *Mamm* should be afraid to cross Mabel. *Mamm* had no place to go like Katie did. *Mamm* was married to Jesse now, and she had to find a way to get along.

Ahead of Katie, Byler's store on Route 8 toward Dover came into view. Soon she was turning Sparky into the driveway. She unhitched in the back parking lot and led Sparky to the fence to tie him up so he could munch on grass while Katie worked. At the sound of buggy wheels, Katie looked up and saw Arlene drive in. She waited as Arlene pulled up and got out of her buggy.

Arlene was her friend among the Amish young people and a fellow cashier at Byler's. They weren't that close because Arlene was on *rumspringa,* which *Mamm* had refused to allow Katie to participate in. And now Katie was attending Mennonite youth gatherings, and Arlene wasn't part of that group. But she was the closest Amish friend Katie had — and a *gut* one at that.

Arlene greeted Katie with a bright smile. "How's married life treating the family?"

Katie stifled a groan. "Okay, I guess." She walked over to the opposite side of Arlene's buggy to undo the harness.

"Come on now." Arlene laughed, obviously picking up on Katie's discomfort. "Kind of sudden, huh? Being dropped in the middle of a family with five children. I can't say I wouldn't complain myself. After all the years you've had alone with your *mamm,* it must be hard to share her. Believe me, it's different when you have brothers and sisters."

"I'm doing fine." Katie laughed halfheartedly. "A few bumps in the road, but I think we'll make it through."

"I know you will." Arlene led her horse forward after Katie took off the tug on her side and held the shafts. When the horse had moved, Katie lowered them to the ground.

Arlene led her horse to the fence quite a ways from Sparky.

While Katie waited, Esther Kuntz roared into the parking lot in her dark-blue Corvette. Esther sure liked to make an entrance with her car. But underneath that bluster was a *gut* heart. She'd already proven herself a good friend many times. If it hadn't been for Esther giving her rides to and from the youth gatherings, Katie would never have met Margaret and Sharon.

Esther could talk her head off with any boy who came around without blinking an eye. Katie envied that ability a little bit. Esther's skill came from natural confidence, not because she was full of herself.

"Good morning!" Esther shouted across the lot after getting out of her car. "Nice to see you again."

"*Gut* morning!" Katie hollered back as a smile spread across her face.

"You look all happy and cheery this morning," Esther said as she walked closer.

"I'm okay," Katie said, happy that her thoughts about Mabel weren't showing on her face now.

Esther was already gushing on. "I really enjoyed your *mamm*'s wedding. It was so quaint and lovely. Especially with your *mamm* up front saying her vows with that tremble in her voice. I guess my voice would also be trembling if I could see half the people watching me while I made my promises."

"And you're not even dating," Arlene teased, having walked up beside them.

"That's because I don't want to." Esther made a funny face at Arlene. "I'm enjoying my freedom too much."

Arlene smiled but didn't say anything more as they walked together to the employee entrance. But Esther wasn't finished talking about the wedding. "I told Sharon and Margaret what an honor I thought it was to be invited, and they thought the same thing. We felt so privileged. I wouldn't have missed the occasion for the world. I don't get to attend Amish weddings very often since I don't have any Amish relatives. Thank you for inviting me, Katie."

You don't know how much you've done for me, Katie wanted to say. But because Arlene was along, Katie kept quiet. Arlene wouldn't understand why Katie would make such a statement.

Arlene held the door open for them, and Katie followed Esther inside, still listening to her chatter. "That cake and the fruit on the table, and the way your young people can sing without any musical instruments. They were a marvel to listen to. I'm going to have to visit more often. If you invite me, that is."

Katie almost laughed. Not that Esther wasn't welcome to attend Amish church services, but it probably wouldn't happen. Regular Amish church wasn't quite like a wedding. No, she was the one who would be attending Esther's youth group, not the other way around. Perhaps now was the time to ask when the next youth gathering was and whether Esther would be kind enough to pick her up. Katie gathered her courage. "I was wondering when the next Mennonite youth gathering is?"

"Let's see . . ." Esther paused. "Oh yes, the next gathering will be on Wednesday night at seven o'clock at Margaret's place. I can pick you up. Oh, and Margaret and Sharon have some awful secret they want to tell you."

"An awful secret?"

"Don't look so scared!" Esther laughed. "I don't know what it is, but it's something wonderful, I'm sure."

Katie caught her breath. "Okay, I'll plan on going. Thank you so much for carting me around like you do. I hope I'm not too much of a bother."

"Not at all," Esther assured her. "But we're going to have to get you a vehicle before too long."

Katie swallowed hard and said nothing as Esther disappeared around the corner of the aisle on her way to the Deli Department. A car? That was never going to happen . . . or would it? At least not in the near future. It was hard to see that happening anytime though. There would never be a car purchase . . . well, probably never.

So what in the world was she doing running around with the Mennonite youth? It didn't make sense to get involved with that youth group. But Katie knew only that her attendance at the youth gatherings had always seemed blessed. *Da Hah* surely was guiding her since He'd blessed her with such good friendships. And — as a bonus — the friendships and gatherings gave her a life away from Mabel.

Yah, she would likely face more disapproval from Jesse and *Mamm,* but it would be worth it.

CHAPTER FOUR

As four o'clock approached that afternoon, there was a rush of customers coming through the checkout stands. Most of them, thankfully, had only a few items in their carts. Katie greeted the next lady in her line with a smile and a cheerful, "Hi! How are you today?"

"Just fine," the lady said. "And how are you?"

"A little tired," Katie admitted as she scanned the woman's items. "But I get off soon."

"Going home to a good supper, I'm sure," the woman said with a laugh.

"*Yah.*" Katie kept a smile on her face. "*Mamm* will have a *gut* supper ready for me — and for all the rest of the children."

The woman beamed. "You come from a large family then? Are you perhaps the oldest?"

Katie's smile faded a little. What was she

supposed to say to that? That *Mamm* had just remarried so she had a new *daett* and was trying to adjust?

"You don't have to be embarrassed," the woman said gently, still beaming. "I also come from a large family, dear. Isn't that common among your people?"

The woman is obviously making the wrong assumption about my hesitation, Katie thought. "*Yah,* it is," she finally managed to get out.

"That's just wonderful!" the woman said as Katie finished checking her groceries. "I'm sure you can't wait to get back home to the farm after working here all day."

"It will be nice to get off my feet," Katie said.

"You have a good evening then," the woman said as she left.

Katie turned to the next customer. At the same time, she caught a glimpse of a young man across the aisle checking out at Arlene's register. Her hand stopped in midair and the rest of her body froze. Ben Stoll! Katie's heart raced. Ben did stop in sometimes, so it really wasn't anything unusual. Would he notice her this time?

"Hi!" Katie greeted her customer after realizing she'd been staring at Ben. Her voice croaked a bit. Thankfully the man standing

41

in her line didn't seem to notice. Katie scanned his two items. He paid with a credit card and left.

Katie sneaked another look in Ben's direction. He was still there, chatting away with Arlene like they were *gut* friends, which they probably were. Even though Arlene already had a boyfriend, it was obvious she was enjoying her chance to chat with Ben. Any girl would. He was the best-looking young man in the county, Katie thought. For years now he'd had a grip on her heart that wouldn't let go. Ben was an impossible dream, Katie knew, but one she had never been able to shake.

Was there reason to hope Ben would notice her? More wild thoughts like that raced through her mind as Katie greeted her next customer. Ben never had. To him she was merely Emma Raber's weird daughter, but now she and *Mamm* were part of a normal family. Arlene herself had said months ago that she'd noticed Katie was changing. And the Mennonite youth didn't seem to view her as odd like the Amish youth did. Was there a chance Ben might see her in a different light too? Or, more realistically, actually notice her for the first time? Hadn't *Mamm*'s miracle with Jesse happened? Perhaps there was a miracle ahead for her too? Or was she only keeping an impossible dream in her heart like the one *Mamm* had held onto regarding Daniel Kauffman?

Ben shared one last laugh with Arlene before disappearing out the door without a glance toward Katie. Thankfully the store was still busy, and Arlene didn't notice Katie's red face. Arlene didn't know about her crush on Ben, but she certainly noticed things like red faces — especially if they happened right when a handsome young man walked past.

"Hi!" Katie greeted as another customer walked up. She pushed away thoughts of good-looking young men — especially Ben.

The customer didn't have much to say beyond returning her smile, and Katie quickly checked her items. Arlene glanced her way, but Katie kept her face turned toward the register, trying to steady her breathing. Hopefully her red face had faded by this time — or at least enough so Arlene wouldn't notice.

Katie kept herself busy checking out two more customers in her aisle. Her face felt perfectly normal now, but her smile might still be a little nervous when she turned toward Arlene.

Katie jumped as the manager, Mrs. Cole,

came bustling around the corner. "Time for you to close, girls! Off with the two of you."

Katie checked out of her register, grabbed the cash drawer, and followed Arlene to the office in the back. Would Ben still be outside when they were finished counting the cash and balancing their registers? Perhaps he'd be chatting with someone or even just hanging around. She wanted to see him, but she would also die of embarrassment if she turned all red in front of him and Arlene. And later, the questions Arlene would ask wouldn't be easy to answer. And Arlene didn't take half answers either.

Katie took a quick glance around as they walked out of Byler's employee door. No sign of Ben's buggy. A pickup truck was parked near their buggies, and a man was sitting in the driver's seat. He appeared to be waiting for someone, so perhaps his wife was still inside the store. Two Amish men sat in the truck bed. Katie stopped midstride. Ben Stoll was one of them!

Ben smiled as he caught sight of Arlene. "Time to go home, huh?" Ben called out.

Arlene hadn't noticed Ben, and she jumped at his voice. "Of course it's time to go home. Did you think I lived here?"

Ben laughed. "Now don't go telling me you have to do chores all evening when you get home."

"I know I have to work harder than you do, Ben!" Arlene snapped. "You don't even have chores when you get home. You have the easy life that carpenters get to live."

The other man joined in her laughter, but Ben didn't say anything.

Katie remained frozen in place. What was wrong with her? Why couldn't she speak up and join this conversation? She would be doing that if this were at a Mennonite gathering. But here there were too many bad memories from her growing-up years to battle. Usually when she tried to enter into discussions with Amish youth, everyone went on talking as if she weren't even there. *Nee,* she couldn't take the pain that would throb in her heart when that happened. It was even worse than when *Mamm* had asked her to leave the kitchen this morning. She noticed the other boy in the back of the pickup glancing her way. Oh! She was already making a spectacle of herself by hesitating. He'd seen her, and yet it probably hadn't registered. So now what was she supposed to do? Just walk past them to her buggy without saying anything?

Before Katie decided, the driver of the pickup truck motioned for her to come closer. He didn't look happy as Katie approached with slow steps.

"You wouldn't have seen my wife inside, would you?" he asked. "She was only supposed to pick up some cheese, and we're in a hurry."

Here was her chance to get out of this situation. "If you'll describe her, I can go inside and look," Katie offered. "She can't be too much longer, I imagine."

"Oh, you'd be surprised," he said. "I'd go look myself, but I'm a little slow on my feet with my back injury." The man lifted a crutch inside the pickup truck high enough for Katie to see.

"I'd be glad to go," Katie said. "What is your wife wearing?"

"A blue sweater and black slacks. And she's about as round as I am. Constance is her name." He laughed.

Katie was already on her way, almost running across the parking lot. The sounds of Arlene's voice, mixed in with Ben's deeper voice, murmured behind her. "I'm not jealous," Katie told herself. "Arlene can talk with Ben all she wishes." Katie knew her feelings went deeper than that. Somehow she would have to overcome feeling worthless with the Amish kids. When she came back out, she would march right up to the pickup truck and say hi to Ben. It wouldn't make Ben like her or make her crush go away, but she would feel better.

Her face determined, Katie found a woman in a blue sweater and black slacks standing in front of the cheese case. She had three types in her hands.

"Excuse me," Katie said. "Are you Constance?"

"Yep." The woman smiled and looked at her curiously.

"Your husband asked me to tell you that he's in a hurry to leave."

"Oh, Robert." A frown spread over the woman's face. "He's always in a big hurry, but when we get home there's nothing to do but watch television. And if I don't get the right kind of cheese, there will be no end of complaining from him about it."

Katie didn't know what to say so she just stood there.

Constance held up the pieces in her hand. "What do you think? Is Swiss better than Mozzarella? That's what I'm thinking, but Swiss seems so ordinary. It's what we always get, and I wanted something a little unusual for a change."

"I don't know that much about cheese," Katie offered. "Mozzarella is a little unusual tasting unless you've tried it before and know you like it."

A relieved look crossed Constance's face. "That's exactly what I thought. Then we will go with my third choice: Canadian cheddar. What do you think about that?"

"That would be a safe option, I think." Katie offered a smile.

"Please tell Robert I'll be right out," Constance said.

Katie left her weighing the small offering of Canadian Cheddar cheese she had in her hand against a larger one. Her heart pounding, Katie went outside the store and walked across the parking lot, heading straight for the pickup truck. This would be easier if she could gather her courage first, but Robert was probably expecting a message from his wife.

"So did you find her?" Robert asked when Katie paused near him.

"*Yah,* she will be out before long."

Robert groaned.

Katie would have smiled if Ben wasn't sitting just a few feet away from her in the back of the pickup. What power did this man have over her anyway, that he could make her blush red one moment and go cold the next?

"I've got to be going," Arlene said to the young men.

Katie forced her feet to move forward. If

she didn't get this done in the next moment, Arlene would be gone and Katie would be on her own. Nothing was going to happen then. She stepped up beside Arlene and looked straight up at Ben, who was slouched forward in the pickup bed.

"Hi!" she said. To her ears, her voice sounded like a screech.

Ben turned toward her. He didn't say anything for a moment.

I'm going to live through this, Katie told herself. How she wasn't sure, but her heart was still beating. She noticed Arlene was staring at her.

Ben finally spoke. "So your *mamm* got married to Jesse Mast. That means you're thrown in with the rest of the family. Let's see, how many of them are there? A bunch I think."

"There's not that many, Ben," Arlene said. "Only five children, and they're all nice. Jesse wouldn't raise anything else."

"Then I guess he should have raised me!" Ben laughed, and everyone joined in except Katie. She tried, but her throat was too dry.

Behind them came the sound of rattling grocery cart wheels.

"It's about time!" Robert yelled as Constance neared the pickup truck.

Ben jumped down to help with the groceries, speaking over his shoulder, "See you later, Arlene."

Katie found her way over to her buggy, waving along with Arlene as the truck left the parking lot moments later. It didn't matter that Ben hadn't said goodbye to her, Katie told herself. She'd spoken to him. That was enough of an accomplishment for one day.

CHAPTER FIVE

Katie drove toward Jesse's place that afternoon, her mind in a daze. Had she really spoken with Ben Stoll? Right out in the parking lot? And he had answered her — sort of. Was it possible she might have another chance to speak with him soon? And would she ever see the day when he actually enjoyed speaking with her like he did with Arlene? Katie laughed, thinking her voice sounded like more of a cackle. Talking with Ben like that. Ha! Now that would be the day. But the thought was quite delicious to think about. What a dream that would be. Someday she would walk right up to Ben Stoll and be able to say "hi" without a pounding heart. She would get over the fear. Already she was changing, wasn't she? After all, she'd summoned up the courage to attend the youth gatherings at the Mennonite church. A right brave thing for an Amish girl.

She really had the best of the two worlds — the Amish and the Mennonites. And it was so unexpected. *Da Hah* was clearly leading her, even if *Mamm* and Jesse didn't understand. She could keep her friendships with Margaret and Sharon, and she could stay in touch with the Amish youth — including Ben. Someday Ben might even notice how much she'd changed and pay her attention. The day might even come when Ben saw her as Margaret and Sharon did — outgoing, fun-loving, and a *gut* friend. When that happened, how Ben's face would light up! On that day Ben would feel for her what she felt for him.

Katie pulled back on the reins as she slowed to turn a corner. Sparky shook his head, and she let him speed up again. Katie took a deep breath. Oh, these were such wild dreams! But anything seemed possible after what had happened in the last year with Jesse and *Mamm.* And even Arlene was impressed with the progress she was making in growing out of her shell. A few minutes later, Katie slowed down as she approached Jesse's lane. It still seemed strange driving down his driveway and calling this place home. But *Mamm* was here, and Katie now had some happy thoughts in her heart that would no doubt sustain her during the next few hours. She looked around the farm and saw the horse teams working in the fields, their forms small in the distance. Jesse and his two eldest boys would have to begin the afternoon chores before long. Perhaps Leroy and Willis would allow her to help once in awhile. She didn't want to lose her touch completely. And it would be *gut* to get out of the house and away from Mabel if things went the way she expected they were going to.

Katie pulled up beside the barn and climbed down from the buggy. The door slammed at the house, and *Mamm* came across the lawn at a fast walk. Katie studied her face for a moment before beginning to unhitch. *Mamm* didn't look troubled, so everything must be okay. No doubt she was coming out to welcome her home. Perhaps she was trying to make further amends for that *kafuffle* this morning.

"Hi," *Mamm* greeted Katie when she arrived. "How did your day go?" She undid the harness tug on one side of the buggy.

"Okay, I guess." Katie led Sparky forward as *Mamm* held the shafts up to keep them from banging to the ground. Should she share her experience with Ben? Katie hesitated. Hadn't *Mamm* once compared her crush on Ben with her experiences with

Daniel Kauffman? And *Mamm* had told her that Ben Stoll was much like Daniel Kauffman. But she didn't believe that entirely. *Mamm* must be mistaken. No one was like Ben Stoll!

"I'm so very sorry about this morning," *Mamm* was saying when Katie tuned back in. She led Sparky towards the barn.

"You don't have to be!" Katie called. "And you've already spoken to me this morning about the matter, so we're good."

Mamm went on like she hadn't heard. "Mabel and I spoke, and we should all have a long talk together tonight. I'm sure we can arrive at some plan on how to live together in peace."

"I have no quarrel with Mabel," Katie said, pulling off Sparky's harness once they were inside the barn.

"You can't just ignore her." *Mamm* stood in front of Katie. "She's part of the family now."

"I'm not ignoring Mabel." Katie didn't look up. "I was quite nice to her this morning."

"Katie." *Mamm* took her hand. "I know this is hard on everyone right now, but we have to work through it. I know *Dà Hah* will help us. Look at what He's already done! You know how impossible this all seemed only a short time ago."

Katie met *Mamm*'s gaze. "I'll continue to be nice to Mabel, even when she turns her nose up at me. And even when you send me out on the porch so you can be alone with her. Is that *gut* enough?" The words came out a little sharper than she'd intended.

Mamm squeezed Katie's hand. "You're being asked to adjust so fast to this new situation, I know. I never thought things would be like this . . . and so soon."

"Perhaps it's *gut* for me, *Mamm.*" Katie paused. "Let me tell you about the most wonderful thing that happened today."

Mamm held Katie at arm's length, her face uncertain. "What happened? Don't tell me Esther's talked you into going back to a youth gathering? You know Jesse and I don't approve."

"She didn't talk me into anything," Katie said. "But I'm still going to the Mennonite youth gatherings. Don't act so surprised, *Mamm.* I want to keep up my friendships with Margaret and Sharon. I don't have friends like them in the Amish youth group."

"Oh, Katie . . ." *Mamm*'s face had fallen. "And you thought this would be *gut* news for me?"

Katie shook her head. "That news was something else. I talked with Ben Stoll after

55

work, *Mamm.* Can you believe that? And he said a few words to me. I think he might like me once he really notices me."

Mamm groaned. "Oh, Katie. You're not over Ben? I thought that was done with a long time ago. Didn't I warn you about him?"

Katie nodded. "You did. But Ben is different than Daniel Kauffman, *Mamm.* No one is the same."

Mamm's hand trembled on Katie's shoulder. "That's what you think, Katie. Ben Stoll is nothing but trouble. I spent too many years running after a boy, hanging on to every smile he gave me, listening to every word he said, when there wasn't one ounce of love in his heart for me. I should know, Katie. I was loved by your *daett* and now by Jesse. Their love is much more *wunderbah* than anything I ever imagined with Daniel Kauffman."

Katie looked away. "You could be right, I suppose. But you were wrong about Jesse, weren't you? You thought at first it wasn't *Da Hah*'s will that you marry him. Now look at what you have. What if *Da Hah* has something like that in store for Ben and me?"

Mamm groaned as shadows crossed her face. "You take too much on yourself, Katie.

You have a decent *daett* now, one who has great wisdom. I wish you would ask him about that boy. My guess is Jesse will tell you the same things I'm telling you. I don't trust Ben, Katie. You know I don't."

"But that's because of Daniel Kauffman," Katie said. "Ben isn't like that."

Mamm reached over to take Katie's hand. "There are a lot of similarities, Katie. I wish you could see them. I also couldn't get over Daniel — even when he was dating his present *frau.* I even dreamed he would break up with her — right up to the time of his wedding day when he said his vows with her. And then that awful thing I did right in front of them and the bishop himself. Do you want to be like that, Katie? Do you want that reputation?"

Katie didn't say anything. There was nothing she could say. She didn't wish to argue with *Mamm,* but her heart wasn't going to change.

Mamm looked ready to say more, but she changed the subject instead. "Be that as it may, Katie, what concerns me right now are your Mennonite friends. I so wish you'd never met them." *Mamm*'s eyes pleaded with Katie. "I saw Margaret and Susan at the wedding. They are nice enough, but they're not from our world. Surely you can make new friends among the Amish now that so much has changed for us."

Katie shook her head. "Finding friends like Margaret and Susan is quite difficult."

Mamm didn't answer. She stared off into the distance.

"I'm not joining the Mennonites," Katie told her.

"That's what they all say, Katie." *Mamm* looked at her with mournful eyes. "The world has a powerful pull on all of our hearts."

Before Katie could answer, Mabel appeared at the barn door. Catching sight of *Mamm* and Katie, she marched toward them.

"I couldn't find you!" Mabel told *Mamm*, as if she were addressing a small child. "I was wondering where you were."

"Mabel," *Mamm* said, "I was just out here helping Katie unhitch. Then we started talking."

"Well, I wish you would tell me when you leave the house. That's what Carolyn and I do when we're working together."

This is not your sister. This is your mamm! Katie wanted to holler. But this was something *Mamm* had best handle.

"Look," *Mamm* told Mabel, "perhaps we can talk about this tonight when your *daett*

58

can be with us."

"I don't see why *Daett* has to be involved." Mabel wasn't backing down. "It's just the decent thing to do. You could have let me know instead of just disappearing on me."

"Then I will try to be more careful in the future." *Mamm* took Mabel's hand. "Come, let's all go to the house and get supper ready for the men. Katie and I have been talking longer than we should have, and it's high time we get started. We can't have supper late for your *daett* and brothers."

"I never have a late supper," Mabel said. "I started the potatoes boiling before I came out."

Mamm tried to smile over her shoulder at Katie as she motioned for her to follow.

"What were you and Katie talking about?" Mabel asked as *Mamm* led the way.

"Just catching up on Katie's day." *Mamm* gave Mabel a smile, but Mabel didn't look convinced.

"Well," Mabel said, "I'd like to know what it was about. I don't think families should keep secrets from each other."

Mabel was one brash girl, Katie thought. If she were smaller she should be spanked, but at sixteen Mabel was way past that point. And Mabel had been running her *daett*'s household since her *mamm* died, apparently quite competently from how things looked around the house. But Mabel's mind was sure messed up. Thankfully, *Mamm* was now bringing some much-needed correction from the sounds of it.

"There are some secrets in every family, Mabel," *Mamm* was saying. "That's just the way things are. Your *daett* and I have things we talk about, and we don't tell everyone. Your brothers will do the same, as will you and Carolyn in the future. The same thing is true for Katie and me. We have our private matters that concern only the two of us."

Mabel turned around to look at Katie but didn't say anything. The look on her face said enough.

CHAPTER SIX

That evening after supper the gas lantern hissed from its spot hanging from the ceiling above the gathered family. Katie leaned back on the couch, listening to Jesse reading from the Scriptures. She could see through the living room door where the stack of dirty dishes was still sitting on the kitchen counter. Jesse had stuck his head into the kitchen some ten minutes ago to announce that it was time for their evening devotions. *Mamm* had appeared ready to protest the interruption since they always finished the dishes at home right after supper. But there hadn't been a *daett* around all those years, especially one with a mind of his own. *Mamm* had forced a smile and left the dirty dishes.

Mabel looked quite smug after watching the exchange between her *daett* and *Mamm*. She was no doubt used to the schedule and was glad to see that *Mamm* had to give in on something so quickly after the wedding.

Mamm was now sitting on the other couch, a look of contentment on her face. The dirty dishes were apparently forgotten. Little Joel sat on the couch leaning against *Mamm*. *Mamm*'s arm was wrapped around his shoulders. Jesse was sitting in his rocking chair, an empty one reserved for *Mamm* beside him. Jesse had given the empty rocker and *Mamm* a quick glance before he began reading, but he'd said nothing. *Mamm* would sit there in time, but tonight she was taking time to bond with Joel.

Mamm was changing so fast it was breathtaking, Katie thought. All those dark years while she was growing up *Mamm* had often been moody and troubled. But now a look of happiness had begun to find a home on her face. The change made *Mamm* look much younger. Even her step, since she'd said *yah* to Jesse's marriage request had grown ever lighter. And now *Mamm* had stood up to Mabel out in the barn tonight. This was a new thing for her entirely. In the weeks before the wedding, *Mamm* used to shrivel up under the sharp words Mabel had spoken.

Leroy and Willis sat on chairs across the room near the old stove. Mabel had ensconced herself on a chair close to the living room doorway. There had been an empty place on both couches — one between Katie and Carolyn and the other beside Joel. Mabel though, had taken one look and retreated to the kitchen for another chair. She now sat there as if she planned a quick dash back to the kitchen when her *daett* finished reading. No doubt she wanted to stay in charge even with *Mamm* in the house.

Mamm stroked Joel's hair, and he smiled up at her. She smiled back, turning her head to listen as Jesse read.

"Thou shalt go unto my country, and to my kindred, and take a wife unto my son Isaac."

Katie also listened to the familiar story in Genesis of how Abraham sent his servant back to the old country to find a wife for his son Isaac. There the servant had put out a test before the Lord, asking that a suitable young girl would arrive and offer water not just for him but for his camels also. That was quite a task, and not one for the faint of heart, Katie thought. Especially since the water had to be drawn by hand from a deep well. Katie realized she might not have passed the test as Rebecca had. She would have offered water to the man, but to give it to the camels too? That was another matter.

63

But then Katie wasn't Rebecca either. And she wasn't going to be asked to wed Abraham's son, a mighty prince of Israel. Ben Stoll would be a *gut* enough husband for her.

Katie stole a quick glance at Mabel. If Mabel knew what she was thinking, there would be no end of scorn from her. But the girl was watching the kitchen doorway, as if she expected her *daett* to finish at any moment. And sure enough, Jesse closed the Bible.

"We can finish the story tomorrow night," he said. "I know everyone is tired after our first day together as a family. I want us all to get a good night's sleep. We have lots of work to do tomorrow."

"Yah," *Mamm* agreed, rising. "And there are still the dishes to be done."

"They can wait," Jesse said. "It's important that we talk and pray with each other a little before we're totally exhausted from the day."

"Oh . . ." *Mamm* sat on the couch again.

Mabel's smile was smug again, and Katie looked away. She had to find more love in her heart for this girl. It wasn't right the way she was feeling. *Nee,* it wasn't right regardless how Mabel was acting.

"I hope all of you are treating Emma like

the *wunderbah* woman she is," Jesse said.

Mamm flushed, and streaks of red ran up her neck. She looked at the floor.

Jesse smiled, seeming to enjoy her reaction. "Not too many women would be willing to leave their comfortable life with their only daughter and take on a family of five children, along with a grumpy husband."

"That's not true!" *Mamm* said with a chuckle.

Jesse continued. "I see Joel has taken right to Emma like I knew he would. Emma is already more of a blessing to our home than I had dared hope she would be. *Da Hah* has truly given us a great gift. Just as He led the servant of Abraham to find Rebecca for Isaac, so *Da Hah* has given us Emma."

Mamm's face was bright-red now, but Jesse was no longer looking at her. Mabel had her gaze turned to the floor and her face was expressionless. No doubt she was thinking of teacher Ruth, and wishing she was sitting on the couch beside Joel instead of *Mamm*.

Ruth Troyer might be able to run a household better than *Mamm* and even bake better pecan pies — like the ones Ruth brought over in her attempt to capture Jesse's heart — but *Mamm* had succeeded in capturing

65

his attention where Ruth had failed. Not that *Mamm* had tried. She was just better at such things than even she knew.

Jesse interrupted Katie's thoughts. "So let's pray and thank *Da Hah* for our many blessings tonight. And then you women can get back to your dishes." Jesse got down on his knees.

They all followed. Katie buried her face in her hands. Jesse hadn't mentioned a word about the trouble they were having with Mabel, but perhaps he didn't know. *He does care about me,* Katie reminded herself. *He has welcomed me into his home.* He'd made his feelings known before the wedding, and she would always be able to depend on him. Jesse thought *Mamm* the best thing to happen in his life in a long time. He'd said some man would someday think the same thing about her. Ben Stoll, perhaps, Katie added. If he ever really noticed her.

"Great Father in heaven," Jesse was praying, his voice muffled by the rocking chair, "You who made the worlds and all that is in them, hear tonight the feeble sound of our voices. We lift them in thanksgiving to You. How great are the things You have given us. First of all, we give thanks for the gift of Your Son, Jesus Christ, who came down to this earth to walk among us. Your care and

66

compassion for our lost souls is more than we can ever understand. You have shared with us love from Your own heart, and then from each of our hearts to each other. This is a great gift that we can never give sufficient thanks for. You have also given me Emma for my *frau* and to be a *mamm* for my children. And You have given me a love to fill the emptiness of my heart. Truly You have said that it is not *gut* that man should be alone."

Jesse continued on, giving thanks for many other blessings *Da Hah* had given them all. Katie pressed back the tears. She had much to be thankful for in a *daett* like Jesse, and she would have to try even harder to understand and get along with Mabel. Now if *Da Hah* would only grant her heart's desire and bless her with Ben's affections. But that might never happen, and she had to accept that. How much it would hurt if Ben began seeing another woman! Katie wanted Ben to bring her home from the Sunday night hymn singing someday. She wanted him to ask if he could come back again for another evening after that. And someday she wanted him to ask her if she would be his *frau.* She wanted it very badly. Katie took a deep breath and calmed herself. She had to get control of her emotions. Apparently

Mamm's warning about Ben being a lot like her Daniel wasn't that far off target. But she wouldn't act like *Mamm* had, Katie declared silently. Even if Ben never paid her any serious attention, somehow *Da Hah* would continue to give her grace. He had so far, hadn't He?

"Amen," Jesse said, as if answering her silent question. Katie got to her feet along with the rest. She hid her face for a moment to surreptitiously wipe her eyes. Hopefully Mabel wasn't looking. A quick glance toward the girl showed she was already disappearing into the kitchen.

"You can dry the dishes," Mabel told Katie when she walked into the kitchen. Mabel tossed her a towel. Katie tried to smile, standing off to the side as Mabel took center stage at the sink. Mabel washed with a flourish, the soapsuds soon rising high. *Mamm* came in and scraped the skillets without saying a word. Carolyn soon appeared and helped Katie dry.

"So what did you do today?" Carolyn asked, looking up at Katie.

"She works at Byler's," Mabel snapped, as if the place were as offensive as a dirty dish.

Katie didn't reply.

"I would love to work at Byler's," Carolyn said, ignoring her sister's barb. "*Daett* takes us there once in awhile to shop. It's a nice place."

"Thank you." Katie smiled. "Maybe I can take you sometime."

Carolyn shrugged. "I have school. And I'm only twelve, soon to be thirteen, so I couldn't help you work."

Katie laughed. "You could watch for awhile, though I guess all day would be a bit much."

"I would say so." Mabel grimaced. "I think places like Byler's are horrible and worldly and not fit for young people to work at."

"Mabel." *Mamm* spoke up for the first time. "You shouldn't speak about where Katie works like that."

Mabel looked undeterred, sinking the barb in deeper. "Katie's already running around with the Mennonite young people, isn't she?"

Mamm said nothing but her face paled.

Mabel looked pleased. "It's absolutely awful," Mabel continued, "when our own young people can't keep their heads on straight. We have been given so much that others don't have, and then some of them go and throw it away as if it didn't amount to anything at all. As for myself, I'm going to marry an Amish boy and settle down on a farm. We'll raise our children close to the soil, like *Da Hah* meant things to be. We'll grow our own things and stay away from places like Byler's. Well, as much as we can, of course. Everyone has to go out into the world from time to time. But not every day."

"I saw Mabel speaking with a boy on Sunday out in the barn," Carolyn said, a big smile spreading across her face.

Katie waited for Mabel to snap at her sister. Mabel didn't and she even continued to look pleased. Obviously Mabel thought her early conquest of a boy was something of a crowning touch.

"Don't you think you're a little young for boys?" *Mamm* asked.

Mabel lifted her head high. "I've been running the household since *Mamm* died. And I'm much older than my sixteen years — soon to be seventeen — as Carolyn says it. *Daett* always thought he was placing too much of a burden on me, but he learned to trust me. And I can make my own clothes already and run the house like a grown woman. Ruth Troyer even taught Carolyn and me how to make pecan pies."

Mamm's face grew paler at the mention of Ruth and her pies.

"I think you ought to forget about Ruth," Katie said, speaking in her *mamm*'s defense.

"Anyone can make pecan pies."

"Can you?" Mabel asked, turning with a smirk on her face to look at Katie.

"I never have," Katie admitted. "Although it can't be that hard."

"Has your *mamm* ever made them?" Mabel asked, not looking at *Mamm.*

Katie searched her memory for pecan pies. Surely there had been some? *Mamm* knew how to cook great meals. And all the Amish around here were known for their pecan pies. But Mabel was making it sound as if pecan pies were the sum total of success in the kitchen.

"Did you ever make a pecan pie?" Mabel asked, now looking at *Mamm.*

"Years ago," *Mamm* said. "But I don't think I've made one since Ezra passed. That was back when Katie was small."

Mabel didn't say anything, but her face said volumes. *There! Didn't I know it. You are both incompetent women who are in way over your heads in this household.*

"Teacher Ruth makes great pecan pies, and *Daett* loves them," Carolyn said, obviously trying to help but only making matters worse.

What a great ending to the evening, Katie thought. *Mamm* is close to tears, and Mabel is gloating again.

They finished the dishes in silence, and *Mamm* fled back to the living room at the first chance.

"You're a spoiled brat!" Katie said to Mabel, all her *gut* resolutions concerning Mabel flying out the window.

"No one running around with the Mennonites gets any respect from me," Mabel shot back.

Katie bit her lip. Then she turned and left for her upstairs bedroom before she said anything worse.

CHAPTER SEVEN

Katie lay on her bed in the darkness and tried to hold back the tears. The exchange with Mabel had stung more than she expected. How in the world were the two of them supposed to live in the same house? And poor *Mamm,* how did she take it? Katie turned to gaze out the open window. The stars twinkled, shining brightly beyond the dark drapes. A soft knock sounded on the door, and Katie held her breath. Who could be there? Surely not Mabel. Getting up, Katie opened the door and peered out into the dark hallway.

"It's me," *Mamm* whispered.

Kate jumped. Then she stepped back to open the door wider. "Come in."

Mamm stepped inside. "I didn't mean to frighten you. Were you already asleep?"

"Nee." Katie fumbled for a match, found one, and lit the kerosene lamp. She turned the wick low and sat down on the bed.

Mamm was seated in the room's lone chair.

"I had to come up and talk with you," *Mamm* said. "I'm so sorry you're having such a hard time with Mabel."

"Mabel's not giving you an easy time either."

"But I have Jesse . . ." *Mamm*'s words hung in the air for a moment. "I wanted to let you know you have my full support. You're still my daughter whom I love very much."

"Shouldn't you be downstairs with Jesse?" Katie asked. She didn't really wish to discuss the evening's *kafuffles* right now. Going through them had been painful enough.

"Jesse suggested I come up and speak with you."

"Did you tell him what Mabel said in the barn?" Katie turned to face *Mamm.*

Mamm shook her head. "I wouldn't do that. I don't want to make trouble. Jesse just told me to come up out of the goodness of his heart. He's a kind-hearted man, Katie." *Mamm* laid her hand on Katie's arm. "You've been crying, haven't you?"

Katie nodded.

"I'm so sorry about Mabel, Katie. But we have to understand where she's coming from. There are a lot of hurts in her life

74

from the loss of her own *mamm.*"

Katie said nothing for moment. This was all true, and she really should have a softer heart for the girl.

"Have you thought more of what I said about Ben Stoll?" *Mamm* now probed in a different area. "I can't get our talk out of my mind, Katie. You're already suffering enough with Mabel without taking on more trouble."

"You know how I feel about Ben," Katie said. "And it's in *Da Hah*'s hands."

"But you can close your heart to him, Katie," *Mamm* pleaded. "Ben isn't the kind of boy you want to be in love with. You should forget him."

Katie sighed. "I wish it were that easy. But you should know that it's not."

Mamm didn't say anything as she stared at the flickering kerosene lamp. Finally she broke the silence. "You don't have to walk the same road I did, Katie. I can say I didn't know better, but you've been warned. Don't do this to yourself. This boy isn't worth wasting time on. Jesse is concerned about you too."

"You told him about Ben Stoll?"

"Nee," *Mamm* said. "I wouldn't do that, even though Jesse's your *daett* now."

"Then what did you tell him?"

"I just asked about Ben, about what kind of boy he is."

"And Jesse made the connection, of course."

Mamm nodded, her face weary. "Maybe, but that's not the same as telling him about you."

Katie sighed. "I still wish you wouldn't have. People already have a low enough opinion about me without them knowing about my crush on Ben."

"Falling in love is a perfectly normal thing," *Mamm* said, trying to smile. "I'm just sorry it had to happen with Ben. Do try to forget the young man, Katie."

Katie took a deep breath. "I don't know about that, but hopefully there won't be another *kafuffle* this week when Esther picks me up for the youth gathering. Mabel could cause quite a racket, you know."

Mamm looked away, her gaze mournful. "So you haven't changed your mind after our talk?"

"Please, *Mamm,*" Katie begged. "Don't make this harder than it already is. You know I don't want to quit going. I like my friends so much. I feel accepted there." Katie felt she had to go. There were her friendships with Margaret and Sharon, plus she needed a place to get away from the stress at home.

"Is dealing with Mabel pushing you away?" *Mamm* asked. "Did she say more after I left the kitchen?"

Katie looked away from *Mamm*'s searching gaze. "*Yah,* she did. But it's not just that, *Mamm.* It's a lot of things. Me for one. And the friendships I have with Margaret and Sharon. It's so wonderful having friends. I just can't throw that away. And perhaps this is *Da Hah*'s open door to help get me away from my obsession with Ben."

Mamm had tears on her cheeks. "Please don't say *Da Hah*'s behind this, Katie. It's as much my fault as anyone with the way I brought you up. I'm so sorry about that, but I couldn't help myself. I was wrapped in my sorrow and couldn't find my way out. Don't you see what a great miracle happened with Jesse's pursuit of me? Now that's *Da Hah*'s doing. And He can do the same thing for you."

Katie didn't know what to say. She wished she weren't breaking *Mamm*'s heart, but she felt helpless about the matter.

"Don't you think you should go back downstairs?" Katie finally whispered.

Mamm stood up. "I'm going to keep hoping and believing everything will work out. And remember that Jesse welcomes you into

77

his home regardless of how Mabel acts."

Katie managed a smile as *Mamm* left and quietly clicked the door shut. After listening to the soft squeaks of *Mamm*'s footsteps on the stairs, Katie got up and walked over to the window. The stars were still twinkling, each one looking like it was trying to do its best to send out what light it had.

"Please help me," Katie breathed a prayer toward the heavens. "I don't want to bring sorrow to *Mamm*'s heart, and yet I can't just sit still while these opportunities are in front of me. I know that Margaret and Sharon's friendships are from You."

The heavens remained silent as troubled thoughts kept rolling through Katie's mind. Did she really know what she was doing? She was only a young woman, not even twenty yet, and here she was taking on the world her own way.

Katie left the drapes open. She prepared for bed and climbed under the covers. The minutes slipped by, but sleep didn't come. Nothing she did seemed to help. Her mind wouldn't shut off. Finally she got up and closed the drapes. Perhaps that would help. Back in bed, she still tossed and turned, wide awake. She might as well get up and start breakfast. But how silly was that? It was still before midnight. Maybe a glass of milk would help.

Katie slipped out from under the covers and swung open the bedroom door. On the stairs, the squeaks stopped her. There was no way of getting downstairs without someone hearing her. Although *Mamm* and Jesse's bedroom was on the other side of the house, it was near enough to the stair door that sounds carried clearly.

Katie retreated to her bedroom. Now what was she supposed to do? Lie here all night wishing for a glass of milk? She could run the risk of going down the stairs, but if *Mamm* found her in the kitchen the resulting conversation might undo any *gut* effects brought on by the glass of milk. Thoughts of Ben crept into her mind. What was he thinking about right now? Was he asleep or was he also lying awake? *Mamm* was probably right in warning her of the dangers inherent in dreaming and longing for a young man who would never be her husband. So why did this hope keep stirring inside her? Had *Mamm* felt something like this for Daniel? Probably not, Katie figured. The two of them weren't as similar as what *Mamm* claimed they were. And *Mamm* hadn't really found love until she found it with *Daett,* and now she was finding love with Jesse.

Surely it could happen that way with Ben and her! Katie thought. Perhaps she could hasten that day by running around in his circles. She could enter *rumspringa*. But how did one "do" *rumspringa* when it came right down to it? She didn't know. Did a person go to wild parties over the weekends and listen to worldly music? What kind of fun would that be? Katie shuddered at the thought. Surely that wasn't what most of the Amish young folks did during their time of flirting with the world. Most of them probably just wore *Englisha* clothing on weekends and drove cars.

Ben must be spending his time in the world doing things like that. He was too decent to do anything really wrong. He just wasn't like that. So why shouldn't she go out some weekend and see what *rumspringa* was like? Perhaps if Ben saw her in an *Englisha* dress, the lights would go on in his head. He would see that she no longer was just Emma Raber's strange daughter.

Katie imagined herself behind the wheel of a car like Esther Kuntz had. She pictured herself roaring down the road dressed up in an *Englisha* dress with rock music blaring from the radio. Katie kicked off the covers as heat flushed through her body. She could never do something like that. Not in a mil-

80

lion years!

Perhaps she couldn't because she'd lived such a shy life for most of her years. Yet it was more than that. That kind of lifestyle just wasn't right. *Mamm* had taught her that much, even if her teachings couldn't keep her daughter away from the Mennonites. Katie could never be wild, and Ben wasn't wild either. He couldn't be. He was too nice. Katie forced her dark thoughts away. *Da Hah* would have to straighten all this out, and she had best keep her hands out of it. She couldn't do anything about her feelings for Ben.

Katie got out of bed and opened the drapes again. She walked back to the bed, lay down, and watched the stars until she finally fell asleep.

CHAPTER EIGHT

The following week, on a Wednesday night, the sun had set and supper was almost over at the Mast house. Katie kept her eyes on her plate as the chatter of conversation rose and fell around her. Mabel knew she was going somewhere tonight, but other than Jesse and *Mamm,* the others didn't. Before long the headlights from Esther's car would be bouncing into the lane as her friend arrived to pick her up for the youth gathering. They would all know something was up — especially when she stood up and left.

Mamm sat at the supper table with a worried look on her face. When someone addressed her, she tried to smile and respond warmly. *Mamm* was doing a *gut* job of hiding her feelings, but Katie knew her well enough to see the depth of her discomfort. She groaned on the inside. Why did this have to be so hard? It wasn't like she was committing a great sin. Yet likely in their eyes she was. Mabel certainly wouldn't be going to a Mennonite gathering, and neither would Leroy or Willis. Jesse had trained his children better than that.

Mamm would be left to explain the whole situation to the other children. Or perhaps Jesse would take the responsibility upon himself to relieve *Mamm* of the burden. And all of this would happen after she dashed out the door. She didn't like either option. It would be better if they heard the words from her mouth. With that thought firmly in her mind, Katie glanced at *Mamm,* gathered her courage, and spoke. "Um, I have something I want to say." Katie tried to keep her voice from squeaking.

"Yah?" Jesse smiled in her direction as silence settled over the table.

Katie dropped her eyes. Jesse wasn't making things easy by being so nice to her. If he became angry she might at least feel justified in what she was doing. "I'm going out tonight with a Mennonite girl I work with," Katie said. "Her name is Esther. We're going to one of her church's youth gatherings. I wanted to be the one to tell all of you where I'll be."

Mabel looked gleeful. "I thought you were up to something tonight! Does your *mamm* know?"

"Of course," Katie said. "And so does your *daett*. And they don't approve. I'm doing this on my own."

"You're really going to a Mennonite youth gathering?" Leroy stared at her. "How come I've not heard about this?"

"You would know things if you kept your eyes open," Mabel snapped. "Katie has been doing these jaunts even before the wedding."

"Mabel," Jesse spoke up, "you will stay out of this. We will let Katie finish what she has to say."

Mabel's eyes cast daggers at Katie, but she kept her mouth shut.

Katie tried to find her voice and wrung her hands under the table.

"Katie made some friends from work . . ." *Mamm* began, obviously trying to help out.

Katie stopped *Mamm* from speaking further with a shake of her head. "This isn't *Mamm*'s doing or anyone else's but mine. *Yah*, I do have some *gut* friends among the Mennonite youth. But I didn't get to know them by working at Byler's."

"Would one of these friends be a boy?" Leroy had a slight smile on his face.

Mabel's mouth opened as if she were going to say something, clearly agreeing with her brother, but Jesse stopped Mabel with a lift of his hand.

"I don't think this has anything to do with a boy. At least not from what I understand," Jesse said.

"It certainly doesn't," Katie said. "My friends' names are Margaret and Sharon. They were at the wedding, even though you may not have met them since it was such a busy day. They've invited me to a youth gathering tonight. Esther, who also works at Byler's, is picking me up in a minute."

"There has to be a boy somewhere," Leroy announced. "You don't go leaving the faith over some girlfriends."

Mabel smirked behind her hand.

"Katie is not leaving the faith," Jesse said. "If she wants to keep up these friendships, then we shouldn't complain if she visits them once in awhile."

Neither Leroy nor Mabel looked convinced by their *daett*'s mellow words. Katie swallowed hard. Jesse was making this difficult again. But if she didn't speak up now, it would only get harder later. "I . . . I may be attending the Mennonite youth gatherings quite a lot," she managed. "I don't mean anything against the Amish faith by that. I really don't. And I have no plans to leave the Amish or join the Mennonite Church."

"They never do," Mabel stated, her voice dripping with sarcasm. "It just happens all of a sudden. That's how deception comes into the heart."

"Mabel!" Jesse said warningly.

"I can't believe you're allowing this, *Daett*!" Mabel said. "You never would let one of us run around with the Mennonites. And now Katie's bringing this evil right into our house."

With a gasp *Mamm* jumped up from the table and rushed into the living room. Her soft sobs could be heard on the other side of the kitchen wall as silence gripped the people at the supper table. Katie wanted to break out into sobs herself. She should have kept her mouth shut and allowed *Mamm* to handle this after she was gone. Now she had made the situation a hundred times worse.

Jesse was looking at Mabel. "I've told you for the last time tonight to keep out of this. Do you understand?"

"Yes." Mabel looked quite offended. "I'm not a child, *Daett*. But this is terrible. We've never had anything like this happen in our home before."

Jesse said nothing as he continued looking at Mabel.

Under his gaze, Mabel finally glanced away and offered no further response.

"Now, what were you saying, Katie?" Jesse turned back to her.

"I'm very sorry about all this." Katie got to her feet. "I'd better go see what I can do for *Mamm.*"

"Sit down, Katie," Jesse said. He stood up. "I'll be right back."

He disappeared into the living room.

Mabel turned to glare at Katie. "I can't believe you!" Mabel spat out.

Katie looked away. She wasn't going to fight about this. Besides, Esther was coming at any moment. In fact, she should be here already. Katie wondered if she should change her mind and give up this idea tonight. It would temporarily solve things for *Mamm,* but that would only postpone the inevitable. *Nee,* she was going. A look of determination settled on her face. *Da Hah* had opened this door, and she was walking through it. Most of the family, including *Mamm* and Jesse, probably thought she'd pushed the door open on her own, but she hadn't. *Da Hah* had done this for her. She was more certain of that each day. How a thing from *Da Hah* could cause so much trouble was hard to understand, but she wasn't turning back now.

Headlights bounced into the driveway, throwing beams of light through the living room windows. They ricocheted off the kitchen wall, stabbing through the bright glow of the lantern. Katie rose and, without looking at any of them, walked out of the kitchen. *Mamm* was seated on the couch beside Jesse, her head on his shoulder. Her sobs were silent now.

"I'm so sorry about all this," Katie said as she paused for a moment.

"It's okay." *Mamm* looked up, a faint smile on her face.

Katie hesitated. But what more was there to say? Other than staying home, nothing would fully cheer *Mamm*. At least there was one thing to be thankful for. Jesse had done wonders for *Mamm* in the last few minutes. She had never recovered from one of her dark spells so quickly before.

Grabbing her stuff, Katie headed out the door, closing it behind her. She walked down the steps as Esther's headlights lit up the front yard. Katie squinted as she ran toward the car and opened the door. She slid in.

"Howdy there," Esther greeted her. "How are you doing?"

"Okay, I guess," Katie managed to say.

"Trouble again?"

Katie waited until Esther was on the main road before answering. "Everybody's taking my leaving hard, and now there are people around other than *Mamm*."

"I can imagine." Esther was all sympathy. "I guess you'll just have to find your way. Carefully, that is. You are of age, aren't you?"

"Not in my world. We have to be twenty-one."

"Ah, I'd forgotten about that." Esther slowed to pass a buggy coming toward them on the side road. Her headlights illuminated the young man's face for a moment.

"That's the Yutzy boy, Mose," Katie said, turning around in the seat to look back.

"Is he your boyfriend?" Esther asked.

"*Nee*, but I think someone else is after him . . . someone like Mabel."

"He looked kind of old. Are they seeing each other?"

"I don't think Jesse would permit Mabel to see a boy. She's only sixteen." Katie fell silent as a question flashed through her mind. "What is Mose Yutzy doing out here at this time of the night? It could be a perfectly innocent thing, but then . . ."

"Will you turn around and go back?" Katie asked.

"Go back? Have you changed your mind about going out this evening?"

Katie shook her head. "I'd just like to see if Mose drives on past our place. It won't take long."

Esther had a strange expression on her face, but she slowed down.

"I could be completely wrong," Katie told her. "But if I'm not and Mose is secretly seeing Mabel, this might work out to my advantage. I know I shouldn't think in those terms, but I'm feeling desperate at the moment."

Esther laughed and turned the car around in the next driveway.

"And where do you expect to find this young Mose? Parked along the road waiting for his sweetheart to come out?"

"Something like that," Katie admitted. "But probably not quite so obvious."

Esther's headlights cut a path back toward Jesse's house, and Katie sat forward on her seat. How juicy would this be if Mabel really was sneaking out of the house to meet Mose in secret! She could turn the tables on Mabel, but she probably wouldn't. It didn't seem like a nice thing to do. But at least she'd have the option.

"I don't see anything of a buggy," Esther said, slowing down as they approached the driveway of Jesse's farm.

"He couldn't have gotten this far." Katie peered into the darkness. "Drive around the corner before you turn around. I don't want anyone to think it's us coming back to investigate."

Esther did as Katie asked, but she was shaking her head and chuckling quietly.

"I'm not imagining things," Katie said. "So don't look at me like I've lost my mind. I think he's parked back in the woods a ways."

Esther didn't say anything, but she slowed down as they approached the area Katie had pointed out.

"Don't slow down too much." Katie motioned her hand. "But look back in there when we go past. Isn't that a buggy?"

Esther drove faster but took a quick glance into the wooded area.

"It's a buggy, isn't it?" Katie stared into the woods. "That's right where that old lane goes back in. I haven't lived here very long, but I did notice that."

"I do think it's a buggy," Esther agreed. "But I don't think this is any of your business even if what you say is true. They're not doing anything wrong unless her father disapproves. Surely you're not going to tattle on them?"

"*Nee,* I won't." Katie leaned back against the seat. "But I'll keep this in mind in case Mabel gets too rough with *Mamm* and me at the house."

Esther gave her a quick, sideways glance. "Just remember how you feel about attending our youth gatherings. Wouldn't it be nice if your family didn't make trouble for you? Maybe Mabel feels the same way about what she's doing."

"You do have a point," Katie allowed. "I'll try to behave myself."

Esther smiled. She slowed down for the next stop sign. Moments later they were speeding into the night, the car lights cutting a bright path through the darkness.

CHAPTER NINE

Katie hadn't even thought about Christmas. It still seemed so far away. But when Esther pulled into the yard where the gathering was to be held, she saw Christmas lights strung up in the yard — so many it made it seem like daylight. There was a Christmas tree in the front window of the house, half of it glittering with decorations already.

As Katie opened the car door, she heard the sounds of hammering in the distance.

"They're putting down a new hayloft floor," Esther offered.

"That ought to be interesting," Katie said, following Esther toward the barn. A thought flashed through her mind. She'd not only forgotten about Christmas, but also the secret Margaret and Sharon would be telling her tonight. It couldn't be much of anything, she figured.

Ahead of them a girl Katie didn't know came out of the barn.

"Howdy there, Nancy," Esther greeted her. "Where is everybody?"

Nancy nodded a greeting to the girls and said, "Just follow the racket, and you'll find them."

"I don't remember seeing her before," Katie said as they walked further back in.

"She's Nancy Keim, just back from Holland," Esther told her.

"Holland!" Katie exclaimed. "What was she doing over there?"

"Working a year for a Mennonite Youth Outreach in the town of Haarlem."

"That's fascinating." Katie turned around to look back toward the house, but Nancy had disappeared.

Esther pushed open the barn door and led the way inside. Older teens were scattered all over the place. A knot of them were deep in conversation while others were working on nailing down a hayloft floor above them. Several people were carrying in lumber from neat piles off to the side of the barn. They handed them up to those working on the floor.

"Well!" Esther came to a sudden stop. "What a racket. I thought this would be a peaceful evening."

Katie laughed. "I think it's my kind of excitement."

Esther waved toward someone on the other side of the building. When the girl waved back and motioned for them to come over, Esther led the way again. Margaret came rushing toward them before they'd taken more than a few steps.

"Hi, Esther and Katie!" she said. She turned to Katie and gave her a hug. "Oh, I'm so glad you could come!"

"Hi," Katie returned. "And it's so *gut* to see you again."

"I'll see both of you later," Esther interrupted. "I see someone I need to talk to."

"Were you going somewhere with Esther?" Margaret asked.

"Not really," Katie said. "Someone waved at Esther, and we were going over to see her. I couldn't see who she was, so I guess I'll stay here with you. Is there something I can do to help?"

"Of course!" Margaret pointed toward the scattered groups. "We have tons of floorboards to put down and only so much time."

"At least it's well lit in here," Katie said. "That's a little better than the gas lanterns we use."

Margaret smiled. "I told Dad we have to stop by nine-thirty. I'm already falling over from exhaustion."

Katie looked around at the piles of lumber

and the amount of people working.

"Can you finish all this by nine-thirty?"

"Probably not," Margaret said. "But Dad understands that. This will give him a head start on his work tomorrow."

"Okay," Katie said. "I know I can carry lumber, and I'm sure I can nail boards even though I haven't done much of that before."

"Then how about helping with the nailing for awhile?" Margaret pointed out a spot where several girls were gathered. "They're taking turns over there so no one gets too worn out."

"I can do that," Katie said, moving toward the group.

Margaret called after her, "Don't leave before I have a chance to talk with you — someplace away from all this racket. I have something special . . ."

"I'll do that," Katie hollered back even as Margaret's words faded away. She wanted to know what Margaret's news was right now, but she guessed she'd just have to wait.

Where is Sharon? Katie wondered. She didn't see a sign of her anywhere. Well, she would find her later too.

Approaching the group of girls, Katie stopped dead in her tracks. It couldn't be! But, *yah,* there on the other side of the room was Ben Stoll standing in plain sight, his back toward her. She must be mistaken! Ben didn't come to the Mennonite youth gatherings. But it *was* him. Is this the secret Margaret planned to tell her? Katie stood frozen to the spot, thinking about that question. Margaret couldn't possibly know that Ben and I, well, that I like him, Katie decided. Ben is probably just passing through for some strange reason — perhaps here only for one evening. He couldn't be planning to attend often . . . could he?

Several of the girls had turned to greet her.

"Hi, Katie," one of them said. "Did Margaret assign you to help us?"

If she didn't gain control of herself soon, they would notice, Katie thought, forcing herself to walk closer. Ben still hadn't turned around, but she pulled her gaze away from him. "*Yah,* she did." Katie smiled. "What can I do to help?"

"Take a turn with this hammer," another girl told her. "The boys are pushing everything along at breakneck speed. One would think the barn was on fire."

Katie reached for the hammer. The girl handed it over with a sigh, and Katie lowered her head just as Ben turned around. He probably would be surprised to see her — if he even noticed. Her Amish dress was hard to miss. Likely he'd assume she was some other Amish girl. That might get his curiosity up, but once he figured out who she was, that would be the end of his attention.

With vigorous blows, Katie pounded away at the nails, not looking up for even a peek. If Ben wanted to ignore her, well, she would ignore him too. What right did he have to come here anyway? Ben had the whole world in which to roam, while she had only this place. Ben could have any Amish girl's heart he wanted. All he had to do was turn on that smile and speak his charming words. What an embarrassing situation this was. What if the girls around her knew what she was thinking? Her neck was no doubt burning red already, Katie thought, pounding even harder.

Was this why Ben had been riding around in someone's pickup truck the other day? He'd always driven his buggy before when she passed him on the road near Byler's. Was Ben going Mennonite? Surely not! She could never visit again if he was. The shame of being ignored by him in front of Margaret and Sharon would simply be too great. And they would find out soon enough that Ben knew her.

"I think we'll keep you here all night," one

of the girls said, interrupting Katie's thoughts. The girl laughed. "None of us will have to do any work if you keep this pace and pound in all the nails!"

Katie stopped, suddenly conscious of what she was doing and that she was gasping for breath. She would soon be making a scene that even Ben would notice. Handing over the hammer, she stood up, took a couple of deep breaths, and smiled. Thankfully, from the looks on their faces, the girls thought she'd been trying to get the work done quickly and efficiently.

Did she dare sneak another look toward Ben? Perhaps he was gone now or, worse, looking in her direction. What would she do then? But, *nee,* Ben wouldn't be looking at her.

A girl standing beside Katie stepped closer, a smile spreading across her face. "I don't think I know you. Edith is my name."

"Hi," Katie replied, returning the smile. "I'm Katie, and . . ." the words died in her mouth as a voice came from behind them. "Edith, I do declare! You have a nice floor-nailing party going on here. Looks like you might even get done tonight."

Edith was distracted and turned toward the voice. Her smile grew even wider. "Hi, Ben. Good to see you. And, yes, with everyone working so hard anything is possible. Now, if all of us worked like Katie just did, I'm sure we would be done before the hour is out."

Ben laughed softly.

Katie finally turned to face Ben.

"Hi, Katie," Ben greeted as he smiled. "I heard you came to these gatherings."

How did you know that? she wanted to ask. *You don't even know I exist.* She finally managed to say out loud, "I haven't been coming long."

He raised his eyebrows, a question obvious on his face.

She searched for the best thing to say. "It's that . . . well . . . I've become *gut* friends with Margaret and Sharon. And I work with Esther, so she picks me up so I can come."

"And we love having her. All of us do," another girl spoke up. "Are you staying for the whole evening, Ben? I heard there will be ice cream and hot dogs served afterward."

"I think I will." Ben eyes lingered on Katie's face for a moment. Then he broke into a smile — aimed solely at her.

Katie could almost feel her knees buckle. She'd lived under his nose for most of her life, and in the past minute, he'd paid more attention to her than in all those years combined. Ben had noticed her!

"Well, I guess I'll see you later then," Ben said as he moved on.

"Oh, isn't he just the charm?" Edith said, staring after Ben.

"That he is," Katie agreed. Edith didn't seem to hear the emotion in Katie's voice. And underneath her words, Katie's heart was pounding like a drum. Ben Stoll had spoken to her! Was this encounter perhaps part of *Da Hah*'s leading? Here she thought she was running away from a problem — Mabel, the Amish youth, and Ben — and had she really run smack into Ben? Even if it was only for one evening, this was a place where Ben could see her in a totally different light. That was something that would never happen at an Amish youth group gathering. There her reputation and past were too well known. Being Emma Raber's daughter was simply too large an impediment to get over. But she'd gotten around it by coming here. In one flying leap she'd accomplished that just by walking through the doors *Da Hah* had opened for her.

Katie forced herself to breathe and then offered to take another turn at nailing the floorboards. She whacked the nails so hard that she moved rapidly down the space placing one nail after another in quick succession. After fifteen minutes, she was breathless again and handed the hammer to the next girl in the rotation.

Standing up, Katie dared take a peek across the barn floor. She caught sight of Ben talking with one of the boys, laughing as they both carried boards into the barn. Could this really be happening? Was Ben really here? Or was she imagining things? She wasn't. The look on Ben's face had been plain enough to see. He'd been surprised and maybe even impressed at seeing her here. Ben had never been one to hide his feelings. She'd always noticed that about him. Every emotion he had seemed to flash across his face. Unlike her, Ben had probably never had the need to hide what he felt.

Oh, she must give time spent with Ben every opportunity to grow. From now on she'd come to every Mennonite youth gathering there was. Just on the hope he might stop by. Not a chance must be missed. In the rush of her optimistic thoughts, dark ones soon crept in. Is this what *Mamm* used to feel for Daniel Kauffman? Is this what *Mamm* was trying to warn her about? It couldn't be! This was too *wunderbah* a feeling for that. It couldn't be the same. Still, Katie was sure *Mamm* would say it was just that — if Katie ever shared this news with her. But she wouldn't. This would be her secret to hold and cherish in her heart. Someday it would grow into something *wunderbah* — so *wunderbah* she wouldn't believe it herself. *Mamm* had only wished for Daniel Kauffman's love. For Katie, love between Ben and her might happen.

CHAPTER TEN

An hour later, under the bright yard lights, the bonfire had burned low and the coals glowed. Several youth held wooden prongs over the low fire, roasting one last batch of hot dogs. Others sat on benches or on blankets spread on the ground. Several of the boys were standing around, talking and munching hot dogs.

Katie saw a shadow move toward her, and she held her breath briefly before exhaling and wondering who it was. She still had her half-eaten hot dog in her hand. Ben had been on the other side of the fire a moment ago, but now his place was empty. Was the shadow Ben's? She forced herself to take a bite of her hot dog before she looked. Her hand trembled in the darkness. She didn't want to act too eager, but it was so hard to hide her feelings. If Ben came over, she would need to let him know she was inter- ested . . . but not let him know how much or he might run like a spooked horse.

"Have you enjoyed the evening?" Ben asked.

Even though she was expecting it, she jumped when Ben's voice came from right beside her.

He laughed softly. "Sorry, I didn't mean to startle you."

"That's okay," she said. "I loved the evening. Did you?"

"It was nice."

She worked on getting the last of the hot dog down without choking.

Ben stood beside her without moving. "So, how's the new . . . housing situation going?" he finally asked.

That's an odd way to put it, Katie thought. And why did he keep mentioning this? "We're working on it. It's a big adjustment for everyone."

Ben smiled in the darkness. "*Yah,* I know. I was at the wedding, you know."

"*Yah,* I saw you."

"And how about you? It can't be easy getting thrown in with five children from another man's marriage."

Katie swallowed hard. Ben was being kind and sensitive — just as she'd always imagined he'd be. But she didn't want to spill out her troubles to him. "I'll be okay.

Mabel's giving me a hard time. Well, *Mamm* and me. Mabel got used to running the house on her own when her *mamm* died, so it's been difficult. *Mamm* is working with her to help make the transition smoother."

Ben chuckled. "I'm glad to hear they're working things out."

Katie stole another quick glance at his face. The firelight threw soft shadows on his handsome features. She looked away at once. This nearness was almost more than her heart could take. But what did Ben mean by "working things out"? Did he know something about *Mamm*'s marriage to Jesse that he wasn't saying? "Yes, they're 'working things out.' Have you been hearing things?"

Ben didn't say anything right away.

Katie rushed on to fill the silence. "*Mamm*'s very happy with Jesse — happier than I've seen her in years."

Ben nodded. "Look, Katie, I have no problem with your *mamm* marrying Jesse Mast. It wasn't any of my business. It was interesting to watch, though. It's not often Ruth Troyer gets bested. And after she'd set her *kapp* for Jesse . . . Well, congratulations go to your *mamm*."

Katie stole another look at him. Wow, he even knew about the Ruth Troyer business!

It must be all over the community. Of course, that shouldn't be a surprise. The community was small. "Yes, that was an interesting time," Katie admitted. She stared into the glowing coals. She was talking with Ben Stoll! She still couldn't believe it. And for such a long period of time. This went to show how different things were with the Mennonite youth. If this were an Amish gathering, she was certain she wouldn't be saying one word to anyone, much less Ben Stoll.

"It's good to see you here tonight again," Ben said, giving her a sharp glance.

Katie returned his gaze. "A lot of things have been changing with me, I guess. In ways I wasn't expecting either."

"You've been coming for some time now?" Ben asked. When Katie remained silent, he continued, "That's what one of the girls told me."

Katie noticed he was looking at her. She was sure she was turning a brighter red then the burning coals. Well, at least it was dark and he probably couldn't see her very well.

"*Yah,* I have been," she admitted.

Ben motioned toward the food table. "Are you still hungry? There are plenty of hot dogs left. I could cook you one."

"No thanks," she said, watching Ben out

of the corner of her eye. "I've had enough."

"I think I'll get one for myself." Ben patted his stomach. "All this work has made me a hungry man."

Katie waited by the fire as Ben walked over to the table to grab some meat and a roasting stick. She watched as another man walked up beside him. They began talking, and soon were laughing together. This was the Ben she knew — so comfortable around people. Katie continued to watch as Ben and his friend walked over to the bonfire. They were still talking and laughing as Ben cooked his hot dog. When he finished, he didn't return to Katie. Instead he sat down on the grass next to a group of girls sitting on a blanket. They made room for him, and after he scooted closer they were soon chatting away. Katie forced herself to look in another direction. Ben had every right to speak with whomever he wished. And he *had* spoken with her. She would never forget that, not as long as she lived. It was a moment she would treasure, especially if it never happened again.

"Here you are!" Margaret announced.

Katie jumped.

Margaret laughed. "Did I scare you?"

"Nee . . ." Katie chuckled. "Well, just for a second. I was just lost in thought for a

minute."

"He is dreamy," Margaret whispered as she looked toward Ben. "He's Amish, isn't he?"

Katie didn't bother asking who Margaret was referring to. Her gaze made that clear enough. "*Yah*. His name is Ben Stoll," Katie whispered back.

"I saw you talking to him," Margaret continued. "The two of you must know each other well."

"Not really," Katie admitted, but she didn't offer more information. There was no way she wanted to explain her relationship with the people in the Amish youth group. And she certainly didn't want to get into all the feelings that were rushing around inside her heart about Ben.

"I'm glad he could stop by," Margaret said. "Are you ready to hear my news?"

Katie gasped. "Oh, I almost forgot! Yes, I'd like to hear about it. I'm so sorry I didn't track you down to ask you about it. So many things have been going on all evening."

Margaret smiled. "That's okay. I know it's been kind of wild. I'm sorry Sharon couldn't be here tonight so we could tell you together. She so wanted to be, but her *mamm* had a quilt that had to be finished for a customer."

Katie waited expectantly.

"It's like this . . ." Margaret paused. "Katie, did you meet Nancy Keim tonight? The woman who spent a year in Holland?"

Katie nodded but said, "Not really. Esther said 'hi' to her when we came in and told me who she was."

"Did you get to speak with her?"

"*Nee.* There were too many other things going on. Esther mentioned Nancy had been in Holland. That sounds like such an exciting place to go to."

"Yes, it does. And that's why I'm so excited!" Margaret exclaimed. "My big news is that several of us are going to Europe, and we want to invite you to go with us! Do you think you might be able to?"

"Europe!" Katie almost shouted, and several heads turned in their direction. Thankfully, a car started up at that moment, and the roar of the motor drew their attention away.

"Yes, Europe," Margaret said. "Nancy so enjoyed her time in Holland that she wants to go back. She didn't have the time to sightsee much, and she didn't have anyone to tour around with her while she was there, so she's invited Sharon and me to go back with her. We told her about you, and she

110

suggested we invite you too! We plan to fly into Switzerland and tour sites where the Mennonite and Amish faith began. Then on to Holland from there. But we wanted one more person to go, and we decided you'd be perfect. Katie, please say that you will consider going with us!"

Katie was so pleased she was being asked that she couldn't find her voice.

"It's going to be awesome, Katie," Margaret went on. "This is the trip of a lifetime. Just the four of us girls. And Europe is quite safe for travel now, except for pickpockets and the like. But there will be four of us so we can look out for each other."

Katie stammered out, "Margaret, I can't go to Europe."

"Why not?" Margaret asked. "Your mother has just remarried, so she's happy. And surely your new dad isn't making hard-and-fast rules for you. He's probably being real easy on you right now. And you are almost twenty."

"Jesse has been *wunderbah*," Katie said. Her body felt numb right now as she tried to think this through. How could she take off on a trip to Europe? What about her job at Byler's? What about the expense of such a trip?

"I know it's kind of sudden," Margaret

was saying. "It was for us too. But the more we think about it, the more excited we are. You can't say no, Katie. It would break our hearts."

"Oh, my!" Katie rubbed her forehead. "I'm going to have to think about this. Wouldn't it be really expensive?"

"It shouldn't be too expensive. Sharon and I have some money saved up for our share. We're not going until the first of May, so there's plenty of time for all of us to save or round up some money."

Katie's mind was spinning. What an opportunity! But how could she make it happen? For one thing, she'd need *Mamm* and Jesse's approval to go. What would they say about her going to Europe with her Mennonite friends? Attending their gatherings was bad enough in their view. And then there was the money required.

"I really will have to think about this," Katie finally said. "I need to talk to *Mamm* and Jesse and consider whether I can afford it."

"Okay," Margaret said, patting Katie on the back. "That's reasonable. And if you really want to go, I know the Lord will make a way for you somehow."

When Margaret put it that way, Katie remembered the power of prayer. *Da Hah* was already opening so many doors for her. Was this another one? Was He going to provide a miracle to swing this one open? And this was a really big one, at that.

CHAPTER ELEVEN

Thirty minutes later Esther slowed down as they passed the woods near Jesse's driveway. The sports car's headlights cut a swath of light across the fields and into the woods, but this time there was no buggy in sight.

"You didn't really think he'd still be there?" Esther asked, laughing. "That is, if he ever was. I'm beginning to think we imagined the whole thing. I mean, what boy nowadays sits around in the woods waiting for his girlfriend to visit him?"

"Maybe you're right," Katie allowed. After all the things that had happened tonight, knowing that Mabel wasn't sneaking around visiting Mose Yutzy at all hours of the night would be a relief. There was only so much excitement a person could handle.

"Well, here we are." Esther pulled into Jesse's driveway and came to a stop by the barn. "I see someone left a light on for you. That's nice."

"*Yah.* Esther, thanks again for yet another ride. I really appreciate it."

"I don't mind. Let me know when you want me to pick you up again."

Katie opened the door, climbed out, and then closed the car door. She waved and watched as Esther drove away. Then Katie looked toward the house and sighed. *Mamm* would be inside waiting, worried about her evening spent with people who were not of their faith. She would want to know everything that had happened tonight, and she wouldn't be able to see things through Katie's eyes. She wouldn't think Ben being there and speaking with her or Margaret's invitation to go to Europe was anything to rejoice over. To *Mamm* it would be cause for further alarm. She had such a different perspective on things. Most of the Amish believed the Mennonites were — at least to some degree — more dangerous than the *Englisha* when it came to luring someone away from the Amish faith. And wasn't Katie proving the point by sliding right into their clutches? *Yah,* that's how *Mamm* would look at this.

But I'm not sliding anywhere, Katie told herself. She was walking in with her eyes wide open. Margaret and Sharon were her friends. *Yah,* and *yah,* they saw things differently than *Mamm* did. But who was to say their way wasn't just as right? And such thoughts were exactly what *Mamm* was afraid of, exactly what *Mamm* was expecting her to think. And that was also why *Mamm* would be up waiting for her.

Katie forced herself to move toward the house. She wouldn't think the worst until she knew for sure. *Mamm* loved her, and so did Jesse. She knew that. She would need to keep reminding herself of that, especially when things got rough. And she was choosing a most unusual path that would be difficult for *Mamm* and Jesse to understand. She had to admit that. Most Amish girls, given a chance at a new start in life with a *daett* like Jesse, would be thrilled. And Katie *was* thrilled. She just wasn't choosing to do the things everyone expected of her, like submissively going to the Amish hymn singings on Sunday nights and attending the instruction classes for baptism. If she attended instruction classes, she'd be expected to accept what the Amish community thought the will of *Da Hah* was for her — even if that meant being single forever.

Katie's heart rebelled. She couldn't do that. No matter how nice Jesse was to her, she couldn't settle for a life among the

Amish people her age who refused to accept her and let her be herself. Especially before she had a chance to see if anything would become of her relationship with Ben. He had spoken to her at the gathering tonight! His being there was all the sign she needed that *Da Hah* was leading her. And Ben had seen her in a totally new light because she was among the Mennonites. There she was no longer Emma Raber's daughter. No, she was a new woman altogether. There was no way that *Mamm* and Jesse would understand all this, even if she tried to explain it.

Katie crept up the porch steps. She gently nudged open the front door, but the hinges seemed to shriek in the night air. Obviously Mabel isn't sneaking in and out this door, Katie thought. She would have to remember to see if the other door leading outside didn't squeak. From now on she'd use the washroom door when she came in at night. Mabel probably kept those hinges well oiled. Katie silently chuckled at the thought.

The door latched behind her with a soft clink, and Katie tiptoed to the kitchen doorway. She peeked around the corner and saw the flickering light of the kerosene lamp playing over *Mamm*'s bowed head. *Mamm* wasn't praying or she would have looked up by now. Perhaps she'd fallen asleep while crying out to *Da Hah.*

"*Mamm?*" Katie whispered as she entered the kitchen.

Mamm's head flew up as she turned toward the doorway. "Katie! You're back."

"Of course I am," Katie said with a smile. She put her arm around *Mamm*'s shoulder and gave her a quick hug.

"Please sit down." *Mamm* motioned toward the kitchen chair. "Tell me all about your evening."

"But it's late," Katie said after glancing at the clock. "*Mamm,* you didn't need to wait up for me."

"I love you, Katie. Waiting up isn't a problem. And Jesse understands. He cares about you as much as I do."

Katie rubbed her face. Should she share everything with *Mamm*? She sat down. Should she tell *Mamm* tonight about Ben being at the meeting and the proposed trip oversees? Now that *Mamm* was sitting right in front of her, the idea of taking a trip to Europe sounded crazy. How could she, a young, unmarried Amish girl, make a trip to the Old Country?

"What are you thinking about?" *Mamm* asked. She reached over and touched Katie's hands.

Katie and her *mamm* had always shared everything, and *Mamm* obviously didn't want that to change. Neither did Katie. No matter how awkward it would be or how much it might hurt both of them, she decided she wanted to share what was going on.

Katie looked up and met *Mamm*'s gaze. "What a night, *Mamm*. We worked on building a hayloft at Margaret's place. And you'll never guess who was there!

"Who, Katie?"

"Ben Stoll!"

Mamm's eyes widened. "At the Mennonite youth gathering?"

Katie nodded.

"I didn't know he ran with the Mennonites."

"I didn't either."

Mamm didn't look convinced. "Really, Katie? Or is this why you've been going to the Mennonite gatherings all along?"

"Mamm!" Katie protested. "How could you believe I'd lie to you?"

Doubt flashed across *Mamm*'s face, but she soon nodded. "I believe you, Katie. But this is another *gut* reason to stop attending the Mennonite youth gatherings. Didn't you tell me you thought going there might be *Da Hah*'s way of getting you away from Ben?

119

So you must have been wrong, Katie. With Ben there, you're not getting over anything. And you know in your heart that nothing good will come out of your infatuation with Ben."

Katie hung her head. She had been mistaken about going to the gatherings to forget about Ben, no doubt about that. But not how *Mamm* thought. *Da Hah* had been leading her straight toward Ben all along. The memories of *Mamm*'s words of warning raced though her head. They'd been sitting in the living room of the old house not too long after Jesse had started to woo *Mamm*'s heart. *Mamm* had shared the story of her own terrible mistakes when she was young and in love for the first time. She told how she'd loved a boy who hadn't loved her back. How she'd hung on to the hope he would someday marry her — right up to his wedding day when he'd said the vows with another girl. And then, in her distress, she'd made a spectacle of herself in front of the Amish community — and garnered a negative reputation as a result. *Mamm* said she never wanted Katie to go through anything like that.

But Katie was determined not to. Her situation was different! Ben had spoken with her tonight. Until they met at the Mennonite gathering, Katie had just been Emma Raber's odd daughter. That had changed now. Ben had seen her in a different light.

"Do you remember what I told you about such boys?" *Mamm* touched Katie's arm. "You have to listen to me, Katie. You can't go running after dreams like this. They will break your heart."

Katie took a deep breath. "But Ben spoke with me tonight, *Mamm.* And I think he really saw *me* for the first time."

Mamm sighed. "Ben Stoll is not the man for you, Katie. And you don't want him as your boyfriend. Even if he asked to bring you home on a Sunday night, but you know that will never happen. He's not in our league. He's out of reach. You know that."

Katie didn't look at *Mamm;* instead, she stared at the wiggling flame in the kerosene lamp. *Mamm* had always objected when Katie talked about Ben Stoll. And Katie had always blamed it on *Mamm*'s experience with Daniel Kauffman. But perhaps this objection went deeper? Could it be rooted in the fact that Ben was in *rumspringa*? That might be the answer. *Mamm* had never liked the practice, and she'd forbidden Katie to participate in it.

Mamm gripped Katie's hands. "Please don't be offended, Katie. I've told you all this before. I don't want your heart broken and thrown away by some boy. I know it can happen regardless of how careful we are. But letting your heart get tangled up with Ben is really asking for trouble."

"It's already tangled up, *Mamm,*" Katie admitted in a whisper. She stood up. "And there's little I can do about it."

"Oh, Katie!" *Mamm* stood up too and wrapped her arms around Katie's neck.

Katie said nothing as she buried her face against *Mamm*'s shoulder. If she didn't say something about the Europe trip right now, it might never get said. But how could she with *Mamm* already hurting so deeply?

Mamm continued. "I hope you don't mind that I shared my concerns about you, the Mennonites, and Ben with Jesse tonight. Jesse's my husband now, and he's your *daett,* Katie. Jesse and I got down on our knees and prayed for you tonight."

"Thank you," Katie said quietly as the image of Jesse and *Mamm* kneeling beside the couch and offering a special prayer for her went through her mind. Their kindness and concern was simply overwhelming. *Mamm* was waiting, a look of hope on her face that *Da Hah* was already answering her prayer and her daughter was seeing the truth as she did.

Katie choked, a sob catching in her throat. "Oh, *Mamm,* there's even more to tell you. And I'm afraid you won't like it, either. But you should know about it sooner rather than later."

Mamm sat down.

Katie could see by *Mamm*'s stiff back and determined look that she was bracing herself. "Margaret asked me to go along on a trip to Europe with her, Sharon, and another girl named Nancy Keim. Nancy just returned from a mission trip to Holland, and she wants to go back for a visit."

Mamm was openly staring as Katie rushed on. "And I do so want to go! It would fit in with the new me, with the new life that I'm beginning. I never wish to go back to being the 'old Katie' again. She was always on the fringes and never accepted. But the 'new Katie' is different. It's a little like you and Jesse, *Mamm.* You've started a new life. And didn't *Da Hah* bring the two of you together in such a special way? Why couldn't He be doing the same thing for me?"

"Katie . . ." *Mamm* wiped away fresh tears. "Oh, Katie, you're all *fahuddled.* All these changes have been too much for you. You're not being yourself."

"Nee, Mamm," Katie whispered, "I'm not being my old self. I've changed, and I like

it. Can you love the new me? Will you love the new me? I love you in your new life."

Mamm gave her a weak smile. "Katie, you're so young. You have so much to learn, and I wish I could teach you. I so wish you would be willing to learn from me. You would avoid so much heartache that way."

Katie was silent as they both wiped away their tears.

Finally *Mamm* said, "Come, Katie. We've talked enough tonight. It's late. If we don't get our sleep, we won't be of any use tomorrow. We'll talk more about this later after I've discussed it with Jesse."

"Please don't," Katie said. "Can't we keep this just between us for now?"

Mamm smiled again. "I have to talk with Jesse, Katie. He cares about you, and he's my husband and your *daett*. He'll know how to help. He's a very wise man."

With what *Mamm* was going to tell him, Jesse might forbid her traveling to Europe and also tell her she could never attend a Mennonite youth gathering again. Then what would she do? This turn of events was to be expected, Katie decided. She just hadn't thought it would be now. Surely *Da Hah* would give her the strength to bear whatever was going to happen. If He was opening doors for her, and Katie was sure

He was, He would make a way so she could continue to attend the Mennonite gatherings and take the trip with Margaret, Sharon, and Nancy.

Mamm was already at the kitchen doorway, holding the kerosene lamp in her hand. She paused to look back over her shoulder at Katie.

"I'm coming," Katie said quietly as she softly walked after *Mamm*. They parted at the stair door, and Katie crept up the squeaky steps, feeling her way by sliding her hands along the walls. She reached the top. The house wasn't quite familiar yet, but she could find her way without a light, well enough to keep from tripping and flying across the floor anyway.

Katie found the knob to her bedroom door, turned it, and pushed the door open. She paused in the doorway as her thoughts turned to Mabel. Mabel and Mose. The idea wouldn't go away. How did Mabel leave without anyone hearing her? Katie decided she had to know tonight. It was stupid, but did the washroom door really open without a squeak? Perhaps knowing for sure about Mabel's shenanigans would lessen her own troubled thoughts about Ben and *Mamm* and the trip to Europe. At least there would be someone else in the family

who wasn't behaving the way they were supposed to . . . or expected to.

Katie left her bedroom door open and felt
her way back downstairs, carefully avoiding
the stairs that squeaked. In the living room,
a glow of starlight filled the room, distin-
guishable now that her eyes had adjusted to
the darkness. Katie went through the
kitchen, dodging the chair she'd been sitting on.

If she accidently made a racket, *Mamm* or
even Jesse would come to check it out, so it
might be good to have an excuse ready.
Katie eased her way to the kitchen sink. Seeing the shape of a glass sitting on the
counter, she wrapped her fingers around it
and lifted. She gently pushed the faucet up
a fraction of an inch and waited for the faint
sound of water filling the cup. She shut the
faucet off seconds later and drank a few
sips. Now she wouldn't be lying if she had
to tell *Mamm* or Jesse she'd wanted to get a
drink.

Katie felt her way through the washroom
and pushed open the outer door. It swung
on its hinges without a sound.

CHAPTER TWELVE

Two evenings later, on a Friday night, Ben Stoll pulled his buggy to a stop behind a grocery store on the west end of Dover. Along these streets the houses were beginning to glow with Christmas decorations, but Ben didn't notice. The guilt that had been gnawing at him for weeks was in full force. How had he gotten himself into this situation? Around him the shadows behind the store blended in with his horse and buggy, camouflaging them as always, but tonight it no longer seemed the perfect setup he'd once thought it to be. They'd been using this place for two years now. Rogge Brighton had assured him they wouldn't get caught, and so far he hadn't been wrong.

Rogge had approached Ben at an *Englisha* party soon after he'd begun *rumspringa*. Ben hadn't purchased an automobile back then, and he remained without one to this day. It really wasn't his thing to tear around wasting a lot of time and gasoline, though that was what many Amish boys did during their *rumspringa* years.

He had enough friends to ride along with when such trips were necessary. That was *gut* enough for him. Rogge had suggested Ben keep his lifestyle like it was to avoid suspicion, so he had. Now it was time to end this arrangement between Rogge and him. He'd made enough money — much more than he could have made in years of working for a construction company. Something conscience also screamed against.

He told himself again, as he had so often before, that all he'd been doing was picking up a large package here on a regular basis, opening it, and then distributing the smaller packages inside to the people on a list that Rogge gave him. It wasn't that big a deal, and yet Ben knew it was. He dropped off the small packages mostly at parties, but occasionally he delivered to someone's home. Ben knew lives were being affected, and he couldn't ignore the knowledge any longer.

Rogge was only concerned with getting caught, and that hadn't happened. He had the brains for this kind of business. He'd assured Ben that if he did as he was told, he would make a lot of money and not get into trouble. And Ben had listened so far. Obedience was a trait bred deep in all Amish, and for Ben it was still there even as he went about *rumspringa.* Besides the obedience factor, following orders was a small price to pay for such easy money.

Ben leaned out of the buggy door to peer down the street. Where was Rogge? He was late again. They never spoke via cell phones even though Ben kept one under the buggy seat. It was for emergencies, though Ben wasn't sure what that kind of emergency might be. He liked having the cell phone because it gave him the feeling of being a real businessman. The only people he could call were his friends on *rumspringa* though.

He'd known from the start that the stuff he dropped off couldn't be doing anyone any *gut.* He certainly stayed far away from the contents himself, although he had opened one of the packages to see what the stuff looked like. From what he observed in Rogge's clients, the substance sent most young people that used it off into some sort of la-la land. But still they used it — and they would probably use it whether he was involved or not. That had always sufficed as an excuse for his participation. Until lately, that is. An empty feeling had crept into his heart, and that, coupled with the guilt, was overwhelming. Something had to change. He'd lost his faith over this mess he was in. Or perhaps he'd fallen into this mess because he couldn't get his faith straight. He wasn't sure which was right, but one sounded about as bad as the other.

Rogge, though, never seemed to worry about such scruples. And in his presence, Ben had never dared voice his doubts or concerns. But now the time had come for a change. He planned to tell Rogge tonight that he was quitting, and this delivery would be his last. He'd made the decision the other evening at the Mennonite gathering. Noticing Katie Raber these past weeks had done something to him. When he tried to remember Katie from the many years he'd known of her, she was just a distant haze in his mind. He'd never paid much attention to her beyond knowing she was the daughter of the weird widow Emma Raber. He did know enough to remember that Katie had always been quiet . . . reserved . . . withdrawn. She'd been like a silent shadow that hung around the edges of the Amish youth.

What had happened to change the girl so completely? Ben wondered. He hadn't believed his eyes at Jesse's wedding when he'd realized who she was. This was Emma

Raber's daughter, the odd girl he'd seen around — only it wasn't. And, if he wasn't mistaken, she had quite a crush on him. He'd seen it in her eyes. It was a pleasant thought too. Not that he paid that much attention to the fawning of girls. There'd been many of them over the years. But Katie was different. There was a freshness about her, an innocence and vibrancy. He sensed Katie had faced the world and won, but he wasn't sure what that meant or what she'd gone through to get to that place.

However, it made him decide it was time to straighten out his life. At least in some measure. He'd never expected motivation to reach him through a girl — a woman, really — but it had. Plus Katie wasn't that bad looking. And she didn't seem to know it, which made her even more attractive. Always before, when he thought about his faith, the only options he'd considered were joining the Amish church after his *rumspringa* years or leaving the faith. Neither choice appealed to him. Now a third one leaped to mind. He could join the Mennonites. That was what Katie seemed ready to do. He should have thought of the Mennonites before, but they'd always seemed a little stuck-up. But how wrong he'd been. They were a nice bunch of people.

Katie and the Mennonite Church were clearly worth looking into further. And even if the Mennonite angle didn't work out, he was still going to get out of this business and go into something more legitimate and fulfilling.

Ben's thoughts were interrupted when headlights raced around the corner of a building a few blocks away. They blinked out, which was followed quickly by a squeal of tires. That would be Rogge arriving in his increasingly careless fashion. He needed to use much more caution, Ben thought. Rogge did in most things, but he seemed to be slipping lately. It came from too many months of success, Ben figured. Success could dull even the brightest brain. That was another reason for him to move on.

Quick footsteps soon came from the shadows as Rogge's form materialized. He had a large bundle beneath one arm.

"Hey there, my good man!" Rogge greeted Ben, throwing the package on the buggy floor.

Keep your voice down! Ben wanted to say. He stared at the bundle. Inside would be a large packet of twenty dollar bills for his trouble.

"Same setup as usual," Rogge said. "There are some new people this time around, but it's all laid out in the instructions. This ought to be a good week. And next week will be even better. See ya later, man." Rogge stepped away from the buggy and turned to go.

"Wait a minute!" Ben called as loudly as he dared. When Rogge turned back, Ben took a deep breath. "This is my last run, Rogge. I'm ready to do something different. And since I'm not giving you much notice, why don't you just keep the payment for this delivery? I don't want any hard feelings between us."

Rogge stepped closer. "What did you just say?"

"I'm quitting. This is my last run. I'm not doing this any longer. It's time to do something different."

Ben noticed the whites of Rogge's eyes even in the dim shadows. He must be shocked, and clearly this news wasn't being received well. But that was to be expected.

"You have any particular reason for this?" Rogge asked.

"No, it's just time. We've been doing this long enough, and eventually the police might figure it out. Not likely, but why take the chance? Plus I've met someone — a woman — and I might want to settle down." That wasn't quite true, but it might make sense to Rogge. At least more than his other reasons would. Rogge laughed, which was encouraging.

"A woman? She must really be something to give up all of this easy money."

"Maybe," Ben said before joining in the laughter.

Then Rogge stopped laughing. "You're leaving me in quite a fix, Ben. I have orders lined up for the next six months. It's not like I can cut contracts," he snapped his fingers, "just like that. They're not friends like we are. You either spend time in the can or you deliver for these people. Those are the only two options they understand."

Ben hesitated. He was wavering. He glanced down at the bulge in the package where he knew the twenties were. But his conscience screamed and got his attention. "Look, I'm sure you can find someone else to do the deliveries. I need to do something else. I know it's been good between you and me, but I'm having bad feelings about things."

"Really? Like what?" Rogge was staring at him.

"I don't know . . . just a feeling. This business has been going too well for too long. I don't want to press my luck."

Rogge grunted, his face hidden in the

134

shadows. "Maybe, but it's still a shame."

"I have to quit," Ben insisted. He felt a twinge of fear. What if Rogge wasn't going to let him off the hook? What if Rogge decided he wasn't trustworthy? Ben decided there wasn't much his friend could really do. If he made a stink, Ben knew too much to try blackmail. And harming an unarmed Amish man wasn't exactly a deed someone of Rogge's caliber would want on his hands. Plus they were friends. That ought to count for something. He looked down at Rogge. "I need to do something else for awhile."

"Well, how about you give me a few more weeks while I scout around for another courier? Until then, it's back here next week at nine o'clock. Okay?"

Ben tried to say something, but Rogge had already turned and was gone, the sound of his footsteps fading away in the darkness. Minutes later a car engine roared to life, headlights stabbed the darkness, and tires squealed as a sports car took off and disappeared down the street.

Ben slapped the reins and drove his horse west and out of Dover. He should have been firmer with Rogge. He should have insisted that this really was the last time. But now the moment was past. To the steady beat of horse hooves on the street, Ben stared out into the night and watched as the shapes of trees and bushes along the road drifted past like ghostly forms. He shook his head. Why hadn't he stood his ground? But he knew why. Because he was weak. Weak on the inside. Ben thrust the thought away. He *would* quit. It might just take some time to accomplish. He slapped the reins hard against his horse's back. As the horse sped up, Ben vowed he would quit — and soon, very soon. Regardless of what Rogge had to say about it. So what if his decision placed Rogge in a bind. He could find someone else. Anyone could deliver packages.

And Ben decided he'd get rid of some of the money — put it toward a good cause. That would be a *gut* thing, and it might make him feel better. He could go to Deacon Noah and give a donation to the general fund the Amish kept for emergencies among themselves. But, then, giving it to Deacon Noah might not work. He'd probably ask where such a large sum of money came from.

Ben's thoughts were interrupted by the bouncing lights of an *Englisha* automobile in the distance. Long before the noise of an engine reached him, the piercing colored lights of a police cruiser blossomed above the headlights and sent wild shadows dancing in the night air. Ben clutched the reins and pulled back so hard that Longstreet slid to a halt, his shoes scraping hard on the pavement. Ben quickly guided him to the side of the road as far as he could to get out of the way.

Panic hit, and Ben's thoughts swirled. Questions whipped through his mind. Had the police been following Rogge? Had they watched their meeting and the transfer of the package? Were they going to arrest him? Had they already captured Rogge? Had someone turned them in?

Rogge was getting sloppy. He should have had the sense to see trouble was coming. A lucrative business like the two of them were running would eventually attract the attention of other users, rival drug dealers, and even people on the street. And just because he was Amish didn't mean he would avoid prosecution or jail. In fact, being Amish might even make the situation worse since they were known to be God-fearing people who lived quietly and honestly.

The flashing lights came closer and closer. Ben held his breath and tried to move the buggy further off the road without coming to a complete stop or getting stuck. Buggies moved slowly enough at their natural speed that they didn't normally pull off the road and stop like the *Englisha* vehicles had to when emergency vehicles went by.

With his buggy wheels bouncing on the lip of a ditch, the police cruiser roared past. Ben's shoulders relaxed as he took a slow, deep breath. Whew! See, Ben, that's all there was to it. No one knows anything. You're okay. No one's after you. He took another deep breath. Still, it was a close call, and his stomach was tied in knots. He was still going to quit. Rogge would just have to find a way to deal with it. Ben decided to consider this a warning to spur him on in case he wavered in the weeks ahead. Getting caught would do so much damage to his family, to him, and to his future. The risk was too great.

Ben slapped the reins gently against Longstreet's back, and they moved quickly through the night. Ben wanted to get this job over with. Soon this life would be behind him.

CHAPTER THIRTEEN

Katie looked out the kitchen window as she washed the supper dishes. Tomorrow was Sunday already, and neither *Mamm* nor Jesse had spoken a word to her about last Wednesday evening, Ben Stoll, or going to Europe. *Mamm* hadn't even shared Jesse's reaction to Katie's news. Both of them must have decided to ignore the problem for the moment. Perhaps their focus was on more immediate troubles. Mabel was still stalking around with looks of either defiance or distress on her face. Katie hadn't mentioned her suspicions about Mabel and Mose because they were just that . . . suspicions. She might be wrong about that situation.

Tonight Mabel had been assigned by *Mamm* to help Katie with the dishes. The girl had turned up her nose at first, but she hadn't verbally complained. The rest of the family was in the living room, and from the sounds of the voices rising and falling, they were having a *gut* time together. Things weren't going so well between her and Mabel though.

The tension with Mabel had to be faced, Katie figured, so *Mamm* was trying to force a peace between them. Jesse had likely put *Mamm* up to it, as she couldn't imagine *Mamm* having the courage to push Mabel this far on her own. Correcting Mabel was one thing, but assigning her the task of drying dishes for Katie was another. From her tense posture, Mabel didn't like this in the least. Jesse must have given her a stern talking-to since she was doing the job.

Katie stole a glance at Mabel's face. Thunder was written on it. Since Katie was the older of the two, she figured it was on her shoulders to make the first friendly move. She smiled and asked, "Did you have a *gut* day working with *Mamm*?"

Mabel stared out the window and didn't answer.

Katie tried again. "Supper was quite delicious, and I wouldn't be surprised if you made it. It didn't taste like *Mamm*'s cooking."

Mabel glared at Katie. "What were you expecting? That you'd starve when you arrived here? I've been running this household since *Mamm* died."

Katie kept a smile on her face. "I would say you did a very *gut* job."

Mabel gave Katie another hard look. "What makes you so sweet all of a sudden? Are you up to something? Or are you just gloating because I have to wipe dishes for you?"

Katie hesitated. She wasn't up to anything other than trying to cooperate with *Mamm*'s peacemaking efforts.

"So you *are* up to something." Mabel stopped wiping the bowl in her hand and looked piercingly into Katie's face.

Katie's mind raced. If she didn't say something quickly, Mabel would grow more suspicious. Perhaps honesty would be the best option. "I'm just trying to help out *Mamm.* She wants the two of us to get along."

Mabel huffed. "It would have been much easier if *Daett* had listened to us and married Ruth. Then none of us would be going through this painful time."

Katie winced. "I'm sorry, but I disagree with you. I wanted *Mamm* to marry Jesse."

Thunder filled Mabel's face again. "Of course you would want that. You and your *mamm* were nobodies in the community until *Daett* came along to rescue both of you. Now you think that your standing will

141

change because you're part of our family. Only it won't because I'll make sure it doesn't. No Amish boy will ever ask you home on a Sunday night, Katie. There's not a chance in the world. I promise you that."

Katie stood still, shocked at Mabel's virulence.

A gleeful smile spread across Mabel's face.

Clearly she was taking the silence to mean her arrow had struck home. Katie forced herself to speak. "You don't know everything there is to know about me, Mabel. There are lots of things about my life you know nothing about."

"Like what?" Mabel shot back. "That your *Mamm* owned five acres before she married my *daett,* and now she owns more than a hundred? That you were as poor as two church mice, but now you have plans to cut into our inheritance? That you once owned two cows, and now you have a full herd? Are those the parts of you I don't know anything about?"

Katie swallowed hard as sudden tears stung her eyes. Mabel was more cruel than she'd thought possible. And it didn't help that her words were true, though not in the way Mabel meant.

"I don't want your *daett*'s money," Katie said firmly even as a feeling of sorrow swept over her. She'd just doomed any chance of having the funds to go to Europe. Now she couldn't accept an offer of help from Jesse — even if he were willing to finance part of the trip — and he probably wouldn't be.

"That's easy enough for you to *say*," Mabel snapped. "I guess we'll just have to wait and see how much of a burden you and your *mamm* are going to be to us."

Katie kept her voice low. "You shouldn't think so high and mighty of yourself. *Mamm* apparently is *gut* enough for your *daett*. He asked her to be his *frau*. And you didn't see anyone in the community stopping your *daett*."

Mabel looked away without saying anything.

"I'm sorry," Katie said a few moments later. "I guess your words hurt more than I thought they would so I responded in anger. The truth is that I had hoped your *daett* would help us out. And he has. He loves *Mamm,* and everyone can see that *Mamm* loves him. I think that's *wunderbah*."

Mabel put the bowl down and picked up a pan to dry.

Katie continued. "And yes, there is something I was hoping your *daett* might help me with. It just came up this week. But since you're worried about your inheritance,

I won't ask for his help. I'll ask for his permission, but that's all. Any funds needed I'll earn and save myself."

Anger gathered in Mabel's face. "I knew you were up to something. Are you going to tell me or not? What is it? A new dress to wear with your Mennonite friends?"

The pain was stinging deeper, Katie thought. Soon she might burst into tears like a little girl who'd dropped her ice-cream cone. How in the world was she going to live with Mabel in the same house with these kinds of insults and thoughts constantly being hurled her way?

"Can you even afford the soap to wash your clothes?" Mabel dug deeper. "I always thought I smelled something strange on Sundays when you or your *mamm* walked past us."

Why is this girl so cruel? Katie wondered. Mabel seemed almost driven to be vindictive. Katie gathered her emotions together before meeting Mabel's mocking eyes. "Mabel, I've been invited on a trip to Europe. And you're right, the invitation did come from my Mennonite friends. We would be gone for three weeks. The plan is to tour sites in Switzerland where the Mennonite and Amish faiths began."

Mabel blinked hard as surprise filled her

eyes. "I don't believe a word you're saying."

Katie shrugged. "That's okay. It's the truth. I told *Mamm* about it on Wednesday night, and I'm sure she's talked to your *daett* about it by now."

"And you expect him to give you the money?" Mabel's eyes blazed again.

"No. And especially not now. I wouldn't want to dip into your inheritance."

"I should say not! What nerve you have!"

Katie took a deep breath. "I don't want your *daett*'s money, Mabel. All I want from him is his permission to go."

"Then you're not going to Europe," Mabel said. "*Daett* won't allow it."

Katie shrugged. "I guess we'll just have to see what he says then."

Mabel went back to wiping the dishes, but soon the cutting words began again. "I imagine you have lots of wild dreams floating around your head, Katie. But none of them will ever see the light of day. You probably thought you could fulfill them now that you managed to get my *daett* to marry your *mamm,* but it's not going to happen. Not ever, Katie." Mabel paused. *"Never!"*

Katie scraped a plate clean before she slid it into the water. "Why do you hate us so much, Mabel?"

"I don't hate anybody," Mabel said. "It's

not Christian. I just don't like my family being disturbed by low-down people who want to better themselves at our expense."

Katie glanced at Mabel. "And how are *Mamm* and I disturbing your life — other than the obvious, such as moving in, which would have happened when your *daett* married anyone? Do you really believe *Mamm* and I are such low creatures who are far beneath your station in life?"

"You don't have to use such fancy *Englisha* language," Mabel said. "It's not going to change my opinion of you or your *mamm.*"

Katie persisted. "I'm not, Mabel. And I would like to know. Do you really think so highly of yourself and so low of us? And I didn't have to tell you about the Europe trip. I chose to share that with you."

Mabel sniffed. "It's hard to explain how I feel so you'd understand."

"Maybe we should start from here and try to understand each other better," Katie ventured.

Mabel let out a bitter laugh. "I don't want to know either of you better. I already know enough and plenty."

Should she attempt an appeal to Mabel's sensibilities? Katie wondered. Tell her how uncomfortable it was living with someone who held something against her that she didn't have anything to do with? Before she could try, Mabel spoke up.

"Neither of you realize how miserable you're making my life."

"Oh?" Katie turned to face Mabel. "How is that? What do you think we're trying to do to you?"

"You don't have to try to do anything. You just do it." Mabel wiped the dishes furiously.

The girl's anger is so deep, Katie thought. What was it based on? What caused it? Maybe she should tell Mabel she knew about Mose? Perhaps then Mabel would know that she'd kept quiet, and that would help the girl trust her. Surely she'd know she hadn't gone racing to Jesse with the information. But Katie decided that if she said something, it might make the stress with Mabel even worse and really blow any chance of a *gut* relationship. And there was that little chance that she was wrong about Mose and Mabel. *Nee . . .* she would wait.

Mabel cleared her throat. "Okay, I'll tell you *one* of the reasons. But I'm not going to expect any help from you."

"Okay, Mabel." Katie waited.

"It's the *rumspringa* thing," Mabel said. "Everyone knows how your *mamm* feels about that subject. She never let you participate, so I'm worried she's going to persuade *Daett* to keep me home."

And make you different or weird to the other kids like I was, Katie almost said aloud. But Mabel was doing a *gut* enough job reminding her of the facts, so there was no sense in adding to her efforts. "But your *daett* isn't like that. I haven't heard him say anything about not allowing you to participate."

Mabel shrugged. "He allows the boys to participate, but I'm his first girl. And *daetts* treat girls different. And now he's married to your weird *mamm.*"

"Mabel," Katie protested, "*Mamm* wouldn't try to sway your *daett* on how to raise you. She'd do nothing of the sort. She might share her personal feelings on the matter, but she wouldn't push your *daett.*"

"She raised you according to her 'personal feelings.' And look how you turned out. No one wants to be your friend. No one includes you in things. Of course, maybe those are *gut* points I could make with *Daett.* You are not only weird, but now you're running around with the Mennonites. Maybe I could threaten to do the same if he refused to allow my *rumspringa* time."

Katie decided to ignore the stinging barbs.

"Have you spoken with your *daett* about this?"

Mabel shook her head. "He doesn't even know I want to participate in *rumspringa*. I'm the mature girl who was running his household, remember? Having my own life wasn't an option. I was needed here. If *Daett* had married Ruth, I'm sure everything would all have worked itself out. Now it won't. And your *mamm* and you are to blame."

Neither she nor *Mamm* planned anything of the sort, Katie thought, and Mabel knew it. She was making an issue out of nothing to justify her own unjustifiable behavior. But accusing Mabel wouldn't help. "I'll speak to *Mamm* about it," Katie offered. "But I know she doesn't plan to influence your *daett.*"

"She doesn't have to," Mabel said. "*Daett* probably already knows how your *mamm* feels about *rumspringa.* Everyone does. He'll assume she's opposed, and he wants to make her happy. But I want to experience *rumspringa,* and I'll make it happen somehow."

Mabel's self-pity was too much to handle. Katie tried to hold back the angry words, but they burst out anyway. "*Yah,* Mabel, you'll make it happen by sneaking out after dark to meet Mose. Is that what you call 'making it happen'? I call it stupid. When your *daett* catches you, he's going to keep you at home for sure. Right now, by the look on your face, I'm sure you're wondering if I've told on you. *Nee,* I have not said a word to your *daett* or to *Mamm.* And I'm not planning on it. I'm just going to stand back and let you make a mess out of your life."

Mabel was staring at Katie, her face a mask. "You know about Mose and me?"

"Yes. And you just confirmed my suspicions. Now, maybe you should adjust some of your opinions about *Mamm* and me or grow up a bit."

Mabel was still staring.

Perhaps she's in shock, Katie thought. She knew she should feel bad for her outburst, but Mabel had pushed her over the edge. Katie didn't feel like apologizing right now, but she knew she would eventually. Since she'd finished washing the dishes, she turned to go upstairs to the peace and quiet of her room. But just then Jesse's deep voice boomed from the living room.

"Devotion time, everyone!"

Mamm's face appeared a few seconds later in the kitchen doorway. "Are you girls done in here?"

"We're coming." Katie put on her best

150

smile, but she figured *Mamm* wasn't fooled.

"Yes," Mabel said, her face still pale.

CHAPTER FOURTEEN

An hour later, Katie was sitting on the couch listening to Jesse read that evening's scripture. All around the room the other children were listening — Leroy and Willis, Carolyn and Joel. Mabel sat in a corner by herself, her face still looking pale. Katie ignored Mabel, concentrating on the *gut* feeling of having so many people present for evening devotions and prayer. Before the wedding it had been only *Mamm* and her kneeling in silent prayer together. Scripture reading and prayers spoken out loud were done only when a man was present to do it — at least that's what *Mamm* had always claimed. Katie closed her eyes and drank in the moment. After the harsh words Mabel had spoken to her in the kitchen, she welcomed this feeling of peace. She didn't wish to think on or repeat any of the biting conversation Mabel had spewed out, but the thoughts wouldn't stop coming.

How could Mabel believe those horrible imaginings about why *Mamm* had agreed to marry Jesse? And that accusation of *Mamm* wanting to keep Mabel from participating in her *rumspringa*? Perhaps it was a logical fear to enter a sixteen-year-old's mind. *Yah, Mamm* had kept her from participating, but that was before she'd married Jesse. So much had changed since then.

Katie's words to Mabel hadn't been edifying in the least. And Mabel now knew about her Europe trip, and she might very well turn her *daett* against the idea. If Jesse forbade her the trip, there would be no going. Even if she could, by a miracle from *Da Hah,* get the money. *Mamm* had already told Jesse her side of the story, she was sure, so that might have finished off any chance of her going long before Mabel said anything. But Katie decided to cling to hope anyway. The extent of *Da Hah*'s grace was always amazing and sometimes even surprising. And she would certainly need as much of it as possible.

Katie pulled her thoughts back to the present. Jesse's voice rose and fell as he continued to read from the book of Hebrews. "And what shall I more say? for the time would fail me to tell of Gedeon, and of

Barak, and of Samson, and of Jephthae; of David also, and Samuel, and of the prophets: Who through faith subdued kingdoms . . ."

Those were beautiful words, Katie thought. And they seemed to mean so much more when a man read them. That was a silly idea, she was sure, because the Scriptures were the Scriptures, regardless of who read them. Still, she was thankful for the work *Da Hah* had done in bringing *Mamm* and her to this house. If only Mabel felt the same way.

Seated in his rocker, Jesse closed the Bible. He leaned over to lay it on the desk. "Let's come to the Lord in prayer," he rumbled.

Katie knelt with the rest, sending up her own prayer as Jesse's deep voice filled the room.

Help Mamm *and me fit in here,* Katie prayed silently, not daring to whisper the words. *Thank You so much, dear Hah, that You had mercy on us so far and brought us here. We don't deserve everything You've done for us. Help me understand what Mabel is going through and how she's feeling. Her words caused a lot of pain in my heart. But please forgive Mabel in the same way You forgive Mamm and me when we make mis-*

takes. Just help us all, please.

Katie heard the rustle of feet signifying Jesse had come to the end of his prayer. She jerked herself out of her thoughts and jumped up. Maybe she could help little Joel get ready for bed. Maybe her willingness to help with tasks that weren't assigned to her might help Mabel feel more kindly toward her.

Before Katie could offer, Jesse spoke up. "If you'd stay for a moment, Katie, your *mamm* and I would like to speak with you."

Katie caught Mabel's look of anger out of the corner of her eye. With her heart pounding, Katie sat down on the couch again. Leroy and Willis gave her brief glances before heading upstairs and taking Joel with them. Carolyn followed closely behind them. Mabel, though, gave Katie another long glare and then disappeared into the kitchen. Apparently she planned to eavesdrop as best she could.

Jesse smiled in Katie's direction once everyone had left. He didn't seem bothered by the knowledge that Mabel was on the other side of the living room wall. But perhaps he didn't care. They were, after all, family now. They shouldn't expect to keep that many secrets from each other.

Katie tried to keep her breathing even as

155

Jesse shifted in his rocker to face her.

Mamm glanced toward Katie. "I hope this is okay — meeting like this. I don't want you to feel uncomfortable."

Jesse nodded. "*Yah,* I agree. What I have to say needs saying, but we can do it some other time if you'd feel better."

"Nee," Katie managed. "I'm okay. I just hope I haven't done anything wrong."

Mamm smiled but she looked nervous.

Jesse cleared his throat. "I have been well pleased with you, Katie. I like how you help with the work around the house. You do this even when you have your job at Byler's. And even when Mabel is a little disagreeable."

Tears stung Katie's eyes. So Jesse had noticed her efforts. How kind of him to go out of his way to mention them. But then, he'd always been tender with her. Gathering herself together, Katie wiped her eyes.

"We just wanted to speak with you about some things," *Mamm* said, not offering any details and already playing her role well as Jesse's *frau* — allowing her husband to lead out in important matters.

Katie swallowed hard. Somehow *Da Hah* would help her through whatever decision Jesse had arrived at. He was looking at her as he spoke. "You know, of course, that your *mamm* and I disapprove of you attending

156

the Mennonite youth gatherings?"

When Katie nodded, Jesse continued.

"I hope you will soon see the wisdom of our feelings. I try to raise my children in the fear of *Da Hah,* and I know your *mamm* has raised you that way too. I also know that neither of us always do the best job. I hope *Da Hah* has mercy on our shortcomings."

Mamm wiped her eyes and Katie whispered, "I'm sorry for what sorrow I may be causing both of you."

Jesse nodded. "It's your broken attitude about the matter that continues to give me hope, Katie. I know you think you're doing the right thing — for whatever the reason. I disagree, of course, and so does your *mamm.* But sometimes we need to find the end of that road ourselves. That's what our *rumspringa* time is for. So that our youth can find the truth on their own. We help where we can, but they also need to find where their lives fit into *Da Hah*'s will."

Katie didn't look up. At least *Mamm* and Jesse weren't being unreasonable so far.

Jesse cleared his throat and glanced over at *Mamm* before he continued. "This is not intended as a rebuke to your *mamm,* as she was doing the best she could. But I believe it would have been wise if your *mamm* had allowed you a time of *rumspringa* like our youth normally take. Then you might not be wandering around right now trying to find your way through life."

Mamm hung her head, and a brief sob escaped her. Jesse leaned over to stroke her arm.

Katie saw *Mamm* look up and smile at her husband. How blessed they were, she thought. *Mamm* had a husband she respects, and she had a *daett* who was trying to guide the family according to *Da Hah*'s will. *Da Hah* would work everything out in the end, even if she had to walk a road Jesse and *Mamm* didn't understand right now. She would stay in the faith, Katie told herself. She didn't plan to leave.

Jesse began speaking again. "So I will try to bear with you while you search for the truth, Katie. But let's not talk about the Mennonites and their youth gatherings in front of the other children. They may not understand."

Katie nodded. That was the least she could do.

Jesse cleared his throat again. "Your *Mamm* told me about the invitation you received the other night — the trip to Europe with your Mennonite girlfriends."

Jesse paused and Katie held her breath.

"That trip seems a little impossible to me,

as well as impractical. Four girls traveling around the world by themselves? Are you sure someone wasn't a little overexcited? Maybe they imagined this trip?"

"Oh no, it's real," Katie said at once. "Margaret wouldn't be making up something like this. Besides, Nancy Keim has already been there doing mission work, so she's familiar with the area and the people."

Jesse shrugged. "It's just seems a little wild to me, that's all I can say."

"Do you have objections?" Katie asked when silence had settled over the room.

"I do," Jesse said. "But you will need to make up your own mind. It will be best that way."

"Wouldn't it be *gut* to learn about the history of our faith?" Katie asked, using the best argument she could think of at the moment. "I really would like to go."

"That is a *gut* reason," Jesse agreed. "But have you thought about the money for the trip? Where would that come from?"

I could work extra hours at Byler's, Katie wanted to say, but she didn't. Asking to keep any of her money before she was twenty-one would be the same thing as asking for Jesse's money.

"I would take it as a *gut* sign from *Da Hah* if He supplies you with the necessary

159

funds," Jesse said when she remained silent.

Katie nodded. She understood perfectly. Jesse thought the expense of the trip would kill the idea — as it well might. Then she would simply have to submit to the will of *Da Hah*. It was a fair enough test.

"That's all we have then?" Jesse asked as he glanced toward *Mamm.*

Mamm looked up and gave Jesse a warm smile.

Katie rose. "Thank you, Jesse and *Mamm,*" Katie said, giving them both a smile. Slipping upstairs, she closed the door of her room. A moment later footsteps came up the steps, followed by a soft knock on the door.

"Come in," Katie said.

Mabel's face appeared in the doorway, a look of triumph on her face. "What did I say! You're not going."

Katie kept silent. Anything she said would make the matter worse. If Mabel wanted to gloat, she could go ahead.

"And *Daett*'s on my side now," Mabel continued. "Your *mamm* can't persuade him to forbid me my *rumspringa* time. I'm going to tell Mose he can come riding right up to the house from now on." Mabel closed the door without waiting for an answer. Her footsteps faded down the hall.

So *Mamm* hadn't influenced Jesse about Mabel's *rumspringa* time. And for her part, she might still go to Europe by a miracle from *Da Hah* — a *financial* miracle.

At the next Mennonite youth gathering she would tell Margaret and Sharon the news. They would understand if the money didn't become available. They would mourn her not being able to go, but there were worse things in the world. She had aimed a little high on this one — about as high as wanting Ben Stoll to notice her. She couldn't expect *Da Hah* to allow her everything she wanted, right?

CHAPTER FIFTEEN

The following Wednesday, Katie came out of Byler's employee doorway and stepped into the brisk December air. Arlene was close beside her. Thankfully, four o'clock had finally rolled around and their day was finished.

"Hey, look who's waiting for us by the buggies!" Arlene grabbed Katie's arm and suppressed a giggle.

Katie almost stopped walking. Ben Stoll was leaning against her buggy.

"Now, don't pass out," Arlene whispered. "He's not going to eat you."

Arlene obviously didn't know the emotions Ben stirred up in Katie or she wouldn't tease like that. This was serious love she had for Ben, and it clearly wasn't going away. And he wasn't helping things by showing up like this. He probably had business with Arlene, Katie decided. But Ben appeared a little sheepish, which was a look he didn't normally wear around Arlene.

"I'd almost take my chances at snagging him," Arlene said out of the corner of her mouth, "if I thought I had the slightest hope in the world. And if I didn't already have a boyfriend."

Katie kept quiet, her mind and body a little dizzy.

"What do you think he wants?" They were almost within earshot of the buggies and Arlene was still talking.

Katie kept her eyes aimed at the ground and didn't reply.

"*Gut* evening!" Arlene sang out.

Ben smiled. "How are you girls?"

"Just fine," Arlene said.

Katie hung back but she did look up.

"What brings you out here?" Arlene asked.

"I was on my way home and thought I'd stop in and say 'hi'." Ben smiled again.

"Come on, Ben, 'fess up," Arlene said. "You didn't stop in at Byler's to say hi to two lowly girls like us."

"Well then, you're both charming princesses, and I felt I had to stop," Ben responded with a grin.

"Stop teasing, Ben." Arlene was glaring at him now.

Ben was looking at Arlene every time Katie took a quick glance at his face. She knew she ought to say something, but she wasn't nearly as bold here as she was at the Mennonite youth gatherings.

"I'm not teasing," Ben was saying. "I'm sure your boyfriend, Nelson, would agree with me. Now let me help you with your horse, and then I want to speak with Katie."

Katie felt a shock run all the way through her. She stared first at Ben and then at Arlene.

Arlene was clearly shocked. "Katie? You want to speak with Katie . . . alone?"

"It's a free world, isn't it?" Ben asked as he headed to the fence where the girls' horses were tied.

Arlene turned toward Katie and whispered, "What does he want with you?"

Katie stopped gazing after the retreating Ben and looked at Arlene. "I have no idea."

Arlene obviously didn't believe her, but she said nothing more, appearing to still be in shock.

Ben led Arlene's horse to her buggy, and Arlene picked up the shafts so Ben could back the mare in. Katie helped with the tugs that were on her side while Arlene did the other side. Then Arlene climbed inside the buggy, an astonished look still on her face, and drove off toward home.

Katie felt herself relax as Ben turned to

face her.

"I suppose this is a little surprising, me stopping in like this."

"Yah," Katie said, "it is. But I don't mind."

Ben's sheepish look was back again. He was running the toe of his shoe around in a circle on the pavement, his eyes following the movement. Several moments passed before he looked up to meet Katie's gaze. "I'm sure you've heard that there's another youth gathering this Friday night."

"Yah, Esther told me."

"Well, if it's all right with you, I'd like to pick you up this time."

"Pick me up?" Katie's heart pounded furiously. Had Ben really asked what he just did?

"Pick you up and take you there is what I mean. If you don't object, of course."

The world was spinning in front of her eyes. Katie almost wanted to reach for something to hold onto.

"So, what do you say?" Ben asked, sounding just a little unsure of himself.

Katie thought she should answer before he changed his mind and remembered who he was talking to. *"Yah,* of course. Sure!" Her words fell all over each other.

Ben visibly relaxed, a pleased look on his face. "That's great! I'll be looking forward

165

to it. I'll need to pick you up earlier than Esther probably does because we'll be going by buggy."

"That's just fine," Katie answered.

"So let me help you get on the road. I've held you up long enough," Ben said.

She wasn't in any hurry to leave Ben, Katie thought. But she didn't say anything. She waited as Ben went over and untied Sparky and then brought him over to the buggy. Katie lifted the shafts as Ben backed Sparky between them and then worked on hitching him to the buggy. She fastened the tug on her side.

"There you are!" Ben said, coming around and giving her a helping hand up to the buggy seat.

He's being so kind . . . and such a gentleman, Katie thought.

"Don't forget Friday night," Ben said as he backed away from the buggy.

"I won't! See you then. And thank you, Ben." Katie gasped as Sparky suddenly took off. No doubt she was acting like a fool, but then what else could she expect? This was the day she'd dreamed of for so long. The fact that she hadn't passed out was enough to get down on her knees and give thanks to *Da Hah*.

Katie leaned out of the buggy door for a

quick glance back. Ben was still standing there waving. She waved back and quickly pulled her body back inside. For a long time she had to struggle to catch her breath.

From the tension on the buggy lines Sparky seemed to know something was up. He lifted his feet high and almost pranced down the road.

Moments later, a dark cloud crossed Katie's mind. She wondered what Arlene would say tomorrow. She'd been quite summarily dismissed tonight by Ben. No doubt she wouldn't be happy. Katie wondered what she was supposed to do. But she was too excited about Ben's offer to worry about Arlene's feelings for very long. A date with Ben Stoll! Would Arlene expect her to crawl back into her shy and retiring cave and hide in sackcloth and ashes? *Nee, nee, nee!* That was not going to happen!

Katie couldn't stop thinking about Ben all the way home. He'd been such a gentleman — so kind and even a bit hesitant. Her heart raced at the memory of him looking at her and his smile. *Mamm* couldn't have been more wrong about Ben's character. She couldn't really blame *Mamm* for her doubts. She'd never really met Ben, but now she would. Not on the first date, of course. Things weren't done that way.

Ben was taking her to the next Mennonite youth gathering! Yes, the feelings from the rest of the family about Ben might be suspicious at best. But someday — after everyone saw they didn't intend to leave the faith — they would love Ben like she did. Slow down! Katie reminded herself. This was just one date. But one date might lead to another, and another, and . . . Katie hugged herself at the thought, leaving the lines slack for a moment. Sparky took the moment to dash even faster down the road until she reined him in. She settled back into the buggy seat and listened to the steady beat of Sparky's hooves on the pavement. Another dark thought flitted in her mind. What would *Mamm* say about Ben picking her up? This would no doubt be worse news than ever for *Mamm*. *Mamm* didn't want her to have anything to do with boys, much less with Ben. The combination of Ben *and* the Mennonite youth gatherings would surely put *Mamm* in an even greater tizzy.

But miracles were happening. She would remind *Mamm* that her wedding to Jesse had been a miracle. Wouldn't *Mamm* see that the same thing might be happening now for her daughter? Because this *was* a miracle. Even one date with Ben Stoll — if another one never happened — was so *wunderbah* she would treasure it for the rest of her life.

Mamm would just have to accept this. There was no turning back now. Ben's buggy would be coming down the driveway on Friday night. There would be no hiding that from anyone. Katie tried to keep breathing normally as she kept her eyes on the road ahead. The Christmas lights in the windows of an *Englisha* house twinkled off and on and drew her attention for a moment. There were many of these homes on the way home, and usually she would be enjoying the sight of the pretty lights. But tonight she had only one thing on her mind: Ben Stoll.

CHAPTER SIXTEEN

That evening the chatter at the supper table filled Katie's ears. *Mamm* had been all smiles since Katie had arrived home, apparently so caught up in her new duties that she hadn't noticed the dreamy look on Katie's face. And Katie had kept the news to herself, afraid that *Mamm* might say words in front of the others she would later regret. Later they'd have a private conversation about Ben and her upcoming date with him.

Mabel was the only one who wasn't joining in the hearty dinner table conversation. Katie noticed that a dark cloud seemed to come and go on her face. Before long *Mamm* would notice, and the questions would start. And then there would be trouble, if Katie didn't miss her guess. In the meantime, she kept watching *Mamm* as she passed the food around the table and made sure everyone was getting enough.

She was the perfect hostess.

Mamm had never been this way before she married Jesse. They'd never gone hungry at their old place, but food preparation had never been high on *Mamm*'s priority list. Now she seemed obsessed with the subject, glowing with happiness whenever one of the children took extra helpings.

"Awful nice eating we have here," Jesse said, dishing another large portion of mashed potatoes on his plate. "A man could grow fat on this."

Mamm's cheeks glowed, and she lowered her head.

Almost like a teenager, Katie thought. Perhaps someday she would prepare food for Ben like *Mamm* was preparing food for Jesse. That thought made her ears and cheeks burn. Thankfully no one knew what she was thinking. And it was way too early for such thoughts anyway. Ben was only taking her to one youth gathering. Still, knowing that Ben was coming on Friday night made her toes tingle.

Mabel's glowering face came into focus again, interrupting Katie's thoughts. It looked like Mabel was really upset. But over what?

Clearing her throat, Mabel's voice rose above the family chatter as she blurted out the words. "So all those months I made our suppers, there was something wrong with my cooking? Is that what you're saying, *Daett*?"

Silence fell around the table except for *Mamm*'s gasp.

"I was just praising your new *mamm* like I used to praise you and your cooking," Jesse protested. "You shouldn't be offended."

"You never said you would get fat on *my* cooking," Mabel shot back.

Jesse didn't look happy. "Look, we're not having this argument again, Mabel. You did an excellent job after your *mamm* died, as did Carolyn. But I needed and wanted a *frau,* and you needed a *mamm.* My being pleased with Emma's cooking doesn't mean I was dissatisfied with yours."

"You do a very *gut* job," *Mamm* spoke up. "In fact, Mabel made the corn tonight and helped with most of the other things. I know I couldn't do all the work without her — at least not as well."

"There you go, Mabel!" A smile spread across Jesse's face. "So let's not hear anything more about this."

Mabel didn't say anything as the murmur of conversation began again. Moments later she lifted her voice again. "I hope everyone understands I'm an adult when Mose Yutzy

172

shows up tonight to take me out. I know it's not the weekend, so we won't be staying too late."

Silence fell again as everyone stared at Mabel.

"What did you just say?" Jesse asked.

"I'm going out with Mose Yutzy tonight," Mabel said, all traces of frown gone. "You let the boys go on their *rumspringa* time, and I'm also going to have mine. I was putting it off because I had to take care of the house, but I see I'm not needed here any longer."

"This has nothing to do with *rumspringa*," Jesse said.

Katie thought he sounded like he was trying to keep his voice even. Apparently there was more going on between Jesse, Mabel, and Mose Yutzy than Katie had been aware of.

"Then what has it got to do with, *Daett*?" Mabel's frown was back in full force. "You've never told me I couldn't see Mose."

"That's because I didn't know you were interested in him."

"Well, I *am* interested," Mabel said. "I was waiting for the right time to tell you. And now that you're married, I'm letting you know."

Jesse cleared his throat. "Mabel, I forbid

you to see Mose. And if I find you aren't listening, I'll also forbid you from participating in *rumspringa.*"

Mabel jumped to her feet.

"Sit down!" Jesse ordered. "We will be having no fits in this house."

"But *Daett*!" Mabel protested, flopping down in her chair. "You're only doing this because of Emma's weird ideas about *rumspringa.* What other strange ideas is she bringing into this house that are taking ahold of you? It's just as I feared. Look, *Daett,* at how Katie is turning out. She's ready to join the Mennonites!"

"Mabel, enough! This is not about *rumspringa.* This is about Mose."

Mamm jumped into the conversation. "Please, Mabel. I wouldn't try to influence your *daett* one way or the other on the subject of *rumspringa.* That's one thing I decided *before* I married him — that I wouldn't interfere with the way he raises his children. In fact, I think he's done a much better job than I could ever have done with all of you."

"Then why am I not allowed to see Mose?" Mabel asked.

"Because he's not right for you. You're not going to see Mose. Get that through your head, Mabel," Jesse declared.

"But why, *Daett*?" Mabel leaped to her feet again. "Why are you saying this?"

"Please, Jesse," *Mamm* reached over and clung to Jesse's arm, "listen to her at least."

"You can say that again!" Mabel leaned forward to emphasize her words. "After all the work I put in to keep this house running after *Mamm*'s death, this is how I get treated? Like a child?"

Jesse looked confused. He looked at *Mamm*. "I guess I need to be more considerate. So what is it about Mose that so impresses you? Let's hear your side of the story."

Mabel took a deep breath and sat down. "Let's see . . . He's *wunderbah,* and sweet, and he likes me." Mabel's voice strengthened. "And he is coming tonight. We've already planned it."

Jesse gave a short laugh. "Maybe he's coming, but he's leaving just as quick. I haven't heard any solid reason in the boy's favor yet."

Mabel's face flashed thunder again, but she said nothing.

Mamm spoke up, her voice cautious. "Why are you forbidding your daughter this thing, Jesse? She seems to care for the boy."

Jesse snorted. "The boy is a disgrace, Emma. His *daett* is among the best farmers in the community, but Mose, his second boy, hardly lifts one foot in front of the other. He's among the laziest boys around. His *daett* hasn't been able to teach him much of anything. Mose can't cut a crop of hay without getting it soaked at least once before he gets it in the barn. And that's with his *daett* and brothers watching his back. The boy barely gets out of bed in the morning, I'm told. He's a lazy young man, and I don't want Mabel to see him."

Jesse stopped talking as the sound of buggy wheels rolling down the driveway could be heard.

Mabel turned bright red, her mouth set and her eyes flashing.

"That must be Mose," Leroy smirked. "I'm sure he'll be happy with his friendly welcome."

Mabel stuck her tongue out at him, and Leroy roared with laughter.

"Quiet now, Leroy!" Jesse pounded the table with a fist. "We will not be making fun of the young man or Mabel. Mose is what he is. Now, Mabel, go out and explain the matter to him. Send him on his way."

"Mabel?" *Mamm* stared at Jesse. "Do you think that's wise, Jesse? To make Mabel do this?"

Mamm is right, Katie thought. Only *Mamm*

didn't know exactly why she was right. Katie was sure Mabel would use the opportunity to plan a secret meeting with Mose.

Jesse paused, a thoughtful look on his face. "I believe it's best if the boy hears the news from Mabel."

Mabel had leaped up before the words were out of her *daett*'s mouth and raced out the washroom door.

Leroy choked back a laugh. When Willis glanced at him, Leroy leaned over. "I was looking forward to learning the famed Mose farming methods, but now my hopes will leave with the evening wind."

Willis turned his head to hide his own laughter.

Jesse glared at both of them.

As the minutes ticked past, Katie's mind raced. What did this mean for her own plans? Did she even dare bring up the subject of Ben picking her up on Friday night? Perhaps this was the time. Maybe Jesse would be disinclined to create another fuss around the dinner table. Katie decided to wait for Mabel's return.

The conversation rose to a low murmur around the table as Katie wondered how it was going between Mabel and Mose. Finally, her footsteps could be heard in the washroom. The door opened, and Mabel slipped into her seat at the table.

"So it's taken care of now, Mabel? You handled it with Mose?" Jesse asked.

Mabel nodded, refusing to look at her *daett* or anyone else.

Now was Katie's moment. She cleared her throat and took a deep breath. Then she exhaled and began. "I have something to share too. I don't know if this is a good time or not, but it does relate to what's happened this evening."

Katie paused and glanced at *Mamm.* "Ben Stoll asked if he could pick me up to go to a youth function on Friday night. I said yes. I hope that's not a problem."

Mabel made a choking sound, but Katie didn't dare look at anyone except *Mamm* and Jesse. She especially didn't want to see the look on Mabel's face.

"We're being invaded by female snatchers!" Leroy said.

Willis howled with laughter.

Katie kept looking back and forth from Jesse to *Mamm.* Had her risk worked? Might Jesse approve of Ben? And if he did, would Mabel dare say anything bad about her?

"I think Ben could teach us some *gut* farming techniques," Leroy said when he could control his laughter.

Willis laughed again and punched Leroy

in the shoulder. "What can a carpenter teach us about farming?" he asked.

"That's enough, boys," Jesse told them. "It's not right making fun of people." He cleared his throat and looked at Katie and then Mabel. "From what I know of Ben, he's a fine boy. Mose could take a lesson from Ben on hard work."

Katie's cheeks glowed with the praise. Jesse approved of Ben! Wasn't that a miracle in itself? Now if Mabel would stay out of the way, she would be fine. Katie took a quick peek at Mabel. The girl met her glance with a look full of daggers. Clearly the battle between them was anything but over.

Katie looked away and thought about Ben driving down the lane Friday night. She smiled. With Ben coming, she could put up with Mabel and then some.

CHAPTER SEVENTEEN

Katie paced the floor of her room, still dressed in her work clothing. Ben wasn't due for another hour. She'd been downstairs, but she couldn't stand another minute of the tension in the kitchen. *Mamm* kept looking at her like her last friend had died, and Mabel had done nothing but give her glares since just before dinner.

Mamm's face had been filled with sorrow when Katie came home from Byler's, and it had grown more haggard as time progressed. The boys and Carolyn hadn't seemed to notice during dinner as they filled the kitchen with their happy chatter. Mabel, though, had begun her piercing looks there — between shooting barbed retorts back at her brothers, that is. On their part, Leroy and Willis certainly weren't making things easier for Mabel and her pining for Mose. And since Katie was planning an evening with Ben Stoll, it was no wonder that Mabel was in short temper tonight.

"Cultivating went pretty *gut* today," Leroy said to Willis, keeping an innocent tone in his voice. "Though I could use someone to teach me *gut* farming methods."

Willis smirked. "*Yah,* I did think you left that plow row a little crooked. Surely a Yutzy would know how to tell us to improve such a thing."

Mabel glared at Leroy and Willis. "Neither of you are half the man Mose is. He'd have plowed the whole field today instead of going around in circles like the two of you did."

Broad grins spread over the boys' faces.

If Mabel knew what was good for her, she'd keep quiet, Katie wanted to tell her. This easy target for entertainment would be too hard for either of her two oldest brothers to resist.

Sure enough, Leroy hid his laughter with a loud cough. "If his horse could make it over here, Mose might still prove himself helpful."

"He'd probably throw all four horseshoes on the road," Willis choked out between snickers.

Leroy feigned shock. "So that's where the twisted-up metal shoe came from? The one that was lying in the driveway?"

While Leroy and Willis howled with laughter, Mabel turned her anger on Katie. "This is all your fault."

Katie knew there wasn't any truth to Mabel's words. It was her bitterness speaking, and she needed help right now, not condemnation. And Katie could see where Mabel might get that idea. Jesse would probably have been easier on discipline if *Mamm* wasn't in the house. With the responsibility of the household on *Mamm*'s shoulders, Jesse was seeing Mabel as a child again — a child in need of serious correction.

Mamm's sorrow was what worried Katie the most. Her sad face and distressful looks cut deep into Katie's heart. *Mamm* was really why she'd fled from the kitchen tonight. It wasn't to escape the thundercloud of Mabel's wrath, but to avoid the searing pain of *Mamm*'s disapproval. Because, if the truth be told, *Mamm*'s opinion still pulled on Katie. *Mamm* was Jesse's *frau,* to be sure, but she would always be her *mamm* too. They were bound together by ties that couldn't be broken. So why did she feel like they were being torn apart by a strong force neither of them could control?

Mamm couldn't get over her disapproval of Ben anymore than Katie could resist going out with him tonight. Soon *Mamm* would be coming up the stairs to discuss the matter. At least Katie would be surprised if *Mamm* didn't try to get in one last plea for her to abandon her plans.

Katie paused long enough to push aside the curtains of the window to see if Ben was coming yet. Soon he'd come driving up the lane, and she would run out to climb into his buggy. A thrill was running all the way through her already even at the thought as tears stung her eyes. Why couldn't *Mamm* see through her eyes and rejoice about this *wunderbah* thing between Ben and her? A miracle had happened between *Mamm* and Jesse, even though *Mamm* had resisted. Why couldn't she see that this might be the same grace from *Da Hah* being offered to her?

There was a soft squeak on the stairs, and Katie flew back to sit on her bed. She would feel better sitting here rather than standing while she listened to what *Mamm* had to say.

"May I come in?" *Mamm* asked through the door.

"Yah," Katie replied. She clutched the bed quilt with both hands.

The bedroom door creaked open, and *Mamm* came in. She sat beside Katie. For a long moment neither of them said anything.

Finally *Mamm* cleared her throat. "I see

you fled the kitchen. Were you wishing to get away from me?"

"Oh, *Mamm, nee.*" Katie threw her arms around *Mamm*'s neck. "You know that's not true. I just couldn't stand seeing you so sorrowful. I love you!"

Mamm held Katie for a long time. "It's *gut* to hear you say such a thing."

"I will always say it." Katie let go of *Mamm*'s embrace and folded her hands in her lap. "And I will always mean it in my heart. I want to make you happy and do what you say is best, but I also want to see Ben, *Mamm.* I'm so torn up about this. Can you not understand how much I like him?"

"You will always be my precious daughter," *Mamm* told her. "I only wish this boy wasn't between us like he is."

"Why can't you see what a miracle this really is? Please try, *Mamm.* Ben actually asked to pick me up! And you know Jesse approves of Ben."

Mamm winced. "I suppose I could tell you again about the mistakes I made with Daniel — running after the boy all those years, thinking I loved him when it was nothing but a schoolgirl crush. True love, Katie, doesn't happen with those types of boys. They only want to have everyone's approval and attention. Good looks and popularity can make life too easy, so they seldom create depth of character. You're only going to get your heart broken by Ben, Katie."

What was she supposed to say? Katie wondered. *Mamm* didn't understand how she felt about Ben. She hadn't seen how kind and hesitant he'd been the other night. *Mamm* thought Ben was like Daniel Kauffman, when he wasn't at all. Ben was much more *wunderbah* than *Mamm*'s Daniel had ever been.

"I see you still don't believe me," *Mamm* allowed. "And in a way I don't blame you. I also was blind to Daniel's faults all those years. I have only *Da Hah*'s mercy to thank that I was spared death by heartache and given the chance to find true love. And not only once with your *daett* but again with Jesse."

Katie gave *Mamm* a quick hug even as she protested. "Daniel turned out decent, didn't he? Even if he wasn't the right man for you, he's an upstanding church member now. Maybe you saw something that wasn't true because you were so upset?"

Mamm shook her head. "I don't think so, Katie. No doubt Daniel has matured by now, and I'm sure his *frau* has helped him. But she came from his world of wealth, Katie. I hardly even dared speak with her

185

while we were in the young folks' group. Every Sunday she wore a new dress, or so it seemed to me at the time. Her *daett* owned one of the most prosperous farms in the community. I'm sure *Da Hah* worked a great grace in Daniel and his *frau*'s life — just as He has done in mine. But they belonged together, just like I belonged in your *daett*'s world. Just like I now belong in Jesse's world. You don't belong in Ben Stoll's world, Katie. And you never will. Their social circle just isn't yours and mine."

"But I'm different from you," Katie countered quietly when the silence had hung long in the room. "And so is Ben. I wish you could see that. He's so kind. You're seeing only the past and what you lost. You're not seeing that love is always a miracle. Just as it was with you and *Daett,* and just as it is with you and Jesse. That's how I feel about Ben. I wasn't old enough to see love grow between you and *Daett,* but I do see how it is growing between you and Jesse."

Mamm stared at her, puzzlement in her eyes.

Katie rushed on. "Love is always a miracle, *Mamm.* And what if *Da Hah* is allowing love to grow between Ben and me? Do you think such a miracle wouldn't be possible?"

"Who has been saying these things to

you?" *Mamm* asked. Her face was a mask of great concern. "Have you already been speaking of love with Ben?"

Katie shook her head. "*Nee,* of course not! We've only spoken a few times. These are thoughts that just came to me."

Mamm didn't look convinced. "Did an *Englisha* person say these things to you while you were working at Byler's?"

Katie laughed out loud. "No, *Mamm.* I wouldn't speak of such things with anyone at work."

"Then what is happening to you?"

"Maybe I'm in love." Katie sat straight up at the thought. "Is this what happens when a person is in love?"

Now *Mamm* laughed. "Sometimes. But I doubt if you've had time to really fall in love with Ben. You don't know him well enough. Love doesn't happen that quickly."

Katie wanted to argue and share about all the years she'd spent admiring Ben from afar. There had been plenty of time for love to grow in her heart. She stroked the quilt and then dared a quick glance at *Mamm*'s face. She was actually smiling a little! Maybe there was hope she'd understand after all.

"Are you still hoping to go on that trip to Europe?" *Mamm* asked.

Startled, Katie glanced up at her *mamm.* Where had that come from?

"That's one dream I hope comes true," *Mamm* said. "And I promise I won't stand in the way if you can find the money to go."

"Thank you, *Mamm*! That means a lot. I hope I can go too!" Katie smiled, glad the subject had changed.

Mamm continued. "I couldn't believe Jesse said you could go. I didn't have anything to do with persuading him that you should be allowed to go."

"Does this mean you might also change your mind about the Mennonite youth gatherings?"

Mamm didn't wait very long before answering. "*Nee,* Katie. Not much can change my mind on such a thing. But if you truly visit the places where our faith began, perhaps it will make you appreciate our beliefs more. I just wish you were going with Amish youth. There's no telling how the Mennonites skew the history of the Amish people."

"Oh, *Mamm,*" Katie threw her arms around *Mamm*'s neck, "the Mennonites aren't like that. Not the ones I've met, anyway."

Mamm smiled, getting to her feet. "Well, we'll see. Now I think you'd better get ready. Ben will be here before long. You don't want to keep him waiting."

When *Mamm* closed the door, Katie rushed around the room with a song on her heart. *Mamm* was at least opening her mind to what she was doing. That was much more than she'd dare ask from *Da Hah*.

"Thank You, *Hah,*" she whispered. "Thank You so very much." Hearing the sound of buggy wheels, Katie rushed to the window. Ben was coming down the drive!

CHAPTER EIGHTEEN

Minutes later Katie raced down the stairs, pausing on the last step to catch her breath. It wouldn't be appropriate to burst into the living room like a young schoolgirl on her first day of term. She also needed to get control of herself so she wouldn't go running outside where Ben might see her. He would think she couldn't wait to climb in the buggy with him. Even though that was true, it would be best if Ben didn't know that yet.

Katie pushed open the stair door and stepped into the living room.

Jesse glanced up from his recliner with a smile. "So we're off for the evening, are we? Be careful now."

"Thank you," Katie replied. A warm feeling rushed around her heart to have a *daett* who was so understanding. Without him, her *mamm* would surely be sitting in the kitchen in tears, casting a shadow over this first opportunity to ride with Ben in his buggy. Surely *Da Hah* was having great mercy on her life. Her cheeks must be glowing with happiness! "Have a *gut* evening!" Katie said over her shoulder to Jesse as she moved toward the front door.

Jesse smiled and nodded, but didn't say anything more, having already turned back to reading *The Budget.*

When she went by the kitchen doorway, Katie gave a little wave to *Mamm.* Since Mabel was also in the kitchen, Katie figured *Mamm* was refraining from giving her a sendoff to make it easier for Mabel. Katie caught a brief glimpse of Mabel's fierce glare, but she didn't slow down. The thought of Mabel's continued troublemaking took the flush off her cheeks, and brought her back down to earth with a thud. She shook herself mentally. Mabel was not going to ruin this evening!

Katie closed the front door, her knees going weak as she walked across the porch. Ben was just circling the buggy to pull in front of the house. She pinched herself and kept going. Ben's buggy awaited! This was the same buggy she used to pass on her way to work at Byler's before *Mamm*'s marriage to Jesse. Back then she used to wonder how a girl would feel riding with Ben. Surely she'd be happy for weeks afterward. Now Katie was going to find out! As she approached the buggy, Ben leaped to the ground with a smile and wave and hurried to her side. "*Gut* evening!" he said. He offered Katie his hand, helping her up the buggy step on the passenger side.

"*Gut* evening," Katie responded as she settled onto the seat. Twice now Ben had offered his hand to help her into a buggy. And she'd noticed a slightly bashful look on his face. She was sure she hadn't imagined it.

Ben climbed up the buggy step on the other side and flopped onto the seat. He picked up the reins and gently slapped them against his horse's back. The buggy headed up the driveway at a fast clip.

Katie hung on to the side of the buggy frame with one hand and smiled at Ben.

Obviously trying to make conversation, Ben asked, "How is your *mamm* getting along in her new life?"

"Quite *gut,*" Katie said. "I think she's fallen in love again."

Ben laughed.

Had she really said that? Katie wondered. She didn't know Ben well enough to spill such close family information! And yet the words had just come right out.

"I'm glad to hear it," Ben said through his chuckles. "Our people usually marry fairly quickly after a partner's death, especially the men. But then again, sometimes the women don't."

Katie leaned back and cleared her throat. "It was hard for *Mamm* to consider Jesse's offer of marriage at first. She wasn't planning to remarry or fall in love again. But now *Mamm* sees that the marriage was the best thing for her."

"And for you . . ." Ben glanced at her, his words more statement than question.

"*Yah,*" Katie admitted. "I wanted a *daett* pretty bad — though not just any *daett.* Getting a kind and gentle man like Jesse is a *gut* reason to give thanks to *Da Hah.*"

"I suppose so." Ben kept his eyes on the road. "I never lost my *daett,* so I don't know from personal experience."

"It's not easy, believe me." Katie looked up into his face. Ben was being so understanding, just as he'd been the few times they'd spoken before. Being with him already felt like they were friends who'd known each other for a long time. No wonder she'd felt such a strong desire to be with him all these years. She had to stop herself from leaning against Ben's shoulder like she'd seen many dating couples do on the way home from the hymn singings on Sunday nights. She mustn't take such liberties yet . . . and maybe not for a long time. That Ben was even driving her to the youth gathering was *wunderbah* enough, she reminded herself.

"I heard a little gossip about you this week," Ben said. "Well, I assume it's gossip."

Katie sat upright on the buggy seat. "Good or bad?"

Ben frowned. "I'm afraid it's bad."

"Oh no! I wonder who's been running their mouths?" Katie frowned. "So what did you hear?"

"Ruth Troyer, the schoolteacher, said something about you going to Europe with some Mennonites."

"Oh . . ." Katie leaned back against the buggy seat.

Ben continued. "Ruth claims your *mamm* is corrupting Jesse Mast completely. That he has lost all his *gut* child-training sense since the marriage. And that's why he's allowing you to go on such a trip."

Katie carefully studied Ben's profile. Did Ben not approve of such a trip? What would he think when she told him it was true? That she might go on the trip if she could find the money.

"Did I say something wrong?" Ben asked. He was looking at her quizzically.

"Nee," Katie replied, "it's just that . . . well, on this one . . . umm . . . it happens to be true. I am considering such a trip."

Ben stared at her. "You're going to Europe?"

Katie shook her head. "It's still up in the air. I've been invited by some friends, but I haven't given them an answer yet. Jesse said I could go, but it wasn't because of *Mamm*'s persuading him. Ruth has that wrong. Jesse said if *Da Hah* provided the funds that would be a sure sign the trip is in His will. And that's the problem. I don't have the money."

Ben's face relaxed. "Well, what a surprise! I wouldn't have thought you'd consider such a trip. How did the invitation come about?"

Katie cleared her throat. "I'm not sure of the details. I've known Margaret and Sharon for awhile now. Nancy Keim asked them to go, and I guess they thought I'd enjoy going along so they talked to Nancy. The three of them decided to invite me because they wanted a fourth person to make up the group."

Ben beamed at her. "I think that's fantastic! And you really might go?"

Katie winced. "Remember, I don't have the finances, and I see no way of getting them. But at least Jesse said I could go. So I have permission . . . but no money."

Ben slapped the reins. "I'd say old Jesse is pulling a fast one on you. He knows you don't have the money, so he's saving himself from having to tell you no. Sort of bypassing the risk of turning his new *frau*'s daughter against him by not having to say no."

"Jesse wouldn't do that," Katie protested. "He's not like that at all."

Ben shrugged in the falling darkness.

Katie ran the memory of the other evening through her mind. She saw Jesse's kind face and his understanding look when he inquired about the invitation to go to Europe. Jesse was honest and open. There was no way he'd been pretending to be supportive.

"Sorry for doubting your old man," Ben muttered, interpreting Katie's silence correctly. "I didn't mean any harm."

"He has been very nice to me," Katie said. "And I think he would let me go if I did get the money somehow."

"But you don't have it, so I guess we'll never find out. Sorry about that. I wish you could go. It sounds like fun." Ben's face was briefly visible as they passed an *Englisha* house that had a tree in the yard twinkling

196

with Christmas lights.

"Thank you," Katie responded. "I think so too." Ben was a *wunderbah* friend already. He was so tenderhearted. *Da Hah* had indeed begun the feelings she had for Ben. *Mamm*'s fears had no foundation in reality at all. Katie was trusting *Da Hah* to make her relationship with Ben work in His *gut* timing. And each moment of that journey would most assuredly be a pleasure and a joy.

"Look's like we're about here," Ben said, interrupting her thoughts. He pulled back on the reins a bit. Ahead of them bright lights flooded the front yard of a modest house. Moments later they turned into the driveway, stopping beside a long line of cars parked near the barn.

"We're about the only buggy here," Katie noted as she climbed down.

Ben pulled a tie strap out from behind the seat. "Does that bother you? Would you rather drive around in a blue sports car like Esther has?"

Katie laughed. "*Nee,* a horse and buggy are just fine for me." *And being with you is even better,* she wanted to say as Ben tied up his horse. But she held her tongue as she waited for Ben. Walking into the gathering together was such a great honor. Every-

197

one was going to see that she'd come with the most handsome man there.

"Ready to go?" Ben asked, stepping beside her.

Katie smiled up at him, and they walked together toward the house. Another couple appeared beside them after exiting a parked car on the other side of the barn.

"Good evening there," they said, their voices singing out together.

"Good evening," Ben and Katie replied at the same time. Katie decided they already sounded like a couple because they'd responded in unison. She stayed close to Ben as they walked through the door. Lights were strung across the ceiling, and a volleyball game was already in progress. A Mennonite boy Katie didn't know showed up to shake their hands and greet them.

"We'll get another volleyball game going soon," he told them. "Glad to have all of you!"

The boy moved on to greet other people who were arriving, and Ben led the way toward a smaller group of young people.

"Name's Andy," a boy said as he extended his hand. He motioned toward a girl standing beside him. "This is my girlfriend, Lilly."

"Hi." Lilly offered her hand.

As they shook hands, Ben spoke up. "This

is Katie. She's a good friend of mine. And I'm Ben."

If only he'd said *my girlfriend,* Katie thought. Well, someday he would if *Da Hah* so willed it. Their relationship might even become deep enough where love would grow between them so they would become husband and wife. Don't put the cart before the horse, Katie reminded herself silently. She mustn't think about such things right now.

"Come on!" The boy who had first welcomed them was back. "We're ready for another game."

"Are you playing on my side?" Ben asked Katie with twinkles in his eyes.

"Yah," Katie told him, her heart pounding in her chest. "I'd like that."

CHAPTER NINETEEN

Several hours later headlights pierced the night sky as Ben drove the buggy in the direction of Jesse's farm. Inside, Katie sat peacefully with happy thoughts whirling through her head. What an evening this had been — and it wasn't over yet! Another half an hour or so still lay ahead of them as Ben drove her home. This might be the best time yet. Each moment seemed to take her joy to a greater height. Tonight had been all she'd dreamed it would be and then some.

Ben's voice reached her through the haze of happiness. "What a *gut* evening that was. They're sure a nice bunch of folks."

"*Yah,* they are," Katie agreed. She leaned forward so Ben could hear her as a car roared past them. She didn't add what she really wished to say: But not nearly as nice as being there with you.

Ben glanced toward Katie and smiled as another car passed them, "It sounded like you had quite the conversation going with some of the girls after the game."

"*Yah,* Margaret and Sharon are really excited about the trip to Europe in May. They want to start planning it now."

Ben looked at her. "I think you should go along, Katie." He turned his gaze back to the road.

Katie didn't answer right away, and Ben glanced at her again.

"*Yah,* I remember that money is a problem," Ben said, seeming to read her thoughts. "Maybe you'll find some way of getting the funds. It would be a great adventure, you know."

Katie leaned back in the buggy seat and took a deep breath. Exhaling she said, "Even if I had the money, I'd have to get it in time to have my picture taken, get a passport, and make plane reservations. And what if the big plane crashed into the ocean?"

Ben laughed. "Those big birds crash less than cars do. Statistically speaking, of course. It's quite safe."

Katie kept her voice steady. "The plan is to go to the sites where our faith began. They plan to visit places in the old town of Zurich, including a cave back up in the mountain where our forefathers gathered for meetings. Margaret thinks the cave is featured in Christmas Carol Kauffman's book *Not Regina.*"

"Have you read it?" Ben asked.

Katie shook her head. "I just heard about it at school."

Ben smiled. "It's an interesting story. I don't know whether the featured cave was a real one or not, but it sounded like it was. Christmas Kauffman can make things come alive even if they aren't real. I really enjoyed her writing. I think you have to go see this place if you can swing it."

"You've read the book?" Katie stared at Ben in astonishment.

Ben laughed. "You don't think boys read books?"

"Of course I do, now that I think about it. I was just a bit surprised, that's all."

Ben shrugged as if it didn't matter, but Katie's mind raced. Ben was even more *wunderbah* than she'd thought. He enjoyed reading and learning! And he was being so supportive and encouraging about the trip to Europe, which made her wish even more that she could go.

Ben looked at Katie. "Did you hear the most important point? I think you should go *if* you get the chance."

Katie smiled. "Believe me, Ben, I will. Even though it might be a little scary to be in a strange place so far from home. I hate to ask *Da Hah* for another miracle though. He's been providing so many of them already."

Ben smiled back. "Well, we never know what will happen. I'm glad to hear you're considering the possibility." He slapped the reins, and Longstreet stepped out even faster. "I think I'd better get you home before your *daett* and *mamm* think I've stolen you."

"They wouldn't think that," Katie said as they went around a curve fast enough to make the buggy lean to one side. *Mamm* would think other things, but Katie wasn't about to say that right now. Ben was teasing anyway. Just as he was likely showing off his fast horse. The thought sent a tremble up her back. She'd never had a boy show off for her before.

"He likes to run in the dark," Ben said, seeming to read her thoughts again. "He's a *gut* horse."

"What's his name?" Katie asked, looking at Ben's face. He looked even more handsome in the dim light. He had a slight grin on his face as they raced through the night.

"Longstreet," Ben said.

"Longstreet?" Katie stared openly at him now. "Where did that name come from?"

He took a moment before answering. "It's the name of a Southern general during the Civil War."

"A *Southern* general, Ben?"

Ben gave her a quick glance. "Do you think there's something wrong with that?"

"*Nee,* I suppose not. I don't know that much about the Civil War."

Ben laughed. "I'm a little strange, I suppose. It's not that I like war, but I'm fascinated with the stories of some of the battles during the Civil War. I learned about Longstreet when I was reading about a battle fought under General Lee at Gettysburg. The book was called *Killer Angels.*"

"*Killer Angels?* That's an odd name, and it sounds pretty gruesome."

"Come on now," Ben said in a teasing voice. "Wars happen whether we agree with them or not. There's nothing wrong with learning about them. In fact, it's probably a good thing to know about them."

"But wars are awful, Ben. So many people die from guns and illnesses. It's not our world, Ben. We Amish abhor violence. Should you be reading such things?"

Ben smiled down at her. "You're sounding like my *mamm* now. *Daett* doesn't care though. I keep the books out of sight in my room so *Mamm* won't get upset. Not that all my books are about war. I enjoy reading detective stories too. And even a love story once in awhile, like *Not Regina.*"

"Why do you want to read about war, Ben?"

Ben was quiet as he stared into the darkness.

Katie wondered if she'd said too much. She was curious, but had she overstepped their friendship by questioning his actions already? Ben had every right to be offended. She stole a glance at him. He didn't seem to be though.

"Picture the scene, Katie. It was a glorious day at Gettysburg. There was a whole field of Southern soldiers, thousands and thousands of them. Their flags were flying and their guns were ready. They marched out of the woods ready to do battle to defend their honor. They had over a mile of open ground to cover as they headed toward Cemetery Ridge where the Union soldiers were entrenched. General Longstreet had failed to gain the high ground the day before on Little Round Top. General Lee had ordered one last charge, striking the Federals in the middle. That battle became known as Pickett's Charge, named after one of General Longstreet's commanders. The day was infamous and glorious all at the same time. So like the South of that day — and so like many of us, I think. We would rather die in the heat of battle with banners unfurled than admit our cause is lost."

Katie knew she was staring, but she'd never heard such words before. And from an Amish boy at that.

Ben's horse trotted through the night, his metal shoes striking the pavement in steady beats.

"That's why I named my horse Longstreet," Ben continued. "No one has ever asked me where I got the name. Besides, most of our people aren't familiar with Gettysburg or the other battles of the Civil War."

"You're not planning to join the *Englisha* wars, are you?" Katie asked, bolting upright.

Ben laughed softly. "*Nee,* Katie. You can quit worrying. I do sometimes think about where I fit — or don't fit — in the Amish community. And sometimes I wonder what our cause is all about."

"You mean our faith?" Katie asked.

Ben nodded slowly. "You could put it that way, I guess. Have you never wondered about such things? Whether life is worth living as we do? All this sacrifice — driving buggies, having no electricity in our homes, giving up many pleasures, watching others enjoy the freedom of using technology — is it really worth it, Katie?"

"I've never thought of such things," Katie said. "Where does that put you when it comes to our Amish faith?" If he was considering leaving the community or questioning faith in *Da Hah,* Katie knew her heart was going to hurt more than it ever had in all her life. It would probably never stop hurting. For the first time she considered her limits. If Ben left, could she leave for the *Englisha* world with him? Maybe *Mamm* had been right all along. If Ben was thinking of joining the *Englisha* world, that would be a problem. Visiting the Mennonite youth gatherings was already a big deal for her. Leaving the faith for the *Englisha* world was out of the question.

Ben must have sensed her thoughts because his voice was sympathetic. "I'm sorry for spilling so much on you — and so suddenly. Don't take me too seriously, Katie. I'm not leaving the faith. It just feels *gut,* I guess, to speak of the questions in my heart. To say out loud what I've been pondering. Around the house, I don't dare say anything. *Mamm* and *Daett* would be shocked beyond belief. I just like to think about things, you know."

And you think I'm not shocked? Katie

wanted to ask.

Ben continued. "I'm half tempted to take a trip to Europe myself. Not with you girls, of course, but on my own. I could travel around and find out whether our faith is all it's made out to be and why our sacrifices are so important."

"I think you should," Katie said.

Ben smiled. "I doubt if visiting the Old Country would do much good. I need to work these thoughts through on my own. I do thank you for listening. You don't know how much it means to me to be free to express my thoughts. Especially since it must be quite a surprise to hear these things spoken."

She'd better say something quickly, Katie thought. But what?

Ben didn't seem bothered by her silence. He continued. "Amish women seem to always be the last to think such thoughts. I've often wondered why that's so. Why are men the wild ones? Why do we think all the troubling thoughts while you women calmly keep the home going, the children in clothing, seeming content to love and be loved. Men make the trouble. In the *Englisha* world, they are the ones who fight the wars and stir things up. But even we Amish men do some of that. It's like it's in our blood, and we can't do much about it."

"I've never thought such things or heard about them," Katie said. "I'm glad you feel free to tell me about your thoughts. I do consider that an honor."

Ben looked surprised when Katie slipped her arm through his and leaned her head against his shoulder. She'd been wanting to do this all evening but hadn't dared. Now she had dared at this strangest of moments. Ben had just finished telling her about his doubts and his wandering thoughts. He probably expected her to run into the house screaming when he dropped her off. And that was the weirdest part of this. To Katie, Ben seemed quite lovable right now. Like he needed her like she needed him. Ben had shared things he'd never told anyone else. Wasn't that reason enough to lean on his shoulder?

Ben's arm tightened on hers. "Thanks again for listening, Katie."

Katie looked up at him. "Why not make that trip to Europe soon? I think it might answer a lot of questions for you."

Ben laughed. "It is an interesting idea. But you're the one with the invitation. You should go."

"You're forgetting I don't have any money."

"I haven't forgotten." Ben pulled back on the reins to slow Longstreet as they approached Jesse's place. "I think *Da Hah* will supply what you need."

Katie snuggled against Ben's shoulder and said nothing. There really was nothing to say. It felt *gut* that Ben thought *Da Hah* would supply the money. It probably wouldn't happen, but it was nice Ben was being so supportive and wasn't shocked at the thought.

Just before Ben turned into Jesse's driveway, and out of the corner of her eye, Katie caught a glimpse of a buggy tied up in the trees. It blended in so well, that if she hadn't been certain Mose and Mabel were seeing each other she might have written it off as her imagination. Katie kept her gasp as silent as possible.

Ben turned into the driveway, drove to the house, and stopped. "Can we do this again sometime?" he asked, his voice tender. "And soon, I hope?"

Katie was surprised and pleased that there was a question in his voice, even after all the things he'd told her tonight. She must have spoken the right words of comfort and support. But she couldn't have done anything else. The words had been on her heart and had sprung easily to her lips. She slipped her arm out of his. His very presence enveloped her like a comfortable quilt. "If you wish," Katie responded softly.

Ben smiled. "Absolutely! I'll see you next week then — or whenever the next gathering is. We'll figure it out soon, okay?"

"*Yah,* Ben. *Gut* night then." Katie gave him one last smile before stepping down from the buggy and walking to the house.

"*Gut* night!" he called after her before driving off into the night.

Katie stopped, turned around, and watched his buggy leave. Ben hadn't asked to kiss her tonight, but it was way too early for that, really. Even with how much she wanted him to. But what a *wunderbah* evening! It was exactly what she'd always hoped for.

CHAPTER TWENTY

Katie paused on the porch to look back toward the road. Ben's buggy lights had long disappeared from sight, but the sense of his presence still lingered in the night air. Katie sighed. She was reaching for the doorknob when she caught sight of a flicker of light in the barn. It lingered only a second before vanishing. Was it the lantern light reflecting off a piece of metal? Had it caught her eye because she was so wrapped up in the sweet memories of her evening with Ben? *Nee,* she'd definitely seen something even if it hadn't lasted long. Mabel. That was the only answer. Since she'd noticed the buggy parked among the trees, Mabel must be in the barn with Mose. Had they grown so careless that they didn't handle their flashlights with care?

What should she do? Katie wondered. Should she tell *Mamm*? *Mamm* would surely tell Jesse. It wouldn't be right to tattle on any of Jesse's children — even Mabel. Besides, such transgressions as Mabel's were always found out eventually. It was only a matter of time. She could speak with Mabel tomorrow, but there would likely be a furious denial. And she'd already told Mabel she wouldn't tell, and that she'd let Mabel mess up her life all she wanted. But really that wasn't right either. She'd confront Mabel, Katie decided. That was the thing to do. Maybe she could talk some sense into the girl's head. Katie walked across the yard and pushed the barn door open. The hinges squeaked loudly in the still night. Mabel obviously didn't enter the barn this way.

"Mabel!" Katie called into the darkness. "I know you're here, so you'd better come out and speak with me." She wanted to sound a bit threatening, as if she planned to disclose Mabel's actions to her *daett* if the girl didn't come out right away. Perhaps Mabel would decide it was best to face the problem rather than continue skulking around.

Silence filled the barn. Katie left the barn door open and moved further inside. The faint light from outside only extended a short distance, and Katie paused where its reach ended. If she were in the old barn at the home place, she could find her way around by the feel of her hands. And Molly and Bossy wouldn't have been startled by her presence. But here she wasn't about to wander around without a light. She didn't want to use one of the barn lanterns. Leroy or Willis, supposedly asleep in their beds in the house, might wake up enough to notice a light. And maybe Jesse too. Farmers were that way. They slept like logs until the slightest change happened on the farm. Then they awoke with a start. In fact, someone in the house might already be stirring. After all, Ben's buggy on the drive hadn't been very quiet. Katie went back to the barn door for a quick look at the house. She saw no signs of movement.

"Mabel!" Katie called again, more urgently this time. With a sigh, Katie was turning to leave when a brief rustling sound came from the back of the barn. It was followed by the sound of a door swinging open and shut, soon followed by another door opening — the back barn door. So she'd been right. Mabel was meeting Mose. And if her guess was right, Mose had just taken off. Perhaps Mabel would show her face now. Katie waited and a few seconds later another door squeak was followed by a quick whisper. "Over here, Katie. Quick."

Holding her hands out in front of her, Katie moved toward the spot where the sound had probably come from. Nothing brushed against her fingers, and her feet stayed on level ground. The cow stanchions would be over somewhere to the right, but she had no sure way of knowing exactly where she was. Knocking her shins against the low metal bars wasn't something she wanted to do. Katie was ready to call out again, when a sliver of light appeared ahead of her.

"This way!" Mabel hissed. "I'm inside the feed bin area."

Katie took the last few steps toward the light and slipped through the door. Mabel quickly shut it behind her. On the floor sat a kerosene lamp turned on low. Mabel must have brought it from the house. She would hardly dare hide it out here lest her father and brothers stumble across it.

"So this is where you've been meeting him?" Katie faced Mabel.

Mabel's eyes blazed. "How *dare* you stick your nose into my business! Especially after you've been out cavorting with that Ben Stoll all evening."

Katie cringed, but a reply still slipped out of her. "Your *daett* forbade you from seeing

Mose. He didn't forbid *me* from seeing Ben."

Mabel glared at Katie and stepped closer. "That's because your *mamm* has wrapped *Daett* around her little finger and driven him away from me. *Daett* didn't used to be like this at all. Not before your *mamm* came around. We all got along just fine, and I ran the household with only Carolyn's help. We were doing great. *Daett* told us so all the time. And we would have done even better if *Daett* had married Ruth Troyer."

Katie sighed. "I don't think there's much use talking about this, Mabel. It's not going to change anything. Your *daett* married my *mamm* because he wanted to."

"And with your approval." Mabel's eyes blazed.

"*Yah.* But what difference does that now make? The question is, why are you meeting Mose out here against your *daett*'s express orders? You know that's not going to work."

"Why don't you leave us alone?" Mabel huffed. "We're not doing anything wrong. Just go inside the house and mind your own business!"

Katie looked around the small feed room. There was nothing here but feed bags stacked on the concrete floor, two of which had obviously been used as chairs from the looks of the indentations. They likely had been doing nothing worse than kissing, but that wasn't the point. Jesse would consider disobedience to his orders transgression enough.

"My *daett* need never know this." Mabel's hand swept across her brow. "That is, if you don't go telling him."

"Such things always come out, Mabel. You can't hide them for long."

"How do you know?" Mabel shot back. "Aren't you hiding things in your life?"

Katie shook her head. "No, Mabel, I'm not. Sure, I'm doing things you don't approve of . . . and even *Mamm* and your *daett* don't approve, but I'm not sneaking around."

Mabel snorted. "I don't believe you. No one is such a little saint. Not if she runs around with Mennonites."

Katie shrugged. "I guess you need to decide that for yourself. But you'll have to stop meeting Mose."

"And what plan do you have to stop me?" Mabel said, her eyes narrowed. "Tell *Daett*? Is that it? Or worse, your *mamm* so she can tell my *daett*?"

Katie thought for a moment before answering. "No, like I've said before, I'm not going to do either of those things. I'm just warning you that eventually you'll get caught. I was hoping you'd listen to reason because it's not *gut* what you're doing, and I think you know it. These things always come out in the end."

Relief spread over Mabel's face. "*Gut!* Thank you for not telling . . . if you really mean it. Apparently you have some morals left."

There was no sense in pushing the matter further. Katie had done her part, and Mabel was determined to find her own way. Katie had one more thing to say though. Maybe this was the time. "Mabel, could we . . . perhaps . . . choose to live peacefully together in the same house without all the fuss all the time?"

Mabel didn't think long on that question. "If you mind your own business about my meeting with Mose, then of course. I'll try to be nicer."

"*Gut.* I'm glad to hear that," Katie said.

Mabel nodded. "Just remember your end of the bargain and there won't be any problem. Now, let's go inside before someone sees us."

That sentiment had come a little late in the evening, Katie thought, but she nodded in agreement. Mabel blew out the kerosene lamp and carried it with her in one hand.

With the other, she led Katie out to where the starlight reached inside from the open barn door in the back. Then they walked toward the house together.

Mabel whispered once they were outside, "Go in the front door, while I sneak in through the washroom door. You can create some cover noise for me if someone is listening. They're expecting you to be coming in."

Katie walked across the yard toward the porch, and Mabel disappeared into the shadows of the house near the washroom door. By the time Katie got inside, Mabel would already be well upstairs. Katie took a moment longer than necessary before she opened the front door. There was no sign of Mabel when she stepped inside. The girl must be an expert at moving through the house without a sound. But then Mabel had grown up here. She would know her way around.

Before Katie opened the stair door, a floorboard squeaked from the direction of Jesse's bedroom, and *Mamm*'s form appeared in her nightgown. "Is it you, Katie? I thought I heard a buggy drive in some time ago."

Katie's thoughts swirled before she whispered, "Ben dropped me off a little bit ago, but I didn't come in." She couldn't lie, and yet she didn't want to reveal Mabel's secret either.

Mamm didn't say anything for a moment. Finally she asked, "How did the evening go with Ben?"

"Gut"! Katie replied.

Mamm's face looked pale in the starlight coming through the window. "I hope it works out well for you, Katie. I hope I've been wrong."

"Thank you," Katie said quietly. She knew those words must be hard for *Mamm* to say, and yet she was saying them.

"One more thing," *Mamm* said after a moment's hesitation. "I think you should stay away from the barn when you come home, Katie. Remember, you can only be responsible for so much."

Katie stood speechless as *Mamm* turned and disappeared down the hallway. A floorboard gave a loud squeak before the bedroom door closed. Astonishment flooded Katie's mind. So *Mamm* knew about Mabel, about what she was doing. Yet she wasn't telling Jesse. And *Mamm* obviously didn't want her telling either. How sweet of *Mamm*, Katie thought as she found her way up the stairs. If Mabel only knew how fortunate she was, perhaps she would be more thankful. And, really, this was a huge change for *Mamm.* Not that long ago she had been so determined to keep other people out of their lives. Now *Mamm* had opened her heart to a man and five children who were not her own. Even unlovable Mabel.

What lessons she could learn from *Mamm,* Katie decided. *Mamm* loves me, and I haven't been that lovable lately. Katie opened her bedroom door. Could she do what *Mamm* had done tonight — be nice to her daughter who did things she disapproved of? And in Ben's case, *Mamm* disapproved sharply. Yet she'd found a way to keep on loving.

Katie found the side of the bed with her hands and knelt to whisper a prayer as she faced the star-filled window. "O dear *Hah,* thank You so much for all the *gut* things You are sending into my life. *Mamm* didn't have to marry Jesse, and You didn't have to give her love again. And You didn't have to give me such a *wunderbah* evening tonight with Ben. I know there will likely be much trouble ahead because that's how You help us grow, but right now I thank You . . . so very, very much. Amen."

CHAPTER TWENTY-ONE

The following Monday night, Ben parked his buggy in front of the grocery store in Dover. Rogge would have a fit, but Ben figured a little subterfuge was in order. Christmas was only a week away, and downtown was flooded with late-night shoppers. Following the same pattern like they had for the past two years wasn't wise. What better plan than to transact business out in the open? No one would suspect anything. And if Rogge Brighton didn't like it, well Ben wanted to quit anyway. This might hasten things along. But he couldn't just sit here waiting because that would look suspicious. Ben climbed down from the buggy and entered the grocery store. In the snack aisle, he picked up several candy bars and paid for them at the counter. When he was outside, he unwrapped one and took a bite. He sauntered back to his buggy and climbed in. Perhaps this wasn't wise after all. The time was well past their usual drop-off schedule, and the grocery store would be closing soon. Rogge might not have the brains to figure out he needed to look around for him and make contact in the front parking lot. Ben decided he wasn't going to give in. If Rogge didn't come in a few minutes, he would leave. Perhaps that was the best thing anyway. His date with Katie last week had meant more than he expected. Anxiety and guilt were gnawing at him. What if she learned what he'd been doing? She probably wouldn't ever want to see him again. But she wouldn't find out because he was quitting, getting out. And what could Rogge really do if he stopped cooperating? Beat him up? They were friends, after all.

A soft step behind the buggy interrupted his thoughts, and Ben stuck his head out the door.

"Why aren't you where you're supposed to be?" a harsh whisper asked. "Rogge has been waiting for fifteen minutes already."

"Tell him I want to meet in the front." Ben didn't crane his neck to see the speaker. He didn't have to. Rogge's brother, Lyman, had a distinctive nasal tone to his speech.

"That's not going to work," Lyman whispered back. "Now pull around where you

223

belong, and Rogge will meet you there in five minutes."

Ben stiffened and the tension was reflected in his voice. "Tell Rogge to follow me out of town in ten minutes. I'll be parked in the woods on the right just outside the town limits. No one will see us there."

"What's wrong with the old way?" Lyman had raised his voice.

"Just do it or I'm out of this tonight," Ben snapped. He leaned forward and clucked to Longstreet. The horse jerked forward. Lyman let out a yelp as a buggy wheel clipped his foot. Ben knew he probably shouldn't have been so rough, but he wanted Rogge to take him seriously. As he approached the edge of town, he checked behind him and to the sides before pulling down a small road into the woods. This small, overgrown path led to a hunting cabin. It was kept up enough so that vehicles could pass through one at a time. Rogge would figure out where he'd parked, even if his buggy wasn't seen from the road.

Ben climbed down and waited. Sure enough, the soft rumble of Rogge's car was soon heard coming down the lane.

The car jolted to a halt and Rogge got out, obviously angry. "So what's this all about?" he demanded.

Lyman stayed inside the car, but Ben could see through the windshield that the brother's face was grim. Ben kept his voice steady. "I thought it was time for a different routine. We'll get caught doing the same thing every time."

"You could have called me," Rogge shot back.

Ben stepped closer. "We agreed a long time ago to make no phone calls, remember? No contact except at our scheduled meetings."

Rogge snorted. "This isn't more of that nonsense about quitting, is it? You had me scared there for a bit."

Ben didn't hesitate. "I am quitting in the next few weeks. I don't want to stay in this business forever. It's not right. Now let's get this over with."

Rogge glared at Ben, but he got a large bag from the car and gave it to Ben.

Ben slid it under the buggy seat. "Now, there's something you can do for me."

"Really?" A sly grin spread over Rogge's face.

Ben produced a roll of bills and held them out.

Rogge's grin disappeared. "Why are you giving me money?"

"I want you to have Lyman or your sister

drop this off at a place called Byler's Market. It's that little grocery store just out of town. There's a girl who runs the deli counter. Her name is Esther Kuntz. Have your brother or sister tell her this is to finance the trip for Katie Raber. Esther will understand. And make sure they don't mention where the money came from. I don't want Katie to know."

Rogge's eyes got big. "You're buttering a broad's bread?"

"Something like that."

Rogge's grin was back. "She must be a sweet one. Why don't you give her the money yourself? Might get you more mileage that way."

"I don't want that kind of mileage, and I don't want to explain. Will you just see to it that Esther gets the money and the message to give it to Katie Raber?"

"Anything for you, my longtime and prosperous business partner." Rogge smirked as he turned on his heels and headed to the car without waiting for any additional comments.

Ben almost shouted, "This isn't going to last much longer, Rogge!" But he decided Rogge wouldn't listen anyway. As the last sounds of Rogge's automobile engine died away, Ben checked the client list with his flashlight. There were a few new names with directions to the drop-off places attached. Most of them were at the usual gathering places on weekends. He would have to go to one on Friday and Saturday night. Beyond that, there was one stop to make at a residence, which he could do tonight. He got back into his buggy, turned it around, and drove away. Longstreet's hooves were soon beating steadily on pavement. Ben drifted into deep thought, imagining Katie's amazement and what she would say when Esther announced that someone had dropped off enough money for her trip to Europe. Would she faint? Scream? He smiled. *Nee,* Katie wouldn't do any of that. She'd be thrilled — excited that her miracle had come through. That's how Katie would look at this. She would think it was a gift from *Da Hah* — which maybe it was, Ben thought, but he doubted it. The money was tainted with sin and illegal activities. *Da Hah* probably didn't work that way.

And if he'd tried to give Katie the money himself, there'd be too many questions. Katie was innocent, but she would still ask a lot of questions. She'd want to know where he'd obtained the money because it was such a large sum. Ben didn't feel like lying to her. There were enough sins on his account that needed cleansing without adding that to the pile. And would Katie even take the money from him? They didn't really know each other well. He sensed she'd had a crush on him, but that probably wasn't enough to get her to accept this much cash. And Ben didn't want to take the chance of clouding this special moment for Katie by arousing unpleasant questions or a tense situation.

Yah, Katie looked at things differently from what he did. She wasn't hard around the edges. Her smile was always open and frank. The girl had suffered in her life, that much he'd figured out. Yet she hadn't turned bitter. What would it be like to have such an open attitude? Ben wasn't sure, but it was one of the reasons he was attracted to her.

That and the fact Katie was quite *gut* looking. Her beauty must have been covered up all those years by the drab dresses her *mamm* probably insisted Katie wear. That and Katie's shy gaze that seldom looked up at someone. The girl absolutely glowed when she smiled. Now that he thought about it, Katie had seldom smiled the few times she'd attended Amish youth gatherings. But at the Mennonite youth gatherings she was so different, always laughing

228

and talking. Almost outgoing, in fact.

He guessed the Mennonites were benefiting both of them in ways he'd never considered. Perhaps there was something to *Da Hah* working in a person's life. Katie certainly thought so. Ben shook his head. He'd always had doubts, even though he took care to hide them. There was no sense in alarming his *daett* and *mamm* more than was necessary. *Rumspringa* was a time for sorting out one's faith, was it not? The problem was he didn't have much faith to sort out.

He ought to make a trip to Europe himself someday. Maybe he would find faith there in the land of the Amish founders. They'd been men and women of great faith who survived persecution and torture and faced death without wavering. He couldn't do that. He wasn't even sure he could make his "no" to Rogge stick even though he knew it was the right thing to do. How could he stand up to much of anything else? Certainly he couldn't stand up to the torture of the rack or being burned at the stake.

Ben shuddered. Perhaps Europe wouldn't do him much *gut.* But it would do Katie a lot of *gut.* He could tell that already. She would have her faith strengthened, and she would grow into even more of a glowing woman than she was now. And from her maybe he could draw strength. Maybe he already was. Wasn't it Katie who had inspired his desire to break with Rogge? *Yah,* it was, Ben admitted. And he would accomplish that before long. Katie had no idea how much *gut* she was doing for him. From the look in her eyes, she thought he was doing her a great favor by spending time with her. That was more evidence of her innocence.

Most girls he knew quickly moved beyond the stage of starry-eyed wonder and started making demands on him. And it didn't usually take more than a few dates to get there. But Katie hadn't shown any signs of going that route. Her eyes were as full of joy when he dropped her off the other night as they had been when he'd picked her up. Could Katie love him? Other girls had, but Katie was different. She didn't throw herself at him or beg for his attention.

Katie probably never thought of what she could get out of him other than wanting him near. It sent strange feelings through him, like he was close to something he didn't deserve. Katie was too *gut* for him. He'd never thought that of any other girl. They had all bored him after a few outings. Like his faith, they left much lacking and gave no promise of better things ahead.

But with Katie, something had certainly changed. What, he wasn't quite sure of. But whatever it was, he didn't want it to go away. *Yah,* he would have to be done with Rogge by the time Katie returned from Europe. There was no question about that. The past would be the past, and maybe they could grow close. And if Katie returned as invigorated in her faith as he expected she would, therein might lie his answer. Katie could inspire his own faith. She would tell him the stories of the land where martyrs had died, and the glow in her eyes would be enough to help him along. Somewhere he would find faith. He wanted to, and he couldn't help but find it with Katie as his companion.

Ben pulled back the reins and the buggy bounced to a stop alongside a curb. The address he'd been given was just ahead, and it would be better not to drive in with a buggy. He didn't want anything different about him that someone might remember or use against him. There was no reason this person needed to know he drove around in a buggy or that he was Amish.

It was easier to make deliveries at parties. But he had done this before, so he tied Longstreet to a fence post and took one last glance around. The buggy was far enough off the road to not be seen, and he wouldn't be gone that long. He slipped through the darkness with a small bundle under his arm, and knocked at the garage door like the instructions said.

A bearded, burly man answered with a gruff, "What'd you want?"

"Delivery for Albert Kinsley," Ben said as he glanced down at the package.

"Who's it from?"

"Rogge."

The man reached out his hand and took the package. "Thanks."

Ben made his way back and untied Longstreet. He climbed into the buggy and turned it around on the road before driving off at a fast clip.

CHAPTER TWENTY-TWO

Katie had just shut down her register for her lunch break when Esther came hurrying toward her. Arlene glanced over from her checkout aisle to see what the excitement was all about. Esther took Katie by the arm. "It's your lunch break, right?"

"*Yah.* But what happened? Why are you so excited? Did that handsome man I saw a moment ago at your counter ask you out?"

Esther gave Katie a baleful look. "Oh, forget about that. I didn't even notice him. This is even better!"

"Then you'd better tell me, before you pass out."

Esther laughed. "You're the one who's in danger of passing out. This news is about you!"

Katie thought fast. What could have happened that would put Esther into such a frenzy — that had something to do with her?

"Come with me! I'll tell you and *show*

you." Esther grabbed Katie by the hand and led her to the lunchroom. After they'd taken their lunches from the refrigerator, sat down, and offered silent prayers, Esther said, "Do you want to guess?"

Katie shook her head, her mouth full of sandwich. Esther was always so dramatic about everything. No news could be this great.

Esther leaned closer. "Someone just dropped off an envelope of money and said it's for your trip to Europe. And from the size of the bundle, I'd say there's plenty and then some."

Katie stopped eating. "An envelope of money? For me?"

Esther giggled, thoroughly enjoying herself. "Can you believe it! And I didn't even know who the woman was who brought it to me."

"Why did they give it to you? I don't understand."

"I don't know," Esther said with a shiver of delight. "But who cares? Maybe the person or persons wanted to make sure the gift stayed anonymous. Isn't this wonderful? Now you get to make the trip. And the other three girls will be thrilled."

"Did you know I needed the money?" Katie asked as she stared at Esther.

Esther shrugged. "Well, I mean, I kind of figured that would be an obstacle. Such trips take an awful lot of money. But what does it matter what I thought, Katie? This is a great thing to happen! And to think I got to be part of it."

Katie tried to keep breathing steadily. "Well, thank you for being part of it. But this money . . . I don't know . . ."

Esther interrupted her with a look of alarm, "I hope you don't object to receiving the money, Katie. You're not going to reject it, are you?"

Katie forced a smile. "I just wish I knew who gave it and why, that's all. How can I thank the person? Are you sure this isn't a joke? People don't do things like this."

"No, it's not a joke. See for yourself! Here's the envelope."

Katie reached out and took it. She looked inside and her mouth dropped open.

"I told you!" Esther said, almost shouting.

"But who . . ."

"I wouldn't worry about it. The woman who dropped it off looked quite nice and respectable."

"I guess I can't give it back. Who would I give it back to?"

Esther grinned. "That's more like it."

Katie peeked inside the envelope again.

"See?" Esther looked triumphant. "There ought to be enough and then some."

Katie's head was spinning. "Wow! It's so much. How can I accept this? And who do I thank? This is beyond amazing. *Da Hah* does many miracles, but this . . . this . . . this is way too nice."

"I thanked the lady on your behalf," Esther said as she patted Katie's arm.

Katie's hand trembled, but she managed to put the envelope down. She finished her lunch in a daze.

"Well, I'm out of here," Esther said after taking the last bite of her chocolate chip cookie. "I have a quick errand to run before I have to get back to work."

As soon as she was alone, Katie took another look inside the envelope. This time she counted it to see just how much was there. It was well over five thousand dollars! "Who? Why? Who did she know that even had that much money to spare? Questions raced through her mind. Few people knew about the trip other than her family and some of the Mennonite youth. Did the gift come from one of her Mennonite friends? It must have. Likely Margaret or Sharon was in on this. Or perhaps some of their friends had heard about a young Amish girl being invited along to Europe who didn't have the needed funds . . .

Even Nancy Keim could have been involved — or the organization she served with in Europe. Obviously whoever it was wanted the gift to remain a secret, probably not wishing to draw attention to himself . . . or herself. That was what godly people like the Amish and the Mennonites did.

How blessed she was to have such friends! And to have Jesse for a *daett* who would allow her to go on the trip. And here was the money to make it possible. What a miracle! Just like so much of her life lately. It seemed like one miracle followed another. First *Mamm* got married to Jesse, then Ben sought her out, and now someone had given her enough money to go to Europe! Surely this was a dream! And yet she wasn't awakening from it. Maybe if she walked out to Arlene and told her about it that would help. If Arlene said this was real, then Katie would have to believe it.

As Katie made her way to Arlene's checkout station, she thought better of it. Arlene had a customer who'd just approached too, so Katie went directly to her register.

Arlene looked up at Katie curiously. "What's going on, Katie?"

Katie smiled. "I'll tell you at quitting time."

Arlene shrugged and tended to her customer. When she was finished, she looked over at Katie. "I'll be right back." With that, she slipped down the aisle toward the lunchroom.

Katie opened her register and greeted her first afternoon customer. The white envelope was in her dress pocket, and it would stay there, she decided, until after closing time. In the meantime she would act normally — as if that were possible.

"Nice weather for the week before Christmas," the older lady in front of her said. "Have you been outside?"

"Not since this morning," Katie said as she scanned the items.

"Stick your head out if you get a chance," the lady said. "It's gorgeous."

"I'll try," Katie said. "I suppose I'll get plenty of fresh air on the way home tonight."

The lady glanced up. "Do you walk to work?"

Katie shook her head. "I drive."

"Oh, a buggy?" The lady looked at her carefully, and then her face beamed. "Are you Amish?"

"*Yah,*" Katie said, scanning the last item.

"Sorry for my asking," the lady said. "I hope I didn't offend you. I thought you looked Amish, but I didn't know the Amish worked in stores like this. I thought you Amish stayed on farms, milking cows or standing at a quilting loom. Oh dear, have I insulted you again?" The lady looked worried. When Katie smiled, the customer relaxed and smiled back.

"That's okay," Katie said. "Some of us do work outside the community. But I can see where it might seem strange. Most of us do grow up and work on farms."

"Well, that's wonderful — and you're wonderful." The lady smiled again.

Katie placed the last item into a bag, took the customer's money, rang it up, and asked, "Do you need help out?"

"No, I'll be fine. Thank you, dear."

Katie clutched the envelope in her dress pocket, allowing joy to sweep over her again. This might not be quite like the ways of her community, but she was so blessed she thought she might burst. *Da Hah* was choosing to bless her beyond words. Why He should do that was a mystery. Perhaps it was *Mamm*'s prayers prayed over all the past years, even when *Mamm* didn't know what she was praying for. *Da Hah* was like that, anyway that's what the preachers said often in their Sunday sermons. He often took a long time to answer the cries of His people, and He didn't always give them what they asked for.

Katie pulled herself out of her thoughts as Arlene rushed up. "Why didn't you tell me about the money someone left you, Katie?" Arlene demanded. "How exciting — and you didn't tell me! I had to hear it from Esther."

"That's what I was going to tell you after lunch, but then you had a customer so I decided to wait until closing time," Katie whispered. "Let's keep this quiet and not talk about it here, okay?"

Arlene glanced around. "There's no one here right now. Will you show me the money? I'd like to see it for myself."

Katie retrieved the envelope and handed it to Arlene. Arlene didn't just peek inside, she took all the money out.

Katie hurriedly whispered, "Arlene, put it back! Someone's going to see it."

"I'm counting it," Arlene said, continuing to flip through the bills. "Five thousand dollars, Katie! Good gracious! Where did all that come from?"

"I don't know! The person who left it with Esther wouldn't say. Now put it back in the envelope!" Then Katie grabbed the bills and stuffed them back into the envelope herself.

"Let's see," Arlene said, keeping tabs with her fingers, "it could be those Mennonite friends of yours. But as far as I know, they don't have this kind of money to throw around. How about your new *daett*? Would he give you that kind of money?"

"He said he didn't have it the other night," Katie answered. "And why wouldn't he just give it to me if he wanted to? He wouldn't need the secrecy or want to make it anonymous."

Arlene nodded in agreement. "I suppose we'll just have to chalk this generosity up to a mysterious friend. This is so *wunderbah,* Katie! What nice things are happening to you. And not that long ago . . ."

Katie hung her head. Arlene meant no harm with her words, but they were true. Not that long ago she'd considered herself just the daughter of the weird widow Emma Raber. Only by the grace of *Da Hah* was that changing. She certainly wasn't doing anything special — except trying to live as *Da Hah* wanted her to.

Arlene seemed to have forgotten about the mysterious friend. "And from what you told me the other day, you'll get to see a lot of Europe. Holland, maybe Switzerland, and Germany. What about France and Paris? Oh, Katie, I'm so excited for you!"

"We're not going to Paris, nor will we see that much of Europe," Katie said quietly,

241

watching as a customer came out of an aisle and headed her direction. "We're going to see the places where the Amish forefathers lived."

"You have to have some fun too," Arlene quickly whispered before returning to her register. The customer, an older man, was already unloading his items on the conveyer belt. Katie went over to bag the man's purchases since no one was in her line.

When the man had paid and left, Katie returned to her register. All afternoon both of them kept stealing glances toward each other and smiling at Katie's good fortune.

"Can you believe it?" Arlene occasionally whispered between customers. "I still can't!"

Katie could only smile and shake her head.

A young lady approached with her cart overflowing, and Katie got to work. But even as she scanned the purchases she thought, *Yah,* it would be a long time before she would get over this latest miracle from *Da Hah.*

CHAPTER TWENTY-THREE

That evening as Katie drove Sparky down the driveway, the barn door opened and Jesse stepped out. Sparky was lathered up around the harness straps from the fast trip home. Katie hadn't intended to push him so hard, but he must have picked up on her excitement.

"Driving in like a teenager, are we tonight?" Jesse said as he approached with a smile. "Did you catch young Ben on the road and have a race with him?"

He's teasing, Katie thought as she stepped down from the buggy. She turned to him with a wide smile. What a *wunderbah daett* he was! She'd planned to tell *Mamm* her news first, but since Jesse was here, what better chance would she have?

As Jesse helped her unhitch. Katie cleared her throat. "I have some great news to share."

Jesse looked up. "So that's why you're

home so fast? This news must be quite something."

Katie grinned and looked straight at him. "It is! It's unbelievable! Today someone gifted me with enough money for the trip to Europe!"

Jesse raised his eyebrows. "Now, that is news! Who was it?"

"I don't know," Katie said as she shook her head. "Esther gave me the money at lunchtime. She said a woman she didn't know came up to the deli and handed her an envelope. Esther said the woman told her to give it to me — that it was money to help pay for my trip to Europe. Esther asked who it was from, and the woman said the giver didn't want to be known. And, Jesse, it's quite a large amount! I still can hardly believe it."

"You must have some really *gut* friends among those Mennonites!" Jesse's smile hadn't dimmed a bit.

"So I can go?" Katie asked as she finished unfastening the tug on her side.

Jesse didn't hesitate. "I said you could if you had the money."

"Here!" Katie walked over to him, reached inside her dress pocket, and handed Jesse the envelope.

He flipped through the bills, counting as

he went. "Looks like you're going, all right," he said, handing the envelope back.

"You don't disapprove?" Katie stood beside Sparky, anxiously awaiting his answer.

Jesse had gone around to lead Sparky forward, so his face was hidden behind the horse's neck. But his voice sounded cheerful enough. "If *Da Hah* goes to this much trouble to help you, then He must wish you over there for some reason. And I'm sure seeing the birthplace of our faith is a *gut* thing."

"Thank you," Katie whispered as she held the buggy shafts up.

"Katie, perhaps we should keep this quiet until after supper," Jesse said as he led Sparky out of the shafts. "You can share it with your *mamm,* but let me tell the family after supper tonight. And then we'll go from there. Okay?"

Katie nodded.

"I'll take care of Sparky tonight," Jesse said. "Just in case you want to go tell your *mamm* the news." He gave her one last smile and then led the horse into the barn.

Katie walked across the lawn and entered the house through the washroom door. Inside, the first thing she saw was Mabel's angry face. Why was the girl already angry with her? Katie wondered. And when Mabel stepped toward her, Katie involuntarily took a step back. She caught her breath as Mabel stepped even closer.

"Why was *Daett* helping you unhitch?" Mabel hissed.

Katie glanced around before answering. "I thought we were going to get along better, remember? I didn't tell him about Mose, if that's what you're worried about. And I'm still not planning to."

Mabel looked a little less angry and a little more relaxed. "So he still doesn't know?"

Katie shrugged. "Not from me anyway."

Mabel's eyes narrowed. "You seem to make an awful lot of things your business around here. Why do you have to make such a pest out of yourself?"

Angry words pressed against Katie's lips. It wasn't her fault Mabel was hanging out with Mose when her *daett* disapproved. And it wasn't her fault Jesse disliked Mose. Mabel just wanted to blame *Mamm* and her for it. And what of Mabel's agreeing the other night to get along better?

"At least you have the decency to keep your mouth shut," Mabel snapped. "It's nice you know your proper place in this household."

In the normal Amish way of authority and

respect, Katie shouldn't have to tolerate a younger girl speaking to her like this. But these weren't normal times. She and *Mamm* had basically invaded Mabel's life. Because of that, Katie wanted to treat Mabel with compassion. Still, Mabel was pushing even her limits.

"So what were you talking about?" Mabel demanded, going back to her original question.

"You'll find out soon enough," Katie answered. She knew if she didn't share Mabel was only going to get angrier, but she wanted to respect and honor Jesse's authority more than please Mabel.

Mabel stepped closer. "If you think I'm going to stand around and let you steal my *daett*'s heart away from me, Katie Raber, then you have another guess coming."

Denial bubbled up inside Katie, but she choked it back.

"You might as well go ahead and tell me your little secret," Mabel continued. "If you don't tell me, I'll just ask *Daett.*"

"He's planning to tell everyone after supper," Katie said. "You'll just have to wait until then — or go talk to him now and see what he says."

Mabel's eyes got big. "I don't like this one bit. What are you up to, Katie Raber?"

Katie walked to the sink and looked out the window.

"Well, it can't be much," Mabel asserted, her face brightening. "*Daett* is probably trying to make things easier for you by giving you extra attention. He knows you've had a rough life, you know."

Mabel sure knew how to strike where it hurt, Katie thought. The pain stung deep inside her heart. She checked the quick tears that threatened to spring up. "Your *daett*'s a *gut* man, Mabel. You should be thankful for him."

Mabel smirked. "I *know* that. He's way too *gut* for you. I don't know why he was so willing to bring you and your *mamm* into our home. Pity would be my guess."

Katie turned and ran upstairs. She caught a glimpse of *Mamm* in the living room as she went by, but she didn't even pause. Had *Mamm* heard their exchange in the kitchen and done nothing about it? Likely she had, but would she let Mabel's accusation stand? But then what could *Mamm* really do? Rebuke Mabel? That would only make things worse for both of them.

Katie threw herself on the bed and buried her face in her hands. The tears didn't come though. It was like they were frozen inside her. Mabel's last words had taken the joy right out of her. And she was right. Jesse was too *gut* a *daett* for her, just as Ben was too *gut* to be her boyfriend, and just as she didn't deserve all the blessings *Da Hah* was bestowing on her. After all, she was still Emma Raber's daughter deep down inside. Mabel could see that even if no one else did right now. Katie knew she couldn't go back to that old life, even if she wanted to. That place was gone, and *Mamm* was sitting in the living room downstairs married to Jesse.

Did Mabel have any idea what it was like to live the life she had lived — without a *daett* most of her growing-up years, ignored and unnoticed by everyone in the community, and having a *mamm* who was known as being strange? Katie sat up. Mabel would just have to deal with what was happening. No one could control everything in life. In fact, most people could control very little. And she wasn't controlling what was happening at all — it was just happening. *Da Hah* was in charge, and she trusted Him in *gut* times and bad times, just like the preachers said on Sundays. And this was one of those *gut* times!

Katie trembled with excitement. She had so much joy on the one side with *Mamm,* Jesse, Ben, and now this trip to Europe. On the other side was Mabel. What would

Mabel say when Jesse told the family tonight? She was already angry, so this might make her explode with jealousy and bad temper.

Katie swung her feet over and stood as the sound of footsteps came up the stairs and stopped by the door. A soft knock sounded. It had to be *Mamm.* Mabel would have stormed up the hallway in the mood she was in. And the other children seldom came to her door.

"May I come in?" *Mamm* asked.

"Yah," Katie said, sitting down.

Mamm came in and sat beside her on the bed. She studied Katie for a moment. "I hate it that we have to continue talking with each other in your bedroom, Katie. But I wanted to say how sorry I am for the things Mabel said to you. I know it's not easy living with her."

Katie hung her head. "You're not to blame, *Mamm.*"

Mamm squeezed Katie's arm. "You've been given a lot of blessings lately. Try to remember that. It wouldn't be *gut* for anyone to have everything go well."

Katie met *Mamm*'s gaze, tears now in her eyes. "I know, but it's hard."

Mamm gave her a long hug. "You know Mabel isn't nice to me either."

Katie choked back a sob. "But you have Jesse to comfort you. I have to face Mabel on my own."

"You have Ben now." *Mamm* held Katie at arm's length. "Who would have thought that would happen?"

Katie wiped her eyes. "I thought you didn't approve of him, *Mamm.*"

A smile flitted across *Mamm*'s face. "*Nee,* but I'm working on it. You know I don't change my mind very fast. You should still be thankful for everything that's happening, all the same."

Katie nodded. "*Yah,* I am thankful for Ben. But for Mabel?" Katie glanced at *Mamm.* "I'm trying, I really am. I understand that we're disturbing her life."

"That's why we must have lots of patience with the girl." *Mamm* stood up. "Mabel's going through a hard time right now. She really doesn't want to sneak around with Mose the way she has to."

So Mamm did know all about Mose and Mabel and was choosing to not say anything. If Mabel knew that, surely she would be easier on *Mamm.*

"Come," *Mamm* said, "we'd better help Mabel fix supper."

Katie looked up, her eyes glowing. "*Mamm,* I have some exciting news!" The words spilled out. "I'm going to Europe! *Today* someone gave the money to Esther — to give to me."

"Someone *gave* you the money?" *Mamm* gasped.

"*Yah!*" Katie allowed the joy to flow. "Isn't that *wunderbah*?"

Mamm didn't look convinced.

Katie took her arm. "It's true, *Mamm*! Look!" Katie pulled the envelope out of her pocket and gave it to *Mamm*. "Open it!"

Mamm fingered the envelope Katie handed her. Then she peered inside. "That's a lot of money, Katie! Who gave it to you?"

"The giver wanted to remain anonymous. Esther asked, but the woman just handed her the envelope, told her it was for Katie Raber's trip to Europe, and left. Isn't that amazing?"

"Yes, it is! Oh my."

"Jesse helped me unhitch when I got home, so I told him about it. And he confirmed that I can go since *Da Hah* has provided the money!"

Mamm met Katie's excited look. "I'm so happy for you, Katie. Europe is a long ways away though . . ."

"You'll let me go, won't you, *Mamm*?" Katie asked hesitantly.

"Yes, of course. It sounds like a wonderful

trip." *Mamm* paused, obviously deep in thought. "I wonder what Mabel will say when she finds out. She may find this difficult — especially since she's going through such a hard time right now."

"I don't know either. Jesse said he would tell the family about my going to Europe after supper."

Mamm touched her arm and then gave her a hug. "Jesse will handle things the right way. We needn't worry about that then."

Katie smiled. Jesse would, but there might still be an explosion tonight, if she didn't miss her guess.

"Now, we'd better get downstairs and get supper on." They both stood, and *Mamm* led the way out of the bedroom. They went downstairs, and when they walked into the kitchen Mabel didn't look up. Neither did she speak to them while the three of them prepared supper. Mabel was still carrying around her thundercloud when the men came in from the barn. Carolyn had peeked into the kitchen moments earlier, but she'd probably felt the tension because she'd beaten a hasty retreat to the living room. Now that the men had arrived, she slipped into the kitchen and sat down at the table. Joel followed her cautiously.

"Sit down, everyone! Supper's ready."

Mamm was all smiles.

Jesse smiled back at her, and Katie felt her neck grow warm. *Mamm* and Jesse acted like newlyweds, even if they were older than most. They have a right to a little mushiness, Katie figured, though their actions still made her squirm. *Mamm* is acting more love-struck than I do with Ben, Katie thought. But *Mamm* was also married to her love. That made all the difference in the world.

Mabel shoved a bowl of mixed vegetables across the table before sitting down. It clanked against the potato dish and came close to tipping over.

Jesse said nothing, but Leroy had no such inhibitions. "What's gotten into you, Mabel? You look angry enough to eat a bear."

"Maybe I am!" Mabel snapped, not looking up.

"Everybody calm down," Jesse said. "Let's have prayer."

Mabel got off another quick glare in Leroy's direction before she bowed her head.

Katie held her breath for a moment before taking a deep breath and closing her eyes. *Yah,* this was was going to be quite an evening.

When Jesse said "Amen," everyone lifted their heads. Leroy immediately grabbed the potato dish.

Mabel reached out and slapped his hand. "Let the younger people go first tonight, Leroy! You don't always have to hog everything."

Leroy's face grew red. "Mind your manners, Mabel. You're a mess. Are you on Mose withdrawal or what?"

Mabel's eyes blazed. "Wait until you love someone, Leroy. I'll tell her everything bad I know about you."

Leroy laughed. "A lot of *gut* that will do. I have too many points in my favor for any little twiddle of a thing you say to have an effect."

Mabel opened her mouth to speak, but Jesse cut in.

"Children! Enough of this! You're embarrassing me. What's Emma going to think about how you're acting?"

Mabel looked like she didn't care one way or the other, but she kept silent.

Leroy lowered his eyes. "I'm sorry, Emma. I didn't mean any harm."

Mamm smiled. "I understand. Sisters and brothers sometimes have words, but they still love each other in their hearts."

Mabel's mouth worked, but she managed to halt any sounds. Apparently she'd decided silence was the better option at the moment.

Everyone quieted down as they ate their fill. When everyone had finished eating, Jesse cleared his throat. "I have some *gut* news I wish to share with the family."

Katie looked at Jesse. In about a minute Mabel was probably going to explode. A quick sideways glance at Mabel's expression confirmed Katie's suspicions. Mabel was already upset, and she hadn't even heard what Jesse was going to share. She looked at *Mamm,* who looked pale too. But Jesse was still smiling as he continued. "Katie was gifted today with the money she needs for her trip to Europe — quite a lot of money, in fact. So it looks like we'll have a member of the family traveling to the land of our fathers' faith."

"What?" Mabel leaped to her feet. "That's what you were talking to *Daett* about, Katie? Talking him into giving you *our* money! How dare you! I knew you were after something all along."

"Mabel, you will sit down at once!" Jesse commanded sharply.

Mabel grudgingly sat down.

"I didn't give Katie any money for this trip, Mabel," Jesse said. "And even if I had, that would be *my* choice. Katie is now my daughter too."

"They're destroying our lives!" Mabel pointed first at Katie and then at *Mamm.* Then she jumped up and raced away from the table. The stair door slammed, the sound echoing through the house. Footsteps thudded on the steps before there was the sound of another door opening and then slamming shut. Silence filled the house.

"Now that was a temper tantrum," Leroy said, breaking the quiet. His smile was broad. "Wow!"

Jesse rose, his face red. "I will not have such behavior happening in my house."

Mamm grabbed his arm. "Let Mabel be, Jesse. It's such a hard time for her. I'll speak with her later."

"But . . ." Jesse's eyes were still blazing.

He doesn't look that different from Mabel when he's angry, Katie noted. She watched the exchange curiously to see how it would turn out.

"It's best if a woman handles this," *Mamm* said gently.

Jesse looked at her for a long moment before nodding his head and sitting back down.

"Let's have our evening devotions," he said. "There's been enough ruckus for one night. Mabel can stay in her room if she

wishes to conduct herself in such an un-
godly manner."

CHAPTER TWENTY-FOUR

Katie hung on to the buggy seat as Longstreet trotted through the night. Ben had
picked up Katie, and they were going to
another Mennonite youth gathering. Katie
couldn't be happier. Christmas and New
Year's Day were behind them. Jesse had
insisted on a quiet time for his first Christmas married to *Mamm.* After family devotions, which consisted of Jesse reading the
Christmas story and everyone singing a few
Christmas hymns, family members had
been free to spend the day as they wished.
Katie had thoroughly enjoyed herself by
making Christmas candy in the forenoon
and reading a book in her bedroom after
lunch.

Mabel's temper fit seemed like a distant
memory now. *Mamm* had gone up and
spoken with her at length the night Jesse
had broken the news that Katie had enough
money for the Europe trip. Katie had stayed

downstairs and washed the supper dishes with Carolyn's help. Thankfully, Carolyn had shown little sympathy for Mabel. But she hadn't exactly been friendly either, probably reacting out of loyalty to her sister, Katie decided. By the time evening prayers were over, Mabel had come downstairs with *Mamm.* Both of them had eyes red from crying.

"I'm sorry, *Daett,*" Mabel mumbled before bringing a kitchen chair to the edge of the living room and sitting down. She was as far away from Katie as she could be. The next morning, Mabel hadn't glared or spouted off while they fixed breakfast, but she hadn't looked happy either. And Mabel still looked glum, especially tonight when everyone knew Ben was coming to pick Katie up.

"How are things going?" Ben asked, interrupting her thoughts.

"Okay," Katie said. "I'm still in shock though. I can't believe someone would just anonymously give me all that money. That sort of thing just doesn't happen."

Ben smiled. "I'm really glad you get to go."

Silence settled in except for the steady beat of Longstreet's shoes hitting the pavement. Katie let her thoughts go back to when she'd told Ben the news.

"You look happy tonight," Ben had commented.

"I guess I should look happy! Ben, someone has gifted me enough money to go to Europe!"

"Really? Wow, that's great!"

Ben had sounded happy for her, just as she'd expected he would.

"Who gave it to you?" Ben asked.

"I don't know. The person wanted to keep it a secret, I guess. A woman came into Byler's and gave my friend Esther, who works in the deli, an envelope and told her to give it to me. Esther had never seen her before."

"A mysterious sort of person, *eh*?" Ben said. Then he'd laughed.

Katie added her joyful laughter to his. "I guess so. I suspect it was one of the Mennonite families or maybe the mission organization Nancy works for. Someone had mercy on this poor Amish girl. I still can't believe it!"

"So you're really going then?" Ben had asked, sounding quite pleased with the idea.

Coming back to the present, Katie leaned against Ben. "Ben, I'm a little scared about going to Europe when it comes down to it," Katie admitted. "There are so many things I have to prepare for. I've never traveled far, so this will be quite an adventure. I'm going to ask Sharon and Margaret tonight for a list of things to take along. And I want to let them know how much I appreciate the money someone gave me so I could go. I'm hoping my thanks will get to the *wunderbah* person who helped me out — if it was a Mennonite family."

"You'll do fine." Ben pulled back on the reins to slow Longstreet for a corner. "You will need a passport. I'm sure the others will take care of the traveling details."

"Thanks for the encouragement," she said, hanging on to Ben and the buggy seat at the same time. Ben sure was traveling fast tonight.

His voice broke into her thoughts. "Remember, when you get over there be sure to look around and notice everything. I want a full report about how the Amish were established and how our forefathers lived their faith."

"Okay." Katie swallowed hard, a bit surprised. She remembered when Ben had expressed his doubts about the Amish faith. Was he changing his mind? That would be so great if it were true.

"Thanks for coming with me tonight," Ben said, smiling down at Katie.

Katie's heart pounded. Ben looked like he

considered her presence a great favor. "I–I–I'm the one who should be saying that to you, not the other way around."

Ben glanced at the straight stretch of road ahead of them, and then he moved the lines to his other hand. With his empty hand, he reached for Katie.

Katie thought for sure she'd stop breathing entirely when she felt Ben's hand on hers. She wrapped her fingers around his. How was this possible? Ben Stoll — *the* Ben Stoll — was holding her hand!

"You have more to offer than you think," Ben said, his fingers tightening against hers.

Katie leaned her head against his shoulder. Only when the next curve came up did he let go of her hand. He gave her a brief smile before fixing his eyes on the road.

Katie sat up when the bright lights of a farmhouse came into view. As they drove closer, she saw people carrying lumber, swinging hammers, and sawing wood.

"Someone said we're helping to build trusses tonight," Ben said as he turned down the lane. "Looks almost like an Amish gathering except for all the cars."

"Yah," Katie agreed.

The thought of Amish gatherings almost made her shudder. Ben wouldn't understand what she was feeling. He'd never experienced rejection or had people ignore him like she had. He probably wasn't aware how much she was different here than at Amish gatherings.

The buggy bounced to a stop, and Ben climbed down. He tied Longstreet to a hitch on the side of the barn. Katie waited for him to come over and help her down. Then they walked over to the worksite where everyone seemed to be scurrying around.

"Howdy there!" someone hollered out. "More help, I see."

Ben laughed. "If you don't need any help, we can, of course, just stand around and supervise."

"Grab a hammer!" a young man said as he pointed toward a pile of tools on the front porch.

Katie followed Ben and chose a small hammer.

"Just swing it," Ben teased. "It drives nails."

"*Yah,* I know. I did pretty well last time. You'd better behave or I'll swing it at you pretty soon." Katie lifted the hammer in the air as if to strike him on the arm.

He grabbed his own hammer in one hand, took her hand in the other, and led her over to where a group of young women were pounding away.

"I have a little firebrand here who needs work," Ben announced.

The girls all smiled and made room for Katie.

Ben left to help the boys with the lumber.

"Are you with him?" one of the girls asked, watching as Ben picked up several pieces of truss material and toted them across the yard.

"*Yah,*" Katie said with a smile.

"My name's Ronda Helmuth," the girl offered.

"I'm Katie Raber. Is there something I can do to help?"

"Take a round at swinging a hammer," Ronda said. "My hand and arm are about worn out."

"You can say that again," another girl said as she stood up and stretched.

Katie started swinging away at the nails, following the pattern already established. A familiar voice soon interrupted her work.

"There you are, Katie! I've been looking for you all over the place."

Katie stood up and turned to the speaker with a smile. "Margaret! Hi! It's so *gut* to see you."

"Yes, and you too. What have you been doing with yourself?"

Katie laughed. "It's not like I didn't see

you last week!"

"Time goes by so quickly, don't you think?" Margaret asked, giving Katie a quick hug. "You look happy tonight."

I should be! Katie almost said, but she decided that might be a little forward. "Have you found out who gave me that *wunderbah* gift?" she asked. "And I want to thank you again for inviting me."

Margaret laughed. "I'm not the one to thank for the money, and I don't know who is. Sharon doesn't know either. And if Nancy does, she's not talking."

"It was so nice of whomever it was," Katie gushed. "If you ever find out, be sure to tell me."

"I will," Margaret assured her, taking Katie by the elbow. "Come, let's go say hi to Sharon."

Margaret and Katie headed off as another girl took Katie's place next to the boards with hammer in hand.

Sharon glanced up as they approached and greeted them with a smile. "I'm glad you came. And with Ben Stoll again. Are the two of you getting serious?"

Katie felt heat rising up her neck, so she figured she must be blushing, but Ben was worth being embarrassed over. "I don't know. We haven't been together that long."

"Now, now," Margaret said, "you don't fool me. I can tell by that look in your eyes that you're smitten!"

Katie laughed and changed the subject. "I want to thank both of you again for including me on our trip. I'm so thankful. I so appreciate the person who gave me the funds. And if either of you ever finds out who it was, please let me know!"

"I had nothing to do with it," Sharon said. "But now that we have our full team, we can begin making definite plans."

"I think I'll pack half my wardrobe," Margaret said. "I don't want to get caught over there with nothing to wear."

Sharon giggled. "Just think, none of us except Nancy knows a thing about traveling in Europe. We'll be like silly girls over there, and we'll probably get lost on the first street corner. I can't even speak a word of German."

"Katie can," Margaret said. "And Nancy can."

"It is a little scary," Katie offered.

"We'll have lots of fun," Sharon said. "I know we will. It'll be a trip to tell our children and our grandchildren about — the time their mothers took Europe by storm."

Margaret laughed. "For now we'd better

get to work or everyone will think we're three cackling hens."

"Here's to the world's traveling hens!" Sharon said. "I can hardly wait."

Katie cleared her throat. "Do you know what we need to take? Like a passport and such things?"

"That's about it," Margaret said. "And that won't be too hard to obtain. Certainly not as difficult as praying in all that money."

"Maybe I was praying more than I thought I was," Katie said thoughtfully.

"That's a good girl," Margaret said. "I'm sure we can use your prayers, along with ours, on the trip — for all the trouble we might get into."

"I hope we get into *lots* of trouble," Sharon said. "Like getting lost in the Swiss mountains. We'd have to live off of goat's milk for days, and find our way back out on foot."

Margaret laughed. "Maybe you should change your mind, Katie. This girl might lead us into trouble on purpose."

Katie couldn't hold back her smile. "I think it's going to be lots of fun. I still can't believe I'm really going."

"Well, believe it!" Sharon said, giving Katie a playful punch on her arm.

"Enough of this silliness," Margaret said,

taking charge. "We'll talk more about this later. Let's get back to work."

The banging of hammers soon filled her ears as they helped nail sheets of plywood on the trusses. By the time they were finished, Katie figured it had to be after nine o'clock. It was too late to play a game of volleyball, but no one seemed to mind. With much laughter they gathered around to eat the cake and ice cream Albert and Mindy Brunson, the owners of the place, brought out.

Margaret and Sharon followed Katie to Ben's buggy afterward to give her quick hugs before she climbed in next to Ben. They stood waving as Ben guided Longstreet onto the driveway. They were the only buggy in the long line of cars leaving the Brunson place.

"Maybe I ought to get a car," Ben commented once they were on the road.

"Please don't," Katie said at once. "That would be terrible."

Ben laughed. "I wasn't planning to. You know, I suppose, that we're being a bit strange about everything. We're attending Mennonite youth gatherings, but neither of us are really thinking about joining their church."

"I don't want to think about that tonight."

Katie nestled against Ben's shoulder. "I just want to think about all the *wunderbah* things that are happening. I never want to stop giving thanks for them."

Ben smiled as he reached over and found Katie's hand. They remained close as Longstreet raced along, the only light coming from the ones on the buggy.

CHAPTER TWENTY-FIVE

Thursday afternoon Katie drove Sparky toward Dover, keeping one buggy wheel well toward the ditch as she approached town. A light dusting of snow lay on the ground, but the *Englisha* vehicles still zipped past her with hardly a check in their speed. She already didn't like coming into town on her own, let alone having the snow and traffic to contend with. In fact, she wouldn't have come except Ben insisted he accompany her to get her picture taken and then deliver it, along with the necessary forms, to the Dover Post Office so she could apply for her passport.

The thought of Ben brought a smile to her face. He was so manly, so protective of her. Just like a *gut* man should be! He promised to meet her in front of The Pancake House. From there they would travel together in his buggy to get the errands done.

Katie shivered. What would it be like to have someone point a camera at her? The Amish taught against it, but it must be done if she wished to travel overseas. Surely *Da Hah* would understand that she meant no vanity by having her photo taken. She would make sure no one ever saw the picture except the government officials who had to see such a thing. And they probably saw thousands of photos every day and would think nothing of it.

Mrs. Cole, her supervisor at Byler's, had smiled when Katie asked for time off for the trip. Apparently news had spread through the store's staff about Katie's upcoming adventure.

"Care if I go along to Europe with you?" Mrs. Cole had teased, which was unusual for her. She usually was calm and collected, but a trip to Europe could unsettle anyone's regular pattern.

Katie's routine had certainly changed. There were nights in bed when cold chills would run up and down her back. Other times so much joy bubbled up inside that she had a feeling of almost exploding.

Katie caught sight of The Pancake House outline ahead of her, and in the parking lot sat Ben's buggy. He was already waiting for her.

Ben waved as Katie drove up and then leaped out of his buggy to grab Sparky's bridle. "Whoa, boy!" he said in mock panic.

Katie laughed and threw him the tie rope from under the seat. "I wasn't driving that wildly."

"You drove in here like a wild woman on a mad dash into the world."

"I did not!" Katie protested as she climbed down the buggy step. Ben stirred things in her she didn't even know were there. A sense of humor, for one. There hadn't been much laughter in her life when she and *Mamm* lived alone. But now, since the marriage, joy seemed to be bubbling up around them. Except for Mabel, but Katie wasn't going to think of her right now.

Ben tied Sparky to a light post. "Are you nervous, having your picture taken and all?"

Katie frowned slightly but she was pleased that Ben seemed to understand her so well. It was comforting in a way — having a man who knew her heart.

"You'll be okay." Ben took her hand when she didn't answer. "I'll be right there by your side. I might even have my picture taken!"

Katie gasped. "You wouldn't . . . would you? It's not right except for a *gut* reason."

"Then I'll think of one," Ben said as he

helped Katie into his buggy.

She held the lines while he untied Long-street and climbed in. Handing the reins to him, their fingers brushed against each other.

"I just thought of a *gut* reason." His eyes teased. "I could go along with you!"

"You can't go with us." She glared at him teasingly. "This is a *girls*-only trip."

Ben laughed. "I meant my picture could go. Like with you. That way you wouldn't forget me. Wouldn't you like that?"

Katie thought about it for a moment. "But how would that be right, Ben?"

"You'd like it, wouldn't you?" he said, gently probing her emotions.

"Maybe . . ." Katie admitted, her voice squeaking a bit. Was she giving in to an aw-ful temptation? But how could she resist? In a way, Ben was right. It would be a picture for the trip, and she could destroy it once she came back and had Ben with her in person.

His hand found hers again. "I'm glad you want me along on your trip. Maybe we can take an extra picture of you so I can have one of yours while you're gone."

"What if someone catches us?"

Ben laughed. "We're not members of the church yet. What are they going to do? Burn the pictures? This won't harm anyone."

Katie saw *Mamm*'s face rising in front of her eyes. It had disapproval written all over it. *Mamm* would burn Ben's photo if she found it. But she could hide the photo well. And if *Mamm* did find it, she would be honest and tell the truth — that she couldn't resist when Ben offered something like this. *Mamm* would surely understand that.

"I'll take a peek at your picture every day you're gone," Ben said, his eyes shining. He let go of Katie's hand to gradually bring Longstreet to a halt for a stoplight.

Ben had read her decision without her saying a word. He was very, very *wunderbah*. And his photo in her suitcase would be almost like having him around.

"Here we are," Ben said as he pulled Longstreet to a stop beside a low brick building. "Passport photo coming up."

Katie waited while Ben tied Longstreet to a post, and then she followed him inside.

"*Gut* morning," Ben greeted the lady at the front desk.

She looked up. "Yes, how may I help you?"

"We're here to have passport pictures taken."

"Traveling are we?"

"Katie is," Ben said. "Maybe sometime in the future we'll travel together, but I'm staying home this time."

Katie felt her spine tingle at the words, wondering if traveling with Ben would ever really happen.

"The pictures are taken upstairs," the lady said. "Just go up the steps and turn right."

"Thank you," Ben said. As they moved toward the staircase, Katie held on to his hand.

At the top of the steps they turned right and found the door labeled "Passport Photos." When they entered, another woman greeted them and gave them instructions for the photo, motioning with her hand for them to follow her. In a back room she had a camera set up on a tripod. A chair sat by itself against the wall. "Right over there, if you will. My name's Carol. This won't take too long."

Ben sat down first, taking off his hat. The camera snapped. And then snapped again as Carol took three or four more shots. Katie watched, amazed at how Ben could look so calm with a camera pointed at him.

"Now, it's your turn," Carol said.

Katie approached the chair cautiously as Ben got up. When she was seated, the woman said, "Relax, dear. You look nervous."

Katie could only think that Carol must

not deal with Amish very often. *Of course* she was nervous! This was a first for her. And almost a forbidden first, at that.

Ben intervened by stepping beside Carol behind the camera. Katie kept her eyes on him, which was obviously what Ben meant for her to do.

"Hi, Katie," Ben said, so calm and relaxed, like they were sitting inside his buggy and talking.

Katie took a deep breath and focused on Ben's face. Carol pushed a button on her camera a few times and finally looked pleased with her efforts.

"Make an extra copy of each, please," Ben requested as they followed the woman out of the room.

"I'll be back in a minute," Carol told them.

"Thank you," Katie said to Ben as they sat down. "I couldn't have done that without you."

"You looked like the scarecrow in *Mamm*'s garden last summer."

"I did not!" Katie shot back.

Ben laughed. "You looked quite cute, in fact."

"Now you're making me turn red." She wanted to stay angry with him for at least a minute, but he was so charming.

Carol returned moments later with a white envelope. She handed it to Ben. "You can pay for them downstairs."

Katie held Ben's hand while they went down the steps, stealing sideway glances at the envelope. Ben must have noticed, because he smiled but didn't say anything until he'd paid. Out in the street, he helped Katie into the buggy and then handed her the envelope. She held it in her hand, turning it over several times. Ben joined her on the buggy seat. "Shall we look at them now?" he asked. He held the reins slack in one hand, and Longstreet seemed to understand it wasn't time to leave yet.

Katie groaned. "How will I look? I've never seen a picture of me before."

Ben laughed. "You've looked in the mirror, silly. It's the same thing."

Katie took a deep breath. "I guess so, but I can always change what I see in the mirror. This I can't."

Ben didn't answer as he pulled the pictures from the envelope. He held Katie's up high between his fingers. Katie gasped, and Ben laughed. "Isn't that beautiful? I think I see love shining in those eyes!"

"Don't say such things!" Katie grabbed the picture from him. He let go and pulled a photo of himself out. "Yuck. Now *that*'s ugly."

"It's not." Katie grabbed his picture and held it up for a better look. "You look quite handsome."

"Not as pretty as you are." He moved closer on the buggy seat.

Katie held her breath, looking up at him. Ben was going to kiss her right here and now, she thought. Was this okay? She had so wanted this moment to arrive, but somehow it would have been so much better at home where everything felt safe and sound. Not right after they had *Englisha* pictures taken.

Ben touched her cheek with his hand. "You're lovely, Katie. Don't worry. I'm going to treasure this photo forever." He plucked the picture out of her hand.

Katie relaxed as Ben studied the picture. He hadn't kissed her, but surely it would happen sometime. And she would enjoy it fully when it did.

Ben slipped all the photos back inside the envelope, slid them into his pocket, and slapped the reins. Longstreet took off with a jerk and Katie hung on.

"I'm also going to treasure your picture," she said as they rode through town.

Ben smiled and reached over to squeeze

her hand. It wasn't long before they arrived at the post office. Ben jumped down to tie up Longstreet again. After helping Katie down, they walked hand-in-hand inside and got in line.

Katie let go soon after that, embarrassed by holding Ben's hand right in front of everyone. What would *Mamm* say if she'd been along? Likely she'd be shocked, just like Katie was with herself. Was this what it was like being young and in love? Changing so quickly and so easily?

"Next!" the man behind the counter sang out.

Ben led the way to him and explained what they wanted. The man retreated behind a wall and soon appeared with a short, thin lady carrying a briefcase. She spread a form out on the counter. "Which one of you is getting a passport today? Or are you both?"

"Just me." Katie took a quick sideways glance at Ben to keep her courage up. He squeezed her hand under the counter.

"May I see your birth certificate and photos?" the lady asked.

Katie dug her birth certificate out of her dress pocket, and Ben laid two of her photos on the counter. One of them he'd left in the envelope — the one he would keep. Katie stepped up to the counter and began to fill out the form, not daring to look at Ben. He didn't need to see how much he meant to her. He already seemed much too aware of it.

CHAPTER TWENTY-SIX

Katie awoke with a start when Jesse called up the stairs, "Time to get up, boys!" Moments later the tramp of Leroy and Willis's feet went past her bedroom door. Katie sat up. Had she dreamed about the ruckus late last night? It seemed so impossible now as the first signs of dawn were breaking outside her window. *Nee,* she hadn't dreamed it. It was too painful. At least the outburst hadn't been about anything she'd done. She'd come home with her passport after spending several more hours with Ben. She'd entered the house as usual, said good night to everyone, and then gone to bed.

And then the *kafuffle* started, and Mabel was the one in trouble. Jesse had a right to discipline his children as he saw fit, but then *Mamm* and Katie had gotten involved, and now they were in even worse trouble with Mabel. Mabel wouldn't be forgetting last night for a long time, and all the blame would somehow come straight back on them. That's what Mabel would do, and in a way she was right this time. If *Mamm* hadn't married Jesse, Mabel might have gotten away with much more.

Katie rubbed her throbbing head. The headache was still here, pounding away, no doubt due to last night. Leroy and Willis had even awakened and come downstairs to see what was happening. And everyone knew they slept like rocks. She didn't know all the details yet, but she could guess what happened. Mabel got caught with Mose out in the barn. And that wasn't something Jesse would take kindly to or tolerate.

Katie had been awakened in what had seemed only minutes after she'd gone to bed, but it was closer to midnight according to the clock on the dresser. Mabel's wails had echoed through the house, haunting cries of despair and anger mixed together. Worried, Katie had thrown on her housecoat and rushed downstairs to the kitchen where the sounds were coming from. Jesse and *Mamm* were already there, and a kerosene lamp was burning on the table. Mabel was sitting on the back bench behind the table where Leroy and Willis usually ate. She was sobbing, her hands covering her face.

Jesse glanced up when Katie entered. He

looked ready to say something, but he changed his mind. Instead, he turned back to continue his talk with Mabel.

Katie stopped suddenly, taking in everything at once.

"You ought to be ashamed of yourself, Mabel. Thoroughly ashamed of yourself! Meeting out in the barn alone with Mose like that. It's disgraceful to the family, and to you, and to Mose, and to his family as well. We will have no more of this going on."

"How did you know I was out there?" Mabel wailed.

"That's not the point!" Jesse said. "But in case you're thinking it, Emma had nothing to do with it. And this issue right now is between you and me and no other. I told you firmly and without question to have nothing more to do with Mose Yutzy."

Mabel lifted her head from her arms. "This wasn't fair. Not one bit."

"I'm your *daett,* and I'll decide that." Jesse's voice was firm. "If you weren't so big, I'd spank you *gut* and hard right now."

This produced further wails from Mabel. Rustling footsteps were soon followed by the appearance of Carolyn in her night robe, followed by Leroy and Willis. Joel somehow managed to sleep through everything. Mabel's wails died down some when she looked up and caught sight of her brothers.

"So she *was* out there with Mose," Leroy said before anyone gave him an explanation. "I thought that's what was going on."

Mabel glared at him through her tears. "So it was you who told on me?"

Leroy shrugged. "I didn't know for sure, so I didn't say anything. But I suspected something like that after I found a candy wrapper in the feed bin. Who else would be out there eating candy bars?"

"You are all so cruel! All of you . . . every one of you!" Mabel wailed again.

"Everybody will go to bed now," Jesse announced. "None of us will be worth a hoot on the farm tomorrow."

Mamm offered Mabel her hand to help her out from behind the kitchen table, but Mabel refused. She found her own way up the stairs, and her bedroom door slammed moments later.

"Off to bed," *Mamm* told Katie when she'd just stood there, rooted to the kitchen floor.

Katie found her way upstairs and back to bed. Leroy and Willis had disappeared by then too.

Mamm followed Katie up the stairs holding Carolyn's hand. She tucked the little girl into bed and then made her way back downstairs to her room.

Now it was morning, and surely Mabel would make things worse for *Mamm* and her. Despite Jesse's words, Mabel probably thought Katie had tattled on her.

Katie got up, slipped on her housecoat, opened her bedroom door, and then closed it behind her. She tiptoed downstairs into the kitchen. There was no sign of Mabel yet, which was probably for the best. Let her sleep in this morning. Maybe she wouldn't be quite as grumpy when she awoke. Doubtful, but maybe.

"*Gut* morning." *Mamm* looked up, smiling weakly.

"*Gut* morning," Katie mumbled back. She went over to the kitchen counter and began to crack eggs into a bowl for scrambling.

"Should we get Mabel up?" *Mamm*'s voice trembled.

"I don't think so." Katie continued working.

"You'd better go awaken Mabel," *Mamm* finally said. "She'll feel worse if we fix breakfast without her."

Katie didn't look up. "I don't want her down here. She'll only weep and wail all over the place. You can get her up after I leave for Byler's."

"You know that doesn't work, Katie. And

we have to love the girl. Go call her. And remember to be nice, even if she's in a mood."

Katie groaned but went up the stairs slowly. At Mabel and Carolyn's bedroom, Katie pushed open the door. Mabel's form was visible in the soft moonlight shining through the open window. Carolyn lay curled up on the smaller bed.

"Mabel," Katie whispered. Mabel sat up at once. "It's time to get up," Katie said. She was already retreating by the time Mabel had swung her legs over the side of the bed. Closing the door behind her, Katie headed down the stairs.

"Everything go okay?" *Mamm* asked worriedly.

"She didn't say a peep, but I think she's coming," Katie offered.

Mamm bustled about the kitchen. Moments later, Mabel appeared fully dressed. "*Gut* morning." *Mamm* smiled her brightest.

Mabel said nothing for a moment. "Did either of you tell *Daett* about Mose and me?"

"Of course not," *Mamm* said.

Katie shook her head.

"So how did he find out? Am I supposed to believe Leroy's story about the candy wrapper?"

Mamm looked straight at Mabel. "Leroy suggested something to Jesse after he found the candy wrapper, so Jesse went out to investigate last night. That's all your *daett* knew, and I added nothing to the story."

"*Daett* didn't ask you if you knew anything about this? You're supposed to be his *frau,* after all."

Mamm's face colored. "Your *daett* did ask me if knew anything, but I refused to answer. I told him I wasn't getting between his daughter and him."

"Then you *did* tell him. That's all the information *Daett* needed. He can figure the rest out on his own."

"Maybe you shouldn't have been out there with Mose in the first place," *Mamm* said. "Then you wouldn't be worrying about who tells your secrets."

Mabel's face flashed red. "I wish both of you would go back to where you belong — and out of my kitchen. We were getting along perfectly fine before you showed up and spoiled everything. Now my life is a mess because you waltzed in here as *Daett*'s wife and brought along this weird daughter of yours who's so high and mighty now she hardly speaks with me any longer. She's even dating Ben Stoll and planning to tramp all over Europe with Mennonites. *Daett* never would have allowed something like that until you ruined him."

Mamm listened with a pained look on her face. "I'm sorry you feel that way, Mabel. And I'm trying to understand it, although I can't do much about it. I love your *daett,* and that's the way *Da Hah* planned things."

"Don't be blaming this on *Da Hah,*" Mabel snapped. "Now let me go ahead with the bacon. I used to do all of this myself with just Carolyn's help — just in case you think I'm helpless in the kitchen."

"We know you're not helpless, Mabel." *Mamm* managed a smile. "Maybe things will look better for you soon."

"What's going to bring Mose back? He'll never show up again after *Daett* chased him out of the barn."

"That might be for the best," *Mamm* said. "I think your *daett* knows what he's doing."

Mabel glared but said nothing more as she started work on the bacon.

Katie stayed out of her way but still helped where she could. It would be better, she figured, if breakfast took a little longer than to infuriate Mabel when it could be avoided.

By the time the men came tramping into the washroom from doing chores, there was still the toast to make. The kettle water had just boiled for the oatmeal, and *Mamm* rushed to finish up.

Mabel had a smirk on her face when Jesse walked in because *Mamm* still wasn't done. *Look how your new frau is doing,* Mabel's look told her *daett. I always had things ready on time.*

Jesse ignored Mabel and sat down at the table. Carolyn and Joel appeared before prayer time, slipping into their chairs. Leroy and Willis kept silent until after their *daett* said, "Amen."

The two wasted no time after that, slipping out words between bites of food. "Looks like our little lovebird isn't too chirpy this morning." Willis glanced slyly at Leroy. "Do her feathers look singed to you?"

"I hope *Daett* sent Mr. Lovebird off with a *gut* kick in his pants," Leroy offered.

"How dare you speak of Mose like that!" Mabel exploded.

"Boys, boys," Jesse cut in. "Don't be hard on your sister. She's had a difficult night."

"Sitting on feed bags kissing Mose can't be that hard," Willis smirked.

"You horrid creature!" Mabel wailed. "I wish I'd let you all starve back when I was doing the cooking. Here I worked my fingers to the bone washing your laundry and making your food, and you . . . you

290

can't even be grateful. You little brats!"

"I think she's upset," Leroy said, exchanging another glance with Willis. They both grinned.

"Okay, that's enough," Jesse said. "We will speak no more on the matter. Mose isn't coming around again, and I'm sure Mabel sees the error of her ways. She'll not be hanging out with that boy anymore. Thankfully we've caught this problem in time that something could be done about it."

Mabel looked like she was ready to burst into tears, but she kept her mouth shut.

"Pass me some more of the oatmeal," Jesse said, apparently trying to move the subject to safer ground.

This produced another wail from Mabel. "You like her oatmeal, don't you, *Daett*? Much better than any I used to make. Why did I even try? I should have left this household a long time ago."

"You're only sixteen, and you are going nowhere," Jesse said. "And of course I like Emma's oatmeal. But I also liked yours when you made it. You know I never had any complaints."

Mabel looked somewhat mollified, but the battle was likely far from over. Without her weekly excursions to meet Mose in the barn, Mabel would be even more impossible to live with, Katie knew.

"By the way, Mabel," Jesse continued, "how is it you got out of the house all this time without us hearing you?"

Mabel kept her eyes on her bowl of oatmeal and offered no answer.

"I'll check the washroom door," Leroy offered. "And Willis can check the front door."

Mabel's face was blazing red by the time her brothers returned.

"What did you find?" Jesse asked them.

"The washroom hinges don't squeak," Leroy said. "She's been keeping them oiled."

"Take care of that first thing then," Jesse told him. "There's an old pair of hinges in the barn. No more of this sneaking around is going to happen at this house. And if you oil the hinges, Mabel, I won't go easy on you."

Mabel hung her head, her face pale now.

Reality was sinking in. Mabel wouldn't be seeing Mose in private for years — if ever again, Katie thought. But that didn't mean she was changing her opinion about *Mamm* and her. Likely Mabel would be even angrier than before.

CHAPTER TWENTY-SEVEN

After the new year started, the weeks passed quickly. Ben felt the increasing weight of his delivery job with renewed regret. Was the money really worth the guilt? And there was his friendship with Katie. They'd continued to attend the Mennonite youth gatherings together and even did other things on occasion. Now it was early April, and spring was in full bloom, the last traces of winter finally gone. Just like his life was about to become, Ben thought. The last of the bitter and bad had to leave.

Ben knocked on the door of the trailer. When there was no answer, he tried again. Silence. Ben pounded on the door and called out, "I know you're in there, Rogge. I need to talk to you."

Noise soon rustled inside the trailer, and Rogge jerked open the front door, his eyes bloodshot. "What do you want this early in the day? Can't you figure out that I'm still sleeping?"

Ben didn't back up. "It's five o'clock in the evening. Have you been sleeping all day?"

"It's Saturday," Rogge muttered. "I sleep days and work nights. Remember?"

"That's what I'm here for, Rogge. This time it's for real. I'm not working for you anymore."

Rogge glared at Ben. "We've been over this before."

"I'm not asking this time. I'm sayin." Ben turned to go.

"It's that young girl you're seeing. The Raber girl, isn't it?"

Ben stopped short. "You mind your own business, Rogge, and I'll mind mine. You and I are through. Got that?"

"Must be something, that girl." Rogge smiled, showing all his teeth. "Does she know what you've been doing?"

Ben turned around and stepped closer. "You'd better not tell her, you hear me?"

"And what would you do if I did?" Rogge was still smiling. "Yell at me? Isn't that all a good Amish boy can do?"

Ben turned on his heels, speaking over his shoulder. "Leave Katie alone if you know what's good for you."

"I'll be seeing you next week at the usual

time, Ben," Rogge hollered after him.

"No, you won't." Ben climbed into his buggy. He slapped the reins against Longstreet's back, and the horse lunged forward. Rogge was still staring at them as they hurled out the driveway.

Let him look long and hard, Ben thought. Rogge was getting no more foolishness out of him. Rogge's threat of telling Katie about his past was just that — a threat. He would do nothing of the sort. He had too much to lose if Ben squealed. Of course he wouldn't do that, but let Rogge think he would. Right now he had other things to think of, like his planned evening with Katie. There would be just the two of them together, going nowhere in particular. Katie had warmed quickly to the idea when he'd asked. She seemed uncomfortable around the Amish young people, but when he'd mentioned attending a party where the *rumspringa* young folks were gathering, Katie hadn't looked happy either. There wasn't a Mennonite youth gathering this week. The coming of spring's busy season had slowed everything down, so a planned drive tonight alone was just the ticket. He would have Katie to himself. That should help wash memories of Rogge out of his mind.

Not that he had quite intended things to

fall in that order. He still had flashes of guilt about how the relationship with Katie was going. She had no idea what his past was, and he didn't have the courage to admit what had been going on. He would lose Katie, he was sure. And she was doing him so much *gut* and he enjoyed her company far too much to take a chance on losing her.

Ben slapped the reins again and directed Longstreet toward the Mast place. His horse already seemed to know the way and didn't fight the pull of the lines when he was turned away from home. Ben sighed. He was doing the right thing by quitting the business with Rogge, but he wasn't treating Katie like she deserved. He pulled into Jesse's driveway and parked beside the barn. He waited in the buggy. There was no sign of Katie. Perhaps he should go inside and see what was keeping her. He had his foot on the buggy step when the front door opened. Katie came running across the lawn.

"Sorry I'm late!" she gasped, stopping in front of the open buggy door. "We went a little long on the Saturday cleaning. I must say, keeping house for a large family takes much more time than it did when it was just *Mamm* and me."

"No problem," Ben said, smiling down at

her. "Perhaps I'm a little early. I had another stop to make, but it didn't take as long as I thought."

"Well, I'm ready now." She walked around and stepped up into the buggy. "Where are we going?"

"Maybe it's a surprise," Ben teased.

"Okay, you don't have to tell me," Katie said. "Just being with you is enough. Take me anywhere. I want to enjoy this time with you before I leave to fly across the ocean."

"I'll still be here when you get back," Ben said.

"I know." Katie clung to his arm. "I am a little scared. And it's not getting any better the closer the time comes to leave."

"You'll be in great company with your three friends." He looked over at her. "And you'll see all those sites where our faith was born. Be sure to take notes of everything. I want to know every little detail when you come back."

"Ben, you mentioned that once before. I wondered if you were still having doubts about the faith. Are you?" Katie looked at him, as Ben slowed Longstreet to make a turn.

"Some, I suppose. But maybe having doubts is a good thing. Once I wrestle through those, I think my faith will be stronger. At least I hope so."

She snuggled up against him again. "Your family comes from a long line of people who believed in *Da Hah,* as do mine. That's our destiny, Ben. But *yah,* I will take notes to share with you, if you wish."

"I'd like that very much." He pulled back on the reins. "There's a little clearing in the woods that I know of just up ahead. Do you want to park there for a few moments? It's a beautiful place. We won't stay for long."

"I would love that," she said.

Ben slowed Longstreet and turned down a little dirt road. The trees grew tight along the path, but they soon opened up just like he remembered. Everywhere spring was in full force, with flowers blooming among the undergrowth and the rest of the vegetation bursting with life. Ben pulled Longstreet to a stop in front of an open meadow and let the reins hang on the dashboard. "I should have taken you into Dover to the Dairy Queen. At least we'd have ice cream."

Katie smiled at him. "This is better than ice cream."

Her cheeks glowed in the falling dusk, and he traced them with his fingers.

She didn't pull back, but trembled under his touch.

He took her chin in his hand, and bent

his head toward her lips. She came to meet him, the softness of her lips moving under his.

Moments later he let go and wrapped his arm around her shoulder. Katie melted into his side, tighter than she ever had before.

"I love you, Katie Raber," he said, his voice shaking. Never had a girl affected him quite like Katie. How could he risk losing her by revealing his past? He'd broken all ties with Rogge and that awful drug dealing. She need never know.

Katie looked up at him. "You know I love you, Ben. Too much, I think."

They watched the birds and animals move about for a while until the darkness was too much. Finally Ben sighed. "Well, I think I'd better take you home."

"*Yah,* I think you should," she said.

They both sat up straighter, and Ben reached out and took up the reins. Katie snuggled under his arm. When they reached the road, Ben let Longstreet meander this time. He was in no hurry to end this night.

CHAPTER TWENTY-EIGHT

Katie stood by the window of her bedroom and gazed out over the open fields. The full moon had risen in the sky some hours ago, and it hung well above the tree line but cast light shadows on the ground. It had been several days now since Ben had dropped her off after their buggy ride to that meadow. Even Mabel's sour face when Katie had walked into the house that night hadn't dampened her joy. Ben had kissed her! She kept repeating that to herself. And he had *wanted* to kiss her just like she had wanted to kiss him. How could that be? A boy like Ben Stoll!

Katie wrapped her arms around herself, catching sight of the moon around the corner of the house as it crept higher in the sky. She hadn't told *Mamm* yet about Ben's kiss. Maybe a person wasn't supposed to tell such things to anyone — even her *mamm.* It didn't seem right in a way. That moment their lips met seemed almost holy. The meadow had lain open in front of them, bursting with new life. The trees and *Da Hah* had been their only witnesses. Well, Longstreet had been there, but he hadn't cared one way or the other. He was just glad for a few minutes of rest.

How wrong *Mamm* had been about Ben all those months ago. In those dark days before Jesse came calling, *Mamm* had said Ben would turn out like her first love had — rejecting her, ignoring her, marrying someone else. But Ben wasn't like that. Ben might even ask her to be his *frau* someday. And then she could kiss him every day.

A shadow running across the lawn caught Katie's attention, jerking her thoughts away from Ben. Katie's eyes followed the figure as it neared the barn door and disappeared inside. That had to be Mabel. Was she meeting Mose again? How would Mabel dare to do that? Jesse had strongly warned her about ever sneaking out to be with Mose again.

Perhaps it wasn't Mabel? Maybe Carolyn had decided to run outside for a second? But the form Katie saw had been Mabel's size. Should Katie do something about this? What could she do? Mabel had a mind of her own, and telling someone what she'd just seen might bring about a great *kufuffle*. Besides, she didn't really know what Mabel was doing.

Katie moved away from the window. If Mabel was up to something again, it wouldn't remain a secret for long. Not with Jesse and Mabel's brothers being on the lookout for this very thing. Should she try to stop Mabel again? Perhaps reach her before Mose showed up? She decided it didn't hurt to try again to talk Mabel out of this foolishness. Katie slipped down the stairs. She smiled at Jesse and *Mamm,* who looked up from where they were sitting in the living room. "I'm going outside," she said.

Jesse nodded. "It's a nice night out. I noticed the full moon was out a few minutes ago."

"*Yah,* it is. A nice night for a short walk."

Mabel was acting quite recklessly, Katie thought as she headed through the wash-room door. Meeting like this with Mose before anyone had gone to bed was so risky. And with the full moon in the sky to reveal so much. Was Mabel *trying* to get caught?

Katie pulled open the barn door. Like the washroom door, it gave off a loud squawk. There was no chance of approaching Mabel and Mose's hiding place without them knowing she was coming. That was just as well. She didn't wish to surprise the couple. This way Mose might have time to safely flee before she arrived.

A dim shaft of light stole out from under the door ahead of Katie. Why had Mabel been so careless and allowed the light to show? Arriving at the feed door, she knocked. There was silence at first, and then she heard a muffled sob. Katie, not sure of what to do, pushed open the door.

In front of her a crying Mabel sat on a feed bag, a kerosene lamp burning beside her. "What do you want? Can't you see I want to be left alone?" she demanded through her tears.

"Is Mose gone already?" Katie looked around.

"He was never here, stupid. Do you think he'd come back after getting caught once? Mose is not an idiot. I've lost him forever." Mabel burst into tears again.

Katie sat down on the feed bag beside Mabel. When Mabel didn't object, Katie was surprised. She'd never seen Mabel quite like this. The poor girl was brokenhearted underneath all that anger and hostility.

"I'm so sorry," Katie said. "I really am. I wish you could continue seeing Mose, although I don't know what kind of boy he really is."

"Well, he's not high and mighty like that Ben of yours. But then the two of you fit each other perfectly."

"You know that's not true," Katie said before she thought to keep silent. "I'm not near *gut* enough for Ben."

Mabel smirked through her tears. "You seem to think you're *gut* enough to mess up my life. That takes somebody pretty full of herself."

Katie remained silent.

Mabel continued. "And you're going to Europe. What kind of Amish girl takes off and does that? Not any that I know. We all stay home and prepare for our future lives with husbands and children. We don't go cavorting around in the Old Land."

Katie wanted to say something, but what could she offer? A sarcastic retort? Hardly. The poor girl was obviously crushed already. Katie thought for a moment that maybe Mabel was right, perhaps she was full of herself. Even thinking she could help Mabel might be evidence of that.

"You see my point, don't you?" Mabel was glaring now. "You're quite full of yourself. You think badly about Mose and me for kissing, but in the meantime Ben and you are smooching all over each other. I'm right,

304

aren't I? You and Ben do kiss just like Mose and I do."

Each word was cutting like a knife, and Katie's roiling emotions wanted to lash back at Mabel, but at the same time she wanted to put an arm around her shoulders and comfort her.

"I wish you and your *mamm* would go away," Mabel continued, waving her hand through the air. "Just disappear and leave us alone."

"Maybe I should go back in the house." Katie stood up. "I'm sorry I've created trouble in your life, Mabel. But I don't know what else I can do. I have to be me, and the fact is Ben and I love each other. And, *yah,* we did kiss the other night — for the first time. And it was *wunderbah.* If that's what you experienced with Mose, then I hope your relationship can continue someday."

Mabel was about to speak when the door burst open and Jesse appeared.

"Was Mose out here?" he demanded.

The accusation sent Mabel into fresh sobs.

"Nee," Katie offered. "I saw Mabel leave the house and followed her. It's just the two of us."

Jesse looked relieved. "If Mose isn't here, why are you out here, Mabel?"

"I needed a place by myself so I could sob my heart out," Mabel wailed.

A troubled look crossed Jesse's face, and he sat down on the feed bag next to his daughter. "I love you, Mabel," he said. "I just want what's best for you."

Mabel looked at him with tear-stained face. "Then why can't I see Mose?"

"Because he's not the right man for you. He's not *gut* enough." Jesse gathered Mabel in his arms, and she sobbed against his chest. Katie left them, closing the door and feeling her way across the dark barn. It was *gut* that Jesse was spending time with Mabel. Perhaps they could find healing for their ruffled relationship. As she stepped outside the barn, the moonlight guided Katie across the lawn and up the porch. The swing squeaked in the slight breeze, and Katie glanced toward it before entering the house. Someday she would have enough nerve to ask Ben to sit on the swing with her. Sometime after Mabel had gotten over her pain and perhaps was dating another boy. Every girl ought to sit on a front porch swing with the man she loved, Katie thought. Just like *Mamm* had with Jesse.

"What's going on out there?" *Mamm* asked when Katie walked in.

"Mabel's mourning her loss of Mose, and

Jesse's comforting her. I tried, but I only made things worse."

Mamm looked relieved. "No Mose then?"

Katie shook her head. "I think I'll go to bed."

"How are you and Ben getting along?" *Mamm* asked.

The words burst out before she could stop them. "He kissed me, *Mamm*! For the first time. And it was so *wunderbah.*"

Mamm smiled a little. "I'm glad to hear it's going well. Still, I wish you wouldn't rush things."

Katie hesitated. "Believe me, *Mamm*. Ben isn't who you think he is."

Mamm didn't say anything for a moment. "I hope everything turns out okay for you, Katie. And if it doesn't, remember *Da Hah* will always see you through. Just be very careful of giving your heart away."

"You still don't trust Ben?"

Mamm shrugged. "I've decided to leave my feelings about Ben up to *Da Hah*. Ben seems like a nice enough boy. I'm just waiting, watching, and praying for you."

Katie went over and gave *Mamm* a big hug. "I'm so scared one minute, and so happy the next. Well, mostly happy. Do you think I'm biting off too much with this trip?"

"*Nee,* that I have no doubts about," *Mamm*

assured her. "Nothing but *gut* can come out of a trip to the land of our faith. Be sure to see and learn as much as you can so you can tell us about it all when you come back."

"The Mennonite girls are going to take cameras. Will you look at their pictures?"

Mamm shook her head. "No pictures, Katie. Just remember in your mind or write out what you see. That's the way of our people. From your words will come images much greater than from the *Englisha* man's camera. Our forefathers didn't need those things to believe."

Katie hung her head. "I'm sorry I brought it up, *Mamm.* I won't be bringing home any pictures then. Ben also wants me to tell him what I see and hear. So now I have two people to write for and remember."

"You will have many more than two people," *Mamm* said. "I'm expecting a lot of our women will wish to hear about what you're going to see. Perhaps you can share at the women's sewing sometime."

"At the sewing?" Katie repeated. That was too much to comprehend. Not that long ago she'd been a nobody, and now *Mamm* was talking of her sharing with the women at the sewing. Ruth Troyer and Mabel would melt her with their glares. It was a wonder that *Mamm* had even started going to the sewings. And somehow the women were accepting her, to hear *Mamm* tell it.

Mamm must have noticed her discomfort. "We'll deal with that when the time comes, Katie. Right now we take each day as it comes up. You'll do okay."

Katie nodded and slipped upstairs. A light shone briefly from the barn door when she peeked out the window, then it blinked out. Two forms came across the lawn, walking close together. Jesse must have succeeded in comforting his daughter, just as *Mamm* had given her encouragement.

CHAPTER TWENTY-NINE

Katie nestled against Ben's shoulder as they drove toward home on a May night. They both listened to the steady drum of Longstreet's hooves on the pavement. Ben hadn't said anything since they left the youth gathering. This was the last one she would attend before leaving for Europe on Monday. Though Ben had been his usual jolly self all evening, now he seemed a little sad.

"Is anything wrong?" Katie looked up at his face in the darkness.

Ben smiled down on her. "No, I was just thinking about your leaving. You've come to mean a lot to me."

"Ben, you mean a lot to me too. I'll only be gone several weeks."

"Those will seem like years."

Katie laughed. "I suppose so. I know I'll miss you terribly. Although I'll be so busy being scared that I might not think of much else for awhile."

Ben took her hand. "You'll be just fine. I know you will. And you'll come back a completely different person. You might not even wish to speak with me again."

Katie slapped him on the arm. "Stop teasing. You know that won't be true."

Ben laughed. "You'll do okay. Don't worry."

Katie nestled tighter against Ben's shoulder and watched Longstreet's smooth gait float across the pavement.

"Can you believe this moment? You and me together?" Katie said, breaking the peaceful silence.

Ben squeezed her hand. "I'm just thankful you drive around with me. You do me a lot of *gut,* Katie."

Katie rubbed her cheek against Ben's shoulder. "It's not like that at all. I remember a day when you drove right past me on the road and never even noticed me."

Ben touched her hand. "I guess I was in my own little world, Katie. I'm just glad you finally caught my attention."

When Katie didn't say anything, Ben continued. "I'm not embarrassing you, am I?"

Katie smiled. "*Yah,* a little. But I like it."

"I think you look cute when you're embarrassed."

Katie looked up at him, his handsome face highlighted against the starlit sky.

"Will you write to me while you're in Europe?" he asked.

"Of course I will," Katie said. "But I might be home before some of the letters even arrive."

"It won't matter. I'll read them even if you're already back home. Be sure to write something — even a short little note would do. I'll treasure them a lot, Katie."

"I'll miss you, Ben. You won't be able to write since we'll be moving around a lot. That'll be hard on me."

After a brief silence, Ben said, "Katie, what are we going to do when you get back?"

Katie didn't dare look up at Ben. Was he about to propose? But he couldn't! She was a little young at nineteen for marriage. Her next birthday wasn't until October.

"I was thinking about the Mennonite Church." Ben cleared his throat. "I thought I might join someday, but now I'm not so sure. I guess I'm not sure about much when it comes to faith. I was hoping things would clear up as we went along."

Katie relaxed against Ben's shoulder. "I'm staying Amish, and surely you'll be doing the same thing."

Ben sighed. "I know. So much of our life seems wrapped up with the Mennonite youth lately. I'm hoping you'll find some answers that will clear everything up for me while you're in Europe."

Katie sat up straight. "I'm only going for a short trip, so don't expect too much."

"You might be surprised by what you'll learn." Ben smiled at her.

"I'll be sure to tell you if I do, but I'm just a girl who's also finding her way . . . although I know I'm staying Amish when all is said and done."

"That's what I like about you, Katie. You don't make me feel rotten because of my doubts."

Ben slowed Longstreet to turn into Jesse's driveway. The house lay dark in front of them. Everyone was no doubt in bed. They were a little late getting back, but the evening had been worth it. There had been time for two volleyball games tonight. Ben had played beside her during both games, insisting even when Margaret had teased him about it.

"Here we are." Ben brought Longstreet to a stop. "I was hoping the evening would never end."

"Yah," Katie agreed. And then she thought that surely tonight was the perfect night to

313

ask. "Can we sit on the porch swing for a little while? I know it's late, but we won't be seeing each other for awhile."

"I would love that."

Ben climbed down from the buggy and tied Longstreet to the hitching post. He turned toward Katie and helped her down. Then he took her hand and they walked across the lawn in the starlight. Above the horizon the late moon was out, the three-quarters globe hanging low on the horizon. Before long it would flood the land with light. Already Katie could see Ben's handsome face in the flickering shadows.

Ben followed her up the steps and waited until Katie was seated on the swing before sitting beside her. The chains groaned in the still night air. *Mamm* and Jesse might hear that, Katie thought. But she smiled. They wouldn't come out to disturb them, she was sure.

"It's nice out here." Ben moved the swing with his feet. The chains squawked, and he stopped.

Katie leaned against his shoulder. "You're so sweet. You know that, don't you?"

"I'll miss you terribly, you know."

Katie didn't say anything as she nestled into his shoulder. She wanted to absorb this moment fully, sitting here on the swing with

Ben. She had imagined this so many times, and now it was happening.

"Katie, I want you to know that I'm trying to get my life straightened out." He found Katie's hand in the darkness. "And you're a very big part of that. I want you to know that."

Katie was surprised at the change in Ben's tone. "Ben, I can't imagine that you have much to straighten out. You just need to resolve your doubts about the faith, that's all. And I know that's going to happen."

"The truth is that I've done some things in my life that I shouldn't have . . . that I'm ashamed of. These things are what I'm trying to make right."

She looked up at him. "I can't imagine you've done very many things wrong, Ben. You don't seem like that type of person."

He looked away. "I'm glad you think so, Katie. It makes me feel better, knowing that you care. But I'm far from perfect."

"Did you ever date someone else, Ben? Is that it?" The question flashed through Katie's mind. That was all she could think of that Ben might feel guilty about.

His voice grew tender. "I have, *yah,* but I never found someone as *wunderbah* as you."

Katie reached up to find his face with her hands. His fingers gripped her wrists, as his head lowered toward hers. Katie held him for a long time, kissing him until he pulled away.

"You shouldn't do that to me, Katie," he said.

She didn't answer as she reached for him again. He didn't resist, and his fingers traced her face after their kiss this time.

"That's enough, Katie," he whispered after long moments had passed. "Jesse might come out and catch us."

"I don't care," Katie replied, holding both of his hands. How did she ever have so much nerve, Katie wondered, kissing Ben like this on the front porch? It was as if great courage raced through her, drawing her heart toward his like a magnet. He did something for her no other boy ever had done or ever would do. She was certain of that. And unlike *Mamm*'s experiences with love, *Da Hah* was allowing her to walk where *Mamm* hadn't been allowed to go with Daniel Kauffman.

Thank You! she almost whispered out loud. But if she did, Ben would think she was thanking him for the kiss, which didn't seem quite right. *Da Hah* was the only one who should be properly thanked for this moment.

"I think I'd better be going." Ben got to his feet.

Katie did too, and she followed him to the buggy.

They kissed again before he climbed in.

"Remember, I'll be at the airport to see you off." Ben spoke through the open buggy door as Longstreet dashed forward, anxious to get home.

Katie stepped back, watching until the buggy lights disappeared in the darkness. Ben was troubled about something. She realized that now that he was gone. His presence had kept the feeling at bay, but now she sensed it was something big . . . something important. But what could it be? Likely it was nothing more than Ben's doubts about his faith. That was a weighty question, and one he would surely settle eventually. Ben would come through, she was sure. Katie slipped back across the lawn and went inside. Everything was dark and still, so they must not have disturbed anyone by sitting on the porch.

Back in her room, Katie knelt in the moonlight to pray. "I'm so thankful for the *wunderbah* time tonight with Ben, dear *Hah*. Thank You so much for letting me experience it. And help me with any sorrow You might decide needs to come our way. I really want to learn thankfulness in all things. Would You help me, please? Amen."

Katie climbed into bed and lay awake for long minutes staring at the ceiling. What awful things might lie ahead of her if *Da Hah* answered her prayer by sending something troubling? Had she opened herself to great sorrow? Would there be sickness to endure? Would she and Ben marry only to have a child die? That would be too much to handle. Surely *Da Hah* would only give what she could take. The preachers always said that was how He worked.

With troubling thoughts still running through her head, Katie fell asleep.

CHAPTER THIRTY

On the day of Katie's departure for Europe, the van arrived soon after one o'clock for the trip to the Philadelphia International Airport. Margaret's mother, Nelly, was driving. Nancy and Sharon had already been picked up, and the suitcases of the three girls were piled high in the luggage compartment.

Katie heard them drive in, and she gave *Mamm* one last hug.

"Make it *gut*," *Mamm* said, wiping her eyes. "And don't forget to pull your suitcase on its wheels."

"Don't you want to come out and say goodbye?" Katie asked.

"I'd better stay inside," *Mamm* said. "I've not been around Mennonite women that much."

"I love you, *Mamm*. I guess I'll be going." Katie pressed her lips together as her eyes stung. The last thing she needed was to

319

break down in front of Mabel, who was watching this scene without emotion. At least she hadn't been scowling all morning, which was something to be thankful for.

"Don't enjoy yourself too much," Mabel said, a hint of a smirk on her face.

Katie tried to smile as she rushed toward the door, giving a quick wave over her shoulder. Maybe Mabel's heart would soften while she was away. That would be a miracle in itself! But she mustn't limit *Da Hah*'s work by doubting. Greater things had already happened in her life. Maybe they could start a fresh relationship when she returned.

"Good afternoon!" Nelly sang out from the driver's seat as Katie approached the van. "The big moment has arrived."

"*Gut* afternoon," Katie greeted them all, overcome for a moment with her old shyness. Katie lifted her suitcase into the van, deposited it on top of the others, and settled into her seat, keeping her carry-on with her. She buckled her seat belt as she said "hi" to Margaret, Sharon, and Nancy.

Nelly pulled the van forward, and Katie waved out the window. *Mamm* had come out onto the porch and was waving back.

"You have a nice mother there," Margaret commented.

Nancy agreed. "It must be good to leave with your *Mamm*'s blessing on such a big trip."

"*Yah,*" Katie said. "I've had many blessings lately, and this trip is one of them!"

"Well, I've sure been blessed that all of you have agreed to come along," Nancy said. "I've wanted to make this trip for so long, but I never imagined three such great traveling companions would accompany me. I think it's going to be the trip of a lifetime."

Katie felt a shiver run through her. "I've never even flown on an airplane before. I'm a little nervous."

"Neither has Margaret," Nelly said at once, an encouraging note in her voice. "You'll do fine."

"Mom!" Margaret protested. "You don't have to tell all my secrets."

"It's no shame flying for the first time," Nelly assured her daughter, taking a quick glance in Sharon's direction. "Have you flown before?"

Sharon nodded. "Out west once when our family went to Colorado. But that wasn't crossing an ocean."

"Then it's a first for most of you," Nelly chirped. "And don't worry! It'll be fun."

With the talk of the plane ride out of the way, the girls chattered as the miles passed.

Nelly had the van out on the interstate toward Philadelphia a few minutes after half-past two.

Katie's mind wandered to Ben. He'd promised to be at the airport to see her off. Wasn't that a ways for him to go just for that? The goodbye the other night and again on Sunday would have been fine with her. But that was how Ben was. So nice and always going out of his way to make her feel special. He'd said his carpentry crew was working away from home this week on a job near Philly. He would have the driver take him over to see her off. His boss not only allowed this, Ben had assured her, he even thought it was a good idea. The boss was apparently the romantic sort. Katie smiled at the thought. Ben was the real romantic.

A thought flitted through Katie's mind. What would the other girls think when Ben showed up? She hadn't thought of that before. All of them appeared to have made their goodbyes to loved ones at home. Maybe she ought to say something so they wouldn't be too surprised. Katie didn't ponder the question long. "Ben Stoll said he was coming to see me off at the airport. I hope that's not a problem."

Nancy's face lit up with a smile. "He's your boyfriend, right? The one who brings you to the youth gatherings?"

"Yah," Katie said. The admission sent a thrill through her.

"Katie must be so special," Margaret said, sounding like she was a little jealous. "You ought to see how that boy dotes on her. And he's so handsome!"

Sharon giggled. "Margaret, you shouldn't be jealous."

"I'm not!" Margaret said, making a funny face at her friend. "I was just hoping Lonnie would catch a few hints. But he hasn't so far."

"We shouldn't compare among ourselves," Nancy said, sounding quite wise. "Look at me. I've never even had a boy ask me home."

"That's because they don't know what they're missing," Nelly said from the driver's seat. "Boys nowadays don't have the sense they did in my day. Back then Nancy would have a boyfriend already."

"Nancy hasn't met the right man yet," Sharon spoke up. "Maybe she'll meet him on this trip."

"Dream on, sister," Nancy said, and they all laughed.

"Philly airport coming up!" Nelly called out soon afterward, beginning to follow the airport exit signs. "Any last thing anyone needs before we get to the airport?"

"I had lunch," Nancy said. "How about everybody else?"

"I did too," Margaret spoke up. Sharon and Katie nodded they had too.

Nelly took the last exit for the airport. Minutes later they were at the front entrance of US Airways and pulling their suitcases out of the van. The buzz and racket filled Katie's ears. Katie shivered, looking around her.

Where was Ben going to meet them? Inside somewhere, he'd said. Well, hopefully he knew his way around here, because she hadn't the slightest idea where she was going. If he didn't show up soon, she would have no way of finding him. This place was huge!

"Goodbye, Mom!" Margaret was giving her mom a last hug and wiping away a quick tear.

"Now, are you sure you know how to get where you're going inside?" Nelly asked.

"Sure. Once we check in at the ticket counter and check our baggage, we just go to the gate they tell us to and wait until boarding," Nancy said. "Remember, I've done this before."

"Okay, then," Nelly said, still a bit dubious. "The Lord bless all of you." She then gave each girl a hug, ending with Katie.

The noise of the jets roaring overhead seemed to get worse by the minute. Looking toward an extra loud sound, Katie saw a huge plane pass over the terminal building and climb into the sky.

"We'll be on something like that soon," Sharon spoke into Katie's ear. "I can hardly wait!"

Watching the plane rise into the air, Katie gathered her courage. If something like that could stay in the air once, then it could again even with her on it. She would just have to pray really hard for *Da Hah* to quiet her pounding heart. He'd been blessing this trip so far, and He would surely continue to do so.

"Let's go!" Nancy hollered, leading the way inside.

Katie hung on to her baggage, using the wheels like *Mamm* had demonstrated on the living room floor. It worked better than she'd imagined. It was certainly easier than carrying the heavy suitcase. Katie wondered how *Mamm* knew about pulling suitcases on wheels. *Mamm* couldn't have traveled much, at least not after she was born. Well, *Mamm* was simply full of surprises — that much was for sure.

"Katie!" a man's voice called out.

Katie looked up and smiled. "Ben, you did come!" She stopped in her tracks.

"I told you I would."

"Well, if it isn't Mr. Charming himself," Margaret said with a grin.

"It's so good that you could come," Sharon said. "Katie told us you might be here."

"I wouldn't have missed it for the world," Ben said. "Seeing Katie off on her great adventure. I might have to do this myself someday. Katie, I'm afraid I can't stay to see you board and fly through the air," Ben said. "I have to get back to the job site. But I wanted to say goodbye one more time."

Katie's face fell. "You have to leave already?" Then she smiled. "Of course I don't want to keep you." She wanted to hug and kiss him right then and there, but that wouldn't have been decent. Kissing him when they were alone was questionable enough. And they clearly weren't going to be alone in this crowded airport.

"Maybe I can walk you to the security checkpoint," Ben said.

"That would be nice," Katie said. She followed the lead of the other three girls as they stood in line and then approached the ticket counter where they were given their boarding passes and their bags were checked. When the agent asked to see Katie's passport she winced as she handed it over. The flight agent stared at her photo, and Katie was relieved when the lady handed it back to her.

Ben was still waiting when they finished, and they all followed Nancy as she led the way deeper into the airport terminal. Ben took Katie's hand, and they lagged behind the others. Katie felt sure everyone was staring at them holding hands in public. It was so embarrassing, but no one seemed to be paying attention.

Moments later Katie knew her face must be flaming red when Margaret turned around with a mischievous smile. "If the two of you want to sneak around the corner for a quick kiss, we'll understand."

Katie gasped, but Sharon and Nancy laughed as if it were the most normal thing in the world. Ben pulled back on her hand. He was taking Margaret seriously. Was he really going to kiss her right in front of all these people passing by?

At the next corner, with Margaret laughing over her shoulder, Ben held Katie back. He pulled her closer to him. "I won't see you for awhile, you know. I have to kiss you one more time."

Katie gave in, even with all the people

walking past.

"Have a good trip now," Ben said, letting her go.

Katie reached up and gave him one last, quick kiss before turning around and running after the other girls, her carry-on banging against her side.

"Look who just got kissed!" Margaret teased when Katie caught up.

Katie looked away as her friends laughed good-naturedly. The kiss was well worth the teasing, Katie decided. Kissing Ben was fast becoming something she couldn't resist.

CHAPTER THIRTY-ONE

Hours later Katie awoke with a start, gasping as she opened her eyes. In the window seat beside her on the plane, Margaret smiled at Katie's startled look. She reached over to squeeze Katie's arm. "I'm glad you finally got some sleep. I declare, I haven't slept more than an hour yet."

"Are we still over the ocean?" Katie glanced around, trying to slow the pounding of her heart. Sharon and Nancy were in seats across the aisle, both of them with their eyes closed and heads leaning against the seat backs.

"I don't know." Margaret lifted the window shade a few inches and peered out into the darkness. "I can't tell."

"What time is it?"

Margaret glanced at her watch. "Around midnight — our time at home, anyway."

Katie calculated the time difference in her head. "If we're to land at eight in Zurich, that will be in two hours. I do feel wide-awake. That's strange."

Margaret leaned back in her seat with a smile. "I only know I can't see straight or sleep with the bouncing of this plane."

Katie fell silent, feeling the vibrations of the great plane more intensely now. She trembled to think they were miles above the ocean, flying like the birds, only they were inside the belly of this metal thing, whereas birds got to fly with their heads in the open air. Perhaps it was better this way. Seeing down that far to the waters below wouldn't be *gut.* She might throw up or die of fright. *Da Hah* must not have made mankind to fly or He would have given them wings. And yet she was doing it.

Beside her Margaret had closed her eyes, seeming to drift off — at least for a few moments. The truth was Katie needed the sleep herself. They had a full day scheduled ahead of them once they arrived at Zurich. When the plane landed, they would leap forward in time six hours. How could six hours of the day just vanish? Katie wondered. And yet she was about to see it happen right before her eyes. The plane had lifted off around six o'clock in the evening back in Philadelphia, and they would be in the air only eight hours. That left six hours lost somewhere. It was a very strange feeling indeed.

Katie's mind flashed back to the takeoff in Philadelphia. She'd clutched the sides of her seat, hardly daring to breathe. She had survived as they took off with a mighty roar of the engines and an awful rush along the ground. She'd watched out of Margaret's little window, even though Margaret had advised against it. The truth was Margaret had been a little disturbed herself since this was her first flight too.

With a last bump from below, the plane left the ground and rose ever higher, until the automobiles and houses on the ground had grown smaller than Joel's little play animals — the ones he stored in the basement now that he was too old to play with them. Katie stared out of the window for a long time, watching the objects on the ground. It must be something to be *Da Hah,* she figured, and look down on all these things He had made. From up here it would be easy to reach down and push things around. Only *Da Hah* didn't push things around. He worked *gut* things in the lives of the people He loved.

A flight attendant in her fancy uniform came down the aisle. "May I get you something, dear? A pillow maybe?" she asked.

"Yah." Katie nodded. "That would be *gut.*"

"I'll be right back," the woman said.

Moments later she returned, and Katie tucked the pillow under her head. It did feel better, she had to admit. Drowsiness swept over her, and she must have drifted off to sleep. When she awoke, Margaret was tugging on her arm and pointing out the window. "Wake up, Katie! You have to see this."

Rubbing her eyes, Katie sat up to see daylight streaming in through Margaret's little window. Beyond the glass lay a long ridge of snowy mountains, ragged and beautiful in the distance.

"Those have to be the Swiss Alps!" Margaret gushed. "Or the French ones perhaps. Aren't they just awesome?"

"So we must be in Switzerland?" Katie asked, leaning over for a closer look.

"I don't know. But we're over land at least." Margaret leaned away from the window so Katie could see better. "Those houses down there. Have you ever seen anything like them?"

"It must be the land of our forefathers," Katie said, sitting back in her seat. Excitement was welling up inside her. She must always remember this first sighting!

Over the loudspeaker came a man's voice

speaking in English. "Ladies and gentleman, we are now approaching the Zurich airport. We'll be landing in approximately thirty minutes. Please observe the seat belt sign and stay in your seats until we arrive at the terminal, as we may encounter a bit of turbulence on the way down. Your flight attendants will be coming around for a last-minute check, and your cooperation will be much appreciated. Thank you for flying US Airways out of Philadelphia to Zurich, Switzerland. We hope to have the pleasure of serving you again."

"It's actually happening!" Katie whispered to Margaret as the man's voice went on to repeat the instructions in German. Then Katie stopped to listen, and her mouth fell open. She could understand most of what was being said! Of course, she'd just heard the words in English, so perhaps that helped. Still, this was also an amazing thing. She really was coming back to the land of her forefathers.

"Hang on!" Margaret said as the plane bounced through some turbulence.

A flight attendant passed them, glancing at each seat before moving on. They were serious about this seat belt thing, Katie thought. But little *gut* a seat belt would do if this big thing crashed into the side of one of those mountains. Katie shivered just thinking about it. She pictured a big ball of flame hitting the snow-covered slope as the pilot failed to clear the summit.

Margaret must have been thinking some of the same thoughts because her face was a little pale. When Katie glanced at her a second time, Margaret managed a crooked smile. "We'll be on the ground before long — I hope."

It couldn't come too soon! Katie thought. Margaret closed her little window shade, and they hung on as the plane bumped ever lower in altitude.

Nearly half an hour later, the plane lurched forward and the engines roared in Katie's ear.

"On the ground!" Nancy said across the aisle.

Katie hung on as the plane taxied toward the terminal. She'd made it! By the grace of *Da Hah,* she was in Switzerland. Chills were running up and down her spine. The flying hours were behind her, and soon her feet would be on the ground again.

With a loud ping from an overhead bell, the seat belt lights went out as the plane came to a stop. Everyone undid their seat belts, gathered their belongings, and stood up, but Katie took a second to catch her breath after all of the excitement of landing and arriving.

"I know how you feel," Margaret said. "But we made it. We're here now, and the fun begins!"

"That's right." Katie jumped up, her head almost hitting the overhead compartment.

"Take it easy there," Margaret said with a laugh. "We have a long day ahead of us."

Katie blushed a bit and reached up for her carry-on bag. Finding it, she stepped back so Margaret could do the same.

They stood there and waited until the line in their aisle moved forward. Katie stayed close behind Nancy. If she became lost in this country, there would be no easy way to find the others. She mustn't allow that to happen.

The girls soon were inside the terminal. "We're heading for baggage claim," Nancy said over her shoulder. "Then we'll go through customs."

Nancy led the way to a circling carousel. They waited until all four of them had collected their suitcases off the conveyor belt. From there it was off to stand in a long line at customs.

"Let's go forward in a group," Nancy suggested when their time came. "It'll look better, and we won't have to answer all the questions four times."

That was fine with her, Katie thought, hanging back as the others moved forward. The lady behind the glass booth looked through the four passports Nancy handed her and then began asking questions.

"What is your business in this country?"

"Are you traveling together?"

"How long are you planning to stay?"

"Will you be seeing other parts of Europe?"

"Are you flying home from this airport?"

Finally satisfied, the woman said, "Have an enjoyable stay in Switzerland!"

The girls were on their way, rolling their suitcases behind them.

"Rental car next," Nancy called over her shoulder. Moments later they arrived at another desk. Nancy gave her name, and while the girl at the desk punched in numbers, Katie walked over to the large windows to look outside. She wanted a first peek at the land of her forefathers, but it looked like just a city here. A section of the runway was visible, and long lines of planes were taking off. In the distance lay more of the city. "Well," Katie thought, "we'll see the countryside soon enough."

"Ready to go!" Nancy said about fifteen minutes later. Katie turned and joined the others as they left through some glass doors.

"Number 304," Nancy sang out. "Help me look."

Katie took in the long lines of parked cars with numbers on overhead signs. Her head grew dizzy, but the others seemed to have no such problem. She followed them until Nancy stopped in front of a small sedan. "Looks like this is our buggy for the trip."

Katie laughed with the other girls. This wasn't a buggy by any means. Nancy must be trying to keep their spirits up.

"No use standing around then," Margaret said, throwing her suitcase in the trunk Nancy had just opened. Margaret climbed into the backseat and threw her head back. "I think I could sleep for a year. Yet it's bright daylight, and my watch says three o'clock."

"Jet lag," Nancy said. "We'll get over it in a night or two. But for now, is anybody hungry?"

"I don't think my stomach's in Switzerland yet," Margaret grumbled. "It stayed behind a couple hours."

"Funny, funny," Sharon said. "Well, I'm hungry. And anything would be fine."

"Then off to the market we go. But first let me hook up my GPS." Nancy attached a black screen to the dash of the car, plugged

337

it in, and tapped it. "Nothing," Nancy muttered. "I guess we have to drive outside for a signal."

"Do you know your way around if that thing doesn't work?" Katie asked.

"Don't even mention that!" Margaret said. "I don't want to wander all over Europe holding a map in front of my eyes."

"It'll work," Nancy said confidently. "My brother checked it all out before I left. And if not, I can find my way around. It just won't be as easy."

Nancy pulled aside after they were away from the overhead roof, and true to her word, the screen blinked to life. Nancy punched away on the screen. Soon an authoritative man's voice told them, "Turn right at the next intersection."

"It talks!" Margaret shrieked. "We have a man in the car with us."

"How indecent," Sharon said, laughing.

"I like a man's voice along," Margaret declared. "It feels more secure."

"Let's hope he tells us the truth about the roads," Nancy said, as she took off and made the turn. "Help me watch for stop signs, girls. They're at different places than they are at home."

"Like where?" Sharon asked.

"Like there!" Margaret shrieked. "Stop!"

Nancy skidded to a halt. "I told you to help me watch."

Sharon looked pale, but Margaret had dissolved into giggles.

"She's not going to be of much help, I can see," Nancy said with a smile before she took off again. "I know we don't want to run one of these things. They take pictures of violators, and then we'll have a big bill from the city of Zurich coming our way when we return the car."

"How would they know who we are?" Sharon asked. "It's not our car."

"The rental company," Nancy said, coming to another stop. She pointed. "And there's a market on the right."

The man's voice from the GPS intoned, "You have arrived at your destination."

CHAPTER THIRTY-TWO

Less than an hour later Katie sat on a low stone wall, watching the clear water of a river below her rush past. Centuries-old buildings surrounded her here in the town of Zurich. She could almost feel the presence of those faithful men and women of old who had traversed these streets. Margaret was unwrapping the sandwiches they'd purchased at the small market where English was spoken only upon request. Katie had taken a deep breath and tried her High German on the young man running the register. *"Es ist ein netter Tag drausen,"* she'd ventured.

He'd smiled but replied in English, "You have a good day, girls. And don't get lost."

Katie lowered her head. Her German must be awful for him to reply in English. She should have kept her mouth shut. The young man probably hadn't understood a word she'd said.

"What did you tell him?" Margaret asked, once they were in the street.

"I tried to remark that it was a nice day outside, but apparently my High German stinks. The correct accent has probably been lost after 300 years of living in America."

They all laughed, but Nancy came to her aid. "They actually speak Swiss German in Switzerland, so I wouldn't worry about it. Save your High German for Germany. They might understand it there."

So she hadn't made a complete fool out of herself, Katie thought as she watched water in the river flow past. This was a beautiful town, so quaint and old yet bustling with vigor at the same time. It was already growing on her, and she'd been here only a few minutes.

"Sandwich?" Margaret asked, interrupting her thoughts. "And an apple?"

"*Yah,* I'm hungry." Katie reached for the offered items. "Starving, in fact, now that I think of it."

"And cheese?" Margaret broke off a piece for herself before passing the slab around.

They must make quite a sight, Katie decided. Primitive savages from America. Here were four girls sitting on the river wall in the old town of Zurich, one of them with a camera strapped around her neck, and all

341

of them breaking off cheese with their hands. *Mamm* would pass out in a faint from embarrassment, if she were here. Katie smiled at the thought. *Mamm* would be very happy for her. Ben too, of course. Mabel might not though. Katie shook her head. She much preferred thinking about Ben — and that *wunderbah* kiss at the airport.

"Thinking of home?" Margaret's voice was a tease.

"Yah," Katie admitted. Katie could feel the heat rising on her neck, but maybe the fresh river air was cooling her face so no one would notice. She'd have to think of something other than Ben's kisses or she would be red all day long.

"He is handsome," Margaret said. "Can't say that I blame you for falling hard. I'd have done the same thing."

"I've been very blessed," Katie said. "And I should go buy a postcard. I promised to write to him."

"You do have it bad!" Margaret laughed. "That's a good idea though — sending something home to our families. Although I think I'll make my contact tonight on Facebook. Cheaper that way too."

Obviously she didn't have a computer, and Katie wasn't sure what Facebook was. Ben wouldn't either. Postcards were better for them, even if they might be expensive and required postage. She'd been expecting that expense though. And Ben and *Mamm* would treasure every postcard she'd send, so she'd send lots of them. These were days to treasure for the rest of her life. She might be an old woman before she came on a trip like this again.

"Everybody ready to go?" Nancy was on her feet. "Time to start the tour of the Old Town of Zurich. By the way, this is the Limmat River, in case you wondered."

"I don't care about the river," Margaret said. "But with my body fortified by bread and cheese, let us set forth. Lead the way, oh brave leader."

Nancy laughed. "You'd better save some of that joking energy for walking. We have a ways to go." She opened a guidebook she produced from her purse. "If you look across the river, there is the *Grossmunster* church where our forefathers listened to Zwingli's preaching. That's the place where our faith first began to grow."

Katie gazed across the river at the immense church with twin towers reaching toward the sky. Sharon snapped away with her camera as Nancy continued. "The church is also the burial place of Zurich's patron saints, or so it says here. The hall crypt under the choir dates from the late eleventh century. The church design is an excellent example of early Romanesque architecture."

"Some kind of culture," Margaret commented. "They must have spent years building something like that."

"I think they did," Nancy confirmed. "Cathedrals back in that time were often decades in the building — sometimes even centuries."

"Do we get to see the inside?" Sharon asked. "I'd like to see where our forefathers sat in their pews."

"Later we will," Nancy said. "Let's see the sights on this side of the river first."

"I like the narrow alleys," Margaret noted as they walked along. "Take plenty of pictures, Sharon."

"You ought to take your own," Sharon said, snapping away.

"Why should I work harder than necessary?" Margaret said. "You take excellent pictures, so how could I do better than having copies made of yours?"

"Flatter mouth," Sharon muttered, but she looked pleased.

"Over here we have the *Fraumunster*," Nancy said. "That translates to 'The Church of Our Lady.' They're not sure when it was originally built, but it was donated for a convent by Emperor Ludwig, also known as 'Louis the German,' in 853. The way it looks now comes from the thirteenth century, it says, so they must have made some renovations."

Katie looked up at the single steeple reaching into the sky. Three beautiful stained-glass windows adorned the front. Drawings of angels and the crucified Lord were engraved into the glass along with a multitude of other depictions of medieval life.

"Right impressive," Margaret said. "I do think they had more time than we did."

"They didn't have airplanes in those days," Sharon said as she stood back and snapped away with her camera.

"Maybe they used those six hours of sleep I just lost." Margaret rubbed her forehead. "I think it will take more than a few days to get over that."

"You'll be okay with all these sights to see." Nancy led the way forward with a confident expression. "We can sleep tonight."

"By the way, where are we staying?" Margaret asked.

"At a bed-and-breakfast twenty minutes from here. Don't worry, we'll get there early so you can start your beauty sleep."

"I'm at death's door, and she talks of beauty sleep," Margaret commented with a short laugh.

Nancy led the way up a series of steps and down some side streets, pausing to read her guidebook in front of another church before speaking. "We have here St. Peter's Church. Its claim to fame is its twenty-eight and a half foot clock, the largest clock face in Europe. The minute hand alone is twelve feet long."

"That's where my six hours went!" Margaret stared upward. "Ow! My neck hurts. Let's find something to look at that doesn't break my neck bones."

Nancy laughed. "You'll enjoy the next stop. It's where the old Roman Citadel once stood. Sort of their guard castle with big walls around it. It's up on top of that hill," she said as she pointed.

"Wait until we're up there before you tell us more," Margaret said.

The group walked a bit and then headed up the road that led to the hill. Upon reaching the top, all four girls paused. Before them lay an open, park-like area.

"There's not much to it," Sharon said. "I don't see any walls."

"I suppose those are long gone." Nancy

checked her guidebook. "It's called the *Lindenhof* now. Famous for its giant chess games played under the linden trees."

"Why would you play chess outdoors?" Margaret asked.

"And what's giant about it?" Sharon added.

"I think the answer is right over here," Nancy said as she turned and headed down a path.

Katie trailed behind the others as they approached a group of men on the side away from the river. She saw huge chess pieces sitting on the ground moments before Sharon said, "That's what they are, all right. Chess pieces. They are giant, indeed."

"Shhh . . ." Nancy put her finger to her lips.

They stood and watched quietly for quite awhile as two chess games took place in front of them. Mostly the games consisted of the four players just staring at the chess pieces. Only twice in the ten minutes they watched, did one of the men move a piece.

"How do they have time for this?" Sharon whispered. "It's the middle of the day."

"They must have more time than we do," Nancy suggested, leading the group of girls away from the game. "Or they make time for it."

"I think they're using the six hours of sleep I lost," Margaret murmured again.

"She's going to chew that all week," Sharon commented.

"I think we all need sleep," Nancy said as they climbed down a long flight of steps. "But let's finish this tour before we head out to the bed-and-breakfast. There's still some things we want to see."

They arrived at the river again, and Nancy led the way back toward where they'd eaten lunch. She studied her guidebook as they walked.

"What are you looking for?" Sharon asked, peeking over Nancy's shoulder.

"The plaque they put in for Felix Manz." Nancy glanced around. "There it is, I think."

Margaret reached the plain stone first. It was embedded along the riverbank in a low wall. "What does it say?"

"Can you read it?" Nancy asked Katie.

Walking up to it, Katie tried. "Here were drowned in the middle of the Limmat from a fishing platform . . ." Katie stopped and laughed. "I'm not that good at reading German that's not Scriptures, I guess."

"You're doing okay," Nancy encouraged her. "It says in my book that Felix Manz was drowned here, along with five other

Anabaptists, between 1527 and 1532."

"It actually happened right there." Sharon was gazing across the water as silence settled on the girls. "It's hard to believe I'm really here . . ."

Katie decided she'd have to write Ben about this moment. Here brave men had given their life for the faith. It seemed more real somehow, seeing the place with her own eyes. They must have had great strength to stand up to such pressure. Giving their lives rather than denying *Da Hah*'s ways. Ben would be encouraged by this, she thought.

"Ready to move on?" Nancy asked.

"Yah." Katie broke out of her thoughts. "Can we find a place where they sell postcards? I'd like to mail one home about this."

"Sure! This place might have some." Nancy walked toward a row of shops just off the riverbank.

Katie's eyes caught sight of several selections as they entered one of the stores. She glanced over them, choosing a scene of the river with the twin towers of the *Grossmunster* in the background. There was no sign of the plaque they'd just seen, but this was close enough.

"Would you like to mail this?" the clerk, a cheerful-faced young man asked when Katie purchased the card.

"*Yah,* I would like that." Katie paid and rushed outside to the low wall by the river. She sat down and scribbled a few words on the back of the postcard.

My dear, dear Ben: We are in Zurich right now, sitting along the banks of the Limmat River, where we just saw the plaque dedicated to Felix Manz. Oh Ben, I wish you could see all of this. I love you so much, Katie.

Writing in Ben's address, Katie took the postcard back inside where the other girls were still browsing. She picked out another postcard, this one featuring the huge face of the clock at St. Peter's, then fished the unfamiliar money from her purse and paid the boy the two Euros he asked for after handing him the postcard for Ben.

"Ready to go," Katie whispered to the others once the clerk gave her a receipt. Only Margaret had purchased something. Katie noticed. Tomorrow she would send *Mamm* this postcard. She should have thought of that today, but her thoughts had been more about Ben than of anyone else, even *Mamm.*

"Okay, ready for the *Grossmunster*?" Nancy asked, leading the way across a stone bridge.

350

CHAPTER THIRTY-THREE

Ten minutes later Katie stood with her hands on a small rope as she looked up toward an elevated pulpit. All around her the dark interior of the *Grossmunster* church pressed in. It was enough to dampen a person's spirits completely. And to think that here a few of the first Anabaptist leaders had once gathered to hear the great Reformer Zwingli thunder forth on his sermons. No wonder they hadn't stayed. She would also have left to find a place more comforting.

"You can't go up to the pulpit," Margaret whispered in Katie's ear. "Don't even think about it."

"You're the one who's thinking about it," Katie retorted.

Margaret's mischievous smile was answer enough. Of course

Margaret wouldn't disobey the tour instructions, even if it was self-guided — no matter how much she wanted to stand behind the pulpit Zwingli used.

Katie followed Margaret as they moved away to look at the huge organ above them. Katie gasped at the sight.

"It's awesome!" Margaret said.

"The famous *Grossmunster* organ." Nancy walked up with her guidebook open. "It doesn't look like anything important really happened here. It's just a really big, gorgeous organ."

"I'd like to hear someone play it," Margaret said, not moving from the spot.

Nancy laughed. "We'd probably have to come back on Sunday for that — if anyone plays it any longer. There's nothing here saying whether it works."

It must be a little wicked to even hear such a musical instrument played, Katie thought. But she didn't say anything to the others. They probably wouldn't agree. Still, this might have been one of the reasons the Amish forefathers forsook such a place — to get away from dangers like this. Men should wait for heaven where *Da Hah* probably had something much greater than this set up. There no sin from this world would tempt a person after hearing such beautiful music.

"Okay . . . next." Margaret swung around

on her heels. "I've seen enough of the organ."

"Over here." Sharon motioned them from across the aisle. "I've been looking at these stained-glass windows. I want to get closer."

The three girls followed Sharon, moving up to a roped-off area and gazing at the sunlight twinkling through the colorful glass. Red, green, blue, and white were all blended together.

"There are so many drawings in the glass, it's confusing," Katie said.

"It's still beautiful," Margaret said. "And the time it must have taken to make that stained glass!"

"Don't start again with the 'lost six-hour' joke," Sharon muttered.

"I wasn't planning to," Margaret shot back.

"Girls, girls!" Nancy interrupted. "We're all tired, but let's not get grumpy."

"I'm not grumpy," Margaret said.

They all laughed.

Nancy turned the page in her guidebook. "Okay, let's see . . . what's next? We'd better take a quick look at the crypt in the church basement. It claims to be the largest in Switzerland."

"Lead the way!" Sharon said, motioning for Nancy to go first.

As they went down the steps, the stairwell opened into a basement area that had three pillared arches supporting the ceiling.

"What's there to see in this gloomy place?" Margaret asked.

"A crypt," Sharon said.

"What's a crypt used for?"

"Storing dead bodies," Sharon said.

Margaret shrieked, the sound echoing off the stone walls. "Yikes! That's what I was afraid you'd say. Get me outta here."

Nancy laughed. "Calm down. The bodies aren't here anymore. They were just stored here for awhile, I think."

"You *think*?" Margaret said before fleeing up the stairs.

"I think we'd better go after her," Sharon said. "I'm feeling a little weak myself. I've never been in a crypt before."

Nancy glanced over at Katie. "Are you also going pale on me?"

"I don't think so," Katie said. "I guess I lack imagination."

"I guess I do too then," Nancy said. "But even so, maybe we should go too."

"I agree," Katie said. "It *is* a little gloomy."

They followed Margaret and Sharon outside, and Nancy checked her guidebook. "Zwingli's parsonage is up the hill a bit. And the house where the first baptisms were performed is about three streets over."

"I don't want to see a parsonage," Margaret spoke up. "But let's see where they baptized our forefathers."

"Agreed?" Nancy glanced around.

When Katie and Sharon nodded, Nancy led the way, following the guidebook's instructions. They arrived at the designated place. A fountain stood in the street with a statue over it. Water bubbled with soft gurgles.

"Somewhere in this vicinity," Nancy read, "was the house where Felix Manz's mother lived. It was here on the night of January 21, of 1525, that the first Anabaptist rebaptisms were performed. And water taken from this fountain may well have been used."

"So why that night?" Sharon asked. "I don't know that I've ever heard that explained."

Nancy glanced through her pages. "It doesn't say, but I think Zwingli and the city council had ordered our forefathers to stop the activities they'd been engaged in *or else*. They were doing things like street preaching and pressing for further changes, which the city council was unwilling to entertain. They all knew what 'or else' meant — likely prison time."

"So what happened?" Sharon dipped her fingers in the water of the fountain and held up her hand so the drops splashed on the street.

If the water that night came from this fountain, Katie thought, this must be almost holy water. And yet it couldn't be. Her people didn't believe in making things *Da Hah* had made holy. Such things were a blessing to all mankind and shouldn't serve as a distraction from *Da Hah* Himself.

Nancy had turned another page and started reading aloud:

It so happened that when they had gathered together that a great anxiety came upon them, and they were pressed within their hearts. They knelt and cried out to the most High God in heaven, asking that He would give to show them His divine will and have mercy. After the prayer, one of them stood up and besought Conrad Grebel for God's sake to baptize him with the true Christian baptism. Felix Manz then ran out with a milk bucket and returned with it filled with water. So Conrad Grebel baptized the first men, including Blaurock. Who, after he received his baptism from Grebel proceeded to baptize the rest in the room.

"And then the fur flew," Margaret murmured. "I wish I'd been here for that night but not for what followed."

"It's hard to imagine why baptizing someone produced such a reaction," Sharon said.

"It was the Middle Ages," Margaret said. "They didn't think right back then."

"Horrible things also happen in our day and age," Nancy said, closing the guidebook. "Just north of here, in Germany, Hitler killed more than six million Jews in concentration camps, and even more people he considered undesirable. It's the human condition, I suppose."

"I wish people would stop killing each other," Sharon said, shivering. "The world would be so much the better for it."

"That I can agree with," Nancy said. "Now, shall we go to our bed-and-breakfast?"

"I think we should," Margaret said. "I've seen enough horror for one day."

"Come to think of it, it's terrible but not quite 'horror,' " Sharon protested. "It's what really happened."

"Dropping grown men into rivers so they'll drown is horrible," Margaret said.

"It was for a good cause, I guess," Sharon said.

Margaret snorted.

Nancy tried to hide the smile that leaped to her face. "I think we'd better get some sleep. It seems we're all tired."

"I could fall in bed and never get out for a year," Margaret groaned. "Please take me there."

At that, the girls followed Nancy back to the car. Moments later they were on the road, darting in and out of traffic. The man's voice came from the GPS stuck on the windshield, guiding them all the way.

"Turn left at the intersection one hundred yards ahead."

"Turn left at rotary, then take the first exit."

"Divided highway in two hundred yards. Stay right."

"Go eighty yards, then keep to the highway."

Margaret groaned. "I'm already tired of that voice."

"You're tired of everything right now," Sharon said from the front seat.

"You can say that again." Margaret leaned back but didn't close her eyes.

Katie sat with her eyes glued on the passing scenery. She wanted to see everything, each passing tree and rolling hillside. But there was too much to absorb. "This is really Switzerland!" she finally whispered.

Margaret sat up and joined Katie in watching the passing houses with little flower boxes in the windows.

"Everything is so neat," Katie said. "And they don't waste an inch of ground."

Margaret rested her head back on the seat again. "People have lived here a long time. It's full. We probably wouldn't either."

Before Katie could say anything, Nancy said, "Wettingen coming up."

As if in agreement, the GPS man intoned, "Take next exit, eighty yards ahead."

Nancy took the turn, navigating through a small town until they arrived at a two-story house on a quiet cobblestone street.

"You have reached your destination," the GPS said.

"Bridgette's house, I believe," Nancy said, turning in the driveway. "And her husband is Hans. She said we could arrive anytime after three o'clock."

"It's four now." Sharon glanced at her watch. "Isn't this driveway a little tight?"

"I was looking at the rose trestles over on this side. Aren't they beautiful?" Margaret said. "Forget about the driveway."

Nancy brought the car to a stop. "Everything's tighter in Europe. They have smaller cars, smaller gardens, smaller homes. But they do know how to raise flowers."

"You can say that again," Margaret said as they all climbed out.

Nancy walked over and rang the doorbell. A few seconds later, a woman appeared.

"Are we at the right place?" Nancy asked. "Bridgette is it?"

"*Jah,* Bridgette," the lady said. "But no English . . . me. My husband, Hans, he come tonight. He can talk English."

"Okay then," Nancy said. "May we come in?"

Bridgette nodded, holding the door as they brought their suitcases in. "Follow," she said. She led the girls to their two rooms. "This you like?"

"Yes, yes, certainly. It's wonderful." Nancy set down her suitcase. Sharon immediately set her luggage down and set up her laptop. "I want to see if there's word from home . . . and check for any other email." She looked to Bridgette. "Internet connection . . . um . . . *jah*?"

Bridgette looked at the laptop and nodded, "*Jah, jah.* Hans, he speak tonight." And then she turned and left.

"I would have tried your German with her," Nancy told Katie. "But with their Swiss variation, it probably wouldn't have worked."

"It's just as *gut,*" Katie said. "I'm probably too nervous to say things right anyway."

"A bed!" Margaret flopped down and groaned. "I'm not moving . . . not for months."

"We have to go out for supper," Nancy said. "They only serve breakfast here."

"I want sleep, not food," Margaret said with a moan.

"Then take a short nap," Nancy suggested. "We'll leave for supper in an hour."

"Bye, bye." Margaret rolled over and gave a little wave with her hand.

"I think we'd better leave her alone," Katie whispered.

"This is your room also, Katie," Nancy said. "So you'd better make yourself boss. I think Margaret has more bark than bite."

"I think I'll solve the problem by taking a little nap myself," Katie said.

Nancy left to join Sharon. Katie lay down on her bed, hoping for rest to come even though her mind swirled with excitement.

She'd just started to doze off when Sharon burst in without knocking. Nancy was right behind her. "Hey, you've got to come over here and see the news from home!"

"What happened now?" Margaret muttered, unhappy to be roused.

"You won't believe this. I pulled up the news from the Dover newspaper. There's been a big drug bust there."

"So?" Margaret asked, still not stirring. "I doubt it's anyone we know."

"Well, no," Sharon admitted. "But it's got the whole community in an uproar."

"It doesn't concern me right now." Margaret sat up to shoo Sharon and Nancy out of the room.

"Well, to be honest, I'm just too worked up to sleep now," Katie said. "I'm going outside to look at the roses."

"I think I'll join you," Nancy told her.

The two girls walked outside into the warm afternoon sunshine. On the trellis fastened to the side of the adjoining house, the roses looked even more beautiful than they had when the girls drove in.

"They're lovely," Nancy said, not moving as they took in the sight.

"*Yah,*" Katie whispered. "So peaceful. It's like they're telling us *Da Hah* is here with His tender touch."

"I like that," Nancy said. "So how did you enjoy this afternoon's tour?"

"I loved it. I'm so thankful I got to see where our faith began. Both *Mamm* and Ben want to hear all about it when I get back. I'll have so much to tell them."

The beauty of the roses caused Katie's thoughts to turn to Ben. He'd once plucked a wild rose for her, stabbing his finger with a thorn in the process. "I love you, Ben," she whispered to the roses before following Nancy back inside.

That evening after Margaret was asleep, Katie pulled Ben's picture out of her suitcase and took a peek by the bright moonlight pouring in the window. He looked even more handsome than she remembered.

CHAPTER THIRTY-FOUR

The following morning the early sunlight warmed the air as Katie rolled down the car window on her side. It was still a little chilly, but she wanted a *gut* look at this little town they were traveling through. Everything was neat as a pin, with bushes growing close to the houses and the occasional flower box in a window here and there. The old town of Zurich had gone past the window on Margaret's side ten minutes ago as Nancy had made her way through creeping traffic. Katie had even caught a brief glimpse of the twin towers of the *Grossmunster* along the banks of the river as they drove past.

Margaret now leaned forward in the backseat, as Nancy parked along the side of a steep hill. "So tell me again where we're at."

"Zollikon," Nancy replied. "It's south of Zurich about three miles. And we just passed the farmhouse where the first Anabaptist congregation was formed, but I couldn't find a parking spot any closer."

"I don't mind. I need to stretch my legs anyway," Sharon said.

All four girls were bright and chirpy after their night's rest — and also from a very yummy breakfast Bridgette had served them. There had been no eggs like an American breakfast would have, but instead there were strange breads, sliced meats, and chunks of cheese. Nobody had any complaints though. Katie figured she might even gain weight if this kept up, which placed walking in a whole new light. It became a great necessity now.

Nancy was laughing as they climbed out of the car. "I think everyone will get plenty of walking by the time this day is done. We have lots to see today!"

"So what is there to see here?" Margaret asked, as they followed Nancy down the hill.

"A house, basically." Nancy consulted her guidebook as they stood in front of the two-story home. "The government has placed a plaque up there, over the door. It says, 'Here on January the 25th of 1525, one of the earliest meetings was held, and a congregation soon formed.' "

"And most of the people were soon martyred or driven out," Sharon offered, aiming her camera at the plaque.

"I thought you were the sunny person!" Margaret said. "I'm still shuddering over how they dropped Felix Manz in the river yesterday. Can you try a little cheerfulness this morning while my breakfast settles?"

"You're quite a carnal person," Sharon snapped. "People shed their blood on this spot, and you're thinking of breakfast."

"Girls!" Nancy interrupted. "Let's try to be nice and cheerful."

"That's what I'm trying to be," Sharon said.

Margaret turned up her nose. "Not very hard, you're not."

Katie giggled, which was exactly what she probably shouldn't do considering the seriousness of the moment. But this argument suddenly struck her as immensely funny. Neither of the two girls were making a lot of sense.

"I'm glad someone finds this funny," Margaret said, obviously trying to keep her glare up, but failing. They all dissolved into giggles except for Nancy.

"You're all a disgraceful bunch," Nancy said, leading the way back up the hill. "What if someone saw us? They'd think we had no respect for our faith."

"I'm sorry," Katie offered, but Nancy had

a trace of a smile on her face by the time they were all inside the car.

"I suppose it's good to laugh once in a while," Nancy concluded as she pulled away from the site. "It's better than fighting with each other."

"Sorry," both Margaret and Sharon said at the same time.

"We'll do better from now on," Sharon added.

"We'll all get along just fine," Nancy said. "And we don't want to spoil the fun even when we're visiting sacred sites. It makes life more interesting."

"How far to our next site?" Sharon asked, ready to move on with the day.

"All the way around this lake," Nancy said. "And with this traffic it might take awhile."

"May I look at the guidebook while you drive?" Sharon asked.

"Sure." Nancy handed it over with the pages open.

"Tell us where we're going next," Margaret said, leaning forward on the seat.

Sharon cleared her throat. "It's look like we're heading to the little town of Hirzel, south of Zurich. It hangs on the top of a hillside, it says here, picturesque and beautiful. The views are spectacular with the Swiss

Alps visible in the background. Its significance to the Anabaptist faith lies in the designation it soon received as a *Taufer* nest. Which is what the Reformers in Zurich called a town that had a high population of Anabaptists."

"What's a *Taufer*?" Margaret asked.

"That's what they call the Anabaptists around here," Nancy replied, taking the car around a tight curve. " 'A baptizer' would be the literal translation. So these towns became known as 'baptizer nests.' They were places our people would congregate as they fled from persecution."

"How awful!" Sharon said. "This is horrible. It says the authorities would come in, confiscate the property of the *Taufers,* banish them, and then use the confiscated funds for at least a portion of a new church structure."

Nancy took another tight curve, climbing higher on the hillside. "That was the authorities' accepted method of evangelization back in those days. Once the church was built, they used it to win back the hearts of the people who were left. I guess everyone felt honored to have their own church."

"That's bad," Margaret said, as they entered a small village.

"And here's the church." Nancy pulled

into a small lot and parked.

"Here's something I missed," Sharon said, before they climbed out of the car. "This town is also the birthplace of Johanna Spyri, the author of *Heidi*. Her home is still here today. Oh, Margaret, I want to see this. I loved that book as a little girl!"

"I want to see the church first," Margaret said, gazing across the parking lot.

"It's nice enough," Sharon said. "But a portion was built with blood money. I don't think I like that."

"Well, you have to have a little understanding of the times these people lived in," Nancy offered. "Anyone want to see the inside of it?"

"Why not?" Margaret said.

And they all followed Nancy inside.

"Stained-glass windows," Sharon noted. "I still don't think they should have done this with the money stolen from our ancestors."

"It's not as fancy as the big cathedrals are," Nancy said. "So something good can be said about the church. And maybe there was some other good also accomplished. People might still have found God here. Just not quite like we do."

"I suppose so," Sharon allowed, following the others outside again. "No one's perfect,

I guess. I just don't think they should have chopped off their heads."

"No one said anything about chopping off heads," Margaret said. "We only heard about drowning yesterday."

"That's coming, don't worry. I can feel it."

"I'm afraid she's right," Nancy agreed. "Medieval times were a little different."

The group was silent as they climbed the hill past the sign that pointed to the Spyri home. They paused occasionally on the long climb to look back at the view and catch their breath.

"It's absolutely gorgeous up here," Sharon gushed. "No wonder Ms. Spyri could write like she could. Listen to those cowbells and look at the Alps over there. I can see Heidi now running through the meadows."

"Or climbing up to the blind grandfather's hut on the mountain," Nancy added.

"It does my soul good," Margaret said. "I think I've found one of my lost hours right now. It leaped right back into my body."

They all laughed and approached the house where Katie translated the sign for them. "There's a lady's name written on top, then 'Birth house of her daughter, Johanna Spyri' written below that."

"It's even more lovely from up here."

Sharon walked away a few steps, snapping pictures. Katie soon followed, and they climbed farther up the hill behind the house. All of them spent a long time looking out over the valley at the rolling meadows with perfect patches of farmland.

"It's almost like a picture book," Sharon commented. "What would it be like to live up here? You'd be close to heaven every day."

"Don't forget the chopping off of heads that's coming up," Margaret said. "People who lived here probably did that."

"You would have to say that!" Sharon sighed, "And you've spoiled a perfect moment."

"Tempers down, please," Nancy said. "Now, let's get back to the car and grab ourselves some lunch. Then we'll be on our way again."

"I want to stay here all day," Sharon said dreamily, but went along when the others started down. She was soon whispering and laughing to Margaret as Nancy and Katie lagged behind.

"Those two will keep us entertained, don't you think?" Nancy said.

"They love each other," Katie said. "They are my two best friends. They did something very special for me during a very hard time in my life. I'll never forget that."

"The Lord does that for us sometimes," Nancy agreed. "He sends us what — or who — we need."

They soon arrived at the bottom of the hill, climbed back into the car, and headed down the mountain. Margaret and Sharon were admiring the view with loud exclamations the whole time. Katie was enjoying herself just as much; she just didn't make as much noise about it. That was probably from being raised Amish, which wasn't wrong — just different from the Mennonites.

The awe and the gasps continued from Sharon and Margaret as Nancy drove through the countryside. Nancy soon stopped at another little market where they purchased lunch.

"Let's not eat now," Nancy suggested when they came back outside. "We'll be at the cave before long, where I'm sure there's a picnic area. And we might even be up in the mountains by then and have another gorgeous view to go along with our food."

"Suits me," Margaret agreed. "Though I hope it's soon. I'm starving."

"You should be," Sharon said. "It's getting close to one o'clock here."

"That's means seven in the morning at

home," Margaret said, as they climbed back into the car. "Breakfast time! I can smell the bacon and eggs."

Nancy laughed. "I'm afraid that's something you won't see in this country. They don't know much about American breakfasts."

"I noticed the pieces of bacon this morning that Bridgette had laid out for us," Sharon said. "I declare they were raw."

"You didn't see me touch them," Margaret said as Nancy got back on the road again.

Sharon punched the address of the cave in the GPS, and the man started talking again. He guided them into the countryside, through several small towns, and down a road that had a sign that pointed toward a *Tauferhohle.*

"Baptizer cave," Katie translated as the road turned into a cow path.

Nancy bounced to a stop after several minutes, and they climbed out.

"Follow the signs," Sharon said, taking the guidebook with her.

The signs led them straight up the mountain, and a picnic table didn't appear until they were almost out of breath.

"The view!" Margaret said, collapsing onto the bench. "At least it's fantastic."

"Well worth it," Sharon agreed as Nancy

pulled out the lunches. They ate in silence, soaking in the beauty around them. When they finished, Nancy led the way forward again. The trail wrapped around the mountainside, guarded with wooden side rails, until they reached a low-ceiling cave with a little waterfall trickling over the front.

"This is it," Nancy announced as they all crowded inside. They stood close together, even though there was plenty of room. The place had a cold feel to it, and yet it also felt sacred at the same time. Here their people had gathered during a time of fierce persecution to sing and pray to *Da Hah*. Katie tried to memorize the scene to describe it to Ben and *Mamm*. They would be so thrilled.

Sharon tried to take a few pictures but gave up. "It's too dark," she said.

"We should sing a song," Nancy suggested, and she led out with the first line of "Amazing Grace."

Katie joined in and soon tears came to the eyes of all four girls. This was indeed a most sacred spot. When the last notes had died away, they started down the trail clinging to the side of the hill.

"This place was featured in Christmas Carol Kauffman's book," Katie said. "At least Ben thinks it was."

"How does Ben know such things?" Margaret asked, hanging on to a wooden guardrail. "He's a man."

"Sometimes men surprise you," Nancy offered.

"All I know is what he told me," Katie said. "Ben likes to read."

Nancy led the way back down to the car, and they arrived without any mishaps other than Sharon slipping on a few loose stones, her camera flailing about. Margaret grabbed her in time to offer a steady hand.

On the drive back, Margaret dozed off and Katie almost joined her. Only the countryside was too fascinating not to keep an eye on it. They arrived back at the bed-and-breakfast and poured into the house. Katie collapsed on her bed, only to be roused by a pale-faced Sharon several minutes later.

"Katie, I think you'd better come to my room for a minute. Something terrible has happened at home."

The girls all exchanged glances, and the four of them went into the next room where Sharon's laptop was open.

Horrible images flashed through Katie's mind. What could be wrong? Had something happened to the community? Had someone's farm burned?

"You'd better sit down," Nancy said, helping Katie onto the bed. Katie's heart raced. This could not be good considering the way Nancy was trembling and concerned for her, trying to soften whatever blow was to come.

Sharon glanced at the girls. "Katie, I don't know quite how to tell you this or even if I should. Perhaps I should just wait and let you find out when we get home."

Katie took a breath. "No, whatever it is, tell me now."

Nancy sighed. "According to the Dover newspaper's website, one of the men arrested in the drug bust I told you about yesterday was Ben Stoll."

CHAPTER THIRTY-FIVE

The following morning, dawn was breaking outside the window when Katie awoke. The sun sent streaks of light sneaking past the drawn drapes. Across the room, a faint form wrapped in blankets came into focus. Margaret's long, black hair was tossed over the side of the bed, her face hidden from view.

Katie sat up as the memories of last night flooded in. Ben had been arrested at home on drug charges. The horror rushed over her again. Of course, it couldn't be true. It just couldn't. The four girls had talked late into the night, looking desperately for a possible explanation. Maybe there had been a mistake somewhere. Sharon had exchanged messages with her folks on Facebook and so had Margaret. In the end there was no mistaking the news. Ben was sitting in jail in Dover.

Katie ended up crying herself to sleep. How could it have happened? She'd kissed him goodbye at the airport. She'd melted into his arms the last time she saw him. And now he was accused of being a drug dealer? Drugs — the plague that destroyed people's lives and fried their brains? Ben had been involved in that? And since he apparently had, why had she not known? She'd driven around in Ben's buggy, likely the very one Ben used to transport the evil stuff. There might even have been some under the seat while she'd been with him and snuggled up to his side, thinking Ben was the most *wunderbah* man in the world. Why hadn't she sensed something was terribly wrong?

Katie wanted to scream, and scream, and scream. Perhaps she could just go to sleep and never wake up again. And now here she was in a foreign country, so very far from home at a time like this. And yet she didn't want to be home while this was happening. How could she ever face *Mamm*? She'd apparently been right about Ben all along. And Katie had so misjudged Ben. How could she ever trust anyone again? If all this about Ben were true, it was going to ruin not only his life, but hers as well.

Yah, the world had gone dark now. It seemed full of evil and crawling with lusts. No wonder the preachers spoke of such awful things in their sermons, warning the people of the dangers in the world. She'd thought them a little negative at times, but they must have known all along of things she couldn't even imagine. And now she was looking one of those evils in the face.

Mamm wouldn't shun her, Katie figured, nor would Jesse. Mabel, though, was another matter. She would feel justified in every objection she ever had about *Mamm* and Katie moving in with her family. Now Mabel's escapades with Mose in the barn looked like child's play compared to her romance with Ben. But no one had known, Katie tried to justify to herself. No one!

How could a man be so deceiving, so full of lies, so living like his evil didn't even exist? Why hadn't she felt this wickedness when she kissed him? Instead, Ben had seemed so full of love and tenderness.

Across the room, Margaret rolled over and sat up, her hair falling all around her shoulders. "Is it morning?" she asked.

It's night! Katie wanted to scream. *It's dark. The morning is never coming.* But she whispered, *"Yah."*

Margaret gave her a long look and came over to sit beside her. "I'm sorry, Katie. I'm so sorry."

"It's not your fault that men can be so evil . . . so deceptive," Katie said, trembling as the words rolled out of her. This was pure hatred, and that was not the attitude a Christian should have.

And yet Margaret wasn't shocked at all. "I think I'd hate his guts myself. In fact, I think I do a little just for what he did to you."

"Oh, Margaret!" Katie grabbed Margaret and pulled her close in a hug. "I hate myself for feeling this way, and yet I can't help it. Ben is a liar, a thief, a horrible person, and . . . and I loved him."

"You didn't know. And neither did anyone else."

Katie's eyes grew big as a new thought occurred to her. "Margaret! The money for the trip! You don't suppose it came from Ben . . . from his drug dealing?"

"Oh, Katie, it couldn't be . . . could it?" Margaret was staring at Katie.

Katie bit her lip. "But it *has* to be. No one else had that kind of money, and only a handful of people knew about the trip. And Ben was one of them."

Margaret shook her head. "There has to be some other explanation, Katie. Don't jump to conclusions."

Katie pressed back the tears. "It's no use, Margaret. Illegal drugs are just so evil. And it makes this trip bad — the way I got the money. I just want to die."

"Katie, please." Margaret held Katie tight. "You can't blame yourself. This is Ben's fault. Don't allow him to destroy your life on top of everything."

"It's already destroyed," Katie sobbed. "And for me this trip is over. I have to go home, Margaret. I have to."

"No, you don't have to." Margaret held Katie at arm's length. "Listen to me. Blaming yourself only makes the situation worse. It solves nothing. I know your heart is torn, but don't run home, Katie. You're here — and maybe for a reason. Let the Lord work His good work. You can't make things better by running away. Besides, I want you along, Katie. The rest of my heart would break if you left."

Katie wiped away her tears. "I . . . I . . . don't know what to do. Maybe you're right. If I were at home, my anger might be worse than it is now. Is that possible?"

"Just stay with us, Katie," Margaret pleaded. "I think you need us right now."

Katie took a deep breath. "Don't tell anyone else about the money — that it came from Ben. I'm already embarrassed enough."

"My lips are sealed." Margaret tried to smile. "Maybe we should get ready for the day and eat breakfast. Are you hungry?"

"My insides have turned to iron. I couldn't possibly eat."

"But you have to, Katie, or you'll wither up and die."

"That sounds pretty *gut* right now."

"Oh, dear Lord," Margaret closed her eyes, "please help Katie right now. This is awful news we received last night. And I don't think any of us can bear this on our own. Comfort her heart, please. And also ours. Amen."

"Thank you," Katie whispered, the tears rushing down her cheeks. Somehow Margaret knew exactly what she needed at this moment. A prayer to *Da Hah* that she was too broken to make for herself. And Margaret had made it for her, being the great friend that she was.

A soft knock on the door sounded, and Nancy's worried face appeared when it opened. "Is everything okay?"

"We're getting dressed and will be right out," Margaret said.

Katie tried to smile, but the effort was mighty weak.

Nancy seemed to understand and smiled in sympathy before closing the door.

Katie dressed as Margaret prepared for the day. Brushing out her hair, Katie did it up under her *kapp,* and when she was finished the two girls went down to break-fast. Nancy and Sharon were already there. They stood when Katie walked in.

"Please," Katie said, "sit down. And please excuse me if I get a little weepy today. I just can't control the way I feel."

"Of course not," Sharon soothed. "And you should be torn up. Any of us would feel the same way."

"It'll take a long time to absorb fully the news from last night," Nancy said. "But the Lord can bring healing over time, even though it seems impossible right now."

Katie hung her head, holding back the tears. She wanted to trust *Da Hah,* but it seemed a little impossible right now. *Da Hah* had seemed to lead Ben and her together. How could she have been so wrong? How could her understanding of *Da Hah*'s lead-ing have been so wrong?

Nancy continued. "The question now is, where do we go from here? What about our plans for today? I can hardly imagine Katie wanting to see sights with how she's feeling. And yet I don't want to leave her here alone. Shall we all take a day off and rest?"

"You will do no such thing!" Katie said at once. "We will keep to the plans we had. There is no sense in Ben destroying more than he already has."

"That's a mighty brave thing to say," Sharon spoke up. "But I'm fine with staying here for the day."

"So am I," Margaret added.

"But we're not going to," Katie told them. "That would only break my heart further. You may have to put up with me gushing tears once in awhile, but that's better than sitting around here."

"Are you sure?" Nancy asked.

"It's decided," Katie declared. "Let's eat and then we're going." Putting her words into actions, Katie filled her plate with a small piece of bread, some meat, and a chunk of cheese. Opening a container of juice, she waited until the others were ready. They prayed and then began eating.

Bridgette soon stuck her head through the doorway. "It goes good?"

"We're doing very well," Nancy replied.

After she left silence hung over the table. Katie struggled to swallow a few times. The cheese stuck in her throat until she washed it down with juice. The others gave her sympathetic glances.

"We can leave everything here today except our purses," Nancy said, when everyone had finished. "We're coming back tonight. Tomorrow we'll spend the night in Interlaken, at the foot of the Alps."

"*Gut.* Let's go!" Katie said, trying to sound happier than she felt. As they made their way to the car, Katie rubbed her head, and when they were seated in the back, Margaret having read her thoughts, popped open her purse. "Ibuprofen for what ails you. It's non-drowsy." Katie held out her hand. "Give me something that knocks me out. Double dose."

"Now, now," Margaret said with a smile, giving Katie two of the pills. "Sleep will come tonight when you need it."

Nancy pulled out on the street as Sharon punched in the first destination on the GPS. The man's voice began talking at once. "Turn right, sixty yards, then proceed to the rotary."

The man sounded a little like Ben, Katie thought, and she now hated the voice. But that couldn't be. This voice had been speaking in the car for two days now, and she hadn't once thought of any resemblance to Ben. Was every little thing going to remind her of Ben now? Would it ever end?

Katie laid her head back against the seat as Nancy pulled out onto the four-lane highway traveling toward Bern. Watching the signs flashing by, Katie told herself, *It wasn't my fault what Ben did. Somehow I'm going to make it. I can't spoil the fun for the other girls. It cost too much for them to fly over here to waste the trip. I have to try . . . I have to enjoy something of the day. Think beautiful sights and smile.*

As if Margaret knew what Katie was thinking, she whispered, "You'll make it, Katie. The Lord will help you."

Katie glanced away, squeezing back the tears.

CHAPTER THIRTY-SIX

An hour later Nancy pulled the car into an underground garage and announced, "So let's see what Bern, Switzerland, has to offer."

The girls piled out of the car, Katie vowing to act cheerful despite her true feelings.

"We have some interesting things to see," Nancy continued. "But if it gets to be too much, please let me know and we can go back." All eyes were on Katie as she said this, and each girl understood Nancy's meaning.

"I'll be okay!" Katie set her chin with determination. She *would* be okay. It wasn't every day that people got to see Bern — especially an Amish girl from Delaware. No matter what had happened with Ben, this was still the trip of her lifetime.

"This way," Nancy said, leading the way up some stairs. Once outside, they crossed a busy street and climbed another set of open steps to the street above them. They stopped in front of a huge cathedral with a high tower in front. On each side near the top was a clock.

Sharon searched through the guidebook before announcing, "This is the first Protestant church built in Bern after the Reformation. Like 1727 or so."

"I want to see the inside," Margaret said, running up the steps and pushing open the huge doors.

Katie followed her, taking in the immense interior with its decorative artwork and detailed carvings. This was not a church in which her faith would be comfortable, that was for sure. Yet it had a wonder all its own.

All four gazed for a long time at the dim interior before going outside again.

"Okay, next site," Margaret said, marching up the street.

"This way," Nancy said, turning onto a side street. Katie stayed close to the others as they twisted in and out of the narrow streets. Already she was feeling better. The decision to continue on with the planned activities had been the right one. And the other girls certainly seemed to enjoy themselves, which they should. It wasn't their fault Ben had turned out the way he had.

Nancy led the way out into what was obviously the main street, where large, roofed sidewalks ran along the street. Little shops filled every inch of the available space.

"Amazing!" Margaret proclaimed as they all paused to look. "Absolutely amazing. Now this is how one should enjoy shopping."

Katie imagined *Mamm* here, and her face darkened. She had to stop thinking of home. *Mamm* would also be heartbroken at the news about Ben, and she was no doubt worried about how Katie was taking it . . . if she even knew that Katie might have heard the news.

Nancy pointed up the street. "Albert Einstein's apartment is over there. And I do know that's the famous Bern clock tower up the street."

Katie glanced that way as they climbed down steps and crossed the cobblestone street. All along the street in each direction water fountains splashed and colorful flags hung on the covered walkway. This was a beautiful old town, Katie decided, as they dashed up under the overhanging walkways on the other side.

Sharon soon found the entrance to the Einstein apartment. It had a long set of stairs leading the way up. When they got to the top, a sign said to purchase tickets in the café below. Retreating, the girls entered the café and made their purchases. Nancy led the way back up to the ticket counter and then on to the first display, which consisted of Einstein's desk.

Margaret walked right up close whispering, "Grow, brain cells, grow!"

Sharon laughed. "And you think that's going to help?"

"I figured it might," Margaret said. "Not much else has so far."

Katie followed them into the living room, where Nancy leaned out of the window. "Einstein looked right out of here, gazing toward the clock tower. Can you imagine that?"

She could imagine it, Katie thought. Maybe it was the old room or the feel of the place. Not that she knew much about Einstein, but she could imagine the white-haired man puttering around, thinking about light and slowing down time — thoughts that were way beyond her. Ben would probably understand all that when she told him. And then she remembered how he'd wanted her to tell him everything she saw on the trip. But that wouldn't happen now. He would be hearing nothing about this visit to the birth of the Amish faith. Katie choked back a sob and turned away from the window. She had to think about something other than home or Ben. Thankfully, the other girls hadn't noticed her tears.

As they left and walked down the stairs, Sharon said, "I'm hungry. Let's eat in that cute little restaurant."

They all agreed, and a few minutes later were seated in the crowded café, having already ordered.

"So what's next on the list?" Margaret asked.

Just then the waitress appeared with their food, and when she left, Nancy said, "There's an old church in town we haven't seen yet. It's close to here. And there's the castle out in the countryside that has an old dungeon where our forefathers were kept in prison. Some of them for quite a length of time before they were martyred or released."

"I want to see the castle," Margaret said, taking a bite of her sandwich. "That sounds romantic."

Sharon had been paging through the guidebook with one hand while she ate with the other. She gave a little shriek. "Horrors! This is awful! But we have to see it."

"Please enlighten us," Margaret said.

"They have a figure of the executioner right out here in the street where they used to chop off heads," Sharon said. "It can't be far away."

"Then I'm running the other way!" Margaret proclaimed. "No heads rolling in the street for me."

Nancy launched into a story about the executioner preserved high above the street. "It was in this very street, many years after the persecution started, where one of the Anabaptist martyrs had a vision prior to his execution. When they led him out he boldly told the crowd that the Lord would perform several signs today attesting to his innocence. First, he would place his hat on the street and his head, after being chopped off, would fall into it and laugh."

Sharon choked and turned. Katie too decided she would have a hard time eating the last of her sandwich after that picture flashed in her mind. She laid her food on the table.

Nancy, though, went on. "Secondly, the town's water supply would turn blood red. And both of those things happened. This so shook up the townspeople that this was the last execution Bern had of an Anabaptist, although they used other forms of persecution for awhile."

"Is the story really true?" Margaret asked.

"It's in the guidebook," Sharon offered.

"The book claims the story is well sourced."

"There you go," Nancy said. "I've always been told it was true."

"Here's another one concerning the cathedral we're seeing next," Sharon said.

Margaret groaned. "Not another head chopping, I hope?"

"No, this one's clean," Sharon said. "Just a bad scare. It seems one Sunday morning a week after pronouncements against the Anabaptists from the government had been read in the pulpit, a bad storm blew up and knocked a large stone loose from the top of the cathedral. This piece of rock came crashing down right into the mayor's reserved chair, who, thankfully, was absent that morning. The townspeople feared the wrath of God, and the persecution let up for awhile."

"That's sounds like a story from the *Munster* Cathedral," Nancy said.

Sharon checked and nodded. "That's right."

"Let's go see it when we're finished," Margaret said.

"Sounds good," Nancy said.

Minutes later the girls were walking in the direction of the cathedral. As they turned a corner, there it was before them — the biggest church they'd seen so far. Hundreds of ornate carvings were everywhere, circling over the doorways and hanging from the eaves and water gutters.

"The *Munster* Cathedral," Sharon intoned, reading from the guidebook. " 'Begun in 1421, but the last steeple wasn't completed until 1893. The building continued for centuries, right through the raging turmoil of the Reformation.' That's something to see, if I must say so myself."

The girls went inside and climbed up more than 200 steps to an observation platform. From there the beautiful tiled roofs of the town of Bern lay below them. Each house was picture-perfect, the flower-pots blooming in the windows. Katie could only wonder how this beautiful country could have produced such suffering for her people. But it wasn't really so surprising. Hadn't Ben carried a very wicked heart under his handsome face and charming kisses? And Katie had been deceived.

They soon found their way back down the narrow stone steps, walking out to where the platform behind the cathedral overlooked the river. Here they listened as the bells from the towers above them pounded out the hour.

"Right down there," Nancy said, once the bells had fallen silent, "is where they loaded many of our forefathers onto ships, sending them out for banishment or, worse, as galley slaves."

Katie turned away. She'd seen enough misery for the moment. People must be very, very wicked to do things like this to one another. It was a little too much to handle right now. Sure, she had heard the stories before, but this was almost like seeing it happen herself. In a way she hadn't expected, it made Katie feel depressed. If only she could get away to a place where she could have some peace and not have to think about killing, death, and deception. In truth, she felt she could easily scream or, at least, burst into fresh tears. But she did neither, pasting a smile on instead and following the others back to the car.

They drove out into the countryside, following the instructions of the man in the GPS who now sounded like Jesse.

When they arrived at the castle and toured the dungeon, they were quiet as they looked at the tiny cells, each with a small bench with a hole in the middle and chains dangling on the side.

"For toilet purposes," Nancy said, trying to be helpful.

"Okay. With that, I'm out of here," Sharon said, turning to go up to the next level. The other girls followed close behind. But there they found yet more cells. As they read the guidebook and looked into the cells where great atrocities had happened to people who believed as they did, the girls all became quiet. Finally on the upper floor there was a single window overlooking the valley below. Beautiful farms lay spread before them. The view was picture-perfect, with cows roaming the fields and the soft tingle of their bells reaching even this height.

Suddenly Katie could stand it no more. She broke into loud sobs. Nancy wrapped an arm around her shoulder.

"Why do people do such evil things?" Katie asked through her tears.

"Human beings do awful things to each other," Nancy agreed. "But the Lord is greater than our wickedness."

Katie knew that was true, but she didn't feel it right now. *Da Hah* felt a thousand miles away, as if He had left this world to its own devices and turned His face away from her.

"The Lord will comfort your heart," Nancy said. "In His own time. We must wait for Him."

Katie choked back her sobs as Margaret and Sharon joined them. With their arms around each other, they prayed for Katie.

But when they were done, her heart was just as cold as when they'd started.

CHAPTER THIRTY-SEVEN

The following day the girls drove to the little town of Eggiwil that Nancy wished to visit. It lay in the high plateaus south and east of Bern, where they'd been yesterday. Margaret and Sharon were caught up in the scenery outside. Nancy was mostly paying attention to her driving on the sharp turns of this mountainous country. Katie was coping with the loss she felt over Ben's arrest. Sharon had been checking the news from home on her laptop, accessing both the newspaper and contacting her parents through email. Apparently there was a new development that seemed to end all speculation about this being a horrible mistake. Ben had confessed.

If she could only forget about Ben, Katie thought. But how did she forget a person who had grown so close to her heart? It was like tearing a piece of her own flesh away. There was one bright spot in this whole mess, if such a thing were possible. Thankfully, this had all been revealed before she married Ben. How much worse would things have been if it hadn't? She might even be with child when Ben was in jail serving a long prison term. Katie refused to think on Ben. He was out of her life. They would never see each other again, of that much she was sure. And to think at one time his doubts about his faith had her worried. That objection paled in light of his illegal drug activities.

Nancy slowed to cross a gorgeous little covered bridge, and exclamations of wonder came from Margaret and Sharon. Shortly thereafter, they arrived in the town and Nancy parked near the town center.

"Bathroom?" Katie spoke up.

"Excellent idea," Nancy said. She proceeded to a small shop and asked. Minutes later, when they exited the restrooms, Nancy said, "There's a church up here somewhere I want to see."

"Is this town another of those *Taufer* nests?" Sharon asked.

Nancy nodded. "They had a congregation up here of around forty members before they were all banished, somewhere around the late seventeenth century."

"Eww . . ." Margaret said, as they came in

sight of a picturesque little church. "Not another of those built with blood money?"

"Well, confiscated property helped for this one," Nancy said. "I doubt if there was enough money to build the whole church."

"I don't even want to see the place." Sharon marched away, and the others followed. Back at the car, Nancy drove higher into the mountains, pausing beside the road occasionally to take in the beautiful view of the valley below.

"I can see how a person would want to live up here," Margaret said. "That's an awesome view."

"I guess we can see why some of our forefathers came back even after they'd been banished and were facing fresh persecution. They became too homesick to stay in their new country."

As they drove on, Sharon asked, "Doesn't it get cold up here? I mean it's decent now, but the guidebook claims the winters are pretty harsh."

"Look at that house," Nancy motioned as they went past. "The barn is built right into the mainframe."

"Gross!" Margaret exclaimed. "Now that's going too far. Animals in the living room?"

"There's another one," Sharon added, "and some more. We haven't seen these before, have we?"

"Not that I noticed," Margaret said. "But I guess it would be kind of cozy. Sheep bleating in your sleep. You'd just open your eyes to count them."

They all laughed, and Katie felt a little calmer. The countryside did have a certain wildness to it. Maybe she could move here and get away from the mess Ben had made of their lives. She'd never see anyone from the community again, which wasn't a bad idea. Surely they'd let her into this country since her forefathers had been from here . . . somewhere.

Katie pushed the thoughts away. Her brain couldn't think straight right now, and even wild ideas made way too much sense. Nancy was now driving along the high plateau and heading toward their next site. She had made an appointment weeks ago at a hiding place in a barn the *Taufers* used to use. And from there they planned to drive on to the base of the Alps. The plans were to ride a cable car up a mountain tomorrow.

Nancy had said there was an awesome place up there called Schilthorn.

She slowed to bounce the car down a narrow lane and then stopped in front of an old homestead. "The Anabaptist hiding place," Nancy announced.

Everyone climbed out. A young lady, apparently expecting them, appeared on the front porch and greeted them with "Good morning" in English, but with an accent the girls had gotten used to hearing. "I see you have come. And right on time. My name is Regina. Would you like to see the barn now? And then I have lunch prepared for you."

"That would be great," Nancy said. "We were just admiring your beautiful countryside on the way here."

"*Jah,* it is great to live here. My family has been in the area now for many years." Regina paused to open the barn door. "Are any of you familiar with the story here?"

"Only what we've read in the guidebook," Nancy said.

"Guidebooks are useful, but it is better to see for oneself. That is why you have come, no? So let me tell you the story from the sixteenth century. Back then it is believed there were many such barns as this in the area. All of the others, though, have been lost during remodeling projects and such things. This one is still as it used to be."

Regina led the way to where a floorboard was raised on a swiveling hinge. She showed them the small hiding place below. "As you may know already, the city of Bern would send *Taufer* hunters out into the countryside

402

to capture both men and women."

Margaret groaned as Regina continued. "When the *Taufer* hunters arrived in the area, word would spread quickly, and the people who were being pursued would run into one of these barns. As you can see this piece of floorboard rotates in the middle. When you step on one end, it goes down, and you climb in the hole. When you are inside you push it back up again, latch it from underneath, and no one can find you. Many people used this place, and once the hunters were gone they could flee to a better hiding place."

"At least they didn't chop off people's heads here," Margaret said. "That was awful yesterday. We saw the place in Bern where it used to happen."

"*Jah.*" Regina wasn't smiling now. "That was all a long time ago, but even then it is a shameful part of our history. Today the government is doing much to expose the past, and to make sure it does not happen again. That is why so many of these sites are being preserved and kept up by the government."

Margaret breathed a sigh of relief as Regina continued the tour. When she was finished, she said, "So are you girls ready for lunch now? I have a little something prepared."

"Starving!" Margaret said.

Regina laughed. "This is my family's farm," Regina told them as she led the way inside the house. "We've been here for many years, and we love the place. But what do you think of the country by now? Other than some of the history, of course?"

"Oh, we love the country itself," Nancy said. "It's just hard for us to understand why such suffering had to happen here. Why people could be so cruel to others."

"*Ach . . . jah,* one does wonder." Regina motioned toward a long table. "Please be seated, and I'll have lunch out quickly. I'm sure you have a long way to travel today yet."

"Do you get lots of people through here?" Nancy asked Regina as she was setting out the food.

"*Jah,* lots of them. Maybe one thousand a year or so. It varies, of course."

"Keeps you busy then," Sharon said. "How does it feel living on the very place where such historical things happened? I mean, people hiding for their lives."

"One gets used to it, I suppose," Regina said. "And no one was ever murdered on the property, so there are no ghosts. But, of course, I am teasing."

As she refilled the girls' glasses, Regina asked, "You are heading somewhere else now, of course?"

"Yes. To the Alps," Nancy said. "We have a bed-and-breakfast scheduled for our stay in Interlaken. Then hopefully we can ride a cable car all the way up to the Schilthorn tomorrow."

"*Jah,* this is where the James Bond movie was made," Regina said. "You have seen that? It is world famous, I think. *On Her Majesty's Secret Service* the movie was called."

Margaret sniffed. "I don't watch James Bond."

Regina laughed. "I guess it is more for the men. But my husband has all the movies. He loves them."

"I've seen some James Bond movies," Sharon offered. "Not that I really liked them, but my brother had a few around once."

"See, it's for the men," Regina said.

"It's worth the trip though, from what I've read," Nancy said. "You can see all the mountains from one side to the other."

"*Jah.*" Regina nodded. "On a clear day you can see much. But those are hard to find in the spring like this."

Sharon glanced at the window. "Well, it's

clear outside today."

"Then you should go today," Regina told them. "But that is not possible, of course."

When silence fell over the group, Regina continued. "But do not let me spoil your lovely vacation. Surely there will be a few more days of sunshine before the clouds move in. And even if there are not, the Swiss Alps are something that must be seen. Even with clouds floating by, they are beautiful. Like nothing in the world."

"You are a good salesperson," Margaret said.

"It is a lovely country." Regina beamed. "The best on the earth. One would not wish to live anywhere else."

"See, that's what I said," Margaret said. "I'd love to live here."

"You will also ride the train to the top of the Jungfrau? That is our most famous mountain peak," Regina asked.

"It's quite expensive, and we might not have time with the weather," Nancy said. "But I do want to see the little village of Gimmelwald, which is on the cable car route."

"*Jah,* that is something to see," Regina agreed. "But do not forget the train if you have the time. It is well worth the money which is spent. You are only here maybe once in a lifetime. Correct?"

"I hope to come back again," Nancy said. "But you may be right. I'll see how much time we have. But the cable car and Gimmelwald come first, after we've settled our bill, of course. The lunch was very good, and so was the tour of the barn. Thank you."

"I am glad you enjoyed it." Regina collected their money, and when the girls were ready to leave, she walked them to the door.

An hour of driving brought them to their first full view of the Alps. Katie gasped along with the others, her eyes glued to the car window.

CHAPTER THIRTY-EIGHT

The next day Katie huddled with the other three girls in front of the ticket booth for the cable car to Schilthorn. Outside the open-sided building, the cliffs rose high into the air, leveling off with sheer abruptness. Low clouds scurried across the sky. The clerk pointed to a computer monitor and said, "This is a view from the camera on top of the Schilthorn. The forecast for today is not good, but it may clear later. We do not know for sure."

If her heart wasn't already dragging, it surely would be at this news. This was not entirely unexpected, but it still hurt to have their slim hopes dashed. There hadn't been time last night to take the cable car all the way to the top after they'd arrived at their lodging in Interlaken. Plus the drive up to the cable car took another thirty minutes. Kareem, who ran the bed-and-breakfast, had smiled in sympathy over their plight.

"*Jah,* it is hard to get up on a good day this time of the year."

"We should have come in the summer," Margaret had said.

"Then you'd have tourists all over the place," Kareem told them. "Then I'd not have place here, and maybe I'd not get to see you. And that would not be good either."

Katie was impressed with both Kareem and the care she gave. The house smacked of cleanness and decorum, with rooms on two floors. And breakfast this morning had been the best spread they'd had yet — cheeses, yogurts, and meats of all sorts. Kareem didn't spare for her guests' comfort, that was for sure.

But to miss seeing the Alps would be another blow. Katie was quite ready for things to go right for a change. Last night she'd awakened in the night to break out in sobs, burying her head in the pillow so Margaret wouldn't hear her.

This morning her swollen eyes must have given her away because all three girls had exchanged worried glances at the breakfast table.

"Do you have any suggestions about going up?" Nancy asked the ticket clerk.

"I'm sorry, we make no recommendations," the man said. "But it is always a beautiful sight up there, even with a few clouds."

"Let's do it then," Margaret said. "We haven't come this far to turn back now."

"That's the spirit!" Sharon agreed. "I say yes."

"What about you?" Nancy turned to Katie.

"*Yah,* let's go!"

"That's the girl." Margaret gave her a quick slap on the back.

"Then we will," Nancy said, pulling out her purse.

When everyone had paid, they climbed the steps to the loading platform above them and sat down to wait.

The cable car soon appeared, moving down from the heights of the cliff. Katie stood to watch it arrive, and the others soon joined her. With a smooth, rocking motion it hung to the cables and docked safely with the platform. A man and a woman stepped out and hurried past them.

"That doesn't look too promising," Margaret said as they boarded after showing the attendant their tickets.

"Chin up there, girl," Sharon encouraged her. "We're going up to the top."

Katie held on to the side bar as the cable car climbed again. Watching the car coming down hadn't looked too scary, but going up was another matter. They really were hanging over nothing, and just attached to something solid by some thin cables.

"It'll hold, won't it?" Margaret asked.

"Sure it will," Nancy said. "Modern man has done some wondrous things. Not like the Lord, of course, but great in their own right."

"Today I'll be glad if we get to see the Lord's works and not man's," Sharon said.

The cable car climbed ever higher, soon docking into another platform with a Gimmelwald sign in large letters attached to the wall. When things stopped moving, the attendant ushered them all off. It hadn't been too scary after all, but all four girls gave an audible sigh of relief as they stepped onto the platform.

"Over here is the car to Murren," the attendant said, motioning with his hand. "Or you can tour Gimmelwald and catch another car later. Perhaps the clouds will clear up by then."

"We're going up now," Nancy decided without much thought. It was as if an inspiration had come on her. "We can see Gimmelwald on the way down."

Minutes later that ride up began, hugging the edge of the cliff with spectacular views of the valley below. Katie joined the other girls in gazing out the east side as the cable car climbed higher and higher.

"How would you get up here without a cable car?" Margaret asked.

"I think there's a path." Sharon consulted the guidebook. "Yes, there is."

"Shiver my timbers!" Margaret muttered. "I believe I do prefer this way."

"Me too!" Sharon added.

When the cable car docked at Murren, they switched again, waiting a few minutes until the next car left. It broke out of the tree line soon after departure, revealing a valley below them dotted with occasional cabins. Majestic sweeps of snow began just below the scurrying clouds.

"The clouds are lifting, aren't they?" Nancy made the observation first.

The attendant smiled at the remark. "They have been coming and going all morning. The weather up here is hard to predict."

"We so hope to see at least some good views," Nancy said. "We come from America."

The attendant kept a close eye on his levers, but added, "If you look below in the valley right now, you can see those little animals running around. Those are our version of deer like you have in America."

Katie looked below for several long moments before spotting the animals. They appeared to feed peacefully, unaware that a cable car full of humans was passing over them. How she wished for such an existence. But her trust in *Da Hah* was so shattered right now. How was she ever to get it back again? She wasn't like Job in the Bible. He had been able to receive both *gut* things and bad things from *Da Hah*'s hand. While she had taken the *gut* things quite cheerfully, she knew she was now complaining furiously about what had happened.

But how did one make peace with what Ben had done? How could anything *gut* come out of that? *Nee,* it couldn't. But still she would have to give thanks like Job had. But for her to get to that point might take years and years — if it happened even then.

Something else soon clutched Katie's heart as the cable car continued to climb. The awesome vastness of what was being revealed all around her touched her heart. She pressed closer to the glass. More huts appeared, clinging to the wood line. The clouds were definitely lifting higher, as if making way for them. Rocky cliffs soon joined in with the green trees, blending together at first before disappearing into

413

snow-covered ruggedness. Thin streams ran everywhere, trickling down narrow beds. A solitary road ran along the ridge and disappeared into the clouds.

"One more," the attendant announced as the cable car docked again.

Katie followed the others through the building to the next ride. The cables stretched out into the distance, spanning another massive valley floor. The end of the lines hung to the faint shadow of a round building perched high on a rock.

"The famous Schilthorn," Sharon announced. "Looks like it's still there."

Katie was looking at the surrounding mountain peaks as they were becoming visible through the thinning cloud cover.

"It's clearing!" Nancy said at last. "I think it really is."

Not only were the clouds moving out of the way. What was being revealed took Katie's breath away. The higher they climbed, with the deep valley far below them, the more of the mountains could be seen. They stretched from the east to the west, jagged peaks, snow-covered, one after the other, and even more lay beyond that.

"That's the Jungfrau," the same attendant pointed out with a proud smile on his face. "Our beloved mountain."

Katie looked at the highest peak. It seemed insignificant almost, standing there beside two others. But that was only because they were all so grand, so breathtaking, so unbelievable. *Da Hah* made all of this. This thought raced through her mind as the cable car docked. They jumped out to run over to the observation platform. Katie hugged herself in the thin air, wrapping her coat tight around her. The clouds had lifted completely now, revealing the full stretch of mountains lying in each direction.

Katie walked the length of the platform and then back again. Sharon and Margaret were taking turns snapping pictures from all vantage points. Finally, the majesty of it all broke a dam of tears in Katie, and she let them fall where they may. So what if the others saw her. This beauty in the midst of her pain was tearing at her heart. It was as if the wound that Ben had made was pulled open and the scab removed. Into the torn ugliness a soft oil was being poured. *Da Hah* was reaching down with His hand, right past His glorious mountains. He was molding the pieces of her heart back together with His fingers. Katie wept great sobs that shook her entire body.

Nancy soon noticed the gush of tears and came over to Katie. "Is there something I can do?" she whispered.

Katie shook her head. "Not really. It's just this . . . this awesomeness. *Da Hah* has made this. Something so beautiful in the midst of all the wickedness of our world."

Nancy squeezed Katie's hand. "I know. It's affecting me the same way. And look how the clouds have cleared away. It's a gift from the Lord."

A gift? Katie choked back another sob. She didn't want another gift from *Da Hah.* The last one had proven only to break her heart. And yet here it was again. That same wonder she'd felt at home. That miracle when *Mamm* had finally agreed to marry Jesse and change their reclusive lifestyle. It was the same feeling of joy that she'd felt when Ben first asked if she would ride with him in his buggy.

Her life might seem destroyed now, but *Da Hah* wasn't finished with her. Nor was the world He had made. *Da Hah* could make whole what was broken. Here was the testimony of that truth calling out to her, telling her that *Da Hah* was in control. That He made all things beautiful. The rugged slashes of the valleys below declared the fact. So did the rushing streams of water and the icy cold of the hovering snow cover. The world was *Da Hah*'s, they all declared, and He did all things well.

Katie sobbed out loud, which brought Margaret and Sharon to her side too. All four of the girls held hands until the worst of Katie's crying had died down. Then they walked back and forth, staying together, imprinting the glory of the Alps — and *Da Hah* — into their minds. *Nee,* more than that, Katie thought. They were all four taking this deep into their hearts.

Something was happening to her — and to them. Something she hadn't expected to find in years — maybe never. Healing was coming. It came like cool water in the hot summer sun. Like *Mamm*'s kiss when she was hurt as a little girl. It even felt like Ben's smile before he'd first really looked at her. *Yah,* inside something was changing. It couldn't be put into words, and yet the others seemed to understand.

When all four girls had been fully satisfied with the feast *Da Hah* had set before their eyes, they rode the cable car to the stop below. There Katie wandered out onto the platform and found a plate with German words posted on the wall. She translated for the others with tears running down her cheeks. She was healing, that she knew. She was being made whole, and she would need to get on with life now. And she could because *Da Hah* might have more miracles for her life. In fact, He might never be done with them. She knew that now, even as she whispered the words on the metal plate: "Everything that has breath praise the LORD." Beside it was the Scripture reference: Psalm 150:6.

Below that were the words, "Our Land with its splendor, its mountains, its halls, are the signs of Your might. Your good fatherly ways. So everything in us prays on. Great things You have done for us. K.V. Greyerz."

"That must be one of their local poets," Nancy said when Katie finished reciting the words.

It might be, Katie thought. But at the moment it was also the voice of *Da Hah* speaking to her heart. His fingers were indeed putting the broken pieces of her heart back together. Katie leaned over the platform railing to hide her tears and caught sight of a beautiful patch of flowers below her. The clumps were clinging to the steep mountainside. Colors of blue and purple were blooming with cheery brightness. Katie stared openmouthed as Sharon snapped away with her camera.

How awesome the works of *Da Hah*! Katie thought. He was showing her again on this day of miracles — so that there would be no question about the future. Even the flowers sang the glory of *Da Hah*'s mighty works up here where so little could grow. Could she not also bloom in impossible situations? Katie covered her face and sobbed again.

CHAPTER THIRTY-NINE

Three days later Margaret was craning over the front seat, looking out of the car window as Nancy navigated the rush-hour traffic toward downtown Paris. Many happy hours were behind them. Days filled with joy and laughter. Katie was continuing to heal from the miracle *Da Hah* had performed in the Swiss Alps. Doubtless life would never be quite the same, but at least the sharp sting of the pain from Ben's betrayal was now only a dull ache.

They'd spent yesterday in the King Louis gardens at Versailles, debating whether to make a bold push into Paris itself. After consulting the guidebook and thinking about the high price of the museums, the vote had been unanimous to bypass spending an entire day in Paris. But there was no reason they couldn't try for a glimpse of the Eiffel Tower — since the man speaking from the GPS was taking them unexpectedly within sight of downtown.

"There it is!" Sharon yelled from the front seat as she grabbed her camera. "I caught a glimpse of it!"

"So did I!" Margaret said.

Katie peered between the buildings as Sharon tried for another photo. She thought she saw the faint outline of the spidery tower in the distance. It didn't look like much from here, but then one probably had to get close to see its true beauty. Like most things in life, Katie decided.

Nancy was being kept busy with the traffic, but she didn't seem to mind. Likely they had seen so much in the last few days that Nancy figured missing a glimpse of the Eiffel Tower wasn't such a big deal. Besides, they were headed for Haarlem, the site of Corrie ten Boom's hiding place. That would be the highlight of the whole trip for her, Nancy had told them last night. Seeing again where the brave Christian family had hidden Jewish people and other refugees during Hitler's occupation. In Nancy's eyes, the Eiffel Tower didn't compare to such an act of faith. And likely there was also the day's journey on Nancy's mind, and it wasn't going to be easy. They needed to travel through several major cities in Belgium and the Netherlands. The GPS estimated the travel time at over six hours from the hotel where they'd spent the night in Versailles.

Sharon was trying for one last picture of downtown Paris as Katie laid her head back on the car seat.

"Tired are we?" Margaret asked.

"*Yah,* but I shouldn't be with the *gut* night's sleep I had," Katie said.

"Yes, but we walked more yesterday than any of us have in years, I'm sure," Margaret said.

"*Yah.*" Katie closed her eyes, thinking about the day. They'd entered the front of the Royal Chateau, which Sharon said had belonged to the kings of France for more than a hundred years — until they chopped King Louis XV's head off in the Revolution.

Margaret had groaned at that bit of information, but Nancy assured Margaret that the beheading was not something they would see celebrated or displayed. Rather, the Royal Chateau was all about the glorious past of the French kings.

"Glorious I can do," Margaret had said.

The self-guided tour of the chateau had begun after they paid for the tickets. An excessive amount, Katie had thought, but Nancy had told them it was normal. They'd been accompanied by hordes of other tourists who seemed intent on also seeing this grandeur for themselves. Katie had stayed close to Nancy, as Sharon tried to take pictures and make sense out of what they were seeing using the guidebook. A long hall stretched all the way around the immense building, lined in one place with statues of famous French personages.

"Dandies," Margaret had called them. And everyone had laughed because the description had seemed to fit. French men were apparently quite impressed with their clothing.

Room after room had followed, each done up in the most decorative fashion with vast paintings on the ceilings. Katie blushed after they left the first set of paintings, but several rooms later, with no one paying a partly disrobed woman any attention, she felt better.

Eventually Margaret had burst out, "Bosoms! I've had enough of them now!"

Sharon had giggled, and Katie's blush returned.

They walked into one long room, called the Hall of Mirrors, that stretched on and on for a long way. Katie had paused for a better look. Tall, arched mirrors lined the back wall and matched arched windows on the front side. Katie had strolled up to one of the mirrors, squeezing through the crowd of people. You couldn't see yourself that well, she decided. So the French back in those days must not have known how to make their mirrors, or perhaps the glass had faded through the years.

From there they'd seen the king and the queen's bedrooms. These were huge affairs with drapes hanging down to the floor on all sides. The king's bedroom looked out toward the east, the tall windows letting in the rays of the rising sun. King Louis XIII considered himself the Sun King, so it was appropriate, he thought, that the sun and he should meet first thing each morning.

The queen's bedroom was quite a distance away, adorned in lesser fashion but still beautiful. All the beds looked short, so Katie figured the French people must have been stunted in growth back in those days. Eventually she had found a sign that explained the matter. It was all an optical illusion caused by the tall drapes on the sides of the beds. Each bed was well over seven feet long.

Below the first floor had been the bedrooms of the young men who waited in line for the throne. Some of them had died while they waited. It seemed awful to Katie to get so close to such awesome power and have it slip away after all. But then she shouldn't be thinking about such things. Christian people weren't supposed to lust after the glory of this world.

The gardens behind the chateau had been the most beautiful of all. There had been acres and acres of plants, taking up much more room than Jesse's farm did at home. Fountains were everywhere, with a huge one right behind the steps when she walked outside.

Standing at the steps, Katie could look back and see how immense the chateau was. It stretched from left to right so far that Sharon claimed she had to take three pictures to fit it all in.

The girls had eaten a sandwich lunch among the planted shrubs, having purchased the food from a vendor tucked in along the long rows of tall greenery. Afterward, they'd found another smaller palace by following the guidebook. The tour there had been nothing like the first one in its grandeur, but there had still been plenty to see.

Nancy said this chateau was for the king to get away from the big chateau when things became too crowded. And from there they found another smaller chateau even further in. Apparently this was the chateau to get away from the second chateau. It all got a little confusing after awhile, both in the layout and in finding their way back. The distances were vast.

By the time they were back at the main chateau, Katie figured one could fit two of Jesse's farms in here. And that night the girls had all slept well.

Now having made her way past the Paris traffic, Nancy was driving through open country.

"Bathroom break, anyone?" Nancy asked.

"Most certainly," Sharon said.

Nancy soon pulled into a rest area. They all climbed out and stretched before going inside.

Once on the road again, silence settled over the car. Katie's thoughts drifted to Ben. She shouldn't think about him, but it seemed impossible *not* to think about what had happened. And then too perhaps it would be better to mourn than to hold the memory inside. And remembering felt possible now. Still, she felt bad that she wouldn't be telling Ben her experiences on the trip. He would so have enjoyed the news of the time they had spent on the Normandy beaches. Of course, she would tell *Mamm* and maybe Jesse, but neither of them were as interested in such things as Ben was.

She'd known only the barest of details of that morning when the Allied forces invaded Hitler's occupied Europe. It was Sharon, of all people, who was almost as interested in such things as Ben had been. Nancy at first didn't want to stop, but finally agreed after Sharon had begged.

"It's not decent," Nancy had said. "Stopping in at a place where war was made. Our people don't believe in such things."

"But it's history," Sharon had insisted. "And men gave their lives there to stop the evil that Hitler was doing."

This seemed to persuade Nancy more than anything — the mention of Hitler.

"I guess he was pretty evil," Nancy allowed. "But I still don't think we should kill as Christians."

The sky had been clear on the morning they arrived at the first beach, after they toured the artificial harbor the Allies had built at the town of Arromanches. Omaha, Sharon had said the beach was called. There was a lonely stretch of open water that looked much like the beaches did at home in Delaware. The biggest difference was the German pillboxes on the bluffs that were still there overlooking the beach. They were huge affairs with the tracks of the rotating guns still visible. Margaret had climbed inside one of the smaller ones for a picture Sharon took. The larger pillbox had steps going down into it, which they all used to climb down. Inside, the musty smell of grass and mold filled the place. Looking out the front, it wasn't hard to imagine what things must have looked like on that morning when thousands of young men came rushing ashore. The Germans had been shooting at them from here, killing brave people who wished only to free a country from evil.

Omaha had been the American beach — or one of them. Katie couldn't really remember. But there young men came ashore who had left loved ones at home, perhaps even wives and children. They came here to die on this stretch of sand for the freedom of others. Katie wiped away the unbidden tears as she looked out from the German pillbox.

What made men kill one another? she wondered. Did they really believe it was right? The Allies might have had reason to think so, but how could the Germans think they were right in killing the Jews and all those millions of others? They would see a site soon in Haarlem where a whole family — the ten Booms — had risked their lives to save others. Here men had also given their lives so that others might be free. Katie shivered. It was a great sacrifice, and one she could not begin to understand. Killing was wrong, and yet men did kill . . . and continued to kill even today. It was as if the evil never stopped, and *Da Hah* was left to pick up the broken pieces.

He must be a great *Hah,* Katie decided, to care so much and to keep caring about people who seemed determined to destroy their lives.

They all headed back to the car, and their next stop had been a site above tall cliffs with huge pockmarks in the ground. This came from the bombardment by the Allied ships at sea, Sharon said. It was here that three hundred soldiers had scaled the cliffs using grappling hooks. Only a third of them had survived.

Katie moved close to the cliff, looking down to the dashing coastline below. Men did both brave and horrible things in war, she decided. *Da Hah* would have to straighten all of it out someday. As He was well capable of doing. Hadn't He healed her heart? But thankfully her people didn't believe in all this killing. The more she was seeing of what happened here, the more she was glad for that.

Sharon had wanted to see one more place

before they drove on to Versailles. The place was in the town of St. Mere Eglise, where paratroopers had overshot their target and landed in the middle of the village. And sure enough, the guidebook had been correct. A dummy paratrooper was still hanging by his parachute from the downtown church's steeple. A real one had gotten hung up there during the landing, Sharon said, and had survived by playing dead. With the church bells tolling beside him to rouse the sleeping Germans, the soldier's ears had been rendered deaf for several days.

Which was understandable, Katie thought. She'd heard enough church bells tolling this trip already to know how loud they were. Apparently almost every little town had its miniature cathedral dating from the medieval ages. Europe had once been a very religious continent even though Nancy said it no longer was.

Katie closed her eyes and put her head back. She really needed to get some sleep before they arrived at their next stop. Margaret was already sound asleep beside her.

CHAPTER FORTY

The following morning Katie stood waiting with the other girls and a small group of American tourists. They were all huddled in the little side street in Haarlem, waiting for the twelve o'clock English tour of the Corrie ten Boom home. The tour had been postponed twice already, but surely soon they would be going in.

The girls had spent the morning touring another old church in the town square. The place was immense, as so many of the churches they'd seen were. Mozart was reported to have played the church organ here, according to the guidebook. The instrument wasn't quite as impressive as the one in the *Grossmunster* at Zurich, but almost. Huge tiles covered the floor of the church. They'd almost finished the tour when Margaret realized that these were actually graves, each containing a body from the ancient past. Sharon followed Margaret in a mad dash outside, where they shivered for awhile in the bright sunlight.

Katie lagged behind, asking the lady who had sold them tickets, "Are those really gravestones on the church floor?"

"Oh, yes," the lady said. "That's how things were done long ago. It was considered a great honor and a help for eternal salvation."

"Thank you," Katie had told her, joining Margaret and Sharon outside, where the two were still horrified about the graves they'd walked on.

Nancy had laughed over the whole matter, and they soon forgot about the graves in the church floor. All of them had been distracted by purchasing mementos of their stay in Haarlem at a small shop. Katie purchased a small windmill for *Mamm,* and after several minutes of thought settled on a set of wooden shoes for Mabel. She hadn't thought of Mabel much lately, and perhaps Mabel wouldn't even speak with her once she arrived back home. But if Mabel was by chance on friendly terms, she wanted to arrive with a gift in hand.

Now that Ben was out of her life, perhaps Mabel wouldn't resent her as much. But on the other hand, Mabel might despise her more completely. She might not want any association with her. She might even think Katie knew about the drugs all along and shielded Ben. And that Katie just wanted to bring the family down. Katie sighed. It could be a no-win situation.

Pushing the dark thoughts away, Katie made the further selection of a cowbell for Carolyn with a colorful ribbon to hang it on the wall. For Joel, she chose a little scarf-wrapped boy, carved out of wood, heading down the mountain on his skis. For Leroy and Willis she purchased a box of assorted chocolate delicacies. Jesse was the hardest to choose for, but Katie settled on a beautiful painting of a Dutch windmill. It cost more than she expected, but for *Daett . . .* it was worth it. Katie wiped away a tear, and added a few postcards to her collection before paying for her purchases. One postcard she would mail to *Mamm* right away. The others would serve as smaller gifts when she arrived home.

They'd arrived early at the ten Boom house, so Sharon had led them into a jewelry shop — an unrelated company to the ten Booms now rented the place. Sharon hadn't bought anything, but Nancy purchased an expensive, white-banded wristwatch.

"You did the right thing," Margaret encouraged Nancy as they walked over to wait in line. "You'll probably never come back here again. And now you have a watch from the former ten Boom watch shop to wrap your memories around."

Katie would have smiled along with them if her heart hadn't been sinking at the moment. On the way out she'd caught sight of the most beautiful gold watch chain. It was exactly what Ben needed for his pocket watch. Before the news from home, she would have purchased it for him regardless of the cost.

After more waiting in line, the American tourists gathered around them were getting restless. From the snatches of their conversation, she gathered they were with various church groups. Katie heard Georgia mentioned and Tennessee. Moments later the street door opened, and the face of an older lady appeared. "English tour," she announced with hardly an accent. "Ready to go."

The group surged forward, and the four girls stayed toward the back. The lady first led them to the living room of the home. They were soon all seated in a circle, using the furniture in the room and chairs that had been brought in.

"Good afternoon, everyone," the lady

began. "My name is Estes, and I will tell you first of all about the Corrie ten Boom home, and then we will go upstairs to see the hiding place. No pictures here, please. But you may take all you wish at the hiding place. Does anyone have any questions before we begin?"

No one said anything, and Estes continued. "This is the ten Boom home, of course, where Corrie was raised as the youngest of four children. Corrie's father, Casper, was a devout Christian who had a great burden for all suffering people. But especially he had a heart for God's chosen people, the Jews. He raised his family to practice a peaceful and brotherly love toward his fellowman and to reject all forms of racism and hatred.

"When Hitler invaded Holland in 1940, much opportunity soon arrived for the exercising of these beliefs. The ten Boom home became known as the place where anyone who was hurting or suffering could find shelter. Soon after the invasion, the Nazis issued ration cards since there was a war going on. This produced quite a problem. Because how were the ten Booms to feed the people they were helping without revealing the need for extra cards? Corrie solved this problem with the help of her friend who was a civil servant in charge of the ration cards. Corrie was able to obtain extra cards, which they hid in the house. The Nazis often made surprise searches of homes, and extra ration cards were always a sign of illegal activity. And the Nazis were very strict on the matter. But Corrie and Betsie were able to hide the cards so they were never found. The ten Booms also soon had someone from the Dutch resistance build them a hiding place in the upper floor of their home, which we shall soon get to see. And many, many people were helped by the ten Booms during this time.

"The family worked out an alarm system, using an all clear signal in the front window. That is the red triangle you saw coming in with what looked like a clock face in the middle. It really was a common item used by jewelry stores in those days. If the signal was up, all was clear. But if it was lying down, then there was danger and people looking for help were warned to stay away.

"Also an alarm system was installed that could be rung from the front door. And the ten Booms constantly practiced drills, along with whomever was being given shelter at the time. They had things so well planned that within minutes everyone illegally in the house could be inside the hiding place.

"The ten Booms were betrayed in February of 1944 by a Dutch informer who came to their door for help. Betsie was suspicious but told him to come back later. He did. This time, before she opened the door, Betsie looked out the window and saw an automobile parked out on the street. Betsie knew that no Dutchman drove an automobile by that date in the war. Only the Germans did. And toward the end, even bicycles were taken away from the Dutch people.

"So Betsy rang the alarm by the door before she opened it. Outside the Dutch informer was waiting, and he was joined at once by German officers. They stormed into the house, but everyone had made it into the hiding place in time and the ration cards had been safely hidden.

"Still, the Germans arrested the whole family because they were convinced illegal activities were being conducted in the house. Betsie knocked over the signal in the window, but a German officer noticed and replaced it. Because of that, more than thirty people who came calling on the ten Boom home were arrested by that evening. In the meantime, the women and men in the hiding place didn't know what was going on, and they didn't dare come out. For close to two days they stayed there until the Germans switched their officers for local Dutch guards, figuring no one could possibly be in the home.

"The Dutch guards knew about the ten Booms' activities and their hiding place. So they let the six men and women out, sneaking them out the back windows to safety. Four of those were Jews, two men and two women. One of those men and the two women are known to have survived the war. The other man, we did not know what happened to him. But one day during a tour of the hiding place, this man in the group broke into tears, saying that he was the very person who had once been hidden inside. I must say it was a very emotional experience for everyone.

"But back to the ten Boom family. Corrie's father, Casper, was soon offered his release by the Nazis since he was an old man and close to death. The Nazis made the offer on the condition that he no longer give shelter to any Jewish people. Casper refused and died soon afterward in prison. Corrie and Betsie were taken to the concentration camps. First to one close to here, and then transferred to another near Berlin. There Betsie died, but Corrie was eventually released just a week before the other women in the camp were killed. She later learned that this happened through a clerical error. Corrie was sure that this was instead the hand of God wanting her to tell His story around the whole world, which Corrie then proceeded to do with her writings and her speaking. Later Corrie met one of the cruel guards from the concentration camp.

" 'Can you forgive me?' the man asked Corrie after her speech that day.

"And Corrie thought to herself that she didn't want to. But she prayed to God for strength, and she extended her hand to the guard. When she touched him, Corrie said, a shock like lightning went through her arm, and her heart flowed over with compassion and forgiveness for the man."

Estes stood to her feet and motioned toward the doorway. "And now that you know something of Corrie's story, let's see the hiding place where those people were hidden. And remember you can take pictures there. All of them you wish."

"That was quite some story," Margaret whispered in Katie's ear as they were going up the stairs.

"I know." Katie stole a quick glance in Nancy's direction. It looked like she had tears in her eyes.

At the top of the stairs, half the group had to stand in the hallway, while the rest went inside the bedroom. When the next turn came, Katie slipped in last. She craned her next to see the open hole in the wall through the shoulders of the others.

"And as you can see," Estes was saying, "this brick wall is quite thick. It was built this solid so that when the Nazis pounded on here, it sounded like an exterior wall. And the closet here gave the bedroom a finished look, while there actually was a small trap door beneath the bottom shelf which opened into this sliver of a space. Does anyone wish to step inside?"

There were plenty of nods, and Katie waited her turn before stepping inside with Margaret. The enclosed space enveloped them, with only inches to spare in front and back.

"Yikes," Margaret said. "I wouldn't want to stay in here."

"I know. And for two days."

"I wonder what they did for a bathroom?" Margaret said, scrunching her face.

Estes, who must have heard the whisper, stuck her head in. "There was a small chamber pot over there."

"I still wouldn't want to be in here," Katie said as she crawled out, careful not to drag her dress against the stone wall.

Estes was already leading the second group to the rooftop when Margaret and Katie stepped into the hallway. They squeezed up the narrow stairway and crowded into the open space on top.

"Then here," Estes was telling everyone, "is where those in hiding below could come out for a few hours of sunshine each day. Back then the ten Booms had a low wooden fence built around this enclosure to shield the area from prying eyes. Those hiding here used it by crawling around on their hands and knees. At least they could get outside for a little bit."

It was strange, Katie thought on the way down, how little things like sunshine on a rooftop became great blessings in times of trouble. Would she have that same experience once she arrived home? Here on this trip she was being given so many blessings almost daily. Surely this would continue. I'll make it somehow, Katie told herself as they all slipped back down the tight stairs. *Da Hah* would see her through the rest of this trip, and He would also be there when she arrived home. She'd already seen plenty of signs that this was true.

CHAPTER FORTY-ONE

The following week the girls' car rocketed down the German Autobahn at speeds none of them had ever gone before. Katie forced herself to look away from the road ahead. She knew that Nancy was a good driver, but the speedometer had stayed well above ninety for some time now as the car rattled down the thoroughfare.

What was even more amazing was that in the next lane other automobiles were roaring past like they were standing still. Thankfully, Nancy was staying away from that lane, except for brief moments during which she gripped the steering wheel until her knuckles grew white. Then one of the huge autos would approach from behind and flash its lights. Nancy would make a dive for one of the right lanes. Contrary to the habits on the highways at home, no one was passing on the right-hand side.

None of the other girls seemed overly

concerned. Sharon had her head back on the seat and looked like she was sleeping. Margaret was on Sharon's laptop toggling through the collection of pictures Sharon had taken in the past few days. If the two of them could be so relaxed on this wild ride down the German countryside, she ought to relax herself, Katie decided. Nancy had everything under control.

"Do you want to see them?" Margaret asked, not even waiting for an answer before handing over the laptop.

Margaret leaned over to watch as Katie held the laptop so Margaret could see. "The ones from the Rhine River turned out really well," Margaret said.

Katie nodded, remembering back a few days. There was the hotel sitting one street away from the waters of the Rhine. There were the barges pushing their cargo on the river with little automobiles sitting near their steering houses. Some of them contained the captain's whole family. When the barge docked at the end of the journey their transportation was readily at hand.

"Excellent," Katie murmured, coming to the picture of a castle, and Margaret nodded her agreement. There were many of those perched high above the riverbanks, looking like silent sentinels from the distant past. It was as if they'd been there forever and would be there long after the frail humanity around them had passed on. There was even a medieval castle in the middle of the river, the stories surrounding it equally ancient. Here a German general had outfoxed Napoleon, the guidebook had said. He had built the first major pontoon bridge of its kind to surprise the wily French emperor. Sharon even had a picture of the German general's statue built along the Rhine riverbank in his honor.

Sharon's picture of the cliffs of Loreley was also *gut*. Only the cliffs hadn't been that much to see. The tour boat had played beautiful music as they approached the cliffs. The music had been inspired by this place. Here legend said that a beautiful woman had once sung her song, which carried distracted men to their deaths on the river below.

They had all laughed at that tall tale. No one took it seriously, Nancy had assured them — at least not in today's world. Equally ridiculous was the story of the seven sisters who had been turned into rocks by their father. They now lay in the middle of the river. Sharon's picture showed them more or less lined up, their backs sticking out of the water.

The story claimed that once the seven girls reached marriageable age, they refused every suitor brought to them by their father. Either the men were too fat, or too thin, too short, or too tall. There was always something wrong with them. Finally in desperation the father threw a big party where he planned to marry off the seven girls, whether they wished to or not. In an attempt to escape, the seven took to the river in a boat. They succeeded, but in a fit of rage, their father turned them into rocks as a lesson to all rebellious daughters. According to the guidebook, this was a story that some German parents still use to rein in their children's mischief.

Margaret muttered as Katie toggled to the next picture, "I think I would have taken to the boat myself if my dad tried something like that."

Katie smiled. It was hard to imagine Jesse forcing her into marriage with anyone. He was way too kind and understanding for that. So things had apparently changed a lot since the old days. But then maybe these people hadn't been very Christian either. These stories sounded pretty pagan, even if they were interesting.

Sharon's pictures of the old Roman walls in one town didn't do them justice. They looked much smaller than they had in real life. Although Katie had seen them only from the tour boat, it was hard to imagine that something still existed from close to the time when Jesus walked on this earth. Yet that is what the guidebook claimed.

Continuing to toggle on, Katie came to pictures of the castle Burg Eltz from the day before the Rhine River trip. It had been under construction, and Sharon had tried to capture only portions of the castle that showed no scaffolding, which didn't do the castle justice at all. But they were still nice. The girls had walked down to the bottom of the tall hill where the castle lay and taken the guided tour. Two families still lived there in separate sections of the castle, which made it quite unique, the tour guide said.

Sharon's next pictures showed the land lying around the town of Bastogne in Luxembourg. It was through this rolling country that Hitler had launched his last major offensive in World War II, known as the Battle of the Bulge. Sharon had insisted that they at least drive through, which they did, spending the night in a hotel in Bastogne and briefly visiting the memorial site outside of town. She hadn't wanted to stop, Katie remembered. War and evil were something she didn't want to hear more about. It seemed to the girls that the history of the world was the history of war.

But the place had deeply affected her once they arrived. The haunting memory of more than 70,000 lives lost in that horrendous battle hung in the air. It was as if the whole place still wept in sorrow. Young men had come here, far from home, to die and suffer for a cause. Did their vision hold out unto the hour of death? Katie wondered. Did it seem wasted to them, a thing soon forgotten by the coming generations?

Katie handed the laptop back to Margaret. She'd seen enough for now. Sharon must have pictures on there of the windmills of Holland and of the Corrie ten Boom house. Katie decided she would look at them later. Right now she had to get her mind ready for another day of touring. This one she had no objections to though — at least not now. Perhaps she would wish afterward they hadn't stopped at a concentration camp, but it was too late to change her mind. Nancy was already slowing down for the exit to Dachau as the voice on the GPS intoned instructions. He had been extra quiet this morning on the long stretches of highway, or perhaps she hadn't noticed his voice when she was looking at the pictures.

Nancy parked the car, and they got out

and followed the signs. They entered a low-slung building to purchase tickets. The man at the counter offered them headphones, but all of them declined after Nancy whispered, "We don't have time for all that. Those don't tell you more than the signs do."

"As you wish," the man said. "There is also literature you can take along."

So they armed themselves with what was available and approached the front gate of the camp, which was a short distance away. The sign outside directed their attention to a section of old railroad tracks that had been excavated a few years ago. These were the actual rails used by the trains that brought in loads of prisoners.

They looked like ordinary railroad tracks near home, Katie thought. But after studying the grainy photo of the camp commander's house a short distance away, she could begin to imagine how it might have been. Here long rows of railcars had been brought in, packed with desperate, starving people. Behind them the iron bars of the camp gate looked menacing. They would have appeared even more so coming here as a prisoner, Katie figured. She read the words in German imprinted in the gate's metal work: *"Arbeit Macht Frei."*

"Translate that please," Margaret told her. "Work makes free."

"An appropriate slogan for a prison camp," Margaret snapped. "The liars."

"No one was thinking straight in those days," Nancy said. "I suspect there is much worse to come than slogans."

And there would be, Katie thought, as they entered the immense enclosed prison yard. For hundreds of yards in each direction the tall, barbed-wire fence that kept the prisoners inside stretched high in the air. Smaller wires ran along the lower levels on the other side of a small ditch.

"Electrified," Sharon said, following Katie's glance.

Katie kept silent as Nancy led the way to the concrete prison blocks to the right. They entered to read the writings posted on the walls from prisoners who had suffered here. Katie read several, tales of political persons primarily, who had angered the Nazi regime. The words soon began to run into one another, the tragedy too much for comprehension. So many people had been hated, and so many had suffering from no justifiable cause.

"I've seen all I want," Margaret whispered, long before they reached the end of the long block of prison cells.

449

"I agree," Nancy said, leading them outside. There they took a peek into the main building that now housed pictures commemorating more of the brutality at the camp.

"I'll also pass on that," Margaret said. No one disagreed.

In front of the main building a grotesque steel memorial had been erected. An appropriate gesture to the horror they'd already seen, Katie thought as her stomach was twisting into knots.

Two low-slung wooden buildings were next on the tour, and the girls entered one of the doors, pausing to read the signs. Here prisoners had been housed, lying on these bunk beds. They were required to keep everything immaculately clean, the signs said. This was a form of torture in itself. Even a fraction of an inch difference in height between the bunk beds could bring quick punishment. The favorite method was suspension by one's wrists while they were tied behind the back. This took place in the prison yard.

Margaret looked quite pale by the time they exited to walk toward the back of the prison yard. For a long way they walked past rows and rows of concrete foundations where similar buildings had once stood.

"This is the worst yet," Sharon warned, as they crossed a little bridge. "Here are the ovens and the gas chamber, though the chamber was never used for some reason."

"I wish you wouldn't have told me," Margaret said.

"Sorry," Sharon said. "But I didn't want you passing out."

"I'll try not to." Margaret set her jaw firmly.

Katie glanced at a memorial as they approached the rugged set of buildings. A stone base held the statue of a man with a mournful upturned face. She translated the words etched into the stone. "The dead which were here, now instruct the living."

"God give me strength to see this," Margaret said, hanging on to Sharon's arm. They all stayed close together, stopping at the posted pictures outside that showed the stacked, emaciated bodies of the prisoners. Inside, a row of brick ovens stood along the wall. Metal frames were visible inside the door opening on which bodies had been slid in and out of the fires.

"How could someone do this to their fellow man?" Margaret asked, tears running down her face.

"It's the wickedness of fallen mankind," Nancy said. "This is what sin does if it isn't cleansed by God."

Beyond the ovens was the four-sided room meant to be a gas chamber. It was made to look like a communal bath so that the prisoners wouldn't object to being herded in. At least no one had died here. Margaret and Sharon were both sobbing by the time they exited, and Katie wiped away the tears herself. They gathered in a huddle a short distance away and prayed mostly sobs and crying from the agony they'd just witnessed. But also cries from their own hearts that the day would come quickly when such evil would never be seen on the earth again.

"Come, we had better go," Nancy soon told them. "We have a ways to travel yet today."

Katie trailed behind the others, taking one last look at the high, barbed-wire fence and the pictures of prisoners on the plaques. She read the line below one sign, this one in English. It was very appropriate, Katie thought: "But the souls of the righteous are in the hand of God, and there shall no torment touch them."

CHAPTER FORTY-TWO

With the three-week trip behind them, the plane lurched through fluffy clouds that drifted past Katie's window. She'd been given the window seat instead of Margaret this time. She'd offered Margaret an exchange, but her friend turned her down, saying, "It's your turn, Katie. Enjoy it." Katie had expected she'd treasure the window seat since their flight would be flown completely in the daytime. Now, though, with so much water appearing during every break in the clouds, it would have been nice not to have the constant visual reminder that the ocean lay far below.

The remaining hours of this plane ride would go faster if she thought on the last few pleasant days, she decided. Except for that awful tour of the Nazi concentration camp. None of them had wanted to speak about it again. Their tears had kept flowing on and off on the long drive to their next stop in Northern Austria. There the rugged mountains and clear green rivers soon brought a more cheerful mood. It was hard to stay with dark thoughts for long once you were out in *Da Hah*'s beautiful creation, Katie thought. He must have made it for that reason, or as one of the reasons, to help weary souls through the horrid effects sin would leave on the world.

They'd visited the castles in the area the next day, and that had also helped lighten the mood. Mad King Ludwig had built two castles in his lifetime, obsessing over them to the extent of never marrying. The second castle sat perched high on a mountainside overlooking a gorgeous valley and was never finished on the inside. They'd taken a bus to the top, touring the castle before climbing higher to walk across the suspension bridge the mad king had built over a deep ravine. From there the castle looked even more beautiful, along with the rushing tinkle of the river far below. Sharon must have taken twenty pictures, hardly able to control herself.

The plane gave another bounce, and Katie looked away from the window. The flight attendant was making her way down the aisle, pushing a cart of prepared meals.

"This is going to be the longest day of my

life." Margaret laughed as she glanced at her watch. "We're taking off at ten o'clock, flying for eight hours, and landing at noon. All with the sun still shining in the sky. Sort of feels like Joshua in the Bible telling the sun to stand still."

Katie shivered. "At least we're not having to fight a battle like he did."

"I know." Margaret grimaced. "We saw some awful things on this trip, but also some mighty works of the Lord. It makes me appreciate the good things God has done, especially when I saw them against the backdrop of man's evil deeds."

"Evil deeds." The words brought Ben to Katie's mind. She deliberately turned her mind away from him. She would never see him again; it was as simple as that. Instead she turned her thoughts to home. She looked forward to sharing about her trip with *Mamm* and Jesse. Even the thought of seeing Mabel and the other children was almost pleasant.

"Chicken or beef?" the flight attendant asked, interrupting Katie's thoughts.

"Beef," Margaret said, answering first.

Katie nodded and said, "The same, please."

The girls ate in silence. They'd been together for almost three weeks, and even close friends could grow tired of each other during that period of time. Likely the other girls were also thinking of home and what awaited them. A joyous reunion, for sure, after being gone all this time. There would be a chattering of voices in their homes as they shared everything they'd seen and experienced.

The others would have pictures to share. Sharon had already made arrangements to get copies to Margaret and Nancy. Katie had said no when Sharon offered to print copies for her. Ben's photo was still in the bottom of Katie's suitcase. She'd gotten around to stealing only one peek at it before she'd heard the terrible news. It had stayed buried for the rest of the trip. She should have destroyed it, but she hadn't even wanted a brief glimpse of his face. Perhaps once she was home and unpacking she could finally dispose of it without bursting into tears.

They should never have exchanged pictures in the first place, Katie thought. She couldn't believe they'd been sneaking around like that. Not that it would have changed anything, really, but it would feel better now knowing Ben didn't have her picture. Surely he would get rid of her picture too. At least she certainly hoped so.

Ben had no right to keep such an intimate item of hers in his possession when he'd turned out to be such a disappointment.

Katie finished her meal and leaned back against the seat. The flight attendant came by to pick up the empty plates. After she was gone, Katie contentedly drifted off to sleep. She awoke to the sound of the captain's voice announcing they would be landing at Philadelphia in approximately thirty minutes. Everyone was to keep their seat belts securely fastened, make sure their tray tables were closed, and put their seats in an upright position.

Katie punched the button on the seat, and it snapped into place. Margaret did the same. The plane continued to descend, feeling much like the landing had three weeks ago. *Yah,* it was the same as three weeks ago, but she was not. As the wheels bounced on the runway, Katie realized she felt three years older instead of just three weeks. So much had happened, but the biggest change was the struggle with what to do about Ben. Her life would never be the same.

When the plane stopped and the seat belt light went off, Margaret stood up to reach her carry-on bag. When Margaret stepped aside, Katie did the same. Several long minutes later, the line in their aisle surged forward. Katie kept Margaret's back in view as they walked up the ramp. They met up with the other two and walked through the airport terminal.

The girls retrieved their suitcases at baggage claim and went through customs with no problems. On the other side, they were greeted with a joyous shout from Margaret's mom. She came rushing up, hugging and kissing Margaret and then giving Katie and the others a welcome home hug.

Nelly led them out to the parking lot, chatting up a storm as they went. She shared all the news from the Mennonite community, including the bits and pieces the girls had picked up from Facebook. The girls chattered about their adventures too. Soon everything was jumbled, but they would sort it out as time went on. No one said anything about Ben. Perhaps Nelly hadn't thought of the subject or maybe Margaret had mentioned Katie's connection to him in an email so Nelly was being kind.

As they drove out of the airport and took the interstate toward Delaware, Katie wondered if her relationship with the Mennonite youth would continue. Something had changed inside her. The closer they came to home, the more certain she was. Everything was feeling quite different. Katie forced herself to focus on the chatter between Nelly and the other girls. She even tried to get a word in edgewise, but she soon gave that up. She would save her words for *Mamm* and Jesse. Right now just hearing the happy talk in the van was doing her spirit a lot of *gut.* It kept the niggling dread of having to talk about Ben and deal with Mabel at bay. Perhaps Mabel had changed since she'd left. Katie could only hope.

"Does your mom know you're coming home today?" Nelly asked Katie, cutting into the middle of the conversation as if the thought had just occurred to her.

"*Yah.* This is the date we'd planned, so everything should be fine."

"Okay," Nelly said. "I just wanted to make sure."

The chatter started again and didn't slow down until Nelly pulled into Sharon's driveway. Katie got out to stretch her legs and say hello to Sharon's *mamm.*

At the next stop, it went much the same. Nancy's *mamm* spent quite some time asking questions about the trip and giving everyone time to answer. Katie responded as best she could. *Yah,* she'd enjoyed the trip. *Yah,* she would go again, but she didn't expect that to happen. *Nee,* they hadn't gotten on each other's nerves. Nancy was an angel, and they couldn't have made such a good trip without her. When Nancy's *mamm* was satisfied, Nelly, Margaret, and Katie piled back into the van. Katie's home was next.

Suddenly Katie realized she was so jittery that her hands were shaking. Hanging on to her carry-on bag, Katie forced herself to keep breathing evenly. She'd been through so much on this trip, so there was no sense passing out now.

Jesse's farm soon came into sight, and Katie clutched her carry-on even tighter. There was no sign of anyone as Nelly drove in the driveway, but Katie had no more than opened the van door when *Mamm* came racing out of the washroom door, her apron flying.

"Oh, Katie!" *Mamm* wrapped her in her arms. "I thought you'd never get home!"

"I know," Katie choked. "It seemed like an awfully long time."

Mamm let go to shake hands with Nelly and Margaret, her shyness apparently gone in the joy of her daughter's homecoming.

"Thanks so much for taking care of Katie while she was gone," *Mamm* was saying to both Margaret and her mother. "I can never express my gratitude sufficiently."

"We are the ones who are grateful that Katie was along," Margaret said while Katie retrieved her suitcase. "And I'm sure I speak for the other girls. We had a great time."

"Well, it was very nice of you to invite her." *Mamm* wiped away her tears.

They stepped back as Nelly and Margaret got back into the van. Nelly started the engine, and soon the van was moving down the driveway, turning left onto the main road.

Mamm and Katie turned toward each other for another long hug.

"I'm so glad to be home, *Mamm.* I can never say how much," Katie whispered.

Mamm held Katie at arm's length. "You've changed. I'm not sure how, but something is different about you."

"Oh, *Mamm,* I've lost Ben!" Katie cried. "How can I not have changed? That and the trip . . . I don't think I'll ever be the same again."

"It'll be okay," *Mamm* said as she held Katie close again. "Everything is going to be okay. *Dah Hah* has His reasons for the way things happen. And they are always for the best for all of us who love Him."

Mamm knew what she was talking about. Not that she'd lost a boyfriend to a hideous crime like she had, but *Mamm* had suffered in her own way. And look how *Da Hah* had healed her and brought her love again.

"I know He's watching over us," Katie said, wiping at her tears. "Well, on to the next difficult subject. Does Mabel still hate us?"

A soft smile spread over *Mamm*'s face. "Mabel's inside waiting for you. She wanted to give me this time alone with you before she greeted you."

"Things are different then?" Katie asked hopefully.

Mamm hesitated. "Maybe some. At least for the moment. *Da Hah* is still working miracles. We just have to trust where He leads us and willingly follow Him."

"I know." Katie looked up as Mabel appeared, walking across the lawn toward them. Katie turned from *Mamm* and ran to meet Mabel. They met on the sidewalk and embraced.

"You're home!" Mabel said. "I'm glad you're back. And I'm sorry about Ben. I really am."

"Thank you, Mabel. It's been hard," Katie whispered.

Mabel smiled as *Mamm* came up with Katie's suitcase. The three of them turned and walked into the house together.

DISCUSSION QUESTIONS

1. Should Emma have been better prepared after her wedding to Jesse to deal with the time when the entire family would be together?

2. How well does Katie do with her attitude toward Mabel?

3. Should Katie have suspected there were ulterior motives to Ben Stoll's sudden interest in her?

4. Why would Mabel think she could hide her furtive meetings with Mose Yutzy?

5. Did Jesse correctly handle Katie's request to join the three Mennonite girls for a trip to Europe?

6. Should Jesse have taken a stronger hand

in dealing with Mabel's hostility?

7. What do you think about how Emma handled the conflict with Mabel and between Mabel and Katie?

8. Was Jesse's offhand rejection of Mose Yutzy a reaction to something else?

9. Was Katie in the wrong by confronting Mabel when she'd been with Mose in the barn?

10. Should Katie have accepted the gift that enabled her to join the three Mennonite girls for going overseas?

11. Is Ben falling in love with Katie? Why or why not?

12. Does the strengthening of Katie's faith while the girls tour early Anabaptist sites equip her to better deal with the news of Ben's arrest and betrayal?

13. Have you experienced God's healing touch as Katie did in the Swiss Alps?

14. How much has Mabel's heart softened

toward Katie when she arrives home from Europe?

ABOUT THE AUTHOR

Jerry Eicher's bestselling Amish fiction (more than 500,000 in combined sales) includes The Adams County Trilogy, Hannah's Heart series, The Fields of Home series, and the Little Valley Series. After a traditional Amish childhood, Jerry taught for two terms in Amish and Mennonite schools in Ohio and Illinois. Since then he's been involved in church renewal, preaching, and teaching Bible studies.